THE ASHES OF POMPEII

Mannington Public Library

THE ASHES OF POMPEII

BOOK 5 IN THE BABYLON SERIES

SAM SISAVATH

MANNINGTON PUB. LIBRARY
109 CLARKSBURG ST.
MANNINGTON, WV 26582

The Ashes of Pompeii
Copyright © 2015 by Sam Sisavath

All rights reserved.

No part of this publication may be reproduced, distributed, or transmitted in any form or by any means, including photocopying, recording, or other electronic or mechanical methods, without the prior written permission of the publisher, except in the case of brief quotations embodied in critical reviews and certain other noncommercial uses permitted by copyright law.

Disclaimer: This is a work of fiction. Names, characters, businesses, places, events and incidents are either the products of the author's imagination or used in a fictitious manner. Any resemblance to actual persons, living or dead, or actual events is purely coincidental.

Published by Road to Babylon Media LLC
Visit www.roadtobabylon.com for news, updates, and announcements

Edited by Jennifer Jensen and Wendy Chan
Cover Art by Creative Paramita
Formatting by BB eBooks

ISBN-13: 978-0692382677
ISBN-10: 0692382674

*Thanks go to my last line of defense against bad writing.
You guys know who you are.*

Every war requires sacrifices.

The only way to survive in a post-Purge world is to keep your head down, but that's not always an option.

Still stranded in the Louisiana countryside, Will, Danny, and Gaby race against the clock to get back to their friends, but the road home is treacherous and enemies lie in wait.

Meanwhile, Lara and the survivors at Song Island continue preparations for an inevitable attack. But what does a third-year medical student know about fending off a full-frontal assault?

As enemies close in on all sides, Will and Lara will be faced with life-and-death decisions. The lives of their friends—and possibly the future of humanity—will rest on the choices they make.

A year after The Purge, the Gates have held, the Stones have crumbled, and the Fires have burned, but now the Ashes will consume...

PRELUDE

THE LITTLE GIRL begged her not to do it.

Not with words, because the fear was too much and the simple act of uttering a sound was beyond her ability at the moment. Instead, dirt-caked lips trembled and light brown eyes (large as saucers, as her father used to say) stared back at her as if the girl couldn't comprehend what was happening or why.

Her father. When was the last time she had thought of him? Sometimes, when she least expected it, memories from her past rushed back to remind her of what once was but could never be again. Sometimes these disjointed flashes would stay awhile, but often they were fleeting.

The girl was still staring intently at her.

Brown eyes, large as saucers...

But her father wasn't the reason she lingered on the girl's face. Those eyes, they reminded her of him. Every pair of brown eyes she encountered these days did. She didn't know why exactly, and the not knowing gnawed at her like an elusive tick. There was nothing extraordinary about him. Nothing that she couldn't find in a hundred other men. A thousand. Tens of thousands.

And yet, and yet...

They'd found the girl hiding in the woods outside one of the towns. How she had managed to stray this far, for this long, was a mystery. Moonlight glinted off her large-as-saucers eyes as she peered out from her hiding place, a thick patch of undergrowth that had formed years ago, and would continue to grow as the planet consumed the remains of humanity. Even now, you could barely tell man used to tread these areas.

The ones who had found the girl swayed back and forth in the background. Her brood. They made very little noise. She once thought they were empty husks, useless flesh draped over frail bones, but she had been mistaken. There were still shreds of humanity in them, somewhere; they were just pushed into the background. Unlike her and the other chosen ones, it was difficult for her brood to reclaim what they had lost.

She crouched in front of the girl and watched the little figure shrink back in response, as if she could disappear into the thickets if she tried hard enough. The fear trembled across the parts of her rail-thin body that were visible, and the smell of fresh urine lingered. The girl wore dirty clothes and was barefoot, dried mud clinging to her toes. She folded her arms around scraped knees and peered up while periodically sneaking glances at the things moving quietly in the darkness around them.

"You're safe," she said to the girl. Her voice came out as a hiss and she hated it, but it was beyond her control. The transformation did things to her body at the cellular level, all the way up to the noises she made.

The girl didn't believe her, and her eyes darted to the darkness again before returning. If she was terrified, the little thing was handling it well. She reminded her of Vera, Carly's little sister. Carly had been her friend too, once upon a time.

"Yes," she whispered, trying her best to lessen the hissing. It was difficult, a monumental task, and she didn't know why she was making the effort. But there was something about the girl that she wanted to draw out. "You're safe now. With me." She couldn't tell if the girl believed her that time. "What's your name?"

The dirt-tinged lips quivered and a squeaky voice, like that of a mouse, said, "Mary."

"Hello, Mary. My name is Kate."

She smiled—or thought she did. Her lips didn't always do what she wanted them to these days. It was so much easier to communicate with the others, with her brood. This old form of talking was crude and cumbersome and took too much effort.

"What are you doing out here by yourself, Mary?"

"My dad..." the girl said, her voice growing stronger with each word, her fear slipping little by little.

"Where is he?"

"Out there..."

Gone, a voice whispered inside her head. *We took him two nights ago.*

It wasn't one voice, but many—a cacophony of fractured thoughts that clashed and merged and somehow formed meaning anyway. It came from the swaying figures behind her, from the ones keeping out of sight, as well as the hundreds racing across the darkened woods like children playing. There was no individuality among the brood; there was just the collective, the us. It was one of the few things that she still struggled with.

"Let me take you to him," she said, and held out her hand.

The girl hesitated.

"You'll be safe with me, Mary. I promise."

"You're not like them..."

"No. I'm different. I'm...something else."

"You won't hurt me?"

"No. I promise. Do you believe me?"

A slight tremor from the girl turned into a weak nod.

"Now, take my hand, and let me take you to your father."

Soft fingers caked with a generous layer of dirt wrapped around her own long, slender ones. She was sure the girl's fear would reclaim her and that she would retreat at any second, but the surprising toughness that reminded her so much of Vera caused the girl to tighten her grip instead.

"You're such a brave girl, Mary. So brave."

She pulled the girl out of her hiding place slowly, gently. Long, stringy auburn hair fell over a round face. One day, she would grow up to be a beautiful young woman. One day, boys would flock to her and other girls would be jealous and whisper cruel words behind her back. One day, those big brown eyes *(big as saucers)* would make her popular.

"Where's my dad?" Mary asked. Her voice had continued to grow stronger, more confident.

"We'll find him," she said. She stood up too, extending her long thin frame, the joints *clacking* slightly as she did so.

The girl had to crane her neck to look up at her. "They won't hurt us? The monsters in the shadows?"

"No. They're my children. And they're very obedient."

"You're their mother?"

"Yes."

"How?"

"You have so many questions."

Mary smiled. It was delicate and radiant. "You're not like the others."

"No, I'm not."

"You're friendly."

"Yes…"

"But they're not."

The girl glanced at the dozen or so of the brood that hadn't hidden themselves well enough. Upon discovery, her children scurried back until it was just the night and her and the girl again in the clearing.

"It's okay," she said. "You're with me now. They won't hurt you."

Mary looked up at her again, her smile widening. In the moonlight, she looked cherubic and pure. "We're going to find my dad now?"

"Yes."

"Where did he go? I thought he'd left me."

"No. He would never leave you. No parent would leave their brood."

"Brood?"

"My children…"

"Oh."

She tightened her grip around Mary's wrist and led her toward the darker parts of the woods. There was stirring in the shadows as her children stepped back to make room. She didn't have to tell them. They knew her wants and needs, and they obeyed without question.

"Kate?" Mary said. Her voice had gotten smaller, and she could practically hear *(sense)* the fear creeping back into every inch of her small frame. "You're hurting my hand. Kate? Kate?"

"*Shhh,*" she said, putting one long, bony finger to her lips and looking down at the girl. "It'll be over soon, little Mary. *Shhh…*"

BOOK ONE

THE RUNDOWN

CHAPTER 1

KEO

"SEE THE WORLD. *Kill some people. Make some money."*

Well, one out of three wasn't bad.

Okay, so it was downright pitiful, but then Keo was used to making lemonade out of lemons these days. First there was that whole end of the world curveball, then getting stuck with strangers in a cabin in the woods. He compounded those problems by falling in *(lust)* something with a girl named Gillian.

And now this.

"This" being stuck on a luxury yacht adrift in the middle of the lake with Song Island behind him and God only knew how many guys with guns in front of him. On the plus side, he was well-armed; besides the shotgun, he still had the Heckler & Koch MP5SD submachine gun, and he had added an AK-47 and a silver-chromed revolver with five bullets left to his arsenal. If life before everything went kaput had taught him anything, it was that there was no such thing as having "too many" guns.

Have bullets, will make mess.

In some ways, his life now wasn't all that different than it was a year ago. These days, though, people weren't paying him a lot of money to risk his hide. These days, he was voluntarily risking his precious limbs for…what again? A bunch of people he didn't really know? Sure, he respected them, but was that really worth dying for?

Then again, maybe he had just finally developed something approaching a conscience.

Say it ain't so.

The big guy with the melon for a head was lying half-on and half-off the floor of the upper deck. Or what was left of the head, anyway. The shotgun in Keo's hands had removed most of the top portion, leaving behind something that looked suspiciously like a badly carved jack-o'-lantern. Clumps of blood and brains were spilled across the floorboards on the other side of the spiral stairwell that connected the upper and the main deck directly below.

There had been footsteps pounding up those same stairs a few seconds ago, but they quickly stopped after Melon Head took the buckshot to the side of the face. The hard chargers decided to retreat after that, then went very quiet soon after. They were tiptoeing around down there, most likely getting ready for an assault on his position. So they weren't complete idiots, after all. Too bad. He liked dealing with amateurs.

Keo was crouched in the semidarkness of the *Trident*, the boat continuing to move even with the anchor lowered. He had turned off the whisper quiet engine at the same time, allowing him to hear everything around and underneath him, including his own slightly racing heartbeat.

Jesus, calm down. What is this, your first time in a firefight?

He leaned back from the turn in the hallway that connected the bulk of the deck's floor with the bridge behind him. Keo spent a few seconds slowing down his breathing while keeping one ear open for noises.

Come on, boys, let's not keep daddy waiting. He's getting antsy.

Song Island was directly behind him, but Keo hadn't had the opportunity to check how far he still was from the beach before he dropped the anchor to keep the boat from running aground by accident. They were close, he could tell that from the halo of lights visible on the other side of the bridge's curving windshield, the swath of intense brightness reaching all the way across the room and into the hallway.

There was no doubt Lara and the others would have heard the shooting by now. Even muffled by the walls around him, there was no mistaking a shotgun blast against the quiet night. Just to make sure, though, Keo leaned out from the corner and fired another shot at the wall across the deck, squinting involuntarily at the thunderous *boom!*

There. They'd have to be deaf not to hear that.

He recalled his last conversation with Lara (a.k.a. kid leader), just before he went for a swim (again) in the cold lake water:

"Don't shoot unless you have to," she had said.

"Trust me," he had replied, *"if you hear shooting on the boat, there's a very damn good reason for it."*

He didn't know why, but Keo trusted her. She had proven to be a tough customer with some big brass ones. That was hard to find in a woman, but especially the civilian variety. He didn't even mind that she had manipulated him into helping with the island's defense the last few days. Now that was smooth. Keo was a shoot-first-and-what-was-the-question type of guy, but he'd always had a lot of grudging respect for people who could think two, three steps ahead and give orders with lives at stake (usually his).

He pressed his back against the wall and tried to pick up any slight vibrations that could signal an incoming attack.

Nothing. A big fat zero. Nada. Zilch.

That should have comforted him, but instead it just made him more paranoid.

Come on, boys, what are you waiting for? An engraved invitation?

To keep his mind off what may or may not be happening out there right now, Keo spent a few seconds taking inventory.

He counted four victims, but only three bodies. There were the two in the bridge—the captain (or the guy wearing a captain's hat, anyway), his first mate, and a third man who had come up the stairs. And Melon Head made three stiffs. The captain was kneecapped and whimpering softly in one of the bridge's corners. Alive, but whipped. Just the way Keo liked them.

That was four down and an unknown number still to go. The vanishing footsteps he had heard earlier were proof of that. There was also someone named Rod, a sniper who had been watching the island when the boat was on approach earlier tonight. He was likely on a high perch—possibly on top of Keo right this moment, or maybe somewhere along the side rails. Someplace high to shoot from.

Counting Rod, there were at least two more still running around out there. His one big advantage was that they were going to have to come to him if they wanted to get the *Trident* moving again. That meant retaking the controls on the bridge.

Keo waited for ten more seconds.

Then ten became twenty…

…and still no attack.

At thirty, he got up and moved, slightly bent over at the waist just in case (you could never be too careful when there were assholes running around with loaded guns), making a beeline back to the bridge. The assault rifle and submachine gun *thumping* against his back made more noise than he would have liked; the eerie quiet made them sound like firecrackers, and he wished he had tightened their straps before moving.

Live and learn, pal. Live and learn.

He slipped back inside the bridge and closed the door, then locked it. Not that he expected to keep out a half dozen determined assaulters, but it would give him time to prepare a proper defense. Which, in this case, meant waiting with the shotgun for the first target to appear so he could pull the trigger. Keo was a simple guy that way.

The "captain" was still in the corner, where Keo had left him earlier. The man had taken off his shirt (it turned out he had an undershirt beneath, though it, too, was now stained with blood) and wrapped it over his right kneecap, trying desperately to stop the bleeding. Keo couldn't tell if the man was more freaked out by his injury, the pain, or the inability to stop blood from dripping through his makeshift tourniquet.

Or it could have been the sight of his first mate's body, sitting on the floor with his back against the long console that covered nearly the entire front half of the room. The man, like Melon Head outside, was missing most of his noggin, with pieces of it clinging to the curving glass windshield behind him. It was a hell of a mess, made more surreal against the wash of the island's LED and multicolored lights from the boat's computer screens and buttons. The fragments of a destroyed handheld radio were sprinkled around the body. Too bad, because Keo would have liked to use it to contact the island.

If wishes were assholes...

Bottom line, he was cut off. Or, at least, until either the remains of the boat's crew got their act together and assaulted the bridge or Lara decided to do something from her end. Frankly, he hated the idea of waiting for one of them to do something already. Patience had never been his strongest trait.

The captain flinched even before Keo got close enough to do anything to him. "Don't kill me!"

Keo put a finger to his lips, and the man clenched his mouth shut. He picked up the white captain's hat from the floor and put it back on the man's damp head, then gave him a slight tap on the cheek.

"That's a good boy," Keo said.

"Don't kill me," the captain mouthed.

"Now why would I do a thing like that? You've been so cooperative."

The captain glanced down at his bleeding leg.

"Oh sure, that," Keo said. "You're not the type to hold a grudge, are you?"

The captain looked uncertain about answering, so he didn't.

"Let's put that behind us and move on," Keo said. "Start with this: How many of you are on the boat?"

The man stared back at him, sweat dripping down his forehead despite the cooling mid-October weather. It was still hot in the day, but at night Louisiana dipped to fifty and sometimes hit the forties.

Right now Keo felt a slight chill; then again, he had been submerged in the lake not all that long ago, so that probably factored into it.

"Numbers," Keo said when the man didn't answer fast enough. "I need numbers, *el capitan*. How many are on the boat with you?"

The captain seemed to be seriously brooding over the question. It wouldn't have surprised Keo if the man thought his life might be at stake, depending on his answer. He was a man in his late thirties and wore a beard that was flecked with white strays, and he actually did look like a ship's captain. The only thing missing was a pressed white uniform like the one worn by that guy from *The Love Boat*.

"Come on, spit it out," Keo said. "You don't know, or you don't want to tell me?"

"Sev—eight," the captain finally said.

"Sev-eight? I must have been absent from Mrs. Krapthorpe's math class that day. How many is sev-eight again?"

The captain swallowed. "Seven."

"You sure?"

"Yes."

"I think you're lying."

Keo pushed the barrel of the shotgun against the man's wounded leg. The captain let out what sounded like a low-pitched squeal. Keo didn't know what to make of that noise, but it seemed to be working so he added more pressure.

"Seven or eight?" Keo said. "Think carefully."

"Eight," the captain said, almost shouting the word out.

Keo lessened the pressure slightly. "Rod the sniper is one."

"Yes…"

"Where is he?"

The captain's eyes shifted up to the ceiling.

"Still?" Keo said.

A shrug and a look of uncertainty.

"And the others?" Keo asked.

"Below."

"Doing what?"

"Guard—"

Keo heard a soft *tap!* and glanced up, reaching forward and clamping one hand over the captain's mouth at the same time.

Tap...tap...

It was coming from the roof.

Rod, the sniper.

Keo pulled his hand away from the captain and took two, then three quick steps toward the middle of the bridge. He leaned the shotgun against the nearest wall and unslung the MP5SD. He traced the sound as it moved from the back of the roof toward the front. Slowly, carefully, because Rod the sniper was that kind of a guy.

A second later, an elongated shadow draped over the windshield. It was in the shape of *a human head.*

Keo fired into the ceiling, stitching it from west to east, then north to south until he had emptied half of the magazine. The only noise was the cyclical whine of the German weapon's parts as it unleashed a series of 9mm rounds. The *clink-clink-clink* of bullet casings flicking and bouncing off the floor was louder than the actual gunshots themselves, thanks to the built-in suppressor at the end of the barrel.

There was a soft *thud*, followed by a pair of arms dangling out the windshield where the glass met the roof of the bridge. Blood dripped from the fingers and ran in thin rivulets along the smooth surface all the way to the bottom.

Five down, three to go.

Keo moved quickly to the door and pressed up against it. He stopped breathing entirely and listened, flattening his hands against the wall to search for any hints of vibrations that would signal the impending attack he had been waiting for.

To his surprise, he continued to hear nothing and felt nothing. Either these guys were incredibly patient, or they weren't willing to risk their necks to regain control of the bridge. Frankly, Keo didn't know whether to be impressed by their sense of self-preservation or irritated by it.

He looked over at the captain, who was staring back across the room at him. The man's face was slicked with a new coat of sweat.

That was either all fear, or the man was just a perspiration machine.

"Three to go," Keo said.

The captain's lips trembled slightly, as if he wanted to say something but was too afraid to.

"Catfish got your tongue?"

He got a confused reaction that time.

Keo nodded at the largest chunk of the destroyed two-way radio on the floor next to the first mate's body. "Got another one of those?"

The captain followed Keo's glance, then looked back at him. The man gave Keo a look that convinced him the guy wasn't sure if he should cooperate. Or maybe he was wondering what was in it for him.

Keo decided to help him out and drew the revolver from his waistband, cocking the hammer back. The loud *click!* seemed to echo through the large room.

The captain's entire body went rigid.

"I think that's a yes," Keo said. "But you don't want to tell me where I can find it. Now, normally I'd make you show me how to use the boat's radio, but that console looks awfully complicated, and I'm just not a very techie sort of guy. So…where's the backup radio?"

"Under the console," the captain said.

"See? That wasn't so hard."

Keo moved back across the room, maneuvering around the still-wet glistening pools of the first mate's blood and brass casings that were now everywhere, and slid back a compartment under the large console that controlled every facet of the yacht. Inside, he found a first aid kit, supplies, and, near the back, another two-way portable radio. He fished it out and spent a few seconds trying to recall the frequency the islanders were using.

Keo turned the dial and pressed the transmit lever. "Lara, come in."

Five seconds of silence went by.

Then ten…

Had he tuned into the right channel? The island was well within the radio's reach, so that couldn't have been it. Of course, if they didn't recognize his voice, they might not respond. Maybe they were wondering who the hell had just broken into their lines of communication—

"Keo," a voice finally said through the radio. *Lara*. "You're still alive."

"Surprised?" Keo said.

"Just worried. What's going on over there? What's your situation? We heard shooting. Was that you?"

"It wasn't Santa Claus. Watch out for snipers. I took one out, but there might be more."

"I was wondering what was hanging off the bridge's roof."

"That would be Rod."

"You talked to him?"

"I heard the captain and his first mate talking."

"What else did you hear?"

"Remember our talk? That if I started shooting, there's a damn good reason for it?"

"I remember."

"Well, there's a damn good reason I started shooting."

She didn't answer back right away. After a while, she said, "We're getting ready to head over and board the boat right now."

"I wouldn't do that."

"Why not?"

"There are still three more of them running around outside the bridge. I have no idea where they are at the moment. That means they could be lying in wait for you, so there's no point in taking the risk. At least, not yet."

"What about you? Are you under attack?"

"Not right now. They seem to be hanging back."

He looked over at the door just to make sure. It would have been a hell of a jinx if they burst inside as soon as the words came out of his mouth. But the door was still closed, and there were no telltale vibrations of approaching men.

These guys are either the most patient assholes left in the known universe, or they're quaking in their boots right now.

"What about the yacht?" Lara asked. "It stopped moving."

"I killed the engines and dropped anchor. At the moment, I have possession of the bridge. That means I control where the boat goes; or, in this case, doesn't go. But I don't have eyes on what's happening outside or on the two lower decks."

Another long pause from her. He could almost imagine that brain of hers working, turning over her options, trying to come up with a plan that wouldn't get her people killed. The kid leader was definitely impressive.

"All right," she said finally. "We'll stay back for now. What are you going to do next?"

"I'm going to stay up here and wait for them to make their move. If they're smart, they'll realize they're beat and take one of the life boats and abandon ship."

"And if they're not that smart?"

"I got plenty of bullets," Keo said. "And since I'm surrounded by water in this floating tub, this is one time where the night's my friend."

THE NIGHT SETTLED down into a crawl, with the only noise coming from the occasional slapping of Beaufont Lake's lazy waves against the hull of the *Trident*. It always amazed him just how dead the world was at night. Now mostly devoid of the loud excesses of humanity, there was a peacefulness here that, were he a peaceful-loving kind of guy, he might have appreciated.

Now, though, the pervading silence, with armed men somewhere outside the bridge door waiting to kill him, just made him irritable.

Keo glanced down at his watch. 12:51 A.M.

Six hours before sunrise.

He looked over at the captain, who was trying desperately not to pass out in the corner next to him. Keo didn't know why the man was even fighting an obviously losing battle. In his experience, people sometimes hung onto things when they didn't have to. But then again, most of the world's population didn't see things the way he did. Too bad, because Keo was sure he was right and everyone else was wrong.

"You got a name, cap?" Keo asked.

The man blinked sweat from his eyes, but the prospect of conversation seemed to give him new energy. "Gage."

"As in 12-gauge?"

"Gage. G-a-g-e."

"Cute name."

"What's yours?"

"This isn't a date. I ask the questions and you answer them." Then, "This your boat, Gage?"

"It belonged to this Mexican guy we worked for."

"What happened to him?"

Gage shrugged. "He didn't need it anymore."

Keo smiled. "Gee, I wonder if you had anything to do with that."

"I didn't," Gage said. His eyes flickered to the headless first mate across the room from them. "But Johns did. I...just went along with it."

"Sure you did."

"I had to. Johns was in charge."

"Hey, I believe you," Keo said, though he assumed Gage knew differently by just looking at him. He had heard the two of them talking earlier. They sounded more like partners-in-crime than boss-and-lackey. "What about the others? What were they doing when this totally mutual exchange of boat ownership went down?"

Gage decided to start drifting off at that moment.

Keo stuck a hand in front of him and snapped his fingers. "Hey, wake up. This is no time to be falling asleep, pal. Especially not in the middle of a Q&A. That's just rude."

Gage's eyes opened back up. "What?"

"You were giving me a very good reason why I shouldn't just put you out of your misery right now."

The other man looked alarmed. "I was?"

"Yes. And let me just say, you're doing quite the shitty job of it." Keo drew the revolver with its five bullets and laid it across his lap, tapping the trigger guard with his forefinger for effect. "Wanna try harder?"

Gage suddenly looked very alert, or was trying very hard to give that impression, anyway. "The boat. I can drive the boat."

"I thought you said this wasn't your boat."

"It's not, but I was its captain."

"That explains the hat," Keo grinned.

Gage didn't know how to respond to that, so he didn't.

"What about the other three?" Keo asked. "Your crew?"

"A couple of them. The others, we picked up along the way."

"Like Rod?"

"Yeah."

Keo glanced over at what was left of the first mate. "What about Johns?"

"He's just a friend."

"He *was* just a friend."

"Yeah…"

"Your boat buddies. The ones running outside like busy little mice. Any ideas what they're up to—"

The rattle of automatic gunfire stopped Keo in mid-sentence. His eyes darted to the door before he realized it had come from behind him—from the direction of Song Island.

He got up and hurried to the front of the bridge and looked out toward the island, just in time to see full automatic rifle fire pouring from one of the piers. It was shooting at something bobbing in the water in front of the *Trident*. A second rifle was shooting from the beach, both weapons spraying at what he could now see was an orange raft, its color making it nearly impossible to miss in the darkness. The small craft had been moving toward the island when it was fired upon. Now, it seemed to be floating in place and Keo could just barely make out a figure lying inside.

He unclipped the radio from his hip and pressed the transmit lever. "Song Island, come in." He waited for a response, and when he didn't get one after a few seconds, "Anyone there? What was the shooting about? Song Island, come in."

"Keo," Lara said through the radio. "Are you still on the yacht?"

"Yeah. Why?"

"People were heading toward the island on some kind of boat. They fired at Blaine, so we fired back. It's orange."

"I see it. Survivors?"

"Doesn't look like it." Then, "Shit."

"What?"

"I think we might have hit it one time too many; it's starting to sink."

Keo saw it, too—the raft was being pulled under the lake's surface.

"You said you saw two people onboard?" he said into the radio.

"Pretty sure," Lara said. "Blaine was on the pier, and he had the best view." Then to someone else, "What did you see, Blaine?"

"Two," Blaine said through the radio. "Probably two."

"That leaves one still unaccounted for," Keo said.

"How many lifeboats does a yacht like that hold?"

"Usually one or two. Hold on, let me ask *el capitan*."

"He's still alive?" Lara said.

"Sort of." Keo looked over at Gage. "Hey, how many lifeboats do you have onboard?"

The man didn't answer him.

"Gage," Keo said, louder this time.

When he still didn't respond, Keo walked over and crouched in front of him. Gage looked dead and was leaning over slightly to one side. Keo pressed two fingers against the side of his neck and detected a pulse. Weak, so apparently Gage had decided to go with the flow after all.

"Keo?" Lara said through the radio. "What did the captain say?"

"He's unconscious."

"What did you do to him?"

"I shot him in the kneecap with his own gun."

"Now why the hell did you do that?"

"It seemed like the thing to do at the time."

"Let's...try not to shoot people in the kneecaps unless we have to from now on, okay?"

"Sure, if you want to take all the fun out of this."

She ignored him and said instead, "So what do we do about the last man? *If* there's really only one left?"

"*El capitan* sounded pretty certain. Then again, he looks like the type that might lie." He stood up and looked over at the door again. "Sit tight and wait for morning. We'll figure it out then."

Lara didn't answer right away.

"You good with that?" Keo asked.

"I guess I don't have a choice," Lara said.

He could hear it in her voice—that burden that came with leadership. He had heard it often enough in people who took on the job that few could do, or wanted to do.

"Relax," he said. "It's not coming tonight."

"What isn't?"

"The attack you've been expecting for the last two days."

She paused for a moment, then, "How can you be so sure?"

"The bad guys will have heard the shooting. They'll know something is happening, but they don't know what. And this boat showing up would have freaked them out. Add all of that with the damage they took yesterday from *moi*, and if I was them, I wouldn't attack tonight. I'd wait, because I could afford to wait. It's not like you're going anywhere, right?"

"No..."

"And they know that. So my guess is, they'll wait another day. Which means we don't have to do anything drastic until then."

"Captain Optimism, huh?"

"I don't know what means."

"Inside joke," she said. Then, sounding more reassured than a few seconds ago, "Okay. If we're not moving until sunrise, that means you'll be on your own for the next six hours. Can you go that long without unnecessarily killing people?"

"No promises."

She sighed. "I'll get one of the boats ready, just in case."

'Just in case,' he thought with a smile. *The island motto, apparently.*

CHAPTER 2

LARA

IN THE MORNING light, the *Trident*'s long, sleek, and sharp features gave it the impression of being a massive white sword, ready to pierce the side of Song Island if it so desired. That seemed to be the only thing the island was good for these days—a target to be attacked.

Maybe keeping it is more trouble than it's worth, Will. Maybe it's time to go.

She watched the sun rising in the distance as Blaine, Roy, and Maddie were prepping the bass fishing boat behind her. Everyone was moving on automatic pilot, strung out on coffee and the work in front of them. Bonnie had returned to the hotel to rest, though Lara was surprised Roy was still there. She guessed he was still trying to make up for two nights ago.

"Keo," she said into the radio. "We're about to head over to you now. Any word on the eighth guy?"

"What, no good morning?" Keo said through the radio.

She smiled. "Good morning."

"Good morning to you, too."

"So, about the eighth guy…"

"Not a peep all night."

"Are we even sure there's an eighth guy?"

"I'll ask the captain again when he's awake. I guess he's not a morning person."

She glanced down at her watch. 7:22 A.M.

Sunrise had come about thirty minutes ago, and she had watched it with barely contained glee from inside the boat shack, where she had been sleeping on a cot. Keo was certain the collaborators wouldn't attack, not with the mess he had made at their staging area yesterday and the chaos of last night. His reasoning was sound, but then these days you couldn't always count on logic to save the day.

He had turned out to be right, though, and she had never been more happy to be wrong in her life.

She concentrated on the *Trident* now. It was almost two football fields away but looked much closer, like she could swim to it with a few strokes. Well, maybe Keo could. She had seen the man swim like a fish the last two nights.

"Boss lady," Blaine said behind her. "You coming, or what?"

Lara turned around and walked back to them. They were already inside the boat, Maddie settling in behind the steering wheel while Roy sat on a chair up front with his M4 in his lap. Blaine was seated on another chair at the back, next to the outboard motor that sent out puffs of smoke and coughed loudly, sounding as if it was going to die at any moment.

She climbed into the boat and nodded at Maddie. "Let's go."

Maddie guided the boat away from the pier. The back dipped slightly as it gained speed, and Lara hurried up to the front to help balance out the weight distribution.

Roy looked over at her and shouted over the roar of the engine, "What about the last guy?"

"I don't know!" Lara shouted back. She glanced at Maddie and Blaine. "Keep your eyes peeled! He might be waiting for us!"

"If there's actually an eighth guy!" Blaine said.

"Take no chances! If you see a head, and it doesn't look like Keo's, shoot first and ask questions later!"

The big man nodded back and checked his rifle.

The boat had already carried them halfway to the *Trident*, the yacht growing in size (and sharpness) as they got closer. Lara unslung her own carbine and flicked the safety off without even realizing it.

Jesus. I really have become used to this thing.

"I can't believe that guy took the whole boat by himself!" Maddie shouted at her. "Let's make a reminder to ourselves: Don't piss this guy off!"

"I'm glad he's on our side!" Roy said.

Lara nodded. She thought about telling them how close she had come to not trusting Keo, but she didn't. They didn't need to know the details right now.

Is this what being a leader is, Will? Keeping things from people, for their own good? Making big decisions that could cost everyone their lives and knowing you're solely responsible for the outcome?

How in God's name did you ever manage the burden all by yourself all these months? You should have told me. I would have been there for you...the way I wish you were here for me right now...

"Approaching!" Maddie shouted behind her.

Lara gripped her M4 tighter, and so did Roy next to her.

The *Trident* really was long, though not nearly as wide *(What had Keo called that? The beam?)* as she had thought when looking at it from afar. Even so, it was an intimidating sight, especially the large chain connected to the massive anchor sitting at the bottom of Beaufont Lake at the moment, keeping the white beast from floating away. The yacht had three decks, with the bridge at the very top. Windows lined the sides, sweeping from front to back.

She eyeballed every inch of glass and railing within range, looking—waiting—for that elusive eighth man that may or may not exist.

Maddie steered them alongside the boat, then turned completely around until they were facing the back. They were greeted by a large, flapping flag hanging from a long metal pole, featuring an eagle eating a snake over green, white, and red stripes. The engine shut off and they continued drifting toward what looked like a lounging area, complete with chairs and recliners for sunbathing. A ladder dipped into the water, though it looked like it could be folded back up when not in use.

Roy stood up with his rifle at the ready, while Maddie manipulated the smaller craft over, deftly spinning the steering wheel left, then right, then left again. Lara felt anxious just watching the smaller woman grit her teeth as she cautiously moved closer and closer. Behind her, Blaine remained seated, but like Lara, he was sweeping the visible parts of the yacht looking for something—*someone*—to shoot.

Lara unclipped her radio and keyed it. "Keo, we're at the back of the yacht now."

"I heard you on approach," Keo said through the radio. "Did you see me waving?"

"Uh, no."

"Too bad. I was doing a jig and everything."

She smiled. "I'm sure you were. What about the eighth guy?"

"You don't see him out there?"

"Not a living soul."

"Maybe he's hiding. If *el capitan*'s numbers square up, he's the only rat left that hasn't tried to jump off this sinking boat yet. That means he's either very determined, or a dumbass. Either way, that makes him unpredictable."

"Understood. We'll make our way to you as soon as we can."

"Roger that," Keo said.

Lara put the radio away, then watched Roy sling his rifle and position himself precariously at the front of their boat. She wanted to tell him to be careful, but doing so might undermine his courage, so she didn't say anything. Roy waited, and when Maddie had gotten close enough to the yacht, he jumped. For a second Lara thought he had missed his target, but he landed soundly on the *Trident*, barreling into one of the chairs and causing it to skid along the smooth floor.

"Easy there, Oklahoma," Maddie said.

Roy gave them an embarrassed grin.

"Throw him the line, Lara," Maddie said.

Roy held out his hands to catch the rope Lara tossed over to him, then began pulling them all the way in.

"Blaine, you first," Lara said.

Blaine got up and moved forward before jumping the short distance onto the luxury cruiser. He landed next to Roy, who was already tying up the rope. Lara had to admit, they were working pretty well for people who had never done any of this before. She almost felt like a proud parent.

Adapt or perish, right, Will?

She followed the men further onto the *Trident* while Maddie stayed behind at the lounge area to keep an eye on their boat.

Lara climbed onto the deck with Blaine and Roy before unclipping her radio a second time. "Keo, we're on our way now."

"Take it easy," Keo said. "No rush. The captain woke up, and we're having a nice talk."

"Try not to shoot him again."

"Yeah, yeah."

She followed Blaine and Roy toward the nearest ladder. The bridge would be on the top deck, which meant they had to climb two floors. That was preferable to traveling through the interiors, where anyone could be waiting around any corner. Out here, in the sun, she felt slightly safer.

"What's he saying?" she said into the radio.

"He's spinning a pretty interesting story," Keo said.

"About?"

"How he and his buddies commandeered the boat. They're originally from Mexico, you know."

"I saw the flag. He's Mexican?"

"Nope. Looks like a gringo to me."

"What happened to the owners of the boat?"

"Let's just say they didn't give their pride and joy up willingly."

"They killed them and took the boat?" Blaine asked.

Lara nodded. "Sounds like it."

"A Mexican boat staffed by an American crew?" Roy said from up front. "That's a new one."

Blaine chuckled. "End of the world, man. Everything's upside down these days. Monsters are real, silver's more valuable than gold, and Mexicans are using Americans to clean the poop decks."

THEY DIDN'T FIND the eighth crewman on the first deck. He wasn't on the second one, either. The third also didn't yield a hidden shooter, and they had to go inside this time in order to access the bridge at the front. Walking through the top floor, Lara almost slipped on the congealed blood in her path. Keo had left behind a hell of a mess as he took the boat last night.

Blaine moved diligently in front of her, while Roy stayed behind outside in case someone tried to sneak up on them. He also kept an eye on Maddie. Will would probably have come up with a better system of watching each other's backs; but then, Will was a soldier and she was just a third-year medical student masquerading as one.

She and Blaine had to circle around two bodies before they reached the hallway that connected a roomy area—a combination entertainment center and living room, complete with couches and a big screen TV along one wall—to the bridge. One of the bodies was missing its head and lay half on and half off the floor, the rest of the man draped over a spiral staircase that connected two of the decks. The other body lay on its back in a thick pool of blood. His face was pale, lifeless eyes staring up at her as she stepped over him.

"Keo!" Blaine shouted as he stepped around the second body and into the adjoined hallway.

They heard the sound of a door opening, then Keo appeared. He had that German weapon of his and was clad all in black. He looked dry for someone who had been swimming most of last night. "I was wondering who was stomping around out here. You guys ever heard of a subtle entry?"

Blaine ignored him and said, "We couldn't find the eighth guy."

"I wouldn't worry about him. He'll poke his head up sooner or later."

"Where's the boat's captain?" Lara asked.

"Inside, resting. Got questions? He's in a very talkative mood this morning."

"I'm sure he is," Lara said, reminding herself what a good decision it had been to recruit Keo onto their side instead of making an enemy out of him. It could have gone either way, but she had trusted her instincts.

Maybe you were right, Will. Maybe I can do this leadership thing. Maybe...

◀■■▮ ▮■■▶

THE YACHT'S "CAPTAIN" looked like he had seen better days. Even so, despite the blood loss and obvious pain on every inch of his face, he seemed to be taking captivity reasonably well. If nothing else, he looked well-rested for a man who was missing one of his kneecaps.

Blaine stayed outside the bridge to stand guard, with Roy and Maddie remaining at their posts. If the eighth man was out there, he was biding his time. Which was fine with her. She didn't feel like adding another victim to her growing body count this morning anyway.

Sorry, lake, you'll just have to wait until tonight for more bodies.

Keo nodded at the man in the white hat. "Gage, this is Lara. Lara, that's Gage. Say hi."

"Hi," Lara said.

Gage peered through a sweat-covered face at her. "Hey."

Lara focused on Gage, which helped her to ignore the body sitting against the *Trident*'s control console across the room, along with the chunks of...something sticking to the windshield. She hadn't asked Keo where he had gotten the shotgun and AK-47 he was carrying around with him this morning, but she could guess. There were three bodies on this deck alone.

"What happened last night?" she asked Keo.

"They were Trojan Horsing you," he said. Then to Gage, "Tell her."

Gage nodded. "He's right."

"You're admitting it?" she said.

"Yeah, why not? Everyone's dead. I'm half dead. What's the point in lying now?"

"See?" Keo said. "Gage here's the pragmatic type. He figures that if he doesn't lie, I won't have any reason to shoot him in his other kneecap."

"Yeah, that, too," Gage said, and this time he did managed a full grin, though she noticed it was half-amusement and half-mortal terror. "What else you wanna know, lady?"

"What were you going to do?" Lara asked. "When you got to the island?"

Gage quickly lost some of his enthusiasm and began noticeably squirming in the corner.

"Don't start lying now, *el capitan*," Keo said. "The truth. Nothing but the truth. So help your other kneecap."

"We were going to take it," Gage said. "Then we would take everything else."

"What's 'everything else'?" Lara asked.

"Whatever you had. The food. The supplies. The…people."

"The people? What were you going to do with the people?"

"Not everyone. Mostly…just the women."

"The women…"

"Yeah."

"What were you going to do with the women?" was the next question that she never asked. She knew. Keo knew. They all did, even the dead man with half of his head blown across the windshield.

She turned to Keo. "What are we going to do with him?"

"That's up to you," Keo said. "It's your island he was going to raid. It's also your people he was going to do probably-not-very-nice things to."

She nodded and looked back at Gage.

"Hey, you promised nothing bad would happen to me," Gage said, but she noticed he had said it to Keo and not her. He wasn't even looking at her now. Maybe he was afraid, or maybe he thought his salvation lay with Keo.

He was wrong.

She drew the Glock and shot him.

The bullet hit the wall an inch from Gage's ducking head, and the yacht's captain might have actually squealed.

Footsteps pounded the deck behind them just before Blaine burst through the open door. "Jesus, what's going on?" He looked at Gage, at Keo, then finally at her. "Lara?"

"It's okay," she said, holstering her sidearm. "I was just making a point."

"Oh."

"I need you back outside, Blaine."

The big man nodded, then exchanged a brief look with Keo, who shrugged back at him. "She was making a point," Keo said.

Blaine didn't look convinced, but he left anyway.

Her radio squawked, and she heard Maddie's voice. "Guys? What's happening? I heard a gunshot."

"Everything's fine," Lara said into the radio. "Everyone stay where you are. We're just…interrogating the survivor."

"You sure?" Maddie asked.

"Yes. Keep an eye out for the eighth guy."

"Will do."

"Well, that was fun," Keo said.

Lara stared at Gage, who peered back out at her from the corner of the room. When he saw her looking, he quickly glanced away. If he could have gotten up and run, he probably would have. But his days of running were over with that still-bleeding kneecap.

"He can be useful," Keo was saying.

"How?" she asked.

She hadn't thought about putting Gage to use. The very idea of the man's continued existence offended her at an almost primal level.

"The yacht," Keo said. "You're going to need someone who knows his way around it."

"You know boats."

"I know boats, but I don't know *that*," he said, pointing at the long console behind them. "He does."

"You also told me a boat this size needs a big crew to run it. All of his crew is dead, except for an eighth guy who may or may not exist. How is one man going to keep this thing afloat, even if he does know what all those buttons are for?"

"We're talking about a twenty-first-century luxury yacht here, Lara. It might break down eventually, but it's still in good enough shape right now that you could use it to get to wherever you needed to go. I think that's worth keeping him alive for a little while longer, don't you?"

Keo wasn't wrong. She was already thinking about all the things she could do with a boat this size when she first saw it last night, and seeing it sitting on the lake under the morning sunlight had crystallized so many of those possibilities.

Keep the island if you can, but if you can't…

Hope for the best, but prepare for the worst, right, Will?

Gage was still cowering in the corner, probably trying to figure out if he was going to live past the next few minutes. She could have reassured him, but Lara decided to let him keep wondering instead.

Her radio squawked, breaking the silence, and Carly's voice came through. "Lara, come in." Carly was back on the island in the Tower with Benny, and Lara thought she sounded slightly anxious. "You still there, ol' fearless leader?"

"I'm here," Lara said into the radio.

"I have your boyfriend on the other radio," Carly said. "Should I tell him you already found someone else?"

◂━▮ ▮━▸

"WE'LL GET HOME," Will said through the ham radio. "Whatever it takes. We're not going to leave the island undefended for another day."

He sounded noticeably tired. She could only imagine it was the culmination of what he had gone through the last few weeks, coming through in his voice even if he didn't mean for it to. So much of Will's life was about making the right choices for the right reasons and internalizing most of it, and she hadn't realized how draining all of that was until the last few weeks.

How did you do it all these months, Will? How did you not break down?

She was glad she was by herself on the Tower's second floor. It was easier to talk to Will when no one else was around. She could let her guard down and for just a brief moment strip away the façade of leadership that they had given her, that she wasn't certain she was capable of living up to.

I feel like every choice I'm making is the wrong one. Why aren't you back here with me now, Will? Why are you still out there?

"It's not undefended," she said into the microphone. "I know it's hard to believe, but we're actually not nearly as incompetent as we seem."

He chuckled on the other end. "Yeah, but I have a couple of M240s that'll come in real handy when they try to land on the beach next time."

"What's an M240?"

"It's a machine gun. Spits out enough lead really fast to make things uncomfortable for an invading force. Put two on the beach and we're all set. What do you think?"

Machine guns. On the beach. It was as if she were living in a World War II movie.

"Lara," he said when she didn't respond right away.

"I'm still here…"

"I love you. Have I said that lately? I've always meant to."

He said it with such seriousness that it made her catch her breath slightly.

"I love you, too," she said, barely getting the words out.

"You hesitated for a moment," he said. Was that an attempt at humor? Will was bad at jokes. That was Danny's department.

"I didn't," she said.

"Don't tell me you've found someone else. You always did have eyes for Blaine."

"He's already taken, so you can relax. No one's replacing you yet."

"I hear a warning in there somewhere."

"Good, because I was afraid I was being too subtle."

"Loud and clear, babe."

"Glad to hear it. Now, how much longer until you come home?"

"Soon," he said. "We'll be on the road soon, and then home."

She recycled through their conversation from yesterday. The farmhouse. The soldiers on the roads. The town of Dunbar...

"What happened to the soldiers from last night?" she asked. "I thought you said they had you surrounded at the farmhouse?"

"They did. But they were gone when the sun came up."

"How did you do that?"

"I didn't do anything. They were just...gone. It doesn't matter why."

"Doesn't it?"

"No." He paused for a moment before adding, "What matters is that we should be back on the road in half an hour. If all goes well, we'll be home by three or four today."

"With Gaby and Danny..."

"That's the plan."

This time it was her turn to pause. After a while, she said, "What if it's a trap, Will? The soldiers. What if they pulled back to ambush you further down the road?"

"Maybe. But we'll cross that bridge when we get to it." Then, with more than a hint of approval in his voice, "You're thinking like a soldier now. I like that."

"I've been hanging around you and Danny for too long, picking up bad habits."

"Danny will be happy to hear that. He likes spreading his bad habits around. Among other things. Smelly things."

"I'm sure he does."

"Lara..."

"Yes, Will."

"I love you."

Again, there was something in his voice, a surprising seriousness that made her wonder what was actually going on out there with him, Danny, and Gaby. He had told her what had happened last night at the farmhouse, how they had made it through, and that they were all "in one piece." That should have comforted her, but Will's idea of "one piece" was a little different than hers...and every other person in the world.

Despite all that, hearing him tell her that he loved her made her smile anyway. "I thought we already did this..."

"Do it again anyway."

"I'm tired, Will."

"You're not that tired."

"I slept inside the boat house on the beach last night. Did you know that? I think I clocked a few minutes total."

"Ouch."

"That's what my back says."

He chuckled again. "I'll be home soon."

"Promise?" she said. She realized how silly she sounded as soon as the word left her mouth, but she didn't care, especially down here on the second floor alone with just Will on the other side of the radio.

"I promise," he said. "Whatever it takes, whatever happens, you won't have to face another night alone."

"Because you'll be here with me."

"Yes..."

There was something about the way he said that. *"Yes."* It should have put her mind at ease, because Will making a promise was as close to a sure thing as you could get these days. But the way he said it made her hesitate for some reason.

"Now," he said before she could put her troubled thoughts into words, "what's this Carly was saying about a new boat?"

"It's a yacht." Lara smiled. "And it's big..."

CHAPTER 3

WILL

SUNRISE BROUGHT THE peace and tranquility that he always longed for, but also that nagging sense of incompleteness, because it was another day without Lara. How long had it been now? Weeks? It felt like months. Even his daily communications with her through the radio only left him needing more.

Feeling the morning's warmth against his face after the brutal encounter of the previous night made him smile for the first time in hours. He should be grateful to have another day when so many people didn't have that luxury. Lance was one of those poor souls, but Annie, his girlfriend, had made it through. So had the two girls that had come out of Dunbar with Gaby. Both Danny and Gaby had also made it, though, like him, they had seen better days.

So what else is new?

"Smells like a trap," Danny said through the radio now.

Will picked up the two-way from the front passenger seat. "What does a trap smell like?"

"Warm and fuzzy, and not the nice kind of warm and fuzzy. Slightly odorous, with a hint of sewage."

"Nice imagery."

"I do my best."

"We gotta find out one way or another, right? Can't stay at the farmhouse another day, not after last night."

"I don't know what you're talking about. Last night was a hoot and a half. And you know how much I like my hooting and halfing."

"How far are we from the interstate?" Gaby asked.

He didn't have to look at the folded map on the seat next to him. He had been counting the distance ever since they left the farmhouse this morning. "Ten minutes, give or take."

"Ten minutes to death," Danny said.

"That's the spirit."

"Oh, sorry, did I say that out loud? My bad."

Danny and Gaby were in the Nissan Titan behind him, carrying the two girls and Annie in the backseat. Their truck followed closely behind his, leaving just enough distance for both vehicles to stop on a dime and *(retreat)* maneuver around any obstacles, if necessary. Will drove the Toyota Tacoma by himself, the wind rushing in through the missing driver-side window. The Nissan was the bigger of the two vehicles, so it made sense for it to carry the others, including most of their supplies, while he used the smaller *(and disposable)* mid-size Tacoma.

"Is this really a good idea, Will?" Gaby asked through the radio. "Splitting up like this?"

"We're not splitting up. We're just making it harder for them to hit us with an ambush."

"But if we know there's an ambush up ahead…"

"Can't be helped. We need to get home, and there's only one way to do that. Straight ahead."

"Right into the jaws of death," Danny chimed in. "Oops. Did I say that out loud, too? Damn my charming mouth."

Will understood Gaby's apprehension. In fact, he shared it. But he had spent the entire night, while waiting for the second attack that never came, thinking about this, turning the options over in his head. There were always options, but some were more possible than others.

And time was against them. Time was always against them.

Time…and Kate.

"Like a certain little island that should have stayed quiet. This is what happens when you stick your head out and get my attention, Will. I grab a hammer."

Kate was talking about Song Island. About the message Lara had broadcast out into the world.

How much of it was true? How much of it was just an excuse to attack? Kate wasn't Kate anymore; this Kate, this *ghoul* Kate, wasn't above a bald-faced lie.

But they had to get back home to Song Island. That was the only thing he knew with absolute certainty. Lara and the others had made it through yesterday thanks to a combination of guts and tough decisions, but what were the chances of that kind of favorable circumstances two straight nights?

Maybe, maybe not.

He couldn't risk it, because the stakes were too high…and time was running out.

It was still a kilometer away from their position when Will took his foot off the gas, slowing the Tacoma from thirty-five miles per hour to thirty, then twenty-five, until he had stopped completely in the middle of the two-lane highway.

Route 13.

Not-so-lucky thirteen.

Then again, given how they'd managed to stay alive, maybe it wasn't such a bad stretch of road after all.

He glanced at his left-side mirror. Danny, in the Titan behind him, had also parked and left a twenty-meter space between the two cars.

On cue, his radio squawked, and Danny's voice came through. "Home sweet home."

"Not quite," Will said. "But we're getting there."

"You and what army?"

"You, me, the girls…"

"The bad guys don't stand a chance…says the two idiots in the trucks about to drive right through an ambush."

Will grinned. "Captain Optimism."

"Hey, you know me, always bringing the funk. Just ignore the BO."

"It's getting harder by the day," Gaby said.

"Ouch," Danny said. "You really know how to hurt a guy's feelings."

Will leaned forward against the steering wheel and focused out the front windshield. The portion of the glass in front of him was dirty, but at least it didn't have a bullet hole to obscure his vision like the passenger side half. Danny's bullet had caused that, along with the bloody spot left behind on the seat and headrest.

He unzipped his tactical pack on the passenger seat, pulled out a pair of small binoculars, and peered through them. The same buildings from yesterday rose out of the flat scenery flanking the highway, looking like something humanity simply decided to drop into the middle of nowhere. The last time he was here, men on horseback had been trying to kill Gaby, forcing them to retreat backward. They couldn't do that today. Going back was out of the question. Everything was in front of them, including the gray concrete structure on the other side of the buildings.

Interstate 10.

It would take him west toward a small town called Salvani. From there, it was a straight shot south down to Beaufont Lake and Lara. He needed to reach that stretch of gray concrete in the worst way.

"What do you see, Will?" Gaby asked through the radio.

It was a good question. What did he see, really? Seemingly empty *(Yeah, right)* buildings on both sides of the road, and I-10 beckoning them. This was the first sign of civilization other than the half dozen or so abandoned farmhouses they had passed since they took off this morning.

"Will?" Gaby said through the radio again. "What do you see?"

It's not what I see, it's what I don't see.

Nothing and everything.

"The same feeder road businesses from yesterday," he said into the radio. "And I-10 on the other side."

"What about the posse from yesterday that tried to perforate our little Gaby?" Danny asked. "They didn't seem like the 'wander off and not come back' types."

"No signs of anyone on horseback."

"Hunh. I guess my prayers last night worked. Now all I have to do is sit back and wait for that private jet to take me to Song Island. You guys can hop along if you want. I'll only charge half-price."

"You're a swell guy, Danny."

"Just don't tell anyone. I got a reputation to maintain."

Will reached over and pulled his M4A1 off the floor where it had been leaning against the hump between the two front seats. He laid it on the passenger seat with the stock facing him for an easy, fast grab.

"Well, what are we waiting for?" Danny said through the radio. "We gonna sit here on our hands and wait for your ghoulfriend to try her luck again?"

"'Ghoulfriend'?" Gaby said.

Danny chuckled. "I came up with that, you know."

"Somehow, I figured that, Danny." Then Gaby said, "Are we really going to do this, Will?"

We don't have any choice, Will thought, but said instead, "We have to get home. It's not about the island. There are a thousand islands out there. It's about the people on it. Lara, Carly…"

"…Maddie, Blaine…," Gaby continued.

"Carly," Danny added.

"He already said Carly."

"I know, but she's so special she deserves to be mentioned twice."

"You're such a charmer."

"Why do you think Carly lets me do questionable things to her?"

"I think I just threw up a little in my mouth," Gaby said.

"There goes breakfast," Danny said. Then, "So, back to our little Sophie's choice here. I don't know about you guys, but I got people to see and things to shoot, and if that means pulling a Clint Eastwood and *Gauntlet*ing it through that little two-horse town, then so be it."

"What's *Gauntlet?*" Gaby asked.

"Damn, kid, what are you, a kid?"

"Kind of."

"It's a movie starring the baddest man alive, Clint Eastwood. Ol' Dirty Harry plays a cop—of course—who has to get a witness to court in order to testify and all that good stuff. But in order to do that, he has to brave an army of gun-toting bad guys waiting to shoot him. Which he did."

"Clint had an armor-plated bus," Will said.

"And you got me. Same difference."

"God, you guys are old," Gaby said.

"Shut up and get off my lawn," Danny said.

Will tuned them out for a moment, letting the group of buildings in front of him fill his vision.

Options. What were his options?

There were a couple, but all of them would take time. Too much time. That was the one thing he didn't have at the moment.

"Like a certain little island that should have stayed quiet. This is what happens when you stick your head out and get my attention, Will. I grab a hammer."

Time. They were always running out of time.

Will put the truck back in gear, but didn't take his foot off the brake.

"Well, make up your mind already," Danny said through the radio. "Some of us got places to go and things to do, ya know."

"Stick to the plan," Will said. "Understand?"

"About damn time."

"Will, are you sure?" Gaby asked.

No, he thought, but said, "Yes. Stick to the plan."

"Okay," she said, even though he could hear the obvious hesitation in her voice. "What about the machine guns? I can go out there and man one of them."

She was talking about the two M240s mounted on the roofs of the Titan and Tacoma, each one capable of unleashing a hellacious number of rounds per second. But someone had to stand out there in the open in order to use them. That made them too easy a target. He knew, because both he and Danny had shot the two men who had been manning those guns a day earlier.

"No," Will said. "You'd be too vulnerable back there. All it takes is one sniper on a rooftop and you're done. Stay inside with Danny, and stick to the plan we came up with this morning. You're in the full-size truck for a reason."

"All right," she said, but he could tell she still wasn't the least bit convinced.

He didn't blame her. He wasn't convinced either, but he had spent all night and morning thinking about it, and it was the only path he could come up with.

Time. That was the culprit. There was so little time, and the island was still so far away…

"We'll get home," he had promised Lara. *"Whatever it takes. We're not going to leave the island undefended for another day."*

"Danny," he said into the radio.

"That's my name, don't wear it out," Danny said.

"We can't let the island go undefended for another night. Agreed?"

Danny didn't respond right away.

"Danny," Will said. "Agreed?"

"Yeah," Danny said finally. "Agreed."

"Rangers lead the way."

"Is that why your blinkers are still on? How many times have I told you about that? You're making us look bad in front of the kids."

Will grinned. "Okay, everyone. Ears up, eyes open, and guns within easy reach."

"Roger, Roger," Danny said.

"We're ready back here," Gaby said, and Will almost believed her that time.

If only we had more time.
If only…if only…

He took his foot off the brake and pressed down on the gas pedal, and the Toyota started moving forward again. At first slowly, then picking up speed. Five miles an hour, ten, then twenty, until the buildings in the distance started to grow with every passing second, including two large signs glinting under the sun. There were no indications of movement. Nothing that would tell him people had been gathering all morning.

What kind of game are you playing, Kate? I know you're behind this. In the background somewhere, pulling the strings…

Something one of the blue-eyed creatures had said to him last night was still stuck in his head:

"Don't worry," it had hissed. *"It's not going to end that easily for you, Will. Kate made us promise her this time. I think she has big plans for you."*

He picked up the radio with one hand, keyed it. "Gaby."

"Yeah," she answered.

"Whatever happens, keep moving forward. Don't stop to look back. Keep moving forward, because that's how we survive. Understand?"

She didn't answer right away.

"Gaby," he said. "Do you understand?"

"I understand," she said.

Will put the radio down and refocused on the road ahead. The sun poured streams of light down on the rooftops of the buildings gathered in front of him, and Will looked through the binoculars again, one hand on the steering wheel, and searched for glimpses of figures hiding on top of them.

Something. *Anything.*

Half a kilometer now, and getting closer…

He could make out more of the buildings, including two gas stations facing off across the street from one another—a Chevron and a locally-owned business called Palermo, their signs raised high and proud like dueling billboards. There were no cars parked along the pumps of either gas station that he could see. In fact, there were no vehicles in either parking lot.

Where did all the cars go?

You always found cars where there were businesses. That was one of the undeniable patterns of a post-Purge world. He was so used to seeing them abandoned in front of stores and gas stations and along streets and curbs that the total absence of them here was unnerving.

200 meters…

Route 13 wasn't well-traveled—he knew that all too well after spending two days on it—but the spot next to a major interstate was still good for business. He put away the binoculars as a restaurant popped up to his right, a Domino's to his left, and an auto body garage owned by a man named Ralph alongside a cellphone store.

150 meters…

A restaurant called Louie's, next to a furniture place advertising new and secondhand inventory. They were having a sale for just this weekend…a year ago.

100 meters…

The buildings were one story high, which made their rooftops easier to spot from a distance. He couldn't make out every detail, but if there was someone *(someones)* up there right now, they were well hidden. Of course, Josh's boys would know they were already on their way. You couldn't hide the sound of two trucks moving up a flat and empty road for miles. He didn't discount the hidden presence of scouts around the farmhouse, either, or along the highway as they traveled across it. Men whose job it was to watch and radio ahead.

That's what I would do.

He glanced briefly at the radio. He should call this off. Try their luck some other way. Use one of those other options he had considered this morning. Yes, they would take longer. Not just hours, but days…

Can't afford days.

Not even close…

There was no getting around it. The enemy knew where they were going. Which made the lack of activity, the apparent nothingness of the road since they left the farmhouse, the stuff of nightmares. There was nothing worse than knowing that the bad guys knew you were coming. He had endured plenty of that during his time in Afghanistan.

Fifty meters...

He gripped the steering wheel with both hands and looked over to make sure the M4A1 was where he had left it. He did a last-minute weapons and inventory check, then gave the Titan behind him a second glance to make sure it was still back there.

Forty meters...

Now!

Will gunned it. He slammed down on the gas pedal until he felt it *thud* against the floor. The Tacoma leaped forward like a caged monster finally unleashed, its engine roaring exponentially louder and louder as he flooded it with gas. The truck bucked and fought under him, and it was all he could to do hold on with both hands on the steering wheel for dear life.

He didn't have to look to know Danny was doing the same thing behind him in the Titan. He could always trust Danny. And he would need to, now.

The Domino's to his left disappeared in a streak of red, white, and blue, then the restaurant to his right (something *Onions*; he hadn't caught the rest of the name) did the same thing. Up ahead, the Chevron and Palermo rushed up toward him, their signs beckoning him forward, sunlight glinting off the sharp, metallic edges.

He kept the truck floored, the speedometer rising on the dashboard.

From thirty miles to forty, to fifty, to *sixty*—

The first shot came when he was almost at the gas stations. He didn't know if he had caught them off guard, or if they had been waiting for him to get close all along. Not that it mattered. He had been waiting for it and his foot remained on the gas pedal as the bullet chopped into the side of the Tacoma; there was a loud-ringing *ping!* as it pierced metal.

Crack! A second shot fired, this one coming from his left, as another bullet went *ping!* off the other side of the truck.

There were a third and fourth shot, both producing their own *ping!* as they either ricocheted or punched through another part of his car.

A flicker of movement, and Will caught sight of the first sniper standing up on the square-shaped roof of the platform that covered the gas pumps of the Palermo to his right. The man's form was silhouetted by the sun, and for a second—just a brief second—Will thought it was a ghoul, out here in daylight, armed with a rifle.

The sniper fired down on him on semi-auto. Will braced himself—at this distance, he didn't think it would take much of a shooter to hit the windshield and him behind it—but there was no pain, because the man's bullets weren't landing. Or, at least, they weren't piercing the windshield the way he had expected them to. The man, he realized quickly, was trying to *hit the tire* of the Tacoma.

They're trying to shoot out the tires. Why are they trying to shoot out the tires?

Because they're not trying to kill us. They're trying to take us alive.

Why?

Kate…

"*Don't worry,*" the blue-eyed ghoul had hissed at him last night. "*It's not going to end that easily for you, Will. Kate made us promise her this time. I think she has big plans for you.*"

Kate, this is your doing, isn't it?

"*I think she has big plans for you…*"

He glimpsed more figures rushing out of the Palermo store. Men in camouflage uniforms. Josh's soldiers.

The second sniper was to his left, also standing on the platform over the Chevron's gas pumps. But this one wasn't shooting at him. The man was firing at the Titan coming up behind him.

The *ping-ping-ping!* of bullets bouncing off both moving vehicles rang up and down the street. He was amazed he could actually hear it over the loud roar of the Tacoma.

And there, up ahead—*Interstate 10.*

It was elevated, with a view of more businesses on the other side of its underpass. The turn was coming up. Right would take him onto the feeder road, then up and onto the interstate itself. Salvani was waiting for him on the other side. Then south to Song Island.

Easy as pie. All he had to do was make the turn now and—

There were two of them. Both trucks with large tires that made them look like hulking predators. One was black, and the other cherry red. They were massive against the sunlight, appearing out from behind the gas stations where they had been hiding all this time. There were uniformed men in the back, and though he was surprised by the lack of mounted machine guns, they made up for it with two shooters in the bed of each truck. He almost laughed at the sight of the four men in the backs trying desperately to hold onto the fast-moving vehicles as they were tossed around like rag dolls.

Will knew what they were trying to do. It didn't take Patton to figure out their plan. The snipers were trying to shoot out his tires, and if that didn't work, the two "monster" trucks bursting onto Route 13 directly in front of him right now would cut off his path to the interstate. It was so simple even a CPA masquerading as a soldier could have come up with it.

And I drove right into it. So who's the sucker here?

He grabbed the radio and shouted into it, "Don't stop! Don't you let him stop, Gaby!"

"Will!" Gaby shouted back.

"Get to the island! Whatever you do, get back to the island!"

"Will!"

She might have said something else, but he had already dropped the radio and returned both hands to the steering wheel. His eyes were fixed out the windshield and on the two trucks. They took up positions in the middle of the road and parked nose-to-nose, both vehicles occupying the entire two lanes. The only way around them was up the curb and into the parking lots of either the Chevron or the Palermo, and there were already men in uniforms, carrying assault rifles and racing out of both gas stations. He counted at least half a dozen on each side.

Jesus Christ, Josh, where do you get all these assholes from?

He saw what was in front and to the sides of him, and Will knew what he would find even before he took a quick peek at the rearview mirror. He looked past Danny and Gaby in the Titan and saw two similarly large trucks appearing in the road behind them, blocking off their retreat.

The snipers were still shooting, trying to hit the tires but missing badly.

Amateurs, Will thought, wanting to laugh. Danny could have shot off the tires on a moving vehicle. If he had missed once, he would have corrected for the next shot. But these guys had already wasted half their magazines (if not more), and they hadn't come close to knocking either the Tacoma or the Titan off course.

Better luck next time, boys!

They must have known he wasn't going to stop, because one of the soldiers in the back of the cherry-red truck up ahead said something to the man standing next to him, and they both leaped off the vehicle. Two seconds later, Will smashed the front grill of the Tacoma into the noses of both parked trucks. They had stopped so close to one another (part of the plan, probably) that it didn't take much to get both of them at the same time.

The loud *crash!* of metal against metal spun both vehicles out of the road, and he glimpsed a body flying through the air. Then, his vision blurred at the same time the airbag deployed and slammed into his face. His hands were ripped from the steering wheel by the blinding blow as the Tacoma spun out of control. It seemed to go round and round in a dozen revolutions, but he guessed it was probably more like one or maybe half of one, until it crashed into a streetlight pole, the sound of more metal grinding against metal piercing what little of his senses were still functioning.

He didn't actually have to see the smoke flooding out from the crumpled hood to know it was happening. He could feel the steam filling up the cab, though that took a backseat to the pain pounding through every inch of his face and chest at the moment. The airbag had done its job and kept him alive, but it had also rendered him useless. He scrambled to push the nylon fabric out of his face and reached sideways for the M4A1.

Except the rifle wasn't there anymore.

He was still looking for the carbine when the shooting outside broke through the haze. There was the loud *ping-ping-ping!* of bullets hitting their intended target—which *wasn't him*.

The Titan. They were still shooting at Danny, Gaby, and the girls.

He waited to hear the sound of another crash to signal that the chase was over, that the Titan had also spun out. Maybe one of the snipers would finally get lucky. *Even the sun had to shine up a dog's ass once in its life*, he thought.

But instead, the sound of ricocheting bullets seemed to become more distant with every passing second. Which had to be good news, right? If there was no crash, no screams, and the *ping-ping-ping!* was fading, that could only mean...

Faster, Danny. Get to Song Island. Save them.

Save Lara...

He was dazed from the impact, which made finding the rifle even harder. It was difficult to focus on the passenger seat, the sea of sprinkled glass, or the shattered window on the other side of the vehicle. The passenger-side door may or may not even still be connected to the car.

Was he losing consciousness? No. He had gotten hit in worse ways, and he'd always made it through. Besides, the airbag had saved his life—

Voices, coming toward him.

Will abandoned his search for the M4A1 and groped for his holstered Glock instead. He drew it and turned toward the door, somehow finding the handle despite the fact there were now three levers instead of one. He managed to grab the right one—or were all three the right ones?—and pulled.

A gust of cooling Louisiana wind hit him in the face, piling on the already throbbing pain. He stumbled out of the truck, almost lost his balance but somehow regained it, and saw the first man coming toward him with a rifle at the ready. The man hadn't fired yet, which Will thought was stupid because *he* wasn't going to hesitate.

He lifted the Glock, but before he could fire, something hit him on the side of the head. The blow stunned him and Will staggered to his left, his gun hand falling to his side. Suddenly the sidearm seemed much heavier than it should be. Like a bowling ball. Or maybe a really big metal pole. Gripping it was difficult.

And slippery. Why was it slippery?

A second blow to the same part of the head made him drop the gun. He stumbled, then was sitting on his knees a second later.

How'd he get down here? He didn't have a clue. Things weren't making sense. He still couldn't focus on any one thing, especially not on the dozen or so pairs of feet surrounding him.

More voices. Men's voices.

Garbled at first, but slowly, very slowly, he started to make out actual words and sentences. Which was a hell of a feat, given that he could barely keep his eyes open. He just wanted to lie down and go to sleep. That would be nice. When was the last time he had actually slept? Days? Weeks?

He couldn't remember...

"Why are we keeping him alive?" someone was asking. He didn't sound very happy about it.

"Shut up," someone else snapped.

"I'm just saying, let's just put him out of his misery."

"You're not in charge here."

"Then who is?"

"*She* is."

"'She'? Who the fuck is—" the man started to say, but never finished.

She? Who is she? Why won't someone answer him?

He should know the answer. And maybe he did. It was right there at the tip of his tongue. Or the edge of his brain. Or wherever it was that words came from. Or the letters that would form those words. And make a name.

She. Who is she?

I know that answer!

Hands grabbed and pulled him up, saving him from the hard concrete that was biting into his knees. He had lost the Glock and couldn't find the rifle, but he still had his cross-knife. Ah. The trusty cross-knife. It had saved his and Danny's lives on the first night of The Purge. It would be strapped to his left hip, still in its sheath.

If only he could reach down for it...

"What about the other truck?" a third voice asked. "Should we go after them?"

"Don't worry about them," the second man said. He was clearly in charge. "They're not gonna get far."

They were carrying him across the parking lot now. Which one? The Chevron or the Palermo?

He smelled old motor oil and spilled gas on the ground around him, all these months later.

Despite the cool air, he was still dripping sweat as he was carried across the parking lot. Curiously, his perspiration looked bright red for some reason.

Focus.

Focus!

The fact that he was still alive was all that mattered right now. As long as he was breathing, there were options available to him. He just had to see them—and seize the right one—when they presented themselves, and they would. They always did.

Don't worry, Lara. I'm coming home.

I'll just be a little later than expected, that's all...

CHAPTER 4

GABY

SHE HADN'T SAID a word since Route 13 and was content to watch the vehicles strung along both sides of the interstate flash by in groups of two, three, and every now and then, a lone car that looked out of place. But mostly, there were just empty slabs of gray concrete, and despite the cars, she couldn't shake the feeling of wandering through a barren and lifeless world.

She was numb all over and barely felt the wind against her face, flooding in through the shattered front passenger-side window. There were holes in the windshield and dry blood on the seat behind and under her, but she was used to the stains. It helped that they weren't hers, but instead belonged to the men who had been in the vehicle a day earlier, when they had the misfortune of running across Will and Danny.

Danny drove with a singular determination, both hands on the steering wheel, his eyes seeking out ambushes that weren't there. He was calm and steady, and to look at him, she wouldn't know he was riding in a car that was covered in bullet holes. If most of that was a mask, Danny wore it well.

"Don't stop! Don't you let him stop, Gaby!"

She hadn't had to convince Danny to keep going. He knew the odds and what was at stake, just like she did. Not that the knowing made abandoning Will back there any easier. If it was hard for her, it had to have been hell for Danny.

"Get to the island! Whatever you do, get back to the island!"

"Gaby," a voice said behind her.

She turned and smiled back at Claire, who was sitting in the backseat with the FHN semiautomatic shotgun clutched between her legs, the barrel pointed up at the ceiling of the Nissan Titan. Claire was thirteen, but the girl already had the stern face of an adult and the lines around the eyes to match.

"I'm sorry about Will," Claire said. She flicked absently at a strand of dirty blonde hair draped over her face. "He was a great guy. I really liked him."

"Is," Gaby said. "Will's not dead yet. If he died that easily, then he wouldn't be Will."

Claire nodded back. Gaby couldn't tell if the girl believed her (Had she been convincing enough, or did her own doubts come through despite her best attempts?), or if she was just humoring her. With anyone else—Milly, for instance—the latter wouldn't have been possible, but Claire wasn't anyone else. The girl had lost more than her share, and Gaby didn't for one moment mistake her for just another "kid."

She's like me. We haven't been kids for a long time now.

"How's everyone doing back there?" Gaby asked.

"Scared," Claire said, "but we're okay."

"We're okay," Milly said to the right of Claire.

Milly was thirteen too, with a round face and large eyes. One of these days, Milly would grow up and turn boys' heads. Seeing the two girls side-by-side was always such an amazing contrast. Milly looked fragile and unready for the world, especially sitting next to Claire, with her dirty hair and steely resolve.

"Annie?" Gaby said, looking to Claire's left.

Annie had been staring out the window the whole time, and she flinched noticeably at the sound of her name. She gathered herself and gave Gaby something that was supposed to be a smile. "I'm okay. You?"

"I'm in one piece. We all are, thank God."

"I don't know how," the older woman said. "They were shooting from everywhere. I wasn't this scared back at the farmhouse last night. All those guns, all those bullets... It's a miracle we're still alive. *How* are we even still alive?"

"I don't know. Lucky, I guess."

"I haven't felt very lucky these last few days." She attempted another smile, and it came out equally bad. "But I guess we're owed a little, huh?"

"Yeah," Gaby said. She thought about Lance. The *other* Lance. Annie's boyfriend, and not one of the soldiers who had guarded her back in L15. The good Lance had died last night in a pile of rubble. "Song Island's not far now. We have plenty of gas, and we'll be there by noon today. Right, Danny?"

"Oh sure, you betcha," Danny said without hesitation. "Smooth sailing now, kids. You got 'em, I suggest you smoke 'em."

"Smoke what?" Claire asked.

"He's just being funny," Gaby said. "We're getting there. Just hang on a bit more."

Claire nodded. Annie, next to her, had already looked back outside the window at the seemingly never-ending wave of concrete dividers that separated the east and westbound lanes. Will had once told her about the thousand-yard stare that soldiers would get after a firefight, the result of being shell-shocked by combat. Annie looked like she was having one of those at the moment.

Gaby sat back in her seat and looked at Danny. "Were they just bad shots back there? Was that how we survived?"

"No one's that bad," Danny said. "They were aiming for the tires."

"The tires?"

She took a moment to digest what he had said. The tires? They were shooting at their tires? Was that why they had missed the windshield? Every second during the ordeal, she had waited and waited for the first bullet to punch through the glass or the roof and kill her, Danny, and the girls in the back. It would have been easy, because the snipers were firing down on them without anything at all blocking their view.

Instead, all she could remember was the *ping-ping-ping!* of bullets hitting the sides of the vehicles.

He's right. They were trying to shoot out the tires.

"Why were they doing that?" she asked him.

"Because they were trying to stop us, not kill us," Danny said. "The only reason we survived back there was because they were trying to take us alive."

"They didn't seem to care whether we lived or died yesterday."

"Different day, new orders. The only thing you can count on as a grunt in the field is the higher-ups sitting around in their comfy chairs back at headquarters, changing their minds from day to day."

"So someone changed the orders. Who?"

Danny didn't answer right away. Gaby watched him closely. She looked past the bruises, the broken nose that was still healing, and the cuts that covered a face that always used to remind her of a transplanted California surfer, even though she knew for a fact Danny had never lived anywhere else outside of Texas after his Army days.

"Danny," she pressed. "Whose orders were they following back there?"

"I don't know."

"You're lying."

"I'm not."

"Bullshit. I know you well enough to know when you're lying."

He looked over and grinned. It was a valiant attempt, but it wasn't anywhere close to being the usual Danny grin, and she thought he probably knew it, too.

"You sound like Carly," he said.

"I'll take that as a compliment." Then, "Tell me, Danny."

"I don't know for sure…"

"But you know something."

"Willie boy and I talked about it on and off. She's been dogging him since she went turncoat."

Gaby knew who Danny was talking about without hearing the name. She had heard it often enough. Not from Will or Danny, but from Lara and Carly. The topic never came up on purpose, but something would happen that reminded them *she* was out there. Both women had known her in the early days of The Purge, especially Carly, and they knew what she had become later, and still was now.

Out there, somewhere.

"You know about her and us," Danny said. "More specifically, her and him."

"They were at the underground bunker in Starch, Texas, together. You all were."

"She came back with a vengeance while we were out there looking for you. A few nights ago, she made one of her patented appearances in his dream. Or nightmare. Foggy walkabout." He shrugged. "Whatever you want to call it. She was there, and she showed him that whole mess in Dunbar."

"With Harrison…"

"Uh huh."

She paused. Gaby didn't want to say the woman's name, but she had to make sure. "Are we talking about the same person, Danny?"

He looked at her and mouthed the word, *"Kate."*

She knew the name, but hearing Danny say it—even if he didn't actually say it out loud—made the hairs on the back of her neck stand up.

Kate.

Will's Kate.

And now her men—her human hands and feet in the daylight—had him. That was the bad news. The good news was that knowing that Kate was behind all of this made it easier to accept that Will was still alive back there, and that, ironically enough, buoyed her spirits. Because he was Will, and as long as he was still breathing, there was a chance.

"Someone once told me I'm too stubborn to die," he had said to her not all that long ago. *"Okay, more than one person, actually. There's a good chance it could be true."*

For the first time since the shooting stopped, Gaby found herself smiling into the wind.

THEY DIDN'T STOP for another thirty minutes, when Milly declared she couldn't go another mile without using the bathroom. Of course, there wasn't a bathroom or a roadside rest stop anywhere nearby, so Danny parked the Titan in the middle of the highway, and Milly jumped out and ran behind a blue sedan.

Gaby climbed out to stretch and look over the damage from the ambush. Danny was right when he said the shooters had been trying to disable the car instead of killing them. The bullet holes were all concentrated around the four tires, which by some miracle had all made it through in one piece. She didn't know what they would have done if one of the shooters had actually managed to puncture a tire. Did they even have a spare in the back somewhere? What would have happened if they had lost two tires?

Danny hobbled out of the truck on the other side. For a guy moving on one good leg—the one encased in a makeshift split that was really just floorboards and duct tape—he had driven amazingly well throughout. He was still grimacing with every step, and when he turned his back to her, she heard the *clinking* of pills in a bottle he had retrieved from one of his cargo pants pockets.

She wished she could say seeing Danny hurt was a novel thing, but the sad truth was they were all hurt. Their entire life since The Purge had been a series of running and fighting, and that kind of existence tended to leave scars and bruises. If they weren't struggling against the creatures in the night, they were braving their human lackeys in the day. Thank God those same men couldn't shoot for crap, or they might have been dead a dozen times over by now.

The sun beat down on her as she peered down the highway. Will was back there, somewhere, captured by those very fallible humans right now.

"Someone once told me I'm too stubborn to die."

She smiled again. Those same men were going to find out just how stubborn he was very soon. As long as Will was breathing, she had faith he'd find his way back to the island. Or wherever Lara ended up, anyway.

Gaby glanced around her to make sure they were alone. I-10 consisted of four lanes, two on each side, and had become low to the ground as they left Route 13 far behind. The east- and westbound lanes were separated by a tall divider with a healthy stretch of shoulder on both sides of the concrete barricade. Tall walls of wood flanked them, and it had been ten minutes since they last drove past a business advertising seafood and "Good Eats." There hadn't been anything else since, which made stopping here ideal.

With the truck's engine turned off, they would be able to hear another vehicle coming for miles. More than enough warning to get back in and flee. It still nagged at her that the soldiers hadn't pursued them from Route 13. They had chased after them on foot for a while, but those large trucks that had tried to block their path, the same ones Will had barreled into with the Tacoma, or the ones that had cut off their retreat, hadn't pursued.

They have a plan. Whoever's leading them, has a plan.

Is that you out there calling the shots, Josh? Is that you doing Kate's bidding?

She looked down at her watch: 10:16 A.M.

It felt like evening already. The temperature had lessened noticeably when they stepped out of the farmhouse this morning. It was hovering around seventy degrees at the moment, pleasant enough that she almost didn't realize for the first time in a long time that she wasn't sweating profusely under her clothes while standing out in the open.

According to the map they carried with them, they were already halfway to Lake Charles. It would take another hour of driving at a decent rate of speed to get there. From there, the town of Salvani wasn't far off. Once they made it past that, it was south toward Song Island. Smooth sailing.

Because everything up to this point has been smooth sailing so far, right?

Danny leaned against the driver side door and looked across the hood at her. "How're you holding up, kid?"

"I'm still standing," she said. "You?"

"Got me a busted face, with a busted nose, and a busted leg. Other than that, I feel super duper awesome."

"Glad to hear it."

Danny was looking past her at the girls. Annie had walked over to join Milly behind the sedan, while Claire was standing watch with that shotgun of hers and looking back down the highway, as if she, too, expected someone to appear in pursuit of them at any moment.

"Where are they, Danny?" Gaby asked. "They had trucks. Maybe more, stashed behind those buildings. But they just let us go. Why?"

"I don't know," Danny said. "Maybe because they got what they wanted."

"Will."

"Yeah."

"That would make sense, if she's the one pulling the strings like you thought."

"Oh, it's her, all right," Danny said with absolute certainty. "I told him never to pick up the psychos. They have separation issues. Plus, he shot her. That tends to sour a relationship, which is why I always try to avoid shooting my girlfriends."

Gaby smiled. It came out easily that time, and Danny looked pleased with himself as a result.

I guess we both needed that.

"Come on," Danny said, "let's keep truckin'. Mother always said not to look a gift horse in the mouth. If we can get to Song Island by three or four, I'll be a happy little boy with bells on his feet."

"Should we radio ahead? Tell them we're coming?"

Danny shook his head. "Not yet."

"We should tell them we're coming."

"We will, when we're closer, but...not yet."

"Why—"

"I don't know what to tell her," he said, and climbed back into the Titan without another word.

Lara. Danny was talking about Lara. As much as they both believed that Will would be fine, that as long as he was breathing he would find them *(Maybe even beat us to Song Island)*, a part of Danny had doubts.

But she didn't.

Did she?

"Girls!" Gaby called. "Let's go!"

Milly and Annie headed back, clinging to one another and looking like mother and daughter. Claire stayed behind until the two had passed her, then she turned and jogged over.

"Next stop, Song Island?" Milly asked, looking brighter than she had all day. Or maybe that was just the sun shining in her face.

"Next stop, Song Island," Gaby nodded.

"Sweet," Claire said. "I'm going to drink cold water until I barf."

THE PART OF her that had been trained by Will and Danny, and that had been surviving out here by herself without them, knew that they weren't going to reach Salvani without encountering resistance. The nineteen-year-old in her that was barely a year removed from her senior year of high school was holding out hope that it was a possibility.

She should have known better.

The first shot hadn't finished its echo before the bullet punched through the front grill of the Nissan and Danny jammed on the brake. The truck swerved slightly, Danny fighting the steering wheel for control, face contorted into a tight grimace. He finally managed to stop the vehicle, freezing it in place across the two-lane highway, the nose barely a foot from ramming into the concrete divider.

That allowed Gaby to look out her glassless window and up the road at two nondescript trucks parked about fifty yards from them. They had looked like all the other derelict vehicles they had passed since Route 13, with nothing about them standing out. Which was why Danny had almost driven right up to them when the first shot shattered the calm midday air.

Except these cars weren't abandoned, because there was a man peering back at her from behind a scope, the long barrel of his rifle leaning over the hood of the parked white Ford truck. The other vehicle was some kind of Chevy, and it sat along the shoulder. She thought she caught a glimpse of another figure moving around on the other side of its windows.

A flicker of movement drew her attention, and she didn't have to turn very far to see a third man moving on the other side of the concrete divider, jogging up the highway toward them. The man's head was bobbing up and down as he attempted to stay as low as possible, but he was doing a very poor job of it.

She twisted in her seat and shouted, "Get out the other side! Now now now!"

Then she was turning back around, opening her car door, and lunging out before she even realized what she was doing.

The other side, you idiot! Go out the other side!

Too late. Her M4 rifle was clutched tightly in her hands, though she didn't remember when she had picked it up from where it had fallen during Danny's chaotic struggle to regain control of the vehicle. As soon as her foot landed on the hard highway floor, she expected to pay for her dumb decision. When she heard the *crack!* of the rifle, instead of feeling pain in her chest, there was a *buzzing* sensation right next to her right ear. The bullet sailed past her and hit the roof of the car behind her before ricocheting into the air.

Two more shots rang out as she darted toward the back of the Nissan, the *ping! ping!* coming from behind her. She swore she could smell metal against metal. Maybe that was just her imagination, though she didn't stop to ponder it. Instead, she grabbed at the top of the truck bed and used it to slingshot herself around the corner until she saw the back bumper and kept running until she was on the other side.

She was happy to see that Danny was on the highway and pulling Milly out after him with one hand, the other holding his beat-up M4A1. Claire and Annie were already huddled against the truck, using it as a shield.

"You okay?" Claire asked when Gaby crouched down next to her.

Hey, that's my job, Gaby thought, but it took her a few seconds to stop her racing heartbeat long enough to respond. "I'm good. You?"

"I don't think I was hit."

She looked past Claire at Danny, who was depositing Milly next to Annie. "Danny…"

"I saw two," he said.

"I saw three."

"Where?"

"On the other side of the divider—"

"Check."

"—behind the white truck—"

"Double check."

"And behind the red Chevy."

"Didn't see that one," Danny said. "You still running around with just the holes God gave you?"

She managed a smile. "Yes."

"Good."

Crack! A bullet punctured the front tire on the front passenger side of the Nissan. The truck dipped slightly just before a second shot rang out and the back passenger tire joined it.

"Sonsofbitches," Danny grunted. "And I misplaced my Triple A card, too. Now how are we gonna get to Song Island on just two good tires?"

"Maybe we have some spares in the trunk?" Annie said.

Danny looked over at her, then grinned at Gaby. "Captain Optimism, this one."

"I thought you were Captain Optimism," Gaby grinned back.

"I've since decided to relinquish the title. It's too much work—"

Crack! A third shot cut Danny off, and they heard the *ping!* as the bullet pierced the other side of the vehicle.

It didn't take long for Gaby to smell it: gasoline.

She dropped to the ground and looked under the car and saw

liquid pouring to the highway on the other side. "Danny, they shot the gas tank."

"Oh my God, is the car going to explode?" Annie said, her eyes wide with terror.

"You watch too many movies," Danny said. He looked behind them, back down the highway.

"What is it?" she asked.

"They're pinning us down. Probably because they have reinforcements on the way."

"Is this why they haven't been chasing us? Because they knew that sooner or later we'd run into these guys?"

"Yeah, looks like it," he nodded. "These buggers are a lot cleverer than I gave them credit for."

"Is that a word?" Claire asked.

"What?" Danny said.

"'Cleverer.' Is that a word?"

Danny chuckled. "I got a dictionary back at the island. We'll look it up when we get there, kid." He looked past her at Gaby. "Let's hope either the Ford or the Chevy is still drivable, 'cause we're gonna need a new car if we wanna get there."

"How are we going to get to them?" she asked. "They have us pinned down, remember?"

"Normally this is when I tell Willie boy to come up with a plan, but since he's not..." Danny didn't finish. He shook his head instead, the frustration visible on his face for the first time since Route 13. "Goddammit. I told him that plan of his was shit. You heard me, right? But no, he always had to have a plan. Well, shit on my bread and rye. That didn't work out too well, did it?"

Gaby wasn't sure if he was talking to her, the girls, or...someone else.

"Danny," she said. "What do we do? How do we get out of here? If they're content to just pin us down and wait for reinforcements, we can't just sit here."

Danny blinked up at the sun. "At least the weather's finally nice. I was starting to think this place had only two decent things going for it—bad weather and bad weather."

There was enough of a cool breeze that none of them had started sweating yet despite the harried last few seconds. The sudden shift in weather, from insufferably hot to almost chilly, was a strange feeling because it was already making her think about sweaters, or a jacket, or maybe even some thermal socks—

"Hey! You back there!" a voice shouted. "Can you hear me?"

It was coming from the guy closest to them, the one behind the divider to their left. Thirty yards? Unless the man had moved further up since she last saw him.

Danny scooted closer to the front bumper of the Nissan and leaned out briefly, then pulled back a second later.

"Close?" Gaby asked.

"Twenty-seven meters, give or take," Danny said.

Gaby did the calculations in her head. Twenty-seven meters was…thirty yards. Give or take. So she wasn't too far off. That surprised and pleased her. Will used to say that combat was like playing sports—after a while, you got so used to the speed and chaos that everything started to slow down.

Too bad I can't put this skill on my college resume. Harvard would have been so impressed.

"Did you see if they were wearing uniforms?" she asked.

He shook his head. "Too well hidden."

"Hey!" the man shouted again. "I asked you a question!"

"Fuck off!" Danny shouted back.

They heard laughter, then, "I guess that's a yes."

"What do you want?" Danny shouted.

"You know what we want!"

"World peace?"

More laughter, though this time it sounded slightly forced. The man clearly wanted them to think he was enjoying this, that he had no worries whatsoever.

Yeah, right.

"That too," the man said. "But what I'd really like is for you to throw out your guns so we can have a talk."

"Oh, is that all you want?" Danny said. "Just to talk?"

"Exactly!"

"I'm gonna have to politely decline and ask you to kiss my ass instead."

"Har har," the man said. "You're a funny guy."

"You think?"

"Absolutely. That's why I'm going to shoot you in the face, funny guy."

"Well that's ironic, because that's what I did to your mom last night," Danny shouted back.

The man went quiet.

Danny looked back at Gaby and grinned. "Too much?"

"Come on, leave the moms out of this," Gaby smiled back.

"Yeah, that was definitely uncalled for." Danny glanced at his watch, then back down the highway again to make sure it was still empty. "Can't stay here forever, kid. If their reinforcements aren't already on the way, it won't be long now."

She craned her head a bit and listened, expecting to hear car engines approaching at any second, but the *drip-drip-drip* of the gas on the other side of the Nissan overwhelmed everything. The smell was also getting stronger, which meant the entire tank was going to be empty, or close enough, soon.

"Danny," she said, "what are we going to do?"

He looked at the girls. At Claire, crouched with the large shotgun, which appeared somehow even larger in her small hands. At Annie and Milly, the two of them with their arms around each other. If they were even aware of what was happening, Gaby couldn't tell.

His eyes finally settled on hers. "You and me, kid."

"Yeah..."

"And me," Claire said, looking at Gaby, then Danny. "I know how to use this," she said, clutching and unclutching the shotgun. "I saved Will's life last night."

"Yeah, you did," Danny nodded. "But that's a close-quarters weapon. Those boys are at least half a football field away—"

Crack!

All three of them ducked on instinct, but instead of hearing the familiar *ping!* of a bullet hitting the other side of the Nissan, there was instead just the echo of the gunshot.

"What the hell?" Danny said. "What were they shooting at?"

Before she could answer, there was a second *crack!*, followed by the *pop-pop-pop* of a magazine being unleashed on something. Or someone.

A moment later, there was just the silence again.

Danny and Gaby exchanged another look.

Even Claire, between them, looked confused.

"You take that side, I'll take this one," Danny said.

Gaby nodded and looked at Claire. "Stay here."

"But—" the girl protested.

"No," Gaby said, cutting her off. "One day I'll teach you how to use this," she said, showing her the M4. "For now, all that shotgun's good for is close range. You understand?"

Claire nodded grudgingly. "You'll teach me one day."

"Promise."

Gaby nodded at Danny, then turned around and moved toward the back bumper. She leaned out and looked up the highway. The white Ford was where she last saw it, about fifty yards up the road. The red Chevy was still parked across from it, but there were no signs of the men she had seen earlier.

"Anything?" she said, looking back at Danny.

He was leaning out too, when he pulled back and shook his head. "Squadoosh."

"The guy behind the divider?"

"No signs of him."

"What's going on, Danny?"

"Hell if I know." Then he sighed. "Stay here."

"No," she said, and lunged out from behind the bumper and into the open before he could protest.

Maybe it was a little bit courage, a little bit stupidity, or just a lot of adrenaline. Either way, she was sick and tired of hiding, of being hunted, and Gaby practically ran up the interstate with her rifle in front of her, eyes zeroing in on the two vehicles, looking for a head, a body, or just a limb. Something—*anything*—that she could shoot.

She was, she realized, just too pissed off to think clearly at the moment.

And Danny wasn't trying to stop her. Instead, he had somehow hopped the divider and was moving up the highway at the same time and keeping pace with her, which was amazing given that he was limping the whole time, and she was pretty sure he was in extreme pain by the way he was grimacing with every inch.

"Don't shoot!" a voice shouted.

It was male, but not the same one who had been trading barbs with Danny earlier. This one was coming from behind the Chevy.

Gaby went down on one knee and lined up her scope on the red truck. She was halfway to her target and wanted desperately to find cover, but there was none around her. She was out in the open, but at least she had her rifle. A year ago, the idea of dying with her weapon clutched in her hands would have been surreal. These days, it was the best-case scenario she could hope for.

She screened the car windows, looking for signs of a head—*something*.

But the man was smart and remained hidden.

She sneaked a peek at Danny and saw him moving steadily up the highway on the other side of the concrete barrier. He was twenty-five yards from the truck and getting closer, and it didn't seem like the shooter had noticed him.

"Gaby!" the voice said.

The sound of her name sent chills through her.

What the hell?

Danny had stopped ten yards from the closest vehicle and went into a crouch. She could just barely make out the top of his head on the other side of the structure, but she knew he had reacted exactly the same way she had—confused and surprised by the sound of her name.

"Gaby!" the man called again. "Don't shoot!"

"Who the hell are you?" Gaby shouted back.

"I'm throwing out my weapon!"

"Do it!"

An AR-15 skidded across the highway from behind the Chevy. It didn't stop until it had gotten ten feet from the back bumper. A second later, a Glock followed, landing a few feet from the rifle.

"I'm unarmed!" the man shouted.

"Come out with your hands up!" Gaby shouted, trying to inject as much menace into her voice as possible.

She didn't have a clue what was happening. Where did the other two men go? Was there some kind of gunfight? A betrayal? Was the last remaining man trying to surrender to them? Was this some kind of trick? If it was, it was overly elaborate, because the shooters had them pinned. They had all the advantage and this…this didn't make any sense at all.

What the hell is going on?

"Gaby!" the man shouted again.

There was something in the way he said her name, as if he knew her. As if they were *close*. Except she didn't recognize the voice.

Or did she?

"Yeah?" she shouted back.

"You don't recognize my voice, do you?" the man asked.

Not a goddamn clue.

"Maybe!" she said instead. "Come out and show yourself!"

"Coming out!" he said. "Tell the guy behind the divider not to shoot!"

Danny stood up on the westbound shoulder and took aim as the figure stepped out from behind the truck, his hands raised above his head. She immediately picked up the camouflage uniform, with the familiar white star insignia above a name tag and a patch with the Louisiana boot on one shoulder.

The man walked toward her. The sun was behind him, and instead of providing the clarity she needed, the light instead turned him into a silhouetted figure whose face was hidden almost completely in shadows.

"You really don't recognize my voice?" he asked. She thought he sounded almost hurt.

"No," Gaby said, standing up. She hadn't lowered her rifle, and neither had Danny. She squinted against the sunlight, trying to see his face. "What happened to the other two?"

"I shot them."

"Why?"

"I had to, or they would have killed or captured you. I couldn't let either of those things happen." He paused, then added, "Has it really been that long? You really don't remember me…"

By now, Danny had reached the trucks and climbed back onto their part of the highway. He hobbled his way around the Chevy and then peered behind the white Ford.

"Danny?" Gaby called. "What do you see?"

"Two bodies," Danny said. "Looks like he's not lying. He took them both out."

"I told you," the man said.

"Who the hell are you?" Gaby said.

"Can I come closer?" he asked.

She nodded. "Slowly…"

He continued walking toward her, making a concerted effort not to move his hands too much or lengthen his stride to give the impression of aggression. He was taller than her, though not by very much. Maybe five-ten to her five-seven.

"They made me cut my hair," he said. When he got to within ten yards of her, he stopped and she could finally see his face.

"You," she said, the word coming out as barely a whisper.

"Too bad, too," Nate said, smiling wryly at her. "Chicks dug the Mohawk."

CHAPTER 5

LARA

WILL WOULD HAVE taken Gage into the back of the boat, made him stand next to the railing, then shot him in the back of the head and let the body drop to the water below. And Lara wouldn't have lifted a hand to stop him, or think about it ever again. Will did what had to be done and though it sometimes stayed with him, he never looked back on it with regret. Or, at least, he never let her think that he did.

She wasn't Will, though.

Instead of putting Gage out of his *(their)* misery, she decided to use him, always keeping in mind what the man was capable of. She had no doubts there were crimes he had committed since The Purge that she didn't know about and that he would never willingly confess to, but she knew what he had intended to do to the island. He had admitted as much, and Keo had told her what he had overheard Gage and his first mate, the man without the head inside the bridge, discussing before he opened fire on them.

"They've done it before," Keo had said. "A lot of times, from the sound of it. They might as well be talking about the weather."

"And you're sure?" she had asked, looking him in the eyes because she needed to know with absolute certainty.

Keo had nodded. "I've breathed the same air, eaten with, and lived with guys like Gage. Trust me when I tell you, what they had in store for the island would have turned your stomach."

She believed him. Every word of it.

It took her a full hour to walk the entire 140-something feet of the *Trident*, slipping in and out of its three decks. The interiors were surprisingly roomy, each section broken down for crew, guests, and the owners. She ended up back on the first deck where she had arrived with Maddie and the others earlier before moving through the passenger cabins, then the crew quarters further up front. The second deck (or main, as Keo called it) contained a complete dining room that was part of a large entertainment area with a bar on the side. It was big enough for a dozen people to gather around without bumping into each other.

An owner's cabin took up the majority of available space up front, with a window that opened up onto a terrace overlooking the front of the yacht. She walked past a king-size bed, its well-used satin sheets tossed across the floor. There were spots of dried blood on the expensive carpeting, along with a pile of men and women's clothes. She did her best to not think about who they belonged to or how they had gotten there, or where their owners were at the moment.

"*Trust me when I tell you, what they had in store for the island would have turned your stomach.*"

When she stepped outside the terrace, she had no trouble picking up Jo, Bonnie's little sister, standing guard in the boat shack on the beach. The yacht had been moved a little closer to the island and they could have swam back and forth if they needed to, though of course using the boats was easier—and drier.

Jo saw her and waved, and Lara returned it.

She felt odd standing out there as if this rich man's toy belonged to her, especially knowing what Gage and his "friends" had been using it for. So she hurried back inside, giving the posh bed and furniture a longer second look. Eventually they'd have to dump most of it. The boat was diesel-powered, and although she was sure it probably wouldn't make much of a difference, the idea of leaving all these luxuries onboard felt wrong. Besides, they'd need the extra room sooner or later, and she'd rather everyone fit than be comfortable.

She moved back through the deck, past all the signs of money, from the large screen TVs that curved along with the wall to the bottles of liquor and wine behind the bar (albeit most of them appeared empty) to abstract paintings from people she had never heard of, but knew that each one probably cost more than she had ever made in her life up to this point. That might have changed if she had ever finished medical school and become an honest to goodness doctor. Those dreams were long gone, though, especially now with Zoe taking her place on the island.

So what am I now?

I guess we'll find out tonight.

Her boots left behind white sand from the beach on the expensive flooring. Some kind of glossy wood…or something. The wall paneling that adorned the place looked like it might have cost more to install than her three years of medical school. Her mind wandered back to the yacht's previous owner. Dead now. She hadn't bothered to ask Gage how the man had died. It didn't matter. Dead was dead.

Well, not really, but close.

She stepped outside onto the patio and leaned over the railing. Maddie was below her on the lower deck, busy fastening a plastic raft in place in case they needed it. The lifeboat that was supposed to be in the spot where Maddie was putting the raft now was, of course, lying somewhere at the bottom of the lake, along with its two occupants.

Two down. That leaves one.

So where's the eighth guy?

Lara unclipped her radio and keyed it. "Blaine, come in."

"What's up?" Blaine said.

"Anything yet?"

Blaine and Roy were two decks below her in the engine room, searching for a man who may or may not actually exist. Lara had gone down there and taken a look herself, but it was like stepping into the belly of a submarine—she didn't have a clue what she was looking at. It did make her glad she hadn't actually shot Gage earlier. Whatever the man was—and he was a lot of things, most of it bad— he still possessed knowledge that none of them did. She was going to exploit that until she didn't need to anymore.

After that, well...

"It's dirty down here," Blaine said through the radio, "but so far no signs of the eighth guy. But I can see why he'd be down here, though. This place is a maze. There are nooks and crannies and places I don't even have names for."

"A lot of places to hide?"

"Too many. We'd need more time and manpower to look everywhere. And if he knows the place as well as Keo thinks he does, then he'll know where to hide from us. Or move around without being seen or heard."

She didn't know what she had expected. That the eighth guy would voluntarily give himself up after hiding out all night? She was hoping, maybe, but she always knew it wasn't going to happen.

Of course not. Because that would have been too easy.

"Okay," she said into the radio. "Finish searching what you can, then get back up here. Once you're outside, seal the engine room. If he's down there, we'll just have to be satisfied with locking him in."

"What about the engine?"

"What about it?"

"What if he sabotages it?"

"Why would he do that?"

"I don't know. Isn't that what people usually do in the movies? To keep us from launching a nuke or shooting someone important? Or, in this case, using the boat?"

Sabotage? She hadn't thought of that.

So what else hadn't she thought about?

"Or he could just do enough damage so we can't use it, but he can fix it later," Blaine said.

"Blaine, you're overthinking it."

"Am I?"

"Yes," she said, doing her best to sound confident. Did it work?

Was she just fooling herself? She added, "Finish up and get up here. Whatever happens, we'll deal with it."

"You're the boss," Blaine said.

So everyone keeps reminding me. God help us all.

She clipped the radio back to her hip. Maybe the eighth guy didn't even exist, and Gage was playing games with them. Or maybe the man didn't know how to count. Either way, she didn't like the mere prospect of having someone running around on the boat who could hurt one of her people. Not that she could do anything about it at the moment. At least, not without more manpower.

Below her, Maddie was looking up in her direction. "I always wanted my own personal yacht!" she shouted.

"What were you going to name it?" Lara called down.

"Jaxon. With an *x*."

"Ex-boyfriend?"

"I wish. He didn't know I existed."

"Well, now you have a yacht. That'll teach him."

Maddie laughed, then went back to cinching the craft into place.

Lara looked down at her watch. It was almost ten.

Will had called two hours ago. He wouldn't call again for another few hours, until he was almost at the island. She had wanted to ask him to make it three contacts instead of their usual two, just for today, but had decided against it. Will had other things to worry about out there, like men in uniforms with assault rifles. The less she put on his plate, the more energy he could devote to actually surviving. God knew that was difficult enough on an island that didn't move, but to be constantly hounded and chased out there in the open...

Hurry home, Will.

She glanced over at the shoreline in the distance. She couldn't quite see the burned-down marina or the two-story house with the naked eye, but if she squinted long and hard enough, just maybe...

Her radio squawked, and Carly's voice came through. She sounded anxious and even slightly out of breath. "Lara, come in."

She answered as fast as she could. "What's wrong?"

"Can you hear it?"

"Hear what?"

"I guess you can't hear it," Carly said. "Boat motors. They're coming toward us from the north."

"Did you say 'motors'? Plural?"

"Yeah. Benny says he can see two of them right now." She paused, then added, "Benny says there are men in camo army uniforms on both of them."

Already? In the daylight?

She pressed the transmit lever again, said, "Keo, did you hear that?"

"I'm on my way to the Tower now," Keo said.

He was back at the hotel, having returned earlier to get out of last night's damp clothes and escort Gage over to Zoe in order to get his wound treated. She might have entertained the idea of killing the "captain" earlier, but now that she accepted how valuable he could be, they had to keep him alive, even if he only had one good leg left. She only needed what was inside his head, anyway.

"Blaine, Roy," Lara said into the radio.

"Where do you want us?" Blaine answered.

"Stay on the boat and guard the yacht."

"Are you sure?"

"Yes." Then, "Maddie, get the boat ready."

"Readying," Maddie said, already climbing onto the bass fishing boat tied to the back of the *Trident* below her.

Lara hustled down the rung of stairs. She hadn't set foot on the lower deck for more than a few seconds when her radio squawked again.

"Lara," Carly said through the radio.

"Where are they now?" she asked.

"Still at the same spot. But remember when I said there were two boats?"

"Yes…"

"They just got friends," Carly said. "There are four of them now."

Are they really attacking? In the daylight?

Maybe I was wrong about them. About what they would do. What they could do.

What else *was I wrong about?*

FOUR BOATS. IF they had two men in each one, that was eight soldiers. That was the best-case scenario, anyway. It was more likely there would be more than just two per vessel. Like four. She remembered that night when Karen's people tried to retake the island. There had been around four per boat then.

The worst-case scenario had sixteen heavily-armed men sent to kill them.

In the daylight? she thought again.

For some reason, she found herself hoping sixteen was the right number. Sixteen men, as menacing as that sounded, was preferable to twenty, or thirty, or God help them, forty or more. If Kate really wanted the island and to kill every living thing on it, she had plenty of collaborators willing to help her achieve that end. All those soldiers out there *(like Josh)* running around rounding up survivors who hadn't capitulated to the ghouls yet was proof of that.

But still…*sixteen?*

She was jogging up the pier, having hopped out of the boat even before Maddie finished sidling alongside it. Lara was amazed how comfortable she had become with moving while carrying a full arsenal strapped to her body. The gun belt didn't even feel heavy anymore, and she hardly noticed the M4 thumping against her back. She had even become used to the weight of the ammo pouches, the handgun, and the knife on her left hip.

Look at me, ma. All armed and a lot of men to kill.

She unclipped her radio and keyed it as she leaped off the pier and landed on the cobblestone pathway that wound its way from the beach to the hotel grounds beyond the wall of trees in front of her. "Talk to me, guys."

"Four boats, two men each," Keo said through the radio.

Two men per boat? That didn't make any sense.

Why so few? And why in the daylight?

"Small boats?" she asked.

"Nope," Keo said.

She couldn't tell if he was just as confused as she was. It was hard enough to hear nuance over the radio, but Keo, like Will, had a bad habit of not giving away his thoughts, even up close and personal. And she knew Will. As much as she had put her trust and the lives of her people in Keo's hands, she had to constantly remind herself that he was still a stranger.

"It doesn't look like this is an attack run," Keo added.

"So what are they doing?"

"Watching us back with binoculars."

A scouting mission? Was that it? Was that all this was?

"How far?" she asked.

"About half a kilometer."

"Can you take a shot?"

"You mean you want me to shoot them?" he asked, almost...was that befuddlement?

"Yes," she said, racing between the trees.

She was momentarily alarmed by the sudden dip in temperature as she jogged up the cobblestone pathway. The island had cooled down noticeably in the last few days, but with the plentiful shade provided by the towering walls of trees to both sides of her at the moment, she felt as if she was running through a pristine valley.

"Um, no," Keo was saying through the radio.

"Why the hell not?"

"I can't make the shot. Who do you think I am, an ex-Army Ranger?"

She sighed. "Never mind. Just keep an eye on them for now."

"Now that, I can do."

Bonnie was on the front patio of the hotel waiting for her when she emerged out of the woods. The ex-model had her rifle and looked like she had just woken up, which was probably not too far from the truth. Bonnie was tired, but then, they were all getting by with less sleep these days. It was just another privilege of surviving in a post-Purge world.

Adapt or perish, right, Will?

"I heard on the radio," Bonnie said. "Where do you want me?"

"Stay in the hotel," Lara said as she jogged past Bonnie. "The girls. Watch the girls!"

Bonnie nodded before heading back into the hotel.

It took Lara another few minutes to finally reach the Tower, a tall structure—a combination lighthouse and radio tower—on the northeastern edge of the island. It stood next to a cliff overlooking Beaufont Lake and was tall enough at forty meters to give them a perfect view of the entire island and the surrounding lake and its shorelines. Will called it a perfect sniper's perch, and she supposed that was true. Unfortunately for her, there was no one on the island at the moment who was good enough with a rifle to actually make use of it. Still, it served other purposes, like an early warning device in case of an attack.

Or boats of undetermined motives approaching, like now.

What the hell are they doing out there? If this isn't an attack, then what is it?

She climbed the cast-iron metal staircase up the three floors and was laboring badly by the time she poked her head through the third floor's opening. The Tower's second and third floors had four windows in each direction, and Keo was standing at the north one, now peering out with binoculars. He had changed into dry cargo pants and a sweater and had that German submachine gun slung over his back. For the life of her, she didn't understand why he didn't switch to an M4, which had a much better range.

Even as she thought that, Lara almost laughed at herself. When did she get so comfortable with all of this that she was seriously considering telling a man like Keo what made for a better weapon? A year ago, she had thought every gun had a safety and didn't know the difference between a clip and a magazine.

She had managed to regain some of her composure and wasn't

nearly hyperventilating as much when she stepped through the door. "Where's Benny?"

Carly looked back at her from the south window. "Keo sent him down to the northwest cliff in case they had managed to sneak someone closer when we weren't watching."

"Did they?"

"The kid hasn't seen anything," Keo said.

"Benny's still hurt."

"He's fine enough." He handed his binoculars to her as she walked over. "North. That means they came from the same staging area I told you about."

"The same one you've hit twice now."

"That's the one." He smirked. "I don't know whether to be impressed or annoyed by their refusal to abandon that place. A part of me feels just slighted enough to go back there and hit them a third time."

"Hey, you shoot the grenade launcher, and I'll drive," Carly said.

"I thought you were leaving soon," Lara said to him.

"That's still the plan," Keo said. "But I had a few minutes to kill."

"Thanks."

He gave her a noncommittal shrug, then pointed again. "See them?"

It was impossible to miss them with the binoculars. Even half a kilometer away, they looked clear as day drifting on the water. It wasn't as if they were trying to hide. A couple of the men were standing and peering back at her with their own binoculars, while the rest seemed to be lounging about without a care in the world. All four boats were powered by outboard motors that were shut off, and the only sound was the crashing of waves against the rocky formations at the edges of the island outside the window.

There were only two in each boat, and although they were heavily armed, the way they were just loitering around made them look like fishermen hanging out for the day. Of course, the fact that they were all heavily armed and wearing what looked like army uniforms said otherwise.

"You've seen those before?" Lara asked. "The uniforms."

"Yeah," he nodded. "They're the same ones I've run across."

"But are they Army?"

"As in US Army?"

"Yeah."

"No."

"You sure?"

"I've been around grunts all my life. Those aren't standard army issue. They're assholes dressing up in costumes."

Carly chuckled behind them. "Damn, you and that silver tongue of yours, K-pop."

"I try," he said. Then, "My guess? Whoever's in charge already knows that you know they're coming. Maybe he figures there's no point in hiding it."

"Maybe it's a she," Carly said. "Just because it's the end of the world doesn't mean you can be a sexist pig, Keo."

"My mistake. It could be an asshole chick calling the shots."

"Better."

"So what's the point of this?" Lara asked, lowering the binoculars.

"Maybe just intimidation," he said.

"That makes sense to you?"

"Beats the hell out of me. I just do the shooting. I don't spend a lot of time thinking about the psychology of why, how, and when."

Lara shook her head. "Well, I do spend a lot of time thinking about that, and none of this makes any sense to me." She keyed her radio. "Benny, come in."

"Benny here," the young man answered.

"Are you seeing anything out there?"

"Nothing. I'm halfway to the western half right now, but so far, I don't see anything."

"How's the leg?" she asked.

Benny had come to them with a broken leg, and she hadn't expected very much out of him as a result. But the young man had proven himself more than capable, and with the help of a custom leg brace designed by Stan, he was moving around again. To help maximize his abilities, she had given him jobs that didn't require a lot of constant movement, such as standing watch on the shack at the beach or in the Tower.

"It itches," Benny was saying, "but I'm still mobile."

"Okay, keep looking. I need to make sure they're not trying something."

"Roger that."

"Carly?" Lara said, looking across the room. "Anything along the shoreline?"

"Not a thing," Carly said. "If they're out there, or planning something, they're really being sneaky about it. Sneaky buggers, as Danny would say."

The not knowing gnawed at her. What the hell were they doing out there? Or was Keo right? Were they just trying to intimidate them? Maybe whoever was in charge didn't even know these bozos had come here? Maybe they were trying to figure out what all the shooting last night was about? Did they know about the yacht yet?

She had so many questions, and so few precious answers.

To keep her mind off the growing frustration, Lara keyed the radio again. "Blaine, come in."

"Blaine here," the big man answered.

"Anything on your end?"

"There's nothing coming at us. It's all quiet on this side."

"Okay." She put the radio down and glanced at Keo. He was staring out the window at the men in the boats. They were mostly stick figures with the naked eye, but that didn't seemed to deter him. "So?"

"So?" he repeated.

"You're the expert. What happens now?"

"I'm the expert?" he said, sounding amused.

"Compared to the rest of us? Yes."

"They're going to attack tonight, aren't they?" Carly said behind them.

Keo did that noncommittal shrug again.

"What does that mean?" Carly said, echoing Lara's own thoughts.

"Pretty sure, yeah," he finally said.

Lara waited for him to elaborate, but he didn't. She was about to press him on it when she heard the roar of outboard motors starting up. She looked through the binoculars as the four boats turned around and began moving away, back in the direction they had come.

"They're leaving," she said.

"They'll be back tonight," Keo said.

She handed the binoculars back to him, catching his eyes as he took it. "We could use you tonight."

"Your boyfriend will be back by then."

Hopefully, but I've been living on hope for so long, maybe I'm just deluding myself this time, too, she thought, but said, "I know, but we could still use your help."

"I told you, army guys and me don't get along."

"After what you've done for us, I'm pretty sure Will and Danny aren't going to have any problems with you, Keo."

He didn't reply right away. He hung the binoculars back up on the hook along the wall and looked across the room at Carly, who had also turned around and was watching him intently as well.

He turned back to Lara. "Look, I respect what you guys are doing here, fighting for this island. But you know my feelings about it. Sooner or later, this place is going to fall and you're going to lose people. It's not worth it."

He stopped for a moment and seemed to be trying to gather his thoughts. Lara could tell talking things out wasn't something Keo did on a daily basis and that this was all new territory for him.

"But I can tell I'm not going to change your mind," he continued. "I hate to say it, but I'm a selfish bastard, and I can't die for a cause I don't believe in."

She could see he was struggling with it, which actually surprised her. Will had called Keo a mercenary, and maybe he had been once upon a time. But he had clearly changed a lot since The Purge, even if he didn't want to admit it.

Lara decided to take pity on him. She keyed her radio and said into it, "Maddie, come in."

"Are they attacking?" Maddie asked through the radio.

"No. They left."

"They just left?"

"Looks that way."

"That's good, right?"

"For now." Then, "Maddie, I need you to prep one of the boats for Keo, like we talked about before."

Maddie didn't say anything for a moment. It took about five seconds, and Keo was watching her closely the entire time. Or was there something else going through his mind at the moment that she couldn't read? She hated to admit it, but the only thing obvious on the man's face was that long scar along the left side of his cheek. Other than that, she couldn't read a damn thing from his expression.

"Roger that," Maddie finally said.

"Thank you," Lara said. "Sarah, come in."

"Yes," Sarah answered. She was back at the hotel with the kids, Bonnie, and the others.

"Put some supplies together for Keo. At least a month's worth."

"Is he leaving?" Sarah asked. It was impossible to miss the disappointment in her voice.

"Yes. I need it within the hour, okay?"

"Okay," Sarah said.

Lara clipped the radio back to her hip.

"I could use some more weapons and ammo, too," Keo said.

"You can take whatever you need from the basement."

"The Army Rangers won't mind if I raid their stash?"

"They probably will a little bit, but I won't tell them and since you won't be here to say otherwise..."

"Works for me. I guess all that's left is to say good luck."

"You too." She shook his hand. "Thanks for everything. We couldn't have gotten this far without you."

"Yeah, watch yourself out there, K-Pop," Carly said.

He smiled awkwardly back at her. If Lara thought Keo was bad at expressing his thoughts, he was even worse at saying good-bye, apparently.

She decided to take pity on him again. "I hope you find Gillian, Keo. I mean that."

He nodded. "Thanks."

She watched him step through the door, his footsteps *clanging* against the cast-iron stairs as he went down, and down... She didn't know why, but Lara kept expecting him to pop back up through the opening and confess he wasn't really leaving after all.

He didn't, of course.

When they could barely hear his footsteps, she looked across at Carly. "We need to get ready for tonight."

"Will and Danny should be back by then," Carly said.

"I know, but we need to get everything and everyone ready anyway until they do get here. Besides, it'll give everyone something to do, keep their minds off other things."

"You're the boss, boss."

"Until then, I'll get Stan up here with you."

"What about Benny?"

"Keo had the right idea. He's better out there making sure they don't sneak up on us before nightfall. I should have thought of it myself."

"Yeah, but Stan?" Carly said. "He's an electrician, Lara."

"He's an electrician, I'm a failed medical student, and you were a teenager before all of this. We adapt or perish, remember?"

Carly sighed. "I hate it when you get all bossy."

"Hey, you're the one who made me boss, remember?"

"Me and my big mouth."

Lara glanced at her watch. 11:30 A.M.

It wouldn't be long now until Will radioed to tell them he was almost at the shoreline and for her to get a boat ready to pick him up. She would probably need to use the pontoon, because Will was coming with more than just him, Danny, and Gaby. And there were those M240 machine guns he had promised her.

In just three—maybe four—hours, she would see him again. Finally.

It's about time, Will. You've kept me waiting long enough…

CHAPTER 6

WILL

THEY WERE TALKING amongst themselves when he woke up, and they were still chattering away when he finally summoned enough strength *(A few minutes later? A few hours later?)* to sit up on the dirty tiled floor. He was in some kind of back room, with the only ventilation coming from a small vent along the top wall in front of him. Except the AC had stopped working a year ago, leaving behind just unrecycled, musty air. Slivers of sunlight shined through a closed high window above him, but most of it came from the open door across the room.

His movements were limited by the zip ties around his ankles, though they were nice enough to let him have his hands folded in front of him instead of bent behind his back. He was uncomfortable, but it could have been a worse. A lot worse.

Yeah, that's the ticket.

He was breathing, which was all that mattered. As long as he was alive, there was a way out of this. He just had to see it. Then he would be back on his way, back to Song Island. Back to Lara.

His current surroundings weren't much to look at. The wallpapers were peeling, and debris was strewn along the floor. A pair of empty boxes sat in a corner, but the room was otherwise empty. Figures moved back and forth across the open door, and he could just make out the rest of a store beyond. He guessed he was inside one of the gas stations along Route 13. Either the Palermo or the Chevron.

His head throbbed like someone was inside his skull kicking up a ruckus. Dried blood clung to one side of his face and ran all the way down to his neck. He looked down at his waistline to make sure the nagging wound he was most worried about hadn't resurfaced, but breathed easier at the lack of blood at that particular spot. That meant Zoe's stitches were still holding. Good, because the last thing he needed right now was to start bleeding down there, too.

"Do you always carry thread and needle around with you?" Zoe had once asked him.

Expect the best, prepare for the worst, Zoe.

They had taken his weapons, of course. The gun belt, the pouches, the sidearm, and the sheathed knife. The Motorola radio and comm gear were also gone. When he moved his legs back and forth he didn't hear the familiar *clink-clink*, so they had taken the pills, too. That, more than anything, was problematic. He was still sore from the last few days, and without the relief of the meds, it was going to be tough sledding.

They were nice enough to leave him his watch, though, and Will looked down at it now: 11:05 A.M.

Cutting it close. Lara's going to be so pissed when I don't show up later today as promised.

Sorry, babe, but it couldn't be helped. I did send Danny and Gaby on ahead. At least two of us will be there for you tonight, so don't be too mad at me.

He looked up at the sound of approaching footsteps, just before a man appeared in the doorframe. Will assumed it was a man, though he was much shorter than any soldier he had ever seen. Of course, these men weren't actually soldiers, either, so his past experiences in Uncle Sam's armed forces was probably irrelevant to the current situation.

Shorty leaned against the door and looked in at him. The man was casually shining a red apple against the front of his uniform and stood about five-five, but Will figured that was partially thanks to the boots. Without those, he was five-three, max. He had short black hair and dark beady eyes and a smirk that looked permanently fixed on his face. Even the sidearm appeared to be too big for him, though the uniform seemed to be tailored for his size.

They must have a sweat shop in one of the towns, cranking out these uniforms. Custom made, too. That must be nice.

"Will, right?" the man said. The name "Mason" was stenciled across his name tag. Like the others Will had seen walking by the open door in the last few minutes, Mason's uniform had the Louisiana patch and white star in prominent locations. "How the hell are ya?"

"I had a bottle on me," Will said.

"What, no 'Hey, how you doing?'"

"Hey, how you doing?"

Mason grinned. "That's better." He reached into his pocket and pulled out the familiar white bottle. He shook it, the pills *clink-clinking* inside. "This one?"

"That's it."

"You need it?"

"I could use it."

"Say 'please.'"

"Please."

"Pretty please with a cherry on top?"

Will gritted his teeth. "Pretty please with a cherry on top."

"Good boy."

Mason tossed it over to him. Will caught it with both bound hands. He was surprised when he twisted off the cap and saw the pills inside and not the small rocks he had been expecting. For some reason, he didn't think it would be this easy, and Mason, smirking at him from across the room, seemed to get a kick out of proving him wrong.

"Thanks," Will said.

He tilted back his head and dropped two of the pills into his mouth, then swallowed without chewing.

"Damn, just like candy, huh?" Mason said.

Will ignored the comment, said instead, "You want it back?"

"Nah. You look like you need them more than me."

"That's awfully civilized of you."

Mason chuckled, then took a big bite out of the apple. Juice flowed down his chin and he wiped at it with the sleeve of his shirt. Will's stomach might have growled a bit at the sight.

Definitely not officer material, this one.

"Hey, we're all just trying to get by, right?" Mason said.

"Absolutely."

"Besides, she made it pretty clear she wants you alive. You know who I'm talking about, don't you?"

"Yeah," Will said.

It took a while before he finally matched Mason's voice to that of the man who had given the orders earlier when they pulled him out of the truck. Mason was the one who had responded, when asked about pursuing Danny and Gaby's vehicle, *"Don't worry about them. They're not gonna get far."*

Officer material or not, the man was definitely in charge. Or, at least, in the daylight.

"What about my friends?" Will asked.

"You should be more worried about yourself right now," Mason said.

"I'm multitasking."

"Be careful; you can get hurt doing that." Mason shrugged, giving the impression of indifference, even though Will suspected the man knew—and cared—more about what was happening around him than he wanted to let on. "Don't worry about your friends. I know it looks like we're running a Scooby-Doo operation around here, but there are actual brains at work. What, you thought we were just going to let you get to the interstate and keep going after last night?"

"I was hoping."

"Hope springs eternal. But no." He took another large bite of the apple. "What you saw out there when you tried to come through was just a small part of it. We have people everywhere. If you'd tried to go back to Dunbar, it would have ended the same way. Even if you'd tried to bail through the fields? Same difference. You wouldn't believe the number of guys with rifles I got running around out there. Like cockroaches. With, you know, assault rifles." He chuckled. "You really thought we'd just leave you alone after last night?"

"So you've got it all figured out, huh?"

"Not me. I'm just following orders."

"Hers," Will said.

Mason grinned. "Yeah. Hers." Then, as if he were conspiring with Will, he leaned slightly forward. "You know her, don't you? I mean, *really* know her."

"Yeah."

"I guess she wasn't always like that. What do you people call them? Ghouls?"

"Sounded like a good name at the time."

"Well they are a little…ghoulish. The black-eyed ones, anyway. The others, like her? I don't even know how to describe them."

Mason had gone back to chewing on his apple when the radio clipped to his hip squawked and a male voice said, "Mason, come in."

Will didn't recognize the voice, but the reception was staticky, clearly transmitting just outside the two-way portable's range.

Mason unclipped the radio. "How goes it out there, boys?"

"I just got word from Reeves," the voice said.

"And?"

"He just reached the ambush point, and he says they're gone."

"Who's gone?"

"The others," the man on the radio said. "They made it through the ambush."

They." He means Gaby and Danny.

Will almost smiled outwardly, but managed to hold it in just barely.

He watched Mason closely instead, waiting to see the flash of anger, but the man's only reaction was to curl one corner of his mouth into a half-smirk. Will had always thought of the collaborators as more opportunists than true believers; people who were in it for themselves, using the situation to their advantage. He'd always believed there were more Kellersons among them than Joshes. Mason, without a doubt, fell into the former group.

"Well, shit," Mason was saying. "How'd they do that?"

"Reeves found Harry and Douglas dead," the man said through the radio.

"What about the targets?"

"They ditched the Titan and took one of our vehicles."

Something seemed to bother Mason, or occurred to him suddenly. "Wait, weren't there supposed to be three people down there?"

"Yeah. Nate's missing."

The name made Will straighten up slightly. He hoped Mason hadn't noticed.

Nate? Did he just say Nate?

"Reeves wanted to know what he should do now?" the man on the other end of the radio asked.

"I guess he better find them again," Mason said.

"We have more people waiting in Salvani, right?"

"Last time I checked." He glanced at his watch. "Whatever you do, you better do it fast. You have exactly six hours before it gets dark, and then you'll be answering to her."

"Me? Why me?"

You've got them running scared, Kate. Didn't anyone ever tell you a scared soldier is a poor soldier?

"Hey, I did my part," Mason said into the radio. He looked amused, like all of this was fun and games. "I got what she wanted. You're the one who screwed up with the girl."

'Girl'? Were they talking about Gaby, or Annie, or one of the kids?

Will sat silently and waited for more clues.

"You heard what I said?" Mason said into the radio.

"Yeah, I heard you," the other man finally answered. "Out."

Now that's one hell of a chain of command there, boys.

Mason put the radio away and gave Will that smirk again. "These radios don't work for shit. We had to put in relays just so we can keep in contact with the ones spread out too far. What do you guys have on that island? Ham radios? Now, that's smart."

"Thanks."

"Maybe that's why she wants you so bad. To take over this sad mess we have going on here. You think?"

Will shrugged.

"I guess it doesn't matter," Mason said. "All that stuff's way above my pay grade, anyway."

"I've always wondered what they're paying you."

Mason grinned. "Life."

"Life?"

"Duh. I get to live. Self-preservation, my man. It's a hell of an incentive to do anything, but especially these days." He glanced over his shoulder at the store for a moment before looking back at Will. "Damn, no rest for the weary. We'll have to continue this chat later. I hope you don't mind, but I never had the privilege of asking an Army Ranger for advice before, and I wanna pick that brain of yours later if you got the time."

"Sure," Will said. "I got no plans."

"Hah," Mason said. "I'll be back."

The short man turned and left, closing the door after him. Will listened to the sound of a deadbolt *click-clacking* into place on the other side.

Alone again, he took inventory of his situation.

What did he know with absolute certainty? A couple of things.

First, Gaby and Danny had survived a second attempted ambush further up the interstate. Which meant they were still en route to Song Island. All they'd have to do now was get past Salvani, which, according to the conversation Will had just overheard, meant there were more soldiers waiting for them there.

Secondly, there was that thing about someone named Nate.

Could it be…?

That would depend on how optimistic he was willing to be at the moment.

I'm not ready to take over Captain Optimism just yet, Danny.

Not that knowing what was happening out there did him any good in here. He could hear them moving around outside the door, along with the occasional sounds of car engines in the streets beyond. He tried to re-orient himself with his surroundings, to get a better sense of direction and where everything was. He was still at Route 13, he knew that much. Everything else was open to debate.

Bottom line: He needed more information, and he wasn't going to get it locked in here.

He leaned back against the wall. It was still noon, so there were still over six hours until sunset. Nightfall was the enemy—had always been, would always be. Besides the darkness, and the creatures lurking inside it, *she* would come, too.

"Don't worry," the blue-eyed ghoul had hissed at him last night. *"It's not going to end that easily for you, Will. Kate made us promise her this time. I think she has big plans for you."*

Kate.

Where are you now, Kate? What are you doing? Are you waiting for nightfall, too? Or are you on your way here now, the way you made the soldiers transport your shock troopers to Dunbar in the U-haul?

Somehow, some way, all his actions—what he did or didn't do—always seemed to be spurred on by Kate in one form or another.

Eventually, inevitably, it always seemed to come back to her…

HE OPENED HIS eyes to what sounded like hell on Earth and promptly sought out his watch in the semidarkness of the back room.

11:47 A.M.

Shit.

The realization that he had dozed off despite having been knocked unconscious just hours ago was troubling, because it could have been a sign there was something wrong with him. Or, at the very least, a lingering effect of the blows he had taken to the head.

That, and he knew what those thunderous *brap-brap-brap* sounds coming from outside were without having to think about it. God knew he had heard and been around them often enough. Someone, somewhere, was firing a machine gun, and the *pop-pop-pop* that accompanied it meant a gun battle.

He stared at the door, waiting for it to burst open and for someone to run inside. Maybe Mason, the short guy in charge of this mess they called an operation. People were definitely running around in the store outside; the vibrations of boots racing frantically back and forth were hard to ignore. Shouting, too, though that was mostly lost in the back and forth gunfire.

It was chaos out there, which was both good and bad for him.

It was good that someone was attacking the soldiers. The phrase, *"The enemy of my enemy is my friend"* ran through his head.

Bad, in that he was stuck inside the back room of a gas station while men were shooting machine guns outside in the streets. Depending on how much gas was still left inside the tank under the Palermo *(Or the Chevron, either/or)*, there was a very good chance he could die in a raging fire sometime soon. Double the chances if someone had some kind of incendiary device and decided to stupidly use it.

Okay, so it was mostly bad.

He couldn't tell who was winning or where the shooting was coming from, because it seemed to be some kind of running gunfight.

How many men did Mason have out there, and how many were attacking them? Better yet, *who* was attacking, and what were the chances they could be friends instead of foes? The only group he'd seen proactively attack the soldiers had been Harrison's group back in Dunbar. And that, unfortunately, hadn't ended very well for them.

"What you saw out there when you tried to come through was just a small part of it," Mason had boasted earlier. *"We have people everywhere."*

But how many of those people were here, now? Especially since the ambush had succeeded. He knew for a fact Mason had sent more men up the interstate after Danny and Gaby. So how many were left? How many would Mason think he needed when he had already, essentially, won the day?

Will was still trying to come up with a viable number (or, at least, one that would make him feel better) when the door finally banged open and a familiar camo uniform rushed inside. No, not familiar. Same uniform, but different person inside it. Taller, skinnier, and younger.

The kid (he couldn't have been more than eighteen, maybe seventeen?) spun around and slammed the door shut before stumbling away from it. He was cradling an AR-15 and wore a gun belt with a sidearm, but Will recognized the awkwardness in the way he carried the equipment.

He's green. Really, really green.

"Kid," Will said.

The teenager whirled around, lifting his rifle and aiming it at Will. He looked frightened, even shocked to see Will there. "Jesus! I almost shot you!"

"It's a good thing you didn't. What's going on out there?"

The kid (he was tall for his age, which was amusing when Will thought about the thirty-something but much shorter Mason) lowered his weapon and shook his head. He wiped at beads of sweat along his temple and whirled back around to face the door. Then he hurried over and leaned against the wall and listened to the *pop-pop-pop* of gunfire still raging outside.

The battle hadn't slowed down even a little bit in the minute or so since Will woke up. That meant there were a lot of people out there, and all of them well-armed. Meanwhile, he was stuck in here, hog-tied and weaponless.

Will looked for and finally caught the name written across the kid's uniform: "Michael."

"What's going on out there, Michael?" Will asked.

The kid looked momentarily confused by the sound of his name, then must have realized how Will knew and shook it off. "They're attacking," he said.

"Who's attacking?"

"I don't know. They came out of nowhere. They must have…they must have been crawling along the fields all day toward us."

'Crawling along the fields all day'?

Will watched the kid closely. He was scared. That much was obvious. So Will did what he always did: He took stock of his situation and considered his available options. Because there were always options. You just had to see it.

"Kid," Will said.

Michael didn't react, either because he was too focused on what was happening outside or he was purposefully ignoring him. Will would have put good money that it was the former.

"Michael," Will said, louder this time.

That did it. Michael looked over. "What?"

"Listen."

"I am…"

"No, I mean, *really* listen."

Michael looked confused again.

Doesn't take much, does it, kid?

"You're losing," Will said. "You know that, right? The other guys are winning. You can hear that, can't you?"

Will had said it all with absolute certainty. It was in his voice and on his face. He knew what he was talking about, and Michael would be smart to listen.

Of course, it was all bullshit. It was impossible to tell who was winning the battle outside. He had no idea how many were taking part or even who they were—two very important details needed to predict the outcome of a gun battle. Who were the good guys and who were the bad guys? If there were any good guys at all. For all he knew, Mason and his men could be putting down the attackers right this moment, which would lead him right back to where he started.

But he didn't tell Michael that. No. The kid was frightened and out of his element. Running in here to hide was proof of that. The shaking hands trying desperately to keep their grip on the assault rifle sealed it.

"Your unit's losing," Will pressed. "Mason's losing. If he's not already dead."

Michael didn't answer. Instead, he looked back at the door so Will couldn't see his face to gauge if he was getting through.

"You need to get out of here, kid," Will said. "Before it's too late."

"There's too many of them out there," Michael said. His voice shook noticeably. "I think they're using our trucks. The ones with the machine guns. How'd they get those?"

"I know, I can hear them using it," Will said. More bullshit. He couldn't tell one way or another who was firing the machine guns, but Michael didn't need to know that at the moment, either. "Trust me, kid, I've been through enough of these situations to know a losing side when I hear it. And your side's losing. *Bad.*"

Michael shook his head. "You can't be sure of that."

"I am. And you are, too." Then, with a harder edge to his voice, "You wanna live or not?"

Michael glanced over. He opened his mouth to answer, but then snapped it shut just as quickly.

A second, then five…

"Yes," Michael said finally. "I want to live."

Will held out his bound wrists. "Cut me loose, and I'll get us out of here."

"How?"

"You'll have to trust me on this."

"What? No fucking—"

An explosion ripped through the building and something smashed into the door on the other side. The clatter of shelves falling, glass pelting tiled floors, and someone (or *someones*) screaming in pain. Chunks of the ceiling rained down on them, and Michael threw his arms over his head as if that would save him. Thankfully, the bulk of the store remained in one piece, leaving them to cough in the aftermath of falling debris.

Oh, hell. That was definitely a grenade.

"Kid," Will said, watching Michael pick himself up from the floor and coughing. "It's either get out of here with me, or stay here and die with the rest of your guys. What's it going to be?"

Michael was on his knees and looking for his rifle. He had accidentally tossed it while falling and grabbing for his head. Now he crawled over and picked it up, even as the gunfire continued to rage outside, the *brap-brap-brap* of a machine gun continuing to fill the air as if the damn thing had an endless supply of belt-fed ammo.

"Michael," Will said. "You gotta decide and you gotta decide *now*. You wanna live or not?"

The teenager got up and hurried over, drawing his knife. The blade was trembling as he cut the zip tie from around Will's wrists, then did the same to the one around his ankles.

"What now?" Michael said. "How are we going to get out of here?"

"I need a gun," Will said.

The soldier stared at him.

"A sign of good faith," Will continued.

Michael sighed and drew his sidearm—a Sig Sauer 9mm—and handed it over reluctantly. "Can I trust you?"

Will stood up. "Kind of a little late to be asking that, don't you think?"

The kid made to smile back, but it came out badly forced. "I guess."

"A deal's a deal," Will said. "Come on, let's get the hell out of here before whoever's wiping out your friends finishes the job and comes looking for us next."

He grinned at the kid.

For a moment there, Will actually thought he was in trouble.

Option found. Opportunity seized.

I'll be home soon, Lara.

"HOW MANY OF you are out there?" Will asked.

"Ten," Michael said.

"I saw more than that this morning. A lot more."

"Most of them left after we captured you."

"Where did they go?"

"I don't know. They really don't tell me very much."

Of course not. You're the kid so wet behind the ears he runs into the closest room to hide the first time someone's shooting at him.

"What about Mason?" he asked.

"I don't know. I think he left before the attack. Like I said, they don't really tell me very much."

Will crouched among the ruins of the gas station (the Palermo, as it turned out) and watched through the broken windows as a bullet-riddled blue Ford F-250, its front windshield dotted with the same bullet holes that had punctured its side and front hood, moved slowly down the street. There were two men in the back, one swiveling a heavy M60 perched on the roof of the vehicle.

Christ, no wonder Mason's people hadn't stood a chance. The all-purpose American machine gun was capable of firing 500 rounds per minute with an effective range of over 500 meters and beyond. That single weapon probably accounted for all the broken windows in the stores up and down the street that he could see, not to mention the destroyed cars that hadn't been there this morning, along with the crumpled uniformed bodies visible in the parking lot on his side of Route 13.

The Ford looked like one of the technicals Josh's soldiers had been using, though he'd never seen this one before. While one man was behind the machine gun, a second was slightly crouched behind him with an AK-47. Other well-armed men were walking alongside them, easily keeping up with the truck's slow pace.

This wasn't a charge, it was a victory march through occupied territory.

The gunfight had stopped almost at the same time Will and Michael slipped out of the back room and into what remained of the convenience store. They hid behind a couple of fallen shelves now, within sight of two bodies lying next to the gas pumps outside. The frag grenade had landed inside where it had left behind a crater in the middle and torn apart everything that wasn't nailed down, including the poor soul whose shredded uniform they were looking at.

There were no rifles for Will to find, though he did see the remnants of an M4 stock among the debris. Which meant he had to make do with the Sig Sauer. At least Michael was smart enough to carry spare magazines, which Will had pocketed. The young man continued clutching his AR-15 (as if he knew how to use it, which Will doubted), eyes snapping from the remains of the uniform and out the shattered windows at the technical and its companions.

The sight of the attackers was intriguing. They were wearing civilian garb, including jeans, cargo pants, and long-sleeve shirts. The fact that they had come extremely well-armed and had acquired one of Josh's technicals offered up more questions than answers.

Who are these guys?

"What now?" Michael whispered behind him.

"Do you know who took my rifle?" Will asked.

"Your rifle?"

"Yeah. I had an M4A1 with me when I was captured. It was in the truck."

"I dunno. What's an M4A1 look like?"

Will started to answer, but shook his head instead. "Never mind." He looked back out the store at the figures moving slowly down the street. "We'll let them pass us by. There's no point in engaging. We're outmanned and outgunned—"

He hadn't finished "outgunned" when two of the attackers broke away from the technical and started angling—*right toward them.*

Right. Because why would luck be on my side now?

"Oh no," Michael whispered a few seconds later.

Kinda late there, kid, don't you think?

"What now?" Michael said in a hushed voice.

Will didn't answer right away. He glanced back at the teenager's terrified face, then looked past him at the back room. There was nothing in there that could help him escape. The window was too high to climb out of, and he wasn't going to break down a wall with his bare hands. The only way out was through the front door of the Palermo. Or the broken windows would do just as well.

The technical had continued down the street and out of his view, but the two figures were stepping over dead bodies at the pumps after checking them for signs of life. One was a man, the other a woman. They both looked haggard, as if they had been fighting for days instead of ten, maybe fifteen minutes, tops. The woman looked in her mid-thirties and was wearing a Texas Rangers baseball cap that she pushed slightly up when she stopped in front of what remained of the windows so she could peer inside.

"Anything?" the man, who was older by at least ten years, asked behind her.

"I see a body," the woman said.

"Dead?"

"I said a body, didn't I?"

The man grunted. "So let's go."

"There's a back room."

"What about it?"

"It's open and it looks undamaged."

Shit. Should have closed the door… Too late for that now.

"Be careful," the man said.

The woman didn't answer him. She stepped through one of the broken windows, *crunching* glass under her boots.

Will's mind turned. Spun. Then whirled.

He looked back at Michael again. The kid was trembling badly, causing the rifle in his hands to shake along with him. He looked like he was about to throw up.

Will back to the woman, the man in the background, and the technical out there, along with, from what he could see, at least four more heavily-armed men.

Then he glanced down at the Sig Sauer in his hand. It was a good weapon. He could probably kill the woman, take her weapon (it looked like an M4), and use it on the man outside. But then there was that damn truck and the M60 mounted on top of it. That thing could chew up what was left of the gas station in no time, and him right along with it.

Gotta get to Song Island. Can't do that if I'm dead.

As long as I'm alive, there's a chance...

"Shit," Will said, before he realized he had said it out loud. Or whispered, anyway.

"What?" Michael said, alarmed. "What are we—"

Will grabbed Michael's rifle and jerked it out of his hands. It came easily, as if the teenager was barely holding onto it. Before Michael could protest, Will tossed the rifle along with the Sig Sauer toward the woman. The two weapons skidded across the floor and stopped in front of her. She immediately snapped up her M4 and took aim at them, hiding behind one of the many toppled shelves, though he was certain she couldn't actually see them.

"Don't shoot!" Will shouted. "We're unarmed!"

The woman didn't answer right away. She looked confused. Then, "Step outside. Slowly!"

Will nodded at Michael, who stared back, horrified. "Slowly, like the woman said, okay, kid?"

Michael sighed, but didn't respond. He did, though, stand up when Will did, and they moved slowly—ever so slowly—out from behind the shelves. The woman's hands tightened around the rifle, and Will was almost certain she was going to shoot them down at any second. There was something in her eyes...

I'm a dead man. Any second now...

But she didn't fire. Instead, she held her ground and glared at them over the iron sights of her weapon, even as the older man rushed into the store behind her. "Where'd these jokers come from?" he asked, slightly out of breath despite the relatively short distance.

"Dunno," the woman said. "They tossed their weapons."

"Step forward," the man said, motioning at them with his rifle.

Will and Michael did as they were instructed, the kid still shaking so much it looked as if he was moving in a herky-jerky motion, desperately trying to make each leg move forward one at a time, one at a time.

The older man hurried forward and circled them before patting them down. He found Will's pill bottle and pocketed it, then stepped back. "They're clean."

"Hear me out," Will started to say.

"You don't have a uniform," the woman said, cutting him off.

"No. I'm not one of them."

"So what are you doing here with them, then?"

"I was captured this morning."

The man and woman exchanged a glance. Will was suddenly very thankful he looked like he had been through the blender, with his bruises and dried blood clinging to one side of his face. He really didn't look anything like the clean-cut Michael in his spiffy uniform standing beside him.

"This morning?" the man said.

"Yeah," Will nodded. "I'm not one of them," he repeated, just in case they didn't hear it the first time. You could never be too clear about your allegiances when someone was pointing a rifle at you.

"What about him?" the woman asked, moving her rifle to rest on Michael. "He's one of them."

"He's surrendering," Will said.

"I'm surrendering," Michael said, nodding furiously while his voice trembled badly. "Please don't shoot. I'm surrendering."

"How old are you, kid?" the man asked.

"Seventeen," Michael said. "Please don't shoot," he said again. "I'm surrendering, like he said."

The woman stared at Michael.

Those eyes. Will had seen those eyes before.

Aw, shit, he thought, just before the woman said, "Too bad. We're not taking prisoners."

Then she shot Michael in the head from ten feet away.

CHAPTER 7

KEO

HE WAS READY to say good-bye to Song Island by noon. The fact that he hadn't come to the place with very much, so had very little to pack on his way off it, helped. The short Texan, Maddie, was taking care of the boat while the other pretty blonde, Sarah, was packing his food for him in the kitchen.

With everything he needed being taken care of, all Keo had left to do was to grab some dry clothes from the hotel's lost-and-found room, where there were piles of the stuff. He knew where they came from, even though Lara hadn't mentioned it. Some of them probably belonged to Allie's people, who had come here months ago seeking salvation, only to find death instead. He should have been a little queasy taking dead people's things, but a shirt and cargo pants, along with socks and boots that fit, were hard to come by these days. Besides, it wasn't as if he had ever actually met Allie's people, or the poor saps who had found the island not quite as hospitable as they had expected.

He was surprised when Carrie knocked on the open door and leaned inside. In all the chaos of the last few days, he had forgotten about her and Lorelei.

"Busy?" she asked.

He gave her his best smile. "I got time if you got time."

She walked over and sat on the edge of the bed and watched him stuff a couple of extra T-shirts and a few rolls of duct tape into the bag. The Rangers had really stocked up on the duct tape.

"What's on your mind?" he asked.

"I just wanted to come see you off. We wouldn't have gotten here if it wasn't for you. Lorelei and me. I'm sorry to see you go."

"I made a promise."

"I know. And you always keep your promises."

Not always, he thought. "These days, yeah. I try."

"It's too bad we never got to talk."

"What would we talk about?"

"I don't know. What you were like before. What I was like. What could have been…"

"Ah. Trouble lies in that direction."

She laughed. It was just a little bit forced. "I guess you're right, so maybe we shouldn't go there."

"Probably a good idea."

"It's going to be lonely out there by yourself. The Gulf of Mexico is a big place."

"So maybe you should come with me."

Carrie looked surprised. She wasn't the only one. It took Keo a second to realize what he had said and another second to know that he meant it. It wasn't because he wanted the company. Well, that might have been a part of it, but it was also the undeniable fact that he had brought her and Lorelei here, a place that was about to come under attack. He felt, as difficult as it was to admit to himself, responsible for the two of them.

"It's not safe here," Keo said. "You must know that after everything we've been through the last few days. Especially after last night."

"I know it's dangerous…"

"Dangerous isn't quite the word I'd use, Carrie."

"What, then?"

"Endangered."

"'Endangered'?" She gave him a puzzled look. "I don't understand."

He hesitated and spent some time searching for the right words. What would make her understand? Did she really know what was coming tonight? How was he going to convince her without scaring her at the same time? Or maybe that was exactly what he needed to do right now. Terror might be what she needed.

"They want this place," Keo said. "The soldiers working for the ghouls. And they're going to take it. If not tonight, then the next, or the one after that. Eventually, it *will* happen. These people are fighting a losing battle."

He paused. Was he using the right approach? Was the truth what she wanted to hear? *Needed* to hear?

"Sooner or later, the island's going to fall," he continued. "It's not a matter of if, it's a matter of when. And when that time comes, one of two things will happen to you and Lorelei along with everyone here. They're either going to capture you and take you back to the towns, or they're going to kill you. That's it. There is no third option."

Carrie didn't say anything. Instead, she looked down at her hands. He didn't have a clue what was going through her head at the moment. Keo had never been especially good at reading the opposite sex, and the end of the world hadn't changed that.

"Come with me," Keo said. "You and Lorelei. There's plenty of room on the boat. Lara would probably be okay with giving me extra supplies."

She finally looked up at him. Damn if he had no idea what she was about to say. He guessed picking up women in seedy bars across the world, as it turned out, hadn't been very beneficial to understanding them.

"What's out there?" Carrie said.

"It doesn't matter. It's better than what's going to happen here when night falls. You saw the same things I did out there. The second time I was at the staging area, there were even more soldiers than before."

Her face paled a bit. He had never asked her what had happened to her that forced her and Lorelei to go on the run in the first place. There was that whole thing about the women in the collaborator towns being impregnated, but he always suspected there was something else. He hadn't pushed her about it because he didn't think it was his business.

Now, looking at her, he wanted to ask but managed to bite his tongue. He said instead, "You'll like Gillian. And I hear the Texas coast is nice this time of year."

"We're not going," she said. She pursed her lips into a half-smile. "Lorelei doesn't want to leave, either."

"Carrie..."

"I know the risks, Keo. I also know there's nothing out there for us."

"There's something in Texas."

"You don't know that. You just *hope* there's something waiting for you."

Crap. She's got me there.

He hadn't been in touch with Gillian or Jordan in months, ever since they split up back at Earl's cabin. That was...how many months ago? Too long. So what were the chances Gillian was actually out there waiting for him, like he kept telling people? Or if she was even alive at all? For all he knew, Mark's boat could have sunk on the way over. Or they might have met more of those soldiers, or...

I'm hoping for the best, just like a sucker. I'm no different from these people.

"Maybe she's there, and maybe she's not," Carrie was saying. "You're just like Lorelei and me before you met us, Keo. You're looking for a place to belong, hoping something's there when you finally arrive. Well, we found that. Here on Song Island. You could stay with us. With me."

He didn't answer right away. It was a tempting offer. Gillian may or may not be out there, but Carrie was here, now. That was a certainty. And he'd always been more pragmatic than a dreamer, so what was keeping him from accepting her offer?

Tonight. The answer was tonight.

It's going to be a bloodbath. Only an idiot would stay behind.

"You don't seem to understand what I'm saying," Keo said. "There won't be an island after tonight."

"Maybe," Carrie said. "Maybe not. Lara's friends are coming back."

"The Rangers."

"Yes."

"They won't be enough."

"You don't know that."

"It's just an island, Carrie. There are other islands."

"The one in Texas is just an island, too, but you're doing everything you can to get to it anyway. What's the difference?"

He sighed. Christ. She had an answer for everything. The woman was going to drive him crazy if he spent any more time arguing with her.

And she was right, too. That was probably the most galling part. Dammit, she was right.

"So you're staying," he said. "You've decided?"

"It's not about the island," she said. "It's about the people on it. It's always been about the people. Stay with us, Keo. There might not be anything for you out there, but there's something here, now."

"Not after tonight." He walked to the dresser and picked up the Glock and holstered it. "I guess there's nothing left to say."

"Yeah," she said, the disappointment showing on every inch of her face. So she had come here with a mission after all: To convince him to stay. "I hope you find her waiting for you in Texas. I really do."

He nodded. He wasn't sure what he was supposed to say next, because everything he was thinking of at the moment would have come out sounding too obviously forced.

Carrie, thank God, decided to take mercy on both of them and left before he could come up with something.

HE STEPPED OUTSIDE onto the front patio and breathed in the fresh air. The island had cooled down noticeably, and he was glad he had on a long-sleeve shirt. The grass *crunched* under his boots as he made his way to the beach, using the road that wound around the island like a stone serpent, each different pebble like scales. He glanced over at the Tower and saw a figure moving behind one of the windows. Judging by the height, he guessed it was either Carly or Jo, Bonnie's little sister.

A motor started up as he neared the beach, the noise rudely breaking through the quiet. He walked across the mushy sand and toward the pier, where Maddie was revving one of the boats. It was an ugly aluminum vessel with chipped navy blue colors, but judging by the sound of its outboard motor, it would do just fine.

She shut down the boat when he was halfway to her. "Lara tells me you know your way around boats."

"Just enough to get in trouble."

"Like last night?"

"They started it."

"Right. So," she said, doing a *Price is Right* gesture at the boat, "it's not the best-looking specimen we have on the island, but the motor's good and it should get you where you need to be. That is, unless you run into pirates out there in the Gulf." She glanced at the big *Trident* anchored nearby, moving slightly back and forth with the wind. "Which would have been an absurd idea until last night."

Keo looked over the boat. It was a sixteen-footer, one of those deep-V vessels with a stainless steel stern and bow, and had fishing decks that took up plenty of space. The windshield above the center console was tinted, the glass cracked in places with something that looked like a fresh bullet hole near the center. He decided not to ask about that.

"Don't let her looks fool you," Maddie was saying. "She's a sturdy little one."

"It'll do."

"Where's your stuff and that cute German gun of yours?"

"Back at the hotel," he smiled. "I was thinking about picking up one of those M4s you guys like so much for insurance."

"How many guns do you need, Keo?"

"After everything that's happened, you're actually asking me that question?"

Maddie chuckled. "Sorry, total brain fart." She tossed him the key, then climbed up onto the pier. "Tank's topped off and I'll bring out the extra gas cans when you're ready to shove off."

"How many?"

"It won't get you all the way to the Texas coast, but that's what the 12-volt trolling motor is for. Battery's fully charged, and I'll give you a spare just in case. Also, two livewells, twenty gallons each, to stash your supplies, and plenty of compartments for everything else. First aid kit, flare gun, et cetera. Oh, and two paddles. You know, just in case."

"Looks like you got everything covered. Thanks."

"Boss lady tells me to do it, I do it."

"You believe in her," Keo said, looking at Maddie.

"She's got us this far. Her and Will. I'm not going to start doubting them now."

"That kind of loyalty's hard to come by. I respect that."

"What can I say? They earned it." Maddie nodded at the white yacht. "I'm surprised you didn't want to take that monster."

"Too rich for my blood."

"I think Lara's already coming up with some ideas on how to use it."

"Oh, I'm sure of that." He remembered the look on her face when she had first seen the *Trident* last night. "She strikes me as the kind of girl who thinks two or three moves ahead of everyone, including me."

"I'm just glad she's on our side." Then, "By the way, I've been meaning to ask…"

"What's that?"

"What kind of name is Keo, anyway?"

"George was taken."

Maddie snorted. "You got that down pat, huh?"

Keo smiled. "I don't know what you're talking about. Absolutely no one has ever asked me that question before."

"Riiiiiight. Well, I wish you'd stay. I won't lie; we could really use another gun around here. But I get that you have to go. If I don't see you again, *vaya con dios*, Keo."

"What if I don't believe in God?" he asked.

"I'm sure he'll get over it," she smiled back.

THE LAST TIME he was in the Tower's basement, he had been looking for something with explosive capabilities. This time, Keo was content to pick up an M4 carbine with a decent optic and a collapsible stock. He liked the MP5SD, but there was nothing wrong with loading up on firepower—especially since he didn't know what was waiting for him out there. The absent Rangers had stockpiled plenty of silver ammo, and he loaded up on as much as he could carry.

He climbed out of the basement with the weapon and spare magazines in his cargo pants pocket. As he was closing the door back up, he heard voices coming through a radio from two floors above him. Foreign accents, some thicker than others, floated through the open doors.

The idea that people around the world were contacting each other made him feel strangely optimistic. Of course, those good vibes always faded when he realized what some guys in China, Russia, or France were doing had zero impact on his life at the moment. The world was a vast place, made more distant by the lack of convenient transportation. Unless, of course, you could find a pilot somewhere with a working plane and the fuel for it. Talking to some guy over the radio was one thing; actually getting together to form some kind of plan was another.

Good luck with that, guys. I'm just looking for a girl to hook up with again.

He headed out, feeling strangely content. What Lara and the

islanders did from now on was their business. He had done his part—more than his part, actually—and it was time to go.

There was no one working the nascent garden outside because everyone was sticking to the hotel these days. Keo wasn't entirely sure if that was a good idea and thought about bringing it up, but decided against it. Lara was a smart girl, and she probably knew what she was doing. And if not…

Not my problem anymore. Time to go.

Carrie wasn't in his room when he returned, but there was a large faded gym bag sitting on the bed. Keo opened it and found stacks of sealed beef jerky, along with bottled water, nonperishable canned goods, and a dozen shiny bags of MREs. There was enough inside to last him weeks on the ocean. More than a month, if he conserved. Of course, if he needed a month's worth of food out there, he was already in trouble. Whoever had brought it over had also generously tossed in a couple of metal sporks and a can opener.

Keo shoved the newly acquired magazines into the same tactical pack he had put his spare clothes in earlier, one of many the Rangers had stashed around the hotel. He slipped the nylon bag on and picked up the much heavier gym bag (the damn thing weighed a ton) and left the room.

The faster he moved, the faster he climbed into the boat, the faster he took off, the better things would be. For him. For Carrie. For Lara and the others.

He decided he wouldn't tell Gillian about Song Island when they finally reunited. Hell, he'd like to forget about this place too after tonight, but somehow he didn't think that was going to be possible anytime soon.

◄━━▮ ▮━━►

HE RETURNED TO the beach just in time to see Lara and Maddie cruising toward the *Trident* in one of the bass fishing boats while Blaine watched after them from the yacht's main deck. It was just as well. He had been dreading another encounter with Lara anyway. He respected the hell out of her, so the prospect of having to face her again while he was *(running)* leaving wasn't at the very top of his to-do list.

Bonnie saw him coming and stood up on the boat shack, where she was standing guard. She was easily the tallest woman on the island, but that wasn't what he noticed most about her. He didn't have any trouble believing she used to be a model. In another time, another place, Keo might have decided dying tonight was worth it if that meant the possibility of getting into her good graces.

But that was then, and this was now. And right now, he had to get the hell off this island before he did something stupid...like decide not to.

"So you really are leaving," Bonnie said.

"Afraid so."

"Too bad. We were hoping you might stay awhile."

"'We'?"

"Everyone on the island."

He sighed. He should have run instead of walked to his boat.

"Can't," he said.

"She must be some woman."

"What makes you think there's a woman?"

"Oh, come on. There's always a woman. Plus, Carly told me."

"Ah."

"Is she pretty?"

"What do you think?"

"Must be. I just hope she's actually there."

Great. Who doesn't know I'm the world's biggest sucker?

"Gotta take the chance," he said.

"So this is all on faith?" Bonnie chuckled. "Somehow, I never took you for the kind of guy who went on faith, Keo."

"People change."

"I guess so."

Keo stopped next to Bonnie's shack and glanced in the direction of the luxury yacht moored nearby. Maddie had expertly sidled the boat toward the back, as if she had done it a million times.

"What's going on over there?" he asked. "Still searching for the eighth guy?"

"If he even exists," Bonnie said.

"The captain thinks so."

"But he's not a real captain."

"He had a captain's hat."

"Well, since he had a captain's hat...," Bonnie said, rolling her eyes.

"So what's happening on the yacht?"

"Lara wanted to check something out."

"She didn't say?"

"Not to me. I guess she has a lot on her mind."

"Guess so." Keo started up the pier toward his boat. "See you around, Bonnie."

"Later, alligator," Bonnie said after him. "Don't be a stranger."

He turned around, but continued backpedaling down the pier. "Remember: Shoot first, shoot often, and reload fast."

"Yeah, but I don't have one of those grenade launchers," she shouted after him.

He grinned. "Somehow, I think you'll do just fine without one."

He spun around and tossed the gym bag into the boat, then untied the line before climbing in. He put the M4 down next to the supplies and dug out the key Maddie had given him and powered on the boat. The outboard motor coughed for a bit, then caught a second later and filled the air with a loud ear-splitting roar. It sounded like a winner. Or close enough to get him to Texas.

Bonnie, still watching him from the shack, waved. Keo waved back.

He maneuvered the boat away from the pier and turned it around, then pushed the throttle forward. North took him further inland—with the soldiers waiting up there—but south took him to the Gulf of Mexico. From there it was right toward the Texas coast and Santa Marie Island.

"So this is all on faith? Somehow, I never took you for the kind of guy who went on faith, Keo."

No kidding. Neither did I.

Blaine appeared along the railing on the main deck of the *Trident* as he neared the big boat. The big man waved and Keo returned it, even though doing so made him feel like a fraud. He didn't see Lara or Maddie or the other kid, Roy. Which was just as well. If he had to fake another good-bye wave, he might decide to end it all now with a silver bullet to the temple.

Keep going. Don't look back.
Gillian's waiting. You've kept her waiting enough, don't you think?
Damn straight.
Goddamn, you almost convinced yourself that time, pal.

He pushed the throttle up as far as it would go, and the boat dipped slightly behind him. The loud noise helped to drown out his thoughts, which was something he was very grateful for. Who knew a guilty conscience could be so loud and annoying?

Keep going, he told himself, and repeated over and over again. *Keep going and don't look back.*

Just keep going…

CHAPTER 8

GABY

"Is something wrong with your shoulder?" Nate asked.

Gaby had been massaging her shoulder for the last few seconds. The pain had lessened noticeably thanks to the painkillers, but every now and then (usually when she sat in one place for too long doing nothing, like now), it came back. It was a reminder of last night and the fight with the blue-eyed ghouls, as if she would ever forget it for as long as she lived.

"No, I'm fine," she said.

"You sure?"

"Yes."

There was an edge to her voice that she hoped he didn't catch, because she didn't know where it had come from. She should be happy to see Nate alive and well, but for some reason she wasn't. Not entirely, anyway.

"So that's Danny, huh?" Nate was saying. "The way you talked about him, I thought he'd be prettier."

"He was, until a few days ago."

"What happened?"

A farmhouse. Blue-eyed ghouls. Will killing them, then cutting off their heads to keep an army of the black-eyed ones at bay all night.

You know, same-o, same-o.

"A lot of things," she said. "Like how you're supposed to be dead, but aren't. Why is that, Nate?"

"I'm starting to think you're not happy I'm alive." He smiled. It was his attempt at being charming, but he didn't have his heart in it and she saw through it.

"You're supposed to be dead, Nate. *Why aren't you dead?*"

He sighed. "I guess I wanted to live more."

He shook his head and she could see him struggling with it, too. Gaby felt suddenly very guilty about not responding to his resurrection with the fanfare he had expected, and that she dearly wanted to give him but just didn't know how.

"It's a long story," he said.

"We're not going anywhere."

"Maybe later..."

Gaby sneaked a look at him. She thought it was the absence of the absurd Mohawk that made him look somehow older, but she realized now that she had been wrong. It wasn't the hair at all. Nate just seemed to have physically aged since the last time she saw him.

"Gaby," he said. "It's me. I swear it."

She looked away, feeling very self-conscious about her own appearance. Nate didn't look the same, but neither did she. Far from it. They had both changed so much in such a short time, in every way that mattered. She had the broken nose that still hurt if she touched it (which she did often, always forgetting why it was tingling), and the bruises and scars from the last few weeks that would never heal properly.

What did he see when he looked at her, she wondered.

"You'll tell me everything later," she said.

"I will. I promise."

She nodded before refocusing back on Interstate 10.

Everything was where they had left it thirty minutes ago, including the white Ford truck and the overturned Nissan Titan further down the road, sitting in a pool of its own gasoline. The only thing missing was the red Chevy Silverado truck, which they had taken to replace their now-unusable vehicle.

"By the way, you look good," Nate said.

Gaby sighed. "This isn't the time."

"I'm just saying. You still look good, and I don't say that to a lot of women with more scars on their face than me—"

Her radio vibrated against her hand, cutting off Nate. Danny's voice came through the speakers at half-volume, just loud enough for them to hear. "Heads up. Here comes the cavalry."

The sound of car engines grew in the distance, getting louder as the vehicles got closer.

"More of your friends," Gaby said.

"Not my friends," Nate said, sounding almost…annoyed?

Two trucks, with men clinging to the back, sped down the highway toward the Titan. She watched them through her binoculars and easily identified the camo uniforms they had on. They were identical to the one worn by the man crouched next to her right now. The vehicles stopped ten yards from the Nissan, and the men hopped out and swarmed it. They were moving in something that she could almost believe was an actual tactical formation.

"Nate," Danny said through the radio.

She looked to her left at a patch of overgrown grass about forty meters from her position and halfway to the highway. Danny. He was close enough that he could probably hear everything the soldiers were saying. He had camouflaged himself so well that she couldn't find a single trace of his existence. And if she couldn't spot him—and she knew exactly where to look—there was no chance the men on the interstate were going to.

Gaby handed Nate the radio, and he said into it, "Yeah."

Although they weren't quite whispering, they had adopted a low decibel. She and Nate were firmly established inside their hiding spot more than seventy meters from the highway, far enough that they couldn't be spotted through the yard or so of trees in front of them. Of course, it would be a different story if the soldiers started walking toward them or looked closely with binoculars, but hopefully the missing Silverado would convince them they had taken it. After all, what reason could they possibly have to stick around thirty minutes later?

So what does that make us? Smart or stupid?

I guess we'll find out.

"Who's in charge of this little circus of yours?" Danny was asking Nate through the radio.

"In charge?" Nate said. He thought about it for a moment. "I guess Mason. This short guy. He was running things when they sent us over to replace the ones they lost back in Dunbar. Why?"

Danny ignored his question and asked instead, "How many of you are running around out here?"

Nate winced a bit at the "how many of you" part, as if he didn't like being reminded of the uniform he was wearing. Which was hard, since he was still wearing the damn thing. It even had his name on it, for God's sake.

"They sent ten of us over just in case you made it off Route 13," Nate said. "They left the three of us behind and the rest went on to Salvani, like I said before."

"The not-so-magnificent seven. What were their orders?"

"I have no idea. They don't actually tell me everything. Most of us don't know what's happening until guys like Mason show up and start giving orders. You gotta understand, these aren't actually soldiers. They're playing dress up. I don't think half of these guys could have survived a real Boot Camp."

"What about these mutts we're looking at now? What's their story?"

He was talking about the six men spreading out along the interstate in front of them, probably looking for hints of where she and the others had taken the Silverado. Gaby wondered if any of them actually knew what they were doing.

"Weekend warriors," Will had once called them.

"My guess is that Mason sent them forward to connect with us," Nate said into the radio. "We're using two-ways, but they have limited range. There's probably another group further down the highway, waiting to relay the message back to Route 13."

On cue, one of the men took out a radio and spoke into it. She had no chance of hearing him over the distance, which was good because that meant he couldn't overhear them, either.

"It's a slapdash operation," Nate continued. "I get the feeling they're just making it up as they go." He had looked over at her when he added, "Imagine what they could do if they had someone with actual leadership ability at the helm, instead of some eighteen-year-old kid."

He's talking about Josh.

"That's nineteen-year-old kid to you," Josh would say.

She didn't bother correcting Nate or responding to his querying glance. If he was going to keep secrets from her until later, then she'd return it in kind. Maybe it was a little childish, but what the hell, he was supposed to be dead.

"You gonna tell me what we're still doing here?" Nate said into the radio. "We could be halfway to Salvani by now."

"There's no hurry, kid," Danny said. "You ever heard the story about the hare and the tortoise?"

"Slow and steady wins the race?"

"Sure, there's that, but I was referring to the part where the tortoise hid in the woods and ate a bag of jerky."

They heard what sounded like chewing on the other end of the radio.

Nate gave her a confused look. "Is he eating?"

Gaby shook her head. "It's Danny."

"And that explains it?"

"Yes."

"Hunh."

They sat in the same spot and watched in silence until the newly arrived trucks fired up again and the men climbed into the back. The vehicles took off up the highway, picking up speed as they went. Soon, the only sounds were the slight echoes of their engines reverberating across the calm midday sky. Gaby and Nate didn't move or say a word until they couldn't hear the vehicles anymore. Even then, both of them were hesitant to break the silence—

"There goes the hare," a voice said behind them.

She spun around at the same time as Nate, both of them reaching for their weapons.

Except it was just Danny, standing behind them chewing on a piece of jerky he had taken out of a bag of Oberto.

"Jesus," Gaby said.

"Nah, it's just me," Danny said. "Let's get back to the Chevy before the girls run off in search of better pastures."

He turned around and began moving through the woods.

She got up, and with Nate at her side, followed him. Nate gave her a *How'd he get behind us?* look.

She shook her head.

"What now?" Nate asked Danny.

"They're going west, toward your other friends," Danny said.

Nate flinched again, this time at the word "friends."

Danny was picking his way back to where they had parked the collaborator truck they had taken off the highway, and she couldn't help but find his slow and steady pace to be slightly irritating. Shouldn't they be moving faster? With purpose?

"Looks like they've gathering the buggers into one place," Danny said. "Despite my legendary skills, that's way too many to take on, especially with the women and kids to take care of. And, oh, you too, Natester."

"So we go around them," Gaby said. "We don't actually have to go through Salvani, do we?"

"No. But it's likely they'll have the rest of the interstate covered, too. Leave behind spotters just in case we decide to take a detour or find a shortcut. Right, Nathaniel Hawthorne?"

"I don't know," Nate said. "Maybe. Like I said, they didn't really tell me the whole plan. Go here, stay there, back up these guys. That's pretty much it." Then he added, "And it's just Nate."

"We need to get going, Danny," Gaby said. "Lara and the others are counting on us showing up tonight."

"Get back to the island!" Will had said. *"Whatever you go, don't leave it undefended for another night!"*

"You know anything about that?" Danny asked. The question

was obviously directed at Nate, even though Danny hadn't looked back at them when he said it.

Nate shook his head. "That's beyond my AO. I haven't been anywhere past the interstate since I woke up."

Woke up? Gaby thought, but restrained herself from blurting out the question.

She said instead, "AO?"

"Area of operations," Nate said. "Though they didn't call it that. Like I said, it's a pretty helter-skelter outfit. I don't think they know what the hell they're doing. Mostly, they're just obeying orders from them."

She didn't have to ask who "them" was. She knew. Danny knew, too.

"So what's the plan?" she asked Danny.

"The fastest path to Song Island is the interstate," Danny said. He was still moving unfathomably slow. She wished he would *move faster* already. "We could try going around it, but it's going to cost us time if we have to pick through the small roads. Of course, we'd have to try not to get lost in the process, too. One wrong turn, and it's another hour or two. Or days. Maps aren't nearly as reliable as GPS, and unfortunately I don't think those are up and running anymore. Like you said, kid, we gotta get home before dark."

"So what are our options?"

"They think we already went on ahead, in the truck we took. So the guys at Salvani are expecting us, and the ones that just took off think they're going to cut off our retreat. I'm guessing they also have guys in Lake Dulcet thirty minutes from here, and Lake Charles after that."

"They're not real soldiers by any stretch, but yeah, they're not total idiots, either," Nate said.

"Good to know. So, my guess is when they can't find us, they'll start spreading out, thinking we left the interstate before we reached one of their ambushes. That's the smart move."

"But that's not what we're going to do," Gaby said.

"Nope." Danny bit on another big stick of jerky and nodded

back at Nate. "Nice uniform."

"Thanks?" Nate said.

Danny grinned at them.

◄━━▮ ▮━━►

"YOU TRUST THIS guy?" Nate asked.

"If it wasn't for Danny and Will, I wouldn't be alive more times over than I could count," Gaby said. "Yeah, I trust him."

"That's good enough for me."

She looked at the girls in the backseat. Annie had Milly in her lap, the two of them staring somberly out the window. Like Gaby, they hadn't protested when Danny laid out his plan. Although she looked like she might have bolted at any second, Annie hadn't said a word when given the chance. Milly, too, had kept quiet. But if Annie and Milly looked terrified of where they were heading, Claire was the exact opposite.

"We're almost there," Claire said, smiling at her.

"Almost," Gaby said.

She returned the girl's smile, though inside she couldn't help but wonder where she was leading them. Was Song Island really safer than out here? Or in one of those collaborator towns? If you obeyed and went along with the program, those places weren't so bad. All you had to do was give blood every night…and let some stranger impregnate you…so your child could be born to serve the ghouls.

Like cattle.

That's what they want to turn us into. Docile cattle.

Gaby shivered slightly and was glad no one noticed, including Nate behind the steering wheel next to her. Claire was also too busy wiping dirt off her FNH shotgun to pay attention.

God, Josh, how did you ever convince yourself any of this was okay?

She turned back around in the front passenger seat and got a quick glimpse of herself in the tilted rearview mirror. If seeing Nate in the fresh soldier's uniform still threw her for a loop, seeing herself in one was even more jolting.

There was a hole in the back of the shirt she was wearing now, along with some dried blood. The man Nate had shot in the back had been about her size, though a few inches taller and wider around the hip area. The pants barely fit, but she was able to cinch it mostly in place with the gun belt. Not that she was going to have to wear it for long, which was why she kept her original clothes crumpled on the floor at her feet.

There were hardly any vehicles left along the interstate to look at, or obstructions in the roads to avoid. This stretch of the countryside had been barren of stray cars for the last twenty minutes ever since they drove out of the woods and made their way back onto I-10. According to all the signs, Lake Dulcet was still five minutes ahead of them.

"I know you want to ask," Nate said after a while.

"Later," she said.

"If we live through this."

Gaby sighed and hoped Claire and the others hadn't heard that. But of course they had. They were sitting right behind them, after all.

"We'll be fine," she said, a little louder than she needed to because she wanted the girls in the back to hear her clearly. "Danny knows what he's doing. You just have to trust him."

God, I hope Danny knows what he's doing.

"You really trust him," Nate said.

"We've been through a lot together."

"So have we."

"It's not even close, Nate."

"Not even close?"

"Night and day."

"Even after the pawnshop?"

"Even after the pawnshop."

"Oh."

He sounded genuinely hurt that time, though she couldn't understand why. He had to know, didn't he, that what she had gone through with Will and Danny was beyond anything he and she had shared in the couple days they knew each other before he was taken?

Didn't he know that?

"Let's talk about something else," she said.

"Okay," Nate said. Then, "They're there? Dwayne, Kendra, and the others? They made it to Song Island safely?"

"They did."

"Good. Not knowing what had happened to them kept me up at night."

"After what you went through, you were worried about them?"

"I've been responsible for them for a long time. Old habits are hard to break, I guess." He paused for a moment, then, "How sure are you they're going to attack the island tonight?"

"Will seemed pretty sure."

"I'm sorry about that. Will, I mean."

"You don't know Will. As long as he's breathing, he's capable of anything. I wouldn't be surprised if he beats us to the island."

God, I almost believed myself that time.

"You didn't know about the ambush on Route 13?" she asked.

He shook his head. "I know they were setting up an ambush, but not that you were involved. I told you, they really don't tell us anything. Just where to go and what to do. I didn't even know you were still alive until I saw you through my scope."

"When did you decide?"

"Decide what?"

"To change sides."

"I was never on their side," Nate said. Again, he sounded slightly frustrated with the question—or the accusation, she guessed, was the more appropriate word. "You have to understand what happened to me after Lafayette—"

"Later," she said, cutting him off and leaning slightly toward the dashboard. She peered out the windshield at what she had been waiting to see since they returned to the highway.

Nate saw it, too, and went quiet.

There were two vehicles up ahead, parked nose-to-nose in the middle of the two-lane highway. The shoulders were wide open, but getting to them would be a miracle with the four men standing around the trucks, aiming assault rifles down the interstate at them.

Nate began to slow down. "Ready?"

She nodded, then turned around slightly in her seat. It was a minor move that was *(hopefully)* unnoticeable from outside the car. "Guys, get down, just like we rehearsed."

There was a lot of movement behind her as Annie and Milly sank into the floor behind Nate's seat, and Claire did likewise behind hers. She imagined the thirteen-year-old clutching her shotgun and steeling herself for what was about to come.

Gaby faced fully forward again and gripped the M4 leaning against her right leg. It had been there the entire time, just out of view.

Please let this work. Please don't let us all die in the next few minutes.

The two-way radio on the dashboard squawked, and they heard Danny's voice. "Easy does it, Nathaniel Ramsey. Just pretend you're back at the Colonial Congress of the Confederation."

"What the hell is he talking about?" Nate said to her.

Gaby couldn't help but smile. "I have no idea. Just keep going. Remember who you are."

"And what's that?"

"A traitorous scumbag who sold out humanity."

"Ouch."

"I didn't mean—"

"I know," he said.

She nodded. "I didn't say it before, but it's good to see you again, Nate. I'm glad you're still alive."

He smiled at her, genuinely touched by that. She almost blushed under his gaze.

"Ditto," he said.

Now all they had to do was survive the next few seconds.

I hope you know what you're doing, Danny. God, I hope you know what you're friggin' doing...

CHAPTER 9

WILL

"ONE DOOR CLOSES, *another door opens.*"

Or maybe the better saying was, "*Up a creek without a paddle and nothing to show for it but a wet ass*"?

The point was, he was in trouble. Maybe. There were options in front of him, but as always, the trick was to pick out the best one and go for it. Choose the wrong one, and he was likely a dead man. And Lara would so be pissed off if he went and died on her.

Don't worry, babe, I don't plan on going anywhere anytime soon.

"You're from Dunbar," Will said.

"How'd you know?" This was Leo, the forty-something who, along with the woman, had found him inside the Palermo. He was the talkative of the duo; which was to say, he was the only one who talked.

"The direction you came from, for one," Will said. "That, and your less-than-enthusiastic reaction to the soldiers."

"'Soldiers,'" Leo snorted. "Don't call them that."

"What do you call them?"

"Wannabes. Killers. Pieces of shit. Take your pick."

Will nodded. He would have gone with "weekend warriors" himself, but "wannabe killer pieces of shit" was just as good.

Natasha, the woman, was watching him closely from across the room. Not that there was a lot of space between them. They were sitting on the dust-covered floor of one of those small pick-up centers for Domino's Pizza. The building was on the other side of the I-10, beyond the underpass, and to the right of Route 13. They were close enough to the highway that he could see out the windows at the Palermo and Chevron signs jutting in the air. There were two more men in a Valero gas station across the street from them, both heavily armed individuals that were, like the three of them, waiting for signs of a counterattack from Mason's men.

Dunbar's fighters didn't have the desire to go anywhere anytime soon post-attack, he had discovered. They were at least nice enough to give him back his painkillers and a half-full bottle of water to wash away the caked blood from his face while they waited, though Will spent most of it keeping dehydration at bay.

He sneaked a look down at his watch: 1:06 P.M.

Almost an hour after Leo, Natasha, and the others laid waste to the ten or so men Mason had left behind at the intersection. Since then, no one else had shown up yet. Looking around him at Leo's gnarled face and Natasha's dead-serious eyes, he couldn't shake the feeling he had found himself in the company of people who had embraced a death wish. Attacking the soldiers had been a hell of a gamble and had cost them two of their own, leaving behind just six, including the two in the technical hidden next to their side of the highway now, ready to burst out and open fire at anyone who came down Route 13.

That was the full extent of their "plan," as it turned out. He wondered if he could use that lack of ambition to his advantage. What would a group of people who just wanted to kill some assholes that had laid waste to their city do when those intended targets never showed up?

Maybe I should find out.

"You've been to Dunbar?" Leo was asking him.

"We thought about it, but we never got that far down the highway," he lied.

"Where you from?"

"Mississippi."

"That was you," Natasha said. "We saw a minivan not far from here, at a farmhouse. It had Mississippi plates."

Will nodded. He was hoping they would have stumbled across it on their way down the road. The minivan belonged to a young man named Lance and his girlfriend, Annie. The two had come to Louisiana from the neighboring state with other survivors looking for salvation.

Old story. New characters.

Annie was the only survivor after last night, and she was with Gaby and Danny right now on their way to Song Island.

Song Island. That was the key.

But first, he had to slowly build up his credibility. Maybe Leo and Natasha knew about his and Danny's presence in Dunbar two nights ago, and maybe they didn't. Right now, he needed them to see him as an unaffiliated third party who wasn't a threat. After all, it was hard to take suggestions from someone you'd rather shoot in the head.

"You alone?" Natasha asked him.

He shook his head. He had a feeling she already knew about the other truck—the one Danny and Gaby had managed to escape in earlier. What was that Michael had said?

"They came out of nowhere. They must have...they must have been crawling along the fields all day toward us."

That kind of stealth approach took a long time. It hadn't surprised him to learn Leo and Natasha's group had been approaching Mason's long before his and Danny's vehicles made their mad dash to reach the interstate. Which meant there was a very real possibility the two people watching him closely right now had witnessed the ambush from cover.

So he had to choose his lies and truths carefully. Very, very carefully. He could see it in Natasha's stare—and, to an extent, in Leo's, too. Days later, they were still reeling from what happened back at Dunbar.

"No," Will said, looking Natasha in the eyes, because this version of him that he was trying to sell had nothing to hide. "After we left the farmhouse, we ran across a couple of the soldiers in trucks. We managed to overpower them and take their vehicles. We were trying to escape when they ambushed us."

"How many more of you are out there?" she asked.

"Four."

"Christ, how many did you fit into that minivan?" Leo asked, with just a hint of amusement.

"We didn't just come in one vehicle."

"Why did you burn down the farmhouse?" Natasha asked. She was still staring at him, trying to read him, maybe catch him in a lie. Sunlight streamed through the windows to their right and splashed across her hardened face.

"After they attacked us, we thought there were some left in the basement in the morning," Will said. "We couldn't stay there anymore, so we burned the house down in hopes of getting some of them, too."

It wasn't a total lie. All of it was true, except for the part where he inserted himself into Lance's role.

"You're talking about *them*, them," Leo said. "The creatures."

Will nodded.

"Did you get them?" the older man asked. He sounded almost hopeful. "Did it work?"

"I don't know," Will said. "We never opened the basement door to check."

Eureka, he thought when he saw Natasha casually slide her finger out of the trigger guard of her M4. She probably didn't even know she had done it—an unconscious act that told him she had stopped seeing him as the immediate danger he once was.

Or, at least, he hoped he was reading her reaction correctly. He had to remind himself that he was treading on very dangerous ground here. One wrong lie, one creative story that couldn't be collaborated by evidence or what they already knew, and he'd never make it to Song Island.

Like walking a tightrope fifty stories up…while getting shot at.

Will sat back against the dirty wall, took out the bottle of meds, and downed two more, leaving just three lonely white pills at the bottom. He had been surviving on mostly adrenaline and sweat these last few days that the old wounds throughout his body had begun to fade into the background. He just had to worry about the ones still held together by stitches, especially the one in his side. That, more than anything, was his primary concern.

"What's that?" Natasha asked.

"Painkillers," Will said.

"You hurt?"

"You're not?"

She almost smiled. Almost.

"Who isn't, these days," he said.

"Dead people," she said.

Leo chuckled. "Hallelujah."

The older man was sitting to Will's left and rummaging through a school backpack. Will had been hoping one of them had picked up his tactical pack, along with all the silver ammo inside, but it was gone. Either Mason had thrown it into his own inventory, or it was lost somewhere in all the rubble back in the Palermo.

There were also no signs of his M4A1, which really hurt. From Afghanistan to Harris County to the end of the world, only to lose it at a lousy gas station in the middle of nowhere. He couldn't ask them about it, either, because that would mean he was a guy who knew guns, and the Will he was trying to sell right now was a civvy through and through.

"Here," Leo said, and tossed him another refilled bottle of water along with a vacuum-sealed bag with strips of jerky inside. "Eat up; it might be a long wait."

"Thanks," Will said. He pried the bag open and devoured the jerky. It tasted like deer meat. "You made this?"

"None of that store-bought junk. I've been hunting since I was twelve and learned to make my own jerky when I was thirteen."

"Where did you even find deer?"

"They're around, if you look hard enough. Not easy by any

means, but there are a few still running around out there in the woods. Of course, turns out surviving the bloodsuckers is easier than dodging me."

"He's really proud of his jerky," Natasha said. She unzipped her own pack and took out a similar bag, then produced another long strip of jerky. "He should be. It's better than the crap we hoarded after everything fell apart."

"And that's the closest you'll come to getting a compliment out of Nat, kid," Leo said.

Will smiled, then, "How long are you guys going to stay here?"

Leo and Natasha exchanged a brief look.

They have no idea. They're just making it up as they go. Swell.

"Maybe an hour," Leo said with a shrug. "If they send more over, we'll deal with them the same way we dealt with the others. Too bad we already used up the frag grenade."

"Whose bright idea was that?"

Leo grinned at him. "One guess."

Natasha. Of course.

"I expected the damn gas station to go up like a Roman candle," Leo said. "I guess it's a good thing for you that Nat doesn't throw like a girl. You should have seen that fastball vanish into the Palermo. *Boom.* If it had landed over the storage tanks under the pumps, we wouldn't be having this conversation right now."

"No kidding. Where'd you get your hands on something like that?"

"From the same meatheads we took the truck from. The stuff these guys are carrying around, all those M4s and MGs. They must have hit a fort or something. Who knows what else they have stashed around the state."

Will glanced down at his watch again.

"You in a hurry?" Natasha asked. The edge had crept back into her voice.

"Yes," Will said, meeting her suspicious gaze.

Sell it. She expects you to run from her glare. So don't.

"My friends got away, and I need to find them again," Will said.

"We came here together, survived all this as a group. You guys seem okay, don't get me wrong, but these are my people. I need to catch up to them."

He must have sold it well enough, because Natasha nodded. "They went up the interstate. West."

So they really had been close enough to witness the ambush. Where the hell had they been hiding during the whole thing? The sunburned grass in the fields around them wasn't exactly a sniper's dream. There were thicker woods further up the highway, but there wasn't much of that over here, where the businesses were concentrated.

"Where they headed, anyway?" Leo asked.

And there it is.

"Have you ever heard of Song Island?" Will asked.

◂▬▮ ▮▬▸

THEY WAITED ANOTHER thirty minutes.

Then thirty minutes became an hour.

And no one showed up.

Meanwhile, the carrion birds had begun circling over the corpses left behind in the streets and parking lots of both the Palermo and the Chevron.

Ray, one of the two guys in the Valero across the street from them, jogged over, his lanky six-three frame like a scarecrow against the heavy afternoon sun. "We're leaving," he said as soon as he was inside the Domino's. "They're not coming."

Then he left and ran up the street, toward the parked technical.

Leo stood up, brushing dust off his pants. "Come on," he said to Will, "let's see if you can convince the others about this Song Island. If we're going, it's gotta be as a group, or not at all."

Will pulled himself up from the floor. He was glad to finally be up again. His side stung a bit, but stinging was better than bleeding, and a quick check told him he was still fine. For now, anyway.

"I can be pretty convincing," Will said.

"You better hope so," Natasha said.

There may or may not have been a warning in her voice, and before he could gauge which one was more likely, she had pushed open the doors and stepped out into the street, leaving him behind with Leo.

"What's her deal?" Will asked.

"What do you mean?" Leo said.

"Back there, at the station. She shot that kid in cold blood."

Leo frowned, which didn't do anything for his already heavily lined face. "She lost her daughter two nights ago. The kid was waiting for her in the VFW hall in Dunbar when the soldiers attacked, and… Well, it didn't end happily for her. For any of us. I guess that explains why we're all out here trying to kill as many of the bastards as possible."

Will nodded. He didn't need Leo to give him the details. He knew what had happened in Dunbar two nights ago, because he had been there. Kate's shock troops, Harrison's people being slaughtered…

He walked outside with Leo. "What was she before all of this?"

"State trooper," Leo said. "She actually busted me a couple of times for hunting out of season. I don't think she ever had to draw her weapon before the world went to shit, though. Funny how things work out."

"Yeah," Will said, though the word "funny" wasn't quite what he would have used.

◂━ ━▸

"AN ISLAND? ARE you fucking kidding me?"

"An island. You're out of your mind."

"The radio broadcast? I heard about that."

"I say we keep going."

"Maybe we should go back to Dunbar."

"We have to find someplace else. Dunbar's lost."

"You don't know that."

"Let's find more of these fuckers and kill as many as we can, before they get us."

Because what remained of Dunbar's fighters didn't have anything resembling a leader, everyone spoke at the same time. Which made it difficult for Will to judge who was leaning toward his proposition and who was just shooting off at the mouth.

Natasha, though, had kept out of the fray. She leaned against the Ford's hood and looked solemnly back down Route 13 through the underpass, as if she expected Mason's soldiers to pop up at any moment. By the way she was holding her M4, he guessed she was hoping for exactly that.

"Shit, it's not any more unbelievable than what's happening now," Leo was saying. "Look around you, boys. The impossible is possible. What makes this any less possible, considering everything we've been through? Have you forgotten about those blue-eyed fucks we all saw two nights ago?"

That seemed to quiet them.

I have a champion, Will thought, fighting back a smile. He couldn't have chosen a better person to argue for him, either. Leo was tall, big, older than the rest, and forceful when he talked so you couldn't help but pay attention.

Leo turned to him now. "And it works. The bodies of water. Just the way the woman on the radio says it does?"

"She was right about the silver," Will said.

"You've used silver on them?" Ray asked.

"We have. After we heard the radio message, we started sharpening silver crosses into weapons. All you have to do is stab them and they die. They actually *die.*"

Ray, Leo, and the others exchanged a look. All except Natasha. She was still focused on the underpass, oblivious to the conversation. Will thought she would at least react to his confirmation that silver worked on the ghouls, but no. Natasha was in her own world. Right now, he didn't think anything besides the presence of Mason's men could make her care.

"Dammit," Ray said. "We heard that same broadcast days ago,

but Harrison insisted it was all bullshit, so we never followed through on it. But you're saying it works. You swear it?"

"I swear it," Will said, "and I've used it."

"So, silver bullets?" Leo said. Will could practically see the gears in the older man's head turning. "We could do that. Make silver rounds. It'd be nice to finally be able to shoot and kill the fuckers for once."

"Silver works, just like the woman on the radio said it would," Will said. "If she's right about that, she could be right about the bodies of water, too. All we'd have to do is get to Song Island. You guys are looking for a new place to stay. There it is."

"I have a question," Ray said. "How the hell are we going to survive on an island?"

"It has a hotel and solar-powered electricity."

"And you know this how?"

"We didn't all come from Mississippi. One of us was from here. He was born and raised around Beaufont Lake and he saw them building the hotel over the years, and he says it's mostly finished. As for what you'd eat, that's easy—the lake is filled with fish. When we heard the radio broadcast, it just made sense to retreat to Song Island."

"Sounds like a fool thing to do," another man, Greg, said. He was in his thirties, squat, and looked ridiculous next to the tall Ray.

The other two were Olsen and Barnes, who had been manning the technical all this time.

Olsen was leaning out the front passenger side door looking bored. "They're from Mississippi, what'd you expect?"

Will ignored him, said, "Look around you, guys. There's not a lot of choices left these days. If it's not the creatures, it's the soldiers."

"And hiding on an island is better?" Ray said.

"Better than out here."

"He's got a point," Barnes said. He was resting against the front hood of the Ford. "We barely got out of Dunbar with our hides. This island sounds pretty good to me. I mean, what the fuck? We gonna run around getting into fights all our lives? We did what we could. Maybe it's time to move on."

The others didn't argue Barnes's point, but they didn't exactly shout their agreement, either. A couple of them, like Leo and Greg, sneaked a quick look over at Natasha. If she noticed them, she didn't show it.

"When we get there, how do we reach the island?" Ray asked.

"John, the guy who told us about it, said there are a couple of marinas with boats in the area," Will said. "He also said there are houses along the shoreline, in case we get there and need emergency shelter."

He stopped talking to let all of that sink in. If he didn't know better, he'd think it was working because each man seemed to have retreated into his own internal monologues, maybe even weighing the pros and cons. He hoped at least most of them were leaning toward the pros. He probably had Leo and Ray. The others, though, were a toss-up.

"Clock's ticking," Will said. "If you're going to decide to go, you need to do it soon." He glanced at his watch for dramatic effect. "You know what happens when it gets dark out here. We all do."

They glanced at each other in silence. All except Natasha. Will wasn't sure if she had even heard any of the conversation going on around her.

"Well?" Leo said finally. "Do we go, or continue taking our chances out here?"

"Fuck it," Ray said. "How long we going to last out here like this, anyway? We had it good in Dunbar, but that's gone. Harrison's dead or worse. Rachel, too. What's left?"

"An island," Greg said. He sounded as if he wanted to laugh, but couldn't make himself do it. "Well, shit. I've heard of worse ideas, I guess."

"If we go, we all go," Leo said. "So do we go?"

They nodded one by one.

Except for Natasha. She still hadn't said a word.

"Nat," Leo said, turning to her. "Did you hear—"

"Okay," she said before he could finish.

"Okay?" Leo repeated, just to be sure.

"Yeah, okay." She walked past him and to the back of the truck. "I guess we better hurry, then. Like the man said, the clock's ticking."

The others followed her example and began piling into the truck.

Leo turned to Will and grinned. "You better hope this island's there, buddy, 'cause if it's not, we'll be standing around watching the sunset with our balls in our hands."

Will smiled back at him.

I'm coming home, Lara. Just hold out a little longer, babe.

BY 1:44 P.M., they were back on the highway and heading west. Olsen and Greg were in the cab of the Ford F-250, with Barnes behind the wheel. Will sat in the back with Ray, Leo, and Natasha. They had given him one of the M4s from the gun battle, but there were still no signs of his M4A1. Besides the carbine, he was wearing a dead man's gun belt and a holstered 9mm Sig Sauer, though not the same one Michael had given him earlier.

The optimist in him hoped Danny and Gaby had already arrived back at the marina and were on their way to the island right now. They needed to be there before nightfall. They *had* to, because it was going to happen tonight. He could feel it in his bones. Lara had managed to stall them with the help of the new guy, Keo, but that was a Band-Aid on a gaping wound. She was counting on him to return, and the last thing he wanted to do was let her down.

Dunbar's people had a map of the state and knew the way down to Song Island, and Will had told them about Salvani. He was worried about a potential ambush along the way—Mason had shown enough foresight to set one up for Danny and Gaby earlier—but he didn't tell the others about that. He should have felt guilty about the omission, but he didn't. He was using them, yes. He couldn't avoid that even if he wanted to, and he didn't want to.

He had to get to Song Island. He had to reach Lara before tonight. That was all that mattered.

It was chilly in the back of the truck with the wind ripping at his face, because Will was sitting with his back against the right side of the bed, facing Leo. He had chosen the spot on purpose, because it allowed him to see both in front and behind him. Natasha sat to his right, with Ray next to her. The ammo belt attached to the M60 draped down from the roof and into the can of ammo sitting between them. Dunbar's fighters hadn't said a word since they started on their way, but every now and then he caught them glancing up at the sun, as if to make sure the night hadn't snuck up on them when they weren't looking.

Will passed the time by watching the never-ending stretch of road flashing by, a constant sea of unyielding gray structures. How long would the roads last? The highways, big and small? The buildings? The businesses and homes and vehicles? Man's time was over. It didn't take a genius to figure that one out. He sure as hell wasn't one, and he knew that.

After a while, he became aware of Natasha staring at him again.

"What?" he said, raising his voice a bit to be heard over the roar of the wind in his face.

"There were two vehicles this morning," she said. "You were in the Tacoma."

He nodded.

"You rammed the trucks that were blocking the streets," she continued. "Why?"

"They were in the way."

"But you *rammed* them. You could have tried to go around."

"Maybe. But there wasn't any time. I made a split-second decision."

"Why?"

"Why?"

"Yeah," she said. *"Why?"*

"I don't understand," he said, wondering again just how close Natasha had been to the action this morning to have seen all of that.

"You sacrificed yourself for your friends," she said. "By opening up a lane for them to drive through. Why?"

"I didn't think I was sacrificing anything," Will said. "I just misjudged how badly the truck would go into a tailspin after the impact."

"You screwed up, is that it?"

"Yeah, I guess I did."

He wasn't sure if she believed him. For that matter, did *he* believe it? Or had he really been thinking about sacrificing himself so Danny and Gaby could reach Song Island, instead of all three of them not making it?

It wasn't as if he'd had the time to think about it since this morning. He had been too preoccupied with trying to survive since waking up from the crash.

But now that the question was posed to him...

Doesn't matter. Danny and Gaby are on their way home, and so am I. That's all that matters now.

"You might have gotten through if you had been driving the bigger car," Natasha was saying.

He shrugged. "We had kids in the backseat, and we needed the extra space."

"Still..."

"Yeah, well, they got through. I just hope they made it to the island."

"That was your first mistake."

"What's that?"

"You still have hope," Natasha said before looking away.

"I'm sorry about your daughter, about what happened in Dunbar," he wanted to say to her, but he didn't. Natasha didn't care about his condolences. She had lost a child, and some stranger telling her that he was "sorry" wasn't going to do a damn thing for her.

So Will kept his mouth shut and laid the M4 across his lap instead.

Besides, there was a very good chance he was sending these people to their deaths with an elaborate series of lies and half-truths. Then again, guilt was for survivors, and if he was lucky enough to call himself that after tonight, then he'd embrace it and carry on like he always did.

But first, he had to get home.

Get to Lara.

Whatever it took, he had to get back home to Lara. Nothing else mattered before and after that.

CHAPTER 10

GABY

No one fired a shot as they drove up to the roadblock, and the clatter of gunfire was still unnervingly absent when they parked and climbed out of the truck. She expected to be fighting for her life the moment her foot touched the hard concrete, and when that didn't happen, Gaby had to spend a few seconds adjusting.

It's the uniforms. They're not shooting because of the uniforms.
I can't believe it's working.

The men pointing the assault rifles at them saw the familiar camo print and must have breathed a sigh of relief almost right away. Or it could have been the sight of a very assured Nate walking forward with his rifle held loosely at his side before stopping near the hood. He was non-threatening, but somehow still aggressive enough to draw their eyes to him.

If he was scared, Nate didn't show it, especially when he shouted over at the soldiers, "What the hell, guys? Stop pointing those guns at us! They told us to come up here and back you up, not to get shot in the face!"

'Shot in the face,' Nate?

That was a nice flourish. Someone who didn't belong here would have reacted differently, and not with the righteous indignation that was clearly evident in Nate's voice. That seemed to relax the men even further. Or, at least, she hoped so. She could have been reading the whole situation wrong and not know it until it was too late.

Gaby had her rifle in her right hand, but she held it loosely at her side, almost cavalierly in order to give off the right impression. Like Nate, she was playing a role, trying to sell that she belonged here, that she wasn't afraid of the rifles pointing—relaxed, but *still pointing*—at them. Her body might have seemed calm, but her hand was clutching tightly onto the rifle. Maybe too tightly. She couldn't be sure because she didn't look down, but it felt as if her entire arm had gone numb.

Relax. This is going to work.
Because we're all dead if it doesn't.
God, I wish Will was here...

She was certain there were just the same four men she had seen from inside the truck as they pulled up. If there were more hiding, maybe even on the other side of the divider like last time, that was going to throw everything off. It would mean they had to adapt on the fly, which might not be possible when the bullets started flying.

What was that Lara liked to say? Adapt or perish.

One of the men had short blond hair, and he straightened up behind the hood of one of the trucks—a black GMC that looked fresh off the lot—and peered up the highway at Nate and Gaby. Thirty yards separated them. That was just far enough of a distance for the soldiers to see them *(The uniforms; focus on the uniforms we're wearing)*, but not too close to reveal everything. A part of her was afraid they might spot the bullet hole in the back of the uniform she was wearing. Which was silly, because she was facing them. Unless there was a fifth man back there...

Please don't let there be a fifth man. Please, please...

She could hear nervous movement behind her from inside the truck. It was either Annie or Milly, because it couldn't have been Claire. The thirteen-year-old knew better. Claire was a born soldier, and Gaby could trust her to remain perfectly still as they attempted this charade. All they had to do was keep their heads down when the shooting started.

Just a little bit longer…

"Who sent you?" the blond shouted at them.

"Mason sent us over as reinforcements," Nate said. "In case those guys in the truck came back. They up there, or what?"

"Mason sent you?"

"Who else? You think I'm out here for my health? I'd rather be back in town."

God, he's good at this, Gaby thought, glancing briefly across the truck at Nate. If she didn't know better, she would have believed him, too.

"Where you from?" the blond asked. It was almost conversational, like he wasn't looking at Nate from behind the iron sights of a rifle.

"L17," Nate said.

"We're from L11."

"I've been there. You know Hank?"

"Yeah, I know him," the blond said.

That seemed to do it. Two of the men flanking Blondie started to relax, and one of them took his hands off his M4 lying over the roof of the other truck—a white Toyota pickup—and actually stood back a bit. The third man had also straightened up from behind his cover and now let his rifle hang at his side.

The only one who hadn't shown any signs of easing up was the fourth man. He was older than the other three by at least ten years and had a large beard. He looked as if he was wearing a uniform that was at least a size too small, making him seem bigger than he really was. He was still watching the Chevy from behind the back of the GMC, as if he expected a gunfight to start up at any moment.

The man must have sensed Gaby staring, because he looked over in her direction and they stared at each other across the short distance. She didn't know how long that lasted. Maybe it was just a second, or a few seconds. It could have been just a split second.

Oh, shit.

Gaby responded on pure instinct. She wasn't even aware of what she was doing until she had squeezed the trigger on the M4 and *hit the side of the truck.*

She had fired too fast and missed!

Fortunately for her, the solid *ping!* as her round drilled into the vehicle must have startled the bearded man enough, because instead of shooting back at her, he ducked behind cover. That gave her the precious extra second to flick the fire selector on the carbine to burst fire and squeeze the trigger again.

She strafed the truck with the first three-round volley, swinging her rifle from right to left, shattering the driver-side window in the process. She kept squeezing the trigger even as the other three men were slow to react, as if they couldn't decide between hiding and returning fire. One man was struggling to get a hold of his rifle, while another was racing along the length of the pickup.

Thank God for amateurs, Will.

She was already backing up, moving behind her open passenger door (hoping and praying Nate was doing the same on his side) while continuing to pull the trigger again and again and again—

Then, a second later her own gunfire was lost in the torrential downpour of *brap-brap-brap!* coming from behind and slightly to her left.

Danny.

Gaby threw a quick look back and saw him standing in the back of the Chevy. He was firing the M240 machine gun over the cab, the nonstop *clink-clink-clink* of empty 7.62mm brass casings pouring down and bouncing off the roof and landing in the truck bed around his feet. Some flickered onto the highway behind Gaby, while others somehow managed to rain down the front windshield and *clank* against the front hood.

Danny held onto the heavy weapon with both hands and was moving it right and left, bracing its bucking weight against the truck's roof to keep it under control as he oscillated his fire. He was slightly bent over, eyes looking behind the iron sights of the weapon at his targets thirty yards up the highway.

There was a loud explosion as a tire blew, then another one. Windows shattered against the constant *ping-ping-ping!* of bullets punching through aluminum and metal and steel. All the noise and fury drowned out her own labored breathing. She couldn't even hear (though she could see) Nate, outside the driver-side door on the other side, still firing up the highway. The smell of gasoline wafted across the highway to her nostrils as the two perforated vehicles began leaking fuel.

Gaby didn't realize she had stopped pulling her M4's trigger until Danny finally stopped shooting. By the weight of her weapon, she guessed she still had half a magazine left, so she switched it back to semi-auto and focused on the two vehicles.

Or what was left of them.

The last half dozen or so shots from the M240 were still echoing off the sun-baked highway and the walls of trees to both sides of them when she finally recognized her own shallow breathing. Slowly, slowly, she forced herself to settle down, just as the last gunshots faded.

"Clear it!" Danny shouted. She didn't know why he was shouting until she realized he was probably slightly deaf from firing the machine gun and didn't even know it.

Then there was just the silence again, with the occasional *clinking* as she moved forward, kicking casings out of her path. Nate was moving forward, parallel to her. They exchanged a brief look and nod before continuing on to the GMC and Toyota.

They were wrecks. Worse than wrecks. The tires were blown, every window smashed to pieces, even the ones on the other side. Danny hadn't spared a single round, and she made a promise to herself never to get in front of one of those weapons.

She didn't say a word, and neither did Nate as they scooted toward the shredded metal carcasses. She counted two bodies on her side, including the man with the beard and the blond. There were two more on Nate's end. Thick red blood pooled under and around their still bodies, wet and unnaturally bright against the sun.

Gaby lowered her rifle and looked back down the interstate at Danny and waved. He nodded back and put the M240 away and climbed out of the truck. She didn't have to be able to see his face to know that all those little motions were causing him a lot of pain with his broken leg. Not that Danny said anything as he hobbled over to the driver-side door and looked in at the girls.

She glanced across the lanes at Nate. He was staring at the bodies, and she couldn't quite tell what the expression on his face was at the moment. Regret? Sympathy? Guilt?

"Nate," she said. "We should take their weapons and look for anything else we can use in the trucks, then get out of here."

He nodded back but didn't say a word. He looked inside the Toyota through the broken front passenger-side window, and she did the same to the GMC. There was a case of MREs in the back, along with green cans of ammo. She grabbed a tactical pack from the floor and found it filled with extra clothes that she yanked out and replaced with the MREs before collecting two M4s from the ground.

Nate had picked up a third rifle on his side, but didn't bother with the fourth one. "It's busted," he said before she could ask.

"Let's get out of here," she said, and they took their spoils back to the Silverado, where Danny was waiting for them.

"We good?" he asked them.

"We're good," Gaby said.

"How about you, Nathaniel Bacon?"

Nate shook his head. "I don't know who that is."

"Read a book sometime," Danny said. He glanced down at his watch, then looked up at the feeder road beside them. "We'll cut across Lake Dulcet and make our way south. It'll be close, but if we haul ass, there's no reason we can't reach Song Island by four or five. That sound good?"

"You know where you're going?" Gaby asked.

"Yeah, sure. Just follow the signs, right? I'm good at that, you know. Back in college, they used to call me Follow The Signs Danny."

"'Follow the Signs Danny'?" Nate said.

Gaby managed a smile. "Just go with it."

"Ah," Nate said.

She tossed the bag of food, ammo cans, and rifles into the back.

Annie and Milly were outside on the driver side and Claire was standing next to her, looking at what remained of the soldiers' trucks. Gaby was glad the girl couldn't see the bodies on the other side of the vehicles. Claire was strong, but she didn't particularly want the kid seeing everything if she could help it.

"What's that smell?" Claire asked, wrinkling her nose.

"Gasoline," Gaby said.

"Oh." Then she turned her calm eyes on Gaby. "I could have helped."

"Not until you learn how to shoot a rifle."

"I already know how to shoot a rifle."

"I mean a real rifle."

"You'll teach me?" she said, nodding at the carbine in Gaby's hands. "Soon? I want to help, too."

"Soon," Gaby nodded. "Now get inside so we can get going."

"Next stop, Song Island?"

God, I hope so, she thought, but smiled reassuringly and said, "Yeah, definitely next stop, Song Island."

Claire grinned and climbed back into the truck.

Danny was already settling in behind the steering wheel. "You did good, kid."

"Thanks," she said.

"Don't let it go to your head."

"Perish the thought."

He grunted, then, "Asses down and seatbelts on. Annie, you're up front with me. You know how to read a map?"

Annie climbed into the front passenger seat. She didn't look nearly as shell-shocked or dazed as she had earlier during the first firefight on the highway. Maybe, Gaby thought, Annie was finally warming to what it took to survive out here.

It's about time, too.

"It's just a map," Annie said, taking the folded paper from Danny. "How hard could it be?"

"Pretty hard, if you're blind," Danny said.

Gaby walked over to Nate, who was already waiting in the back of the truck. He held out his hand, and she let him pull her up.

"How old is that girl? Twelve?" he asked, looking into the cab window at Claire on the other side, clutching her FHN shotgun.

"She's thirteen."

"Thirteen. Jesus. You think she's ready for an assault rifle?"

"I wasn't ready for one, either, but I got over it."

"Well, in that case, why don't we just give her a bazooka?"

"If only we had one."

"I was kidding," Nate frowned.

"I wasn't," Gaby said.

SHE SAT IN the back of the truck across from Nate, with the M240, now reloaded with a fresh ammo belt, rattling next to them. The soldiers were, if nothing else, well stocked when they ventured out. Danny drove, with Annie in the front passenger seat directing his turns using the map.

They had taken the feeder road off the I-10 and were now moving through what looked like Downtown Lake Dulcet. It wasn't a particular big city—more like a tourist attraction—and the only sound for miles was the churning of the truck's engine. If Josh's soldiers were in pursuit, they would be able to hear them easily enough. But that couldn't be helped right now. To move fast, they had to be loud, too.

The one bright spot was that it had been almost an hour since they entered the city and there were no signs of pursuers. That supported Danny's theory that the rest of the ambushers were either positioned in Lake Charles further up the interstate or waiting to strike near Salvani. Either way, they had skirted trouble.

Or they hoped, anyway.

Nate sat across from her so they could see both forward and back, as well as both sides of the road. She kept the M4 in her lap, because the very thought of not having it was terrifying. The only sounds for the longest time were the car engine, the wind blasting in her ears, and stray brass casings *clinking* randomly around them. Danny was driving at forty miles per hour in the narrow streets and gassing it when he found bigger lanes.

She should have felt good about making it through a second ambush unscathed, but seeing those men falling under Danny's onslaught hadn't been nearly as triumphant as she had expected. Looking across at Nate now, she guessed he felt the same way, which may or may not be why he hadn't said a word since they climbed into the Chevy.

"You okay?" she finally asked. She had to raise her voice over the roar of the wind to be heard.

He gave her a forced smile. "Yeah. You?"

"We did what we had to. Back there."

"I know."

"Then what's wrong? Is it the four guys we had to kill?"

"I don't care about those guys. I was thinking about the other two. The ones who were with me before."

"What about them?"

"I shot them in the back." He paused. "They never saw it coming. One of them...he was surprised. I could see it on his face afterward."

They chose their fates, Nate, she wanted to say. *They got what they had coming. Would they have felt bad about shooting us?*

But she didn't say those words out loud because she could see how much it was bothering him, and had been for some time now. It didn't surprise her at all that he would feel guilty about it. They had once argued about whether to kill another man who had ambushed them on the highway not all that long ago.

"Did you know them?" she asked.

He shook his head. "Not really. We were thrown together when I volunteered for this."

"You volunteered?"

"I had to. It was the only way to leave L17 and find you."

"L17," she repeated. "The town they took me to was called L15."

"There are dozens of towns in just this state alone. You have no idea how massive the operation really is, Gaby. L17 had over 5,000 people."

Not people, Nate. Cattle. That's what we are to them. Nothing but cattle.

"I'm glad you're alive," she said, and managed a smile that wasn't completely forced.

"You already said that."

"It deserves saying again."

He gave her his best (mostly) unforced smile. "I wasn't sure for the longest time, you know. After I woke up…"

"What happened to you, Nate?"

His face darkened slightly. "The night at the pawnshop. They didn't kill me. They'd been feeding on me for…" He shook his head. "I don't know how long. After they were done, I guess they put me in one of the towns."

He stopped talking and seemed to drift off.

"What happened then?" she prompted.

"I eventually got my strength back. After that, they asked me if I wanted to keep fighting or comply. That was the word they used. 'Comply.' Not ominous at all, right?"

"Who was it?" she asked. "Who asked you?"

"Just some guy," Nate said. "I was lucky your friend Josh wasn't around. I don't think he would have been quite as willing to just let me go on my merry way."

You have no idea, Nate. No idea at all.

Nate was staring at her intently when he added, "After he took you, that kid, did he do anything to you, Gaby?"

"Like what?"

"Anything. Did he do *anything* to you?"

She shook her head. "It wasn't like that, Nate. Josh…"

Wouldn't have done something like that, she wanted to say, but she didn't, because she couldn't be certain. The Josh she knew—the eighteen-year-old kid who had survived with her and Matt, would never have even thought about something so despicable. But that boy was long gone, replaced by a stranger. This Josh was different.

He wasn't *her* Josh.

"No," she said. "He didn't do anything to me."

Nate looked relieved. She wondered how long he had been thinking about that, tormenting himself with what was happening to her at Josh's hands. Gaby didn't know if she should be grateful or annoyed. Maybe she was overthinking it. Nate was one of those gallant types. An idealist. If the world hadn't ended, he would have become an Army officer and served his country dutifully and likely retired a war hero, one that was well-liked by his platoon. Or unit. Or whatever it was they called groups in the Army.

"But anyway, back to their comply-or-die question, it was a no-brainer," Nate was saying. "When I told them about my military background, they were happy to let me enlist. Like I told Danny, most of these guys are average Joes. Office drones, salesmen, construction workers, you name it."

"Why did you decide to become one of them?" Gaby asked. She was thinking about all the soldiers she had seen, the ones she had shot at, and the ones she had killed. The men from Mercy Hospital, the ones in Dunbar, men like Mac and *(the other)* Lance that held her captive in L15...

"It was the only way I was going to get to leave the towns," Nate said.

"I thought anyone could leave."

"That's what they tell you, but it's a lie. You're never seen in town again, but it's not because you found someplace better. You just...disappear. I don't know what happens exactly. No one I've talked to does; but then, we're all pretty low on the totem pole. Maybe the guys higher up know."

I bet Josh knows.

What happens to those who leave the towns, Josh? Where do they go? What becomes of them?

"How did you escape?" Nate asked.

She told him about waking up in L15, then escaping with Peter and Milly before getting captured again in Dunbar by Harrison's men. He smiled when she got to the part about reuniting with Will and Danny later."

"He'll be okay," Nate said. "Will, I mean. I've never met a more capable guy in my life."

"I know," she nodded. "I would worry if it was someone else, but it's not. I wouldn't be surprised if we got to Song Island and found out he already beat us there."

Nate nodded back, but she could tell he didn't actually believe her. Which wasn't a total surprise to Gaby, because she had a hard time believing it herself.

THEY DIDN'T SAY anything again for a while. There was a lot to talk about, but she didn't want to do it in the back of a moving truck with the wind tearing away every other word between them. Besides, there would be time for everything she wanted—needed—to ask him later.

She glanced into the cab window to break the monotony of staring at Nate across from her. Annie was consulting the map in her lap while Danny drove. They were aimed south the entire time, except for a few minutes where they had to take detours. But for the most part, it was always south, toward Song Island. Toward home.

They were approaching the southern city limits of Lake Dulcet, with the downtown far behind them now, when Gaby heard something that made her sit up. It wasn't a gunshot, another car engine, or any of the alarming noises she had been waiting for since they abandoned the interstate for the streets.

It was a man's voice shouting at them.

Nate heard it too, and he looked around before settling on a group of office buildings behind him. There were two figures on the rooftop of what looked like a big box warehouse store, both jumping up and down and waving their arms frantically above their heads to get their attention. The sun was behind them, but both had the shape of men clutching guns in their hands. If the intention was to flag them down, swinging assault rifles wildly back and forth was probably the dumbest thing they could have done.

The Chevy slowed for a bit—not much, just enough for her to notice—but it didn't stay that way for very long. It picked up speed again three seconds later and continued on. Businesses and storefronts flashed by them again, including the one with the two figures on the rooftop still waving after them, though they had stopped jumping enthusiastically when they realized the truck wasn't going to stop.

Nate turned back around and looked across at her. "You think Danny saw them?"

She nodded but didn't say anything. He started to ask another question, but stopped himself and looked down the street instead.

In many ways, he was still the same Nate she remembered (and missed dearly when she thought he was dead), but he had also changed a lot. His smiles didn't come out quite as easily as before, and when they did, she couldn't tell if they were genuine or forced. Maybe somewhere in between. As much as she noticed the slight change in him, he probably saw the same thing in her. Beyond the physical (bruises and broken noses didn't heal overnight), she wasn't the same girl she was when they had first met in Lafayette.

She closed her eyes and leaned her head back against the truck and wanted nothing more than to just go to sleep. Maybe when she woke up she'd finally be at Song Island, back home again. She tried to imagine that the hard steel vibrating behind her was her soft mattress back at the hotel. Of course it was like trying to convince herself the blood and dirt on her tongue was milk chocolate.

"Gaby," Nate said.

She opened her eyes and looked across the small space at him.

"You're still as beautiful as I remembered," he said.

"Bullshit. My nose is broken and I have scars all over me that are never going to heal properly. For the last few days, I've purposefully stayed away from shiny surfaces so I wouldn't have to look at myself."

He surprised her by chuckling.

"What's so funny?" she asked, unable to hide her annoyance.

"That you think you're still not the most beautiful girl running around out here."

"You know we're probably going to die tonight, right?"

"You mean at the island?"

"Yeah."

"So we're racing like crazy to get to this island of yours, just so we can end up dying there tonight?"

"Yup," she said. "How you like them apples?"

He laughed. "I like 'em just fine, as long as you're there. How about you?"

"We're all going to die one of these days anyway. If my time comes, I'd rather it be at home with my friends."

As soon as she said it, Gaby knew she meant it. Every single word of it. She had managed to survive when so many had perished, but if her time came tonight, or tomorrow, or the day after that, she would embrace it with open arms. Just as long as she had the right people by her side. Her friends…

"So where do I fit into that scenario?" Nate asked.

"I don't know," she said, "but we'll figure it out."

CHAPTER 11

WILL

THEY ONLY STOPPED once so Ray and Leo could take a leak. Natasha didn't move from the back of the truck, and neither did Will. He opened one of the MRE bags they had shared with him and spooned out some meat loaf.

"Mississippi, huh?" Natasha said.

He nodded.

"Which part of Mississippi?" she asked.

"South."

"Where, south?"

He chewed slowly, enjoying the taste. Natasha never took her eyes off him the entire time.

"Hattiesburg," he finally said. Then, before she could ask anything else, "We took I-59 down before switching over to the I-10. We were originally headed for New Orleans, but it was too big, and you know what that means."

"The creatures..."

"Yeah. So we headed west instead, looking for someplace smaller where we could get lost."

"You found that along Route 13?"

"Uh huh."

"That's a pretty obscure road. I wouldn't even know it existed if

I didn't live in Dunbar all my life."

"We had a map and we were looking for a quiet place. Route 13 is pretty desolate, which was what we thought we needed." He took a sip from a refilled bottle of water. "It worked for us. For a while, anyway."

"I'm surprised you guys never went into Dunbar."

"We had everything we needed, brought most of it with us. Maybe we'd have to start looking for more supplies eventually, but we never got that far."

"How long were you there?"

"A couple of months."

He wasn't sure if he had been convincing enough, because Will didn't look up at her as he spun his tale. But when Natasha finally took her eyes off him and watched the others coming back from wherever they had gone to do their business, he figured he had probably done a decent enough job.

"I'm sorry about your daughter," Will said.

She didn't reply.

"Leo told me about her," he continued.

"Leo talks too much," she said.

"I heard that," Leo said, climbing back into the truck.

"You were supposed to," Natasha said.

"He understands, Nat," Leo said, settling in across from Will. "He's lost someone, too, remember? We all have."

Natasha didn't respond. Instead, she closed her eyes and folded her arms across her chest and pretended to go to sleep. Or maybe that was just her way of letting them know she wasn't interested in this conversation anymore.

"You lost someone?" Will asked Leo.

The older man nodded. "I guess you could say I was luckier than most. Some friends, but no family to lose when everything went tits up."

Leo opened another bag of MRE and sniffed the contents before peering inside. He must have liked what he saw, because he produced a metal spork from his pocket and devoured the food with a flourish usually reserved for starving homeless people.

Ray climbed up behind them and walked to the front, where he banged on the cab window. "Let's go, guys! We're losing daylight!" He glanced at his watch. "We're cutting it close. I don't like it." Ray banged on the window again. "Drive faster!"

"Fuck off!" Olsen shouted from inside.

The Ford started up and they were moving again a few seconds later. The truck began picking up speed, and although he couldn't see the speedometer, Will guessed they were topping off at around sixty miles per hour, judging by the speed with which the concrete barricade was flashing by in front of him.

Too fast. We're going way too fast.

He wanted to get to Song Island as soon as possible, but he also remembered all the accidents and ambushes he had endured on the road in the last year. Of course, he didn't expect someone with a rocket launcher to pop up in front of them, but the possibility existed because Josh's soldiers had free rein of the state's armory. The machine guns up and down Route 13, including the one perched on the roof of the truck's cab right now, were proof of that.

"Ray," Will said.

Ray looked up from a bag of jerky. "What?"

"We're going too fast."

"So?"

"There could be hazards on the road. Barnes is going too fast."

Ray smirked. "Relax, Mississippi. You want to get down there before sunset, don't you?"

"He's right," Leo said. "Tell them to slow down."

"Jesus Christ, what are you two, grandfathers?" Ray said. "Keep your diapers on. There's nothing on the fucking road. It's been a year since the end of the world, for God's sake." He looked at Will. "And besides, you got all the way over here from Mississippi just fine. We're not even going that far."

Will was hoping Leo would press the issue—it would have been better coming from him—but the older man had already gone back to eating his MRE. Nearby, Natasha had opened her eyes and was staring at him intently. There was something about the way she was eyeballing him that made him think he hadn't really thrown her off the scent at all.

He leaned out and looked up the highway. It was flat and empty, with no vehicles other than theirs for miles in any direction. No wonder Barnes didn't see any problems with going sixty miles an hour along this stretch of road. Maybe he was worried about nothing; maybe Ray was right, after all.

Yeah, that's the ticket.

HE WAS EXPECTING it. He had turned all the possible scenarios over in his head and how he would react to each one, but as mentally prepared as he was for it to happen, the *how* still caught him by surprise. It was worse for Natasha, Leo, and Ray in the back of the truck with him, because when the tires blew, no one was ready for it.

At first there was a loud series of *popping* sounds, like small explosions ringing out one after another underneath them. Then the truck spun, and Will imagined Barnes inside fighting for control of the vehicle. Olsen might have even screamed. Or it sounded like someone was screaming behind him, the voice slightly muffled by the wall between them.

Will went from looking at the divider wall behind Leo to staring back down the highway as the car skidded off course, tires screeching as the brakes clamped down and the stinging smell of burnt rubber filled the air. A moment later, the front bumper dug into the concrete and the F-250 was no longer on the highway.

That was when Will leaped out of the truck. It wasn't anything he had planned, but he was already being flung anyway by the vehicle's chaotic flipping momentum, so he decided to stop fighting it. His one hope of surviving was to get far enough from the tumbling vehicle not to get caught—and dragged—underneath it.

Then he was sailing through the air, the wind rushing against his face, grinding metal filling his ears. He blocked the noises out and curled his body inward, doing his best impersonation of a flying human ball, just before he slammed into the highway on his right shoulder. The pain lanced through his body as he tumbled once, twice, and three times before unfurling his legs and arms in an attempt to stop his momentum.

He finally came to a stop on his stomach and was turned in the right direction, allowing him to see the truck as it rolled down the highway on its side, roof and undercarriage taking turns digging gaping divots in the concrete pavement as it went. Pieces of the F-250 flung wildly into the air around it, falling back down to earth just as the vehicle—or what was left of it—rolled one final time and…settled. It had left large chunks of glass and aluminum and metal in its wake, along with thick bloody swaths from bodies it had dragged.

The M60 that was once soldered onto the roof was nowhere to be found, leaving only the twisted legs of its bipod behind. He was thinking about the weapon, about all the other guns that were inside the truck, and where they were now. Tossed free, most likely, along with his newly acquired M4.

What the hell happened?

He was alive, even if his arms and legs were numbed from the collision. He had somehow been tossed almost across the road and now lay in an unmoving pile against one of the guardrails.

Will managed to pull himself up from the scathing hot floor and onto his knees. His palms were cut and bloodied, and he was pretty sure that the warm sensation dripping down both sides of his face was blood. Although it was hard to concentrate, he looked around anyway, searching for bodies. That long and thick trail of blood had to have come from someone *(someones)*.

The sun glinted off a long strip of something metallic lying in a jagged line back down the highway. Linked square-shaped objects stretched from one side of the two lanes to the other, sharp spikes at the end of them pointing in the air.

Police spikes. Christ, they put police spikes on the road and Barnes drove right over them.

You idiot, Barnes, I told you, you were going too fast…

He was still trying to come to terms with what had happened, how Barnes had screwed them over, when sudden movements in the corner of one eye caught his attention. He turned around as men in camo uniforms were climbing over the middle concrete divider. Had they been there the whole time? Probably, given the presence of the spikes on the road. This was the plan all along. Stop them without firing a shot.

Maybe they're not so dumb after all.

There were a half dozen of them. Or maybe five dozen. He couldn't be certain because they seemed to be multiplying the more he tried to focus.

There was more movement from behind him, the shuffling of boots against concrete. He turned around (something red—blood?—flicked away as he did so) as another half dozen men in camo were rising up from the fields of swaying grass along the feeder road. They looked like serpents coming out of the ground.

Snakes in the grass. With assault rifles.

One of them stepped over a body (Leo? Ray?) that had been tossed all the way across the highway, while a second man paused to check the prone figure's pulse before standing back up and moving on a few moments later.

The first group of men was converging on the truck, resting on its crumpled roof. The loud *crunch crunch* of boots on broken glass and metal were almost as loud as the *drip drip* of gasoline from the overturned Ford's tank. Smoke drifted from the battered hood and one of the wheels, now missing its tire, was still spinning in the air. *How long was it going to keep doing that,* he wondered.

He wasn't entirely sure why he hadn't reached for the Sig Sauer in his hip holster yet. It was within easy reach, so close that it wouldn't have taken much to move his hand toward it. Except that hand was covered in a thick film of blood that *drip dripped* from his fingers to the concrete, where they appeared to sizzle as if they were hitting a frying pan.

Christ, it's hot out here. Didn't the weather just cool down?

You know what they say about Louisiana. If you don't like the weather, just wait a few...

Wait, or is that Texas?

The soldiers were now moving cautiously toward him, but no one had fired a shot yet. He kept waiting for it *(Here it comes, here it comes)* but it never happened. He blinked at the first few faces before they started going out of focus and it became impossible for him to see more than just clouds.

Bloodied red clouds.

He didn't even feel anything when his face hit the concrete the second time.

"IS HE STILL alive?" a voice asked.

"I think so," a second voice answered.

"You think so?" The first man chuckled. "You better hope he lives, or it's your ass on the line. You told me those spikes would work."

"They did work."

"So what happened?"

"I don't know. The guy must have lost control of the truck, or pulled the steering wheel too hard or something. What happened back there wasn't supposed to happen. Not like that, anyway."

"Yeah, well, looks like you just got one of your nine lives back, because he's awake."

Will opened his eyes to sunlight flooding in through tall glass windows. Too bright, and he immediately had to close his eyes again.

He was alive, but at the moment he wished he weren't. Every inch of him hurt and there was an incessant banging in his head, like a thousand drums going off at once, that wouldn't go away. He couldn't open his eyes a second time and didn't want to. His entire body felt sticky, as if he were covered in syrup.

Blood. I'm lying in my own blood.

Can someone spare a towel?

"Who is this guy, anyway?" the second man asked. "Why's he so important?"

"Don't you worry about him," the first one said.

That voice. It sounded familiar.

Mason.

The short dickhead in charge of the ambush at Route 13. In charge of more than that, for all Will knew. Was Mason behind the ambush? And, more importantly, he wondered if the man knew where his M4A1 was…

"Just keep him breathing until nightfall," Mason was saying. "Can you handle that?"

"I'm not a doctor," the other man said. "I'll do what I can, but I'm not guaranteeing anything. The guy was in shitty shape even before the truck flipped."

"He had a little vehicular accident earlier today."

"So he was already hurt. You can't put it all on me."

"The spike strip was your idea, remember?"

"I told you, it wasn't supposed to do that. If this guy dies, it's not my fault."

"Well, shit, Rick, if you can't keep him alive, then what the hell am I dragging you around for? Might as well put someone else in charge of him, right?"

"I'll keep him alive," Rick said quickly.

Will didn't entirely believe Rick, because the man hadn't been all that convincing. It sounded like poor Rick was afraid for his own life and was saying whatever Mason wanted to hear.

Join the party, buddy. You and me, up a creek without pants on.

"So it's true?" Rick said. "She's coming here?"

"You scared?" Mason asked.

"Shit, yeah. Aren't you?"

"If you'd seen all the things I've seen, Rick ol' buddy, you wouldn't be. Now, less questions, more action. Your job is to keep him alive for another three hours. Can you handle that?" Mason's voice sounded like it was coming from across the room this time. "Get it done, or, well, you know."

The sound of something opening and closing.

Then, silence.

Will couldn't be certain how long that lasted, before the man who had stayed behind *(Rick)* said, "You hear that? Three hours. That's all you got left."

Three hours...

"You're welcome, by the way," Rick said. "For saving your life. Truthfully, I don't even know how you're still moving around even before I got my hands on you. I guess the painkillers help, huh?" *Clinking* noises. "You're running out of those, by the way. Don't worry, we got plenty of refills. Lucky you." Then, Rick chuckled. "Well, not really lucky you, but...you know."

Yeah, I know, Rick. Fuck you, too.

He gave up what little fight he still had in him and slipped back, back into darkness.

THE NEXT TIME he woke up, he felt cold, hard floor underneath him. He was getting some feeling back, which meant the thrumming pain coursing through every inch of his body, from head to toe, was worse. Much worse. He wanted to call Rick over and demand those refills he had been promised, but when he tried to open his mouth, the only thing he heard was air escaping his lips. Very, very soft air. Even breathing was difficult.

At least the sticky sensation he had felt all over his body from earlier was gone. He guessed that was because his blood had *(mostly)* dried since he last woke up. Given how much he was bleeding after the highway, he wouldn't be surprised if there were parts of him still leaking plasma.

"Your job is to keep him alive for another three hours," Mason had said.

Three hours.

Three hours until what? He should know this. It was right there, at the tip of his very dry tongue—

Wait. How much time had he lost since the last time he was

awake? Hopefully not too much. That would make escaping difficult if it was—

Night.

It was dark outside the glass windows, the blackness overwhelming everything, including the long stretch of interstate road and the…

Eyes. Black eyes, like endless oceans of tar looking through the tall panes of glass back at him.

Ghouls.

A lot of them. Hundreds. *Thousands.*

So many that the parking lot outside *(A gas station? Was he in another gas station? Christ, how many of these places were there along the highway?)* was carpeted with them—a sea of pruned flesh swaying against one another. They were deathly silent, as if biding their time, waiting for something.

He expected them to attack the store at any moment, to smash their limbs and skulls against the glass to try to bash their way in like rabid dogs. But they didn't assault the store. In fact, they hardly moved at all.

Movement.

He wasn't alone inside. A pair of camo print uniforms shifted in the darkness in front of him. Two men, their backs to him, the barrels of their rifles outlined against the moonlight pouring into the front half of the store. There were shelves to the left of him and the counter along with an abandoned cash register to the right.

Weapons. He needed weapons.

If the soldiers knew he was awake, they didn't show it. Or seem to care. And why should they? He only had to look down to see that his hands were bound with zip ties, as were his ankles. Again. This was becoming the worst kind of déjà vu.

His head continued to throb, and for some reason both his palms were tingling. Oh, of course. When he was flying down the interstate, he had stuck out his hands to slow his slide. That hadn't exactly been the smartest thing he had ever done in his life. As a result, the skin was torn and bleeding, though someone had since treated the flesh and wrapped gauze tape around both hands.

He could just barely make out the stark whiteness of the bandages wrapped around him, and since he wasn't bleeding to death at the moment, he guessed there was more around his waist under his blood-covered shirt. Bandages clung to his temples and cheeks, which he was grateful for, even though he had no interest in seeing himself at the moment. What must he look like, he wondered. Maybe a mummy, only less capable at the moment.

One of the men finally turned around. He was older than Mason, with specks of white in his hair. "Welcome back," the man said.

Will recognized the voice: Rick.

My savior.

"Well, shit, Rick, if you can't keep him alive, then what the hell am I dragging you around for?" Mason had said.

My reluctant savior.

"Didn't think you were going to be awake to see this," Rick was saying. "You're lucky I did a stint as a paramedic, otherwise you'd have definitely bled to death." He looked almost sorry for Will when he added, "Of course, it might have been better for you if you couldn't see this."

"See what?" Will said. Or thought he did. He might have just croaked the words out. He swallowed and tried again. "See what?"

"She's coming for you, kid. You know who I'm talking about, don't you?"

He did.

She.

There was only one "she" that continued to plague him since The Purge. He knew all about her, all right.

"As sorry as I am about what's going to happen to you, I'm anxious to see it for myself," Rick said. "I've never seen them before, you know. The blue-eyed ones."

"Me neither," the other one said. He was sitting much closer to the twin glass doors of the store, his face partially lit by the moonlight. He was younger than Rick, even younger than Will, and there was an eagerness on his face that defied logic.

Didn't this man know there were *monsters outside the windows?*

"I've heard stories," the man added, "but I didn't think they actually existed. Especially her. I've heard them talking about her. She's…different, they say."

You have no idea, buddy. No idea at all.

Will looked past them and out the windows, at the mass of black-eyed creatures. They looked like gargoyles, unmoving and watchful. Except he knew they weren't made of stone; far from it. They were very real and alive *(-ish)*, and he kept waiting for them to spring to life.

Any moment now…

"They're not coming in," Rick said. He had apparently seen where Will was looking. "The doors aren't even locked. There's nothing to stop them from coming in if they want to, but they won't."

"Why?" Will asked. His voice sounded better to his own ears, if a little too gravelly. What he wouldn't do for a little water.

"Because we're in here," Rick said.

"It's the uniforms," the other man said.

"You're just guessing."

"What else could it be?"

He's right. It has to be the uniforms. They recognize them. Or the patches on them. Or…something.

But they know. Somehow, they recognize allies from foes.

Dead, not stupid, remember?

"What did you do?" the young one asked, eyeing Will curiously across the semidarkness of the room. Will couldn't quite make out the name on his shirt. Something starting with the letter "M."

"I didn't do anything," Will said.

"You must have done something. I've never seen this before, or heard of it happening."

"I did what I had to in order to survive."

"Yeah, a lot of that going around," M-something said before turning back to the windows.

"That's it?" Rick said. He was apparently less satisfied with Will's answer as M-something had been. "There has to be more than that.

What aren't you telling us?"

"Ask Mason," Will said.

Rick's face soured at the sound of Mason's name. "He doesn't tell us much."

"Then ask Josh."

"Josh? Who is Josh?"

Will stared at him for a moment, trying to gauge if the man was lying. Either Rick was the world's best actor, or he didn't have a clue who Josh was.

"Never mind," Will said.

Rick shrugged. "Doesn't matter, I guess. Keep your secrets, dead man."

Will leaned back against the cold brick wall and took in the room around him again. The silhouetted store shelves to his left, the boxes of food and candy on the floor—some crushed, others spoiled, which explained the strange smell. The counter to his right, with the heavy cash register on top. Cigarettes in the back. Square-shaped paper *(Money?)* littering the floor around him. In front of him was Rick and M-something, and on the other side of them...

How many were out there right now?

Too many. Always too damn many.

Those sea of eyes staring back at him, as if they could bore into his soul, made him shiver slightly. He wanted to think it was because of the drop in temperature, but of course he knew better.

Weapons. I need weapons.

He didn't have to look far for those. Rick, who was less than a meter away with his back turned invitingly to him, had an M4 in a sling. He couldn't be sure what M-something was holding, but it looked like another carbine. He needed one of those in the worst way.

But then there were the ghouls outside. If they weren't coming in now, would they act differently once he killed the two soldiers? Somehow, the creatures had interpreted the two men as allies *(Dead, not stupid)*, so what would they do if he attacked them? Would they come in to help?

"The doors aren't even locked."

Or would they stay back because they were ordered to?

Ordered? By whom?

Oh, don't be an idiot. You know damn well the answer to that question.

Of course, for any of this to work he'd have to kill Rick, take his rifle, then kill M-something with it. That was going to be difficult since he could barely move, and it wasn't just because of the restraints. His body was sore and numb, and just moving his head was painful. How the hell was he going to take out Rick—

"Will."

He might have stopped breathing at the sound of the voice.

He looked around him, expecting to see its owner in the darkness, but there was nothing, because the voice was *coming from inside his head.*

"Will," it said again. Louder and clearer, as if it were right next to him.

He watched Rick and M-something just to be sure, but neither man had reacted.

Because they couldn't hear the voice.

It was all in his head.

Was he imagining it? Was he going crazy—

"No, Will, you're not."

Kate.

"Yes."

He looked quickly to the ghouls outside the gas station, but they hadn't moved at all. The cluster of frail forms was still pressed against one another like good soldiers. Waiting for orders. Waiting…for her.

Kate.

"I'm coming, Will," she said, her voice like a lovely melody inside his head. *"I'll be there soon…"*

BOOK TWO

THE GUNS OF SONG ISLAND

CHAPTER 12

LARA

As she moved through the *Trident* for the second time, Keo's words from last night kept echoing inside her head:

"Regardless of how many times you push them back, delay them, or repel a full-on frontal assault. You can't do it forever. Sooner or later, if they want this island bad enough, they'll get it. And when that happens, a lot of people will die."

She had resisted it at first, but she knew he was right. She had always known. Even when Will and Danny finally returned, how long could they possible keep Song Island afloat? Sooner or later, Kate was going to throw more men at them. Even if they fought back one wave, what about the next? Or the one after that?

Kate had soldiers. Maybe not authentic soldiers, but they were real enough when you gave them assault rifles and pointed them at a target. Anyone could squeeze a trigger. She knew that personally, as did everyone else on the island at the moment. Bonnie, Jo, Gwen, Carly…and her. It didn't take a lot of skill to storm an island, especially one that didn't *(couldn't)* move. You just needed manpower. And that was something the enemy had an abundance of.

Which was why she had wanted the yacht when she first laid eyes on it last night. Her mind had swirled with possibilities then, and it still did now. Was this what it was like to be Will? Always trying to think of the next move before the bad guys did?

This would be easier if you were here with me, Will. So what the hell's taking you so long?

She was inside the dining room on the main deck of the *Trident* when she heard a boat cruising by outside. She didn't have to look out one of the windows to know who it was.

Keo. Leaving.

Dammit.

Her best-case scenario had been to keep him around, even after Will and Danny came back. With Danny in the Tower with the ACOG-mounted rifle and Will and Keo on the beach organizing the defense, they could have held out for a while.

But not forever. Never forever.

"Sooner or later, if they want this island bad enough, they'll get it. And when that happens, a lot of people will die."

He was right from day one. As much as she wanted him to be wrong, she knew he wasn't.

The trick is to keep everyone alive. So how do I do that? Can I do that? Or am I staring down the barrel of inevitability?

Wow, that was almost poetic, Lara. You should write a poem.

The squawking radio snapped her out of her thoughts. Carly, watching from the Tower. "There he goes, boss lady. We should have thrown Bonnie at him. She would have totally been able to convince him to stay."

Lara smiled and said into the radio, "You know Bonnie's listening to this, right?"

"Oops."

"No, no, I would have done it," Bonnie said through the radio. "Take one for the team, as it were."

"I wouldn't have asked you to, Bonnie."

"You wouldn't have had to. But I don't think he would have gone for it, anyway. It sounds like he's loyal to the girlfriend."

"Wow, a faithful boyfriend," Carly said. "Wonder what that's like."

"Oh, give it a rest," Lara said. "Yours is coming home right now."

"Speaking of which, when are they supposed to radio back? It's past noon, and I keep looking at the radio and it refuses to make a sound. Stupid radio. Are you sure it's not broken?"

"It's fine. They'll radio when they're closer."

"How are you so calm?"

Because I don't have a choice. If I think about Will, I'll just end up paralyzed with worry. Because I love him. Because I can't imagine life without him. Because I'm afraid he'll never come back to me and that possibility terrifies me, and right now, I can't afford to be terrified.

"Relax," she said. "They'll be here. Until then, keep your eyes on the lake. You see someone in a uniform, you shoot him."

"They'll have to come pretty close," Carly said. "I'm not exactly Annie Oakley up here."

"Hey, guys?" Maddie said, cutting into the conversation. "Sorry to break up the girl talk, but there's something you have to see down here, Lara."

"Where are you?" Lara asked.

"The swimming area on the lower deck."

"I'm on my way."

Lara cut through the fancy dining room to reach the back of the boat sooner. She hadn't expected to find something like it onboard, but then she'd never been on a luxury yacht before. The more she explored, the more possibilities she saw. There were so many rooms and spaces that could be put to other uses. It could work, she thought, with enough time and preparation. She just had to make a decision.

Because they'll do what I tell them. God help me, they'll actually do what I tell them.

She climbed down the rung of stairs at the rear of the boat and hopped the last few feet to the lower deck. Maddie was waiting for her with her hands on her hips.

"What is it?" Lara asked, walking over.

"We're not alone," Maddie said. "Keo was right. There's someone else still on the boat."

"How do you know?"

Maddie pointed at a pair of shoe prints on the all-white deck. Lara didn't know what she was supposed to see. There were a lot of prints, which made sense since she, Maddie, and the others had been coming and going all morning.

"What about them?" Lara said.

"They're not ours, Lara."

"How can you tell?"

"We're all wearing boots. Those are tennis shoes."

Lara stared again, but she couldn't tell the difference. "Are you sure?"

"One hundred percent," Maddie nodded.

Lara instinctively put her right hand over her holstered sidearm and looked back at the two decks above and behind them. "How long ago?"

"I just noticed them now, but they look pretty fresh. They weren't here when we came back earlier. That means whoever it was, he was checking out our boat. Maybe looking for a way off."

"Just one pair of prints?"

"Just the one."

Lara unclipped her radio and keyed it. "Blaine, where are you?"

"I'm still on the bridge," Blaine answered. "What's wrong?"

"It looks like that eighth guy exists after all."

"Figures," Blaine said. "What do you want us to do?"

"I'm heading back to the island with Maddie, then I'm sending her back over with Roy. Until then, I want you to lock the bridge door. Don't open it for anyone until we have more men onboard to take this boat apart floor by floor."

"Roger that."

Lara looked into the deck behind them. The windows weren't tinted enough to hide the rooms on the other side, but she had discovered for herself that the *Trident* was deceptively larger in person than it appeared on the outside. There were too many rooms, too many hallways, and too many corners to hide in.

"Come out, come out, wherever you are," she whispered softly to herself.

GAGE, THE "CAPTAIN" of the *Trident*, looked healthy for a man who had just been shot in the kneecap with his own gun less than twenty-four hours ago. He sat on one of the beds they had repurposed from the unused hotel rooms and put into the makeshift infirmary. He was still wearing the same clothes from last night, though one of his pant legs had been cut away to treat his wound.

Zoe looked over from the counter where she was scribbling on a notepad when Lara knocked on the open door. Benny, who sat guard across from Gage, looked up before quickly turning off the PlayStation Vita portable gaming console in his hands. One of the benefits of the island was the electronic devices. They didn't have the Internet anymore, of course, but laptops and computers (and the games on them) were still useable.

Lara pretended she didn't see Benny scrambling to put the PS Vita away and said to Zoe, "How is he, doc?"

"See for yourself," Zoe said. She swiveled around in her stool. "Stan's making him one of those leg braces like Benny's. Once he has that, our fair captain should be up and marauding again in a few days. He'll just be a lot more gimpy, that's all."

If Gage was insulted by being called a "marauder," he didn't show it. Not that he had any right to take offense. The word was appropriate, given what he and the friends had planned to do to Song Island. In the few minutes she'd talked to the man, Gage hadn't lied to her once. Or, at least, she hadn't caught him in an obvious falsehood yet. In fact, the man seemed at home with what he was and what he had done. She hadn't expected that, and a part of her was actually impressed with his frankness.

She sat down on a chair at the foot of his bed. "The eighth man. Does he have a name?"

"I thought you didn't believe he existed," Gage said. "You didn't care about his name back when I told you and that Chinese guy about him."

"Korean," Benny said.

"What?" Gage said.

"Keo's half-Korean, asshole."

"Same difference."

"Answer the question," Lara said.

"Boris," Gage said, turning back to her. "His name's Boris."

"Is he Russian?"

Gage smirked. "Nah. It's just what we call him."

"Why?"

"Did you find him yet?"

"No. But we will. Tell me about Boris."

"What's to tell? He was a crewman on the *Trident* before I even signed up. After we, er, took over, he decided to stay onboard. He knows that boat better than everyone, including me."

"You gave him a choice to stay or leave?"

"Of course I did," Gage said, sounding almost offended. "Everyone who stayed did so because they wanted to. I didn't have to force anyone."

"What happened to the owners of the boat?" Zoe asked.

Gage looked past Lara at the doctor. "We took the boat," he said, as if that should explain everything.

"How did you take the boat?"

"How do you *think* we took the boat? They didn't exactly want to give it up. So we took it."

"What will Boris do next?" Lara asked.

"What do you mean?" Gage said, shifting back to her.

"Will he try to get off the boat? Like the other two did last night?"

"I have no idea. It's not like we're joined at the hip. I captained the boat, and he worked the decks."

"He sweep the poop deck?" Benny grinned.

Lara ignored him and said to Gage, "Is he dangerous?"

Gage shrugged. "It's a dangerous world. Who isn't, these days?"

Lara stared at him for a moment, trying to decide if the man was holding something back. Gage was in his late thirties, with a hardened face that had seen a lot of sunlight over its lifetime. She could imagine this man nonchalantly shooting the *Trident*'s previous owner and assuming command simply because he could. She'd guess that anyone who traveled with him would be capable of that same level of violence.

She nodded and stood up. "Okay."

"What about me?" Gage asked.

"What about you?"

"What happens to me now?"

"I haven't decided yet. Right now, you're still valuable because I might need someone to pilot the boat. But that doesn't mean I'll hesitate to throw you into the water if you endanger my people in any way. I'm betting that with time, I can teach someone to push all those buttons on the bridge."

"Yeah, but there are so, so many buttons," Gage said, grinning at her. When he didn't get the reaction he was expecting, he lost the stupid grin and frowned instead. "Look, truth is, I was a captain before all of this, and I can be your captain, too. I mean, I'm not above taking orders. I did it for most of my life. I can do it again."

"Good to know." She glanced at Benny, who sat up straighter. "Keep an eye on him. If he does anything that's even the least bit threatening toward you or Zoe, you have my permission to shoot him in the other kneecap." She looked back at Gage. "Who needs legs to push some buttons, right?"

Gage swallowed.

"Gotcha," Benny said.

Lara walked back to the door, where Zoe was waiting for her. Lara was glad to see the doctor up and moving around. She might have been a third-year medical student back when the world still made sense, but Zoe was the real deal. Lara had a feeling they would need her in the days to come.

Lara nodded at the hallway outside. Zoe understood and followed her out, and Lara closed the door behind them.

"Any word from Will?" Zoe asked.

"He's on his way back now. He'll radio in when he's closer."

"Good. For a moment there, I thought he might be in trouble. Then I remember who I'm worrying about."

"Will can take care of himself. It's us I'm worried about." She looked back at the door. "You have to be careful around him. Gage. He's dangerous."

"I know. That's what Benny's here for, right?"

"Benny's just a kid."

Zoe smiled at her.

"What?" Lara said.

"How old are you?"

"Twenty-six."

"Jesus, you're just a kid, too. All of you guys, except for Mae and Kendra, are just kids."

Lara smiled. Zoe had a point there. "I guess I haven't felt like a kid in a long time."

"I know. Everyone grows up fast these days. You have to."

We all adapt and grow, or not at all. Adapt or perish.

"Just remember not to relax too much around Gage," Lara said. "He's not our friend."

"Oh, trust me, I know. I just spent an hour with that guy."

"Good. I gotta get back to the boat and look for Boris."

Lara turned to go, when Zoe said, "Hey." When Lara stopped and looked back, Zoe said, "I'm glad Will's fine, and that he's coming home."

"Yeah, me too."

They exchanged an awkward smile before Zoe went back into the infirmary.

Lara continued up the hall. She unclipped her radio and keyed it. "Blaine, come in."

"You headed back?" Blaine answered.

"I have to collect a few more bodies to help with the search. Anything happen while I was away?"

"Nothing exciting. Any word on our mystery man?"

"His name's Boris."

"Boris? What is he, some kind of Russian?"
"Apparently that's just what they call him."
"Hunh."
"That's what I said."

SHE WAS HALFWAY back to the beach when a slight echo, like a warm and wet *popping* sound, from far away drifted across the island. It sounded like it was coming all the way from the other side of the lake.

"Anyone hear that?" Maddie asked through the radio. "I'm pretty sure that was a gunshot."

"Did it come from the yacht?" Lara asked, alarmed.

"Definitely not the yacht," Blaine said through the radio. "I'm on the bridge, and it doesn't sound close."

"Okay, stay where you are, Blaine," Lara said. "Maddie…"

"We can take off as soon as you show up," Maddie said.

Lara smiled to herself and started jogging down the pathway that connected the hotel grounds to the beach.

We're like a well-oiled machine. Okay, maybe that's a bit of an exaggeration, but we're definitely getting pretty good at this.

She said into the radio as she ran, "Everyone hold your positions. I repeat: hold your positions."

Two more shots rang out, followed by a long silence, before two more *popping* noises echoed across the water. It had to have come from the other side of the lake. She remembered hearing the ferocious gunfire between Will and some of Kate's collaborators months ago from the nearby marina, and those had sounded much louder.

She was halfway back to the beach when there was a long series of gunshots. These came faster and furious, the *pop-pop-pop* signaling the unmistakable exchange of automatic rifle fire between two sides.

What was going on out there? It couldn't have been Will. He would have radioed as he got closer. Plus, the shooting seemed to be coming from the other side of the lake. Will had no reason to venture that far out, especially when a simple radio call would bring a boat to him.

Maddie was waiting for her on the pier, looking out at the lake with binoculars as Lara walked up behind her. "Anything?"

Maddie shook her head. "It's too far south. The only reason we can hear it is because we're downwind."

"So it's probably not meant for us."

"I don't think so, no." She looked over. "What should we do?"

Lara didn't answer right away. What should they do? If the shooting was coming from the other side of the lake, it was closer to the Gulf of Mexico than the island. Was what was happening out there worth finding out? What if it was some kind of elaborate trap to lure them out? The last thing she wanted was to send someone out there and have them be picked off by snipers along the shoreline.

What would Will do?

"Lara?" Maddie said. "What should we do?"

"I don't—" The loud *boom!* of a shotgun blast cut her off.

This one was much closer to home.

The Trident.

Even as that revelation hit her, there was a second *boom!* and moments later, the *pop-pop-pop* of automatic gunfire. It sounded like they were coming from the upper parts of the boat.

The bridge.

"WELL, THAT WAS anticlimactic," Maddie said. "That's him?"

"I guess," Blaine said.

"Him" was Boris. Or a man she assumed was Boris, though she couldn't be sure without bringing Gage over to the boat to ID him.

The man was large, almost as big as Blaine, with a bushy red beard and a very pale complexion, which was amazing given that he probably spent most of the last year on a boat, basking in the sun. Or maybe he spent most of his time in the engine room, which would explain how he could have hidden from Blaine and Roy earlier in the day.

Whoever he was, he was lying on his stomach a few feet inside the bridge. Blood pooled under him and his head was turned to one side, black eyes staring almost accusingly across the room at Blaine.

A pump-action shotgun leaned against a nearby wall where Blaine had put it. That shotgun had blasted a hole in the bridge door where the lock and doorknob used to be. Having stumbled inside, Boris (unless, of course, there was a second man running around on the *Trident*) had taken a shot at Blaine only to miss, sending buckshot into another part of the wraparound windshield and adding to the existing damage.

Lara looked at Blaine. "You okay?"

He nodded. "He surprised me, that's all."

"Man, we need to stop people from firing guns on the bridge," Maddie said. "We're lucky no one's shot out the control panels so far."

"I guess he was waiting for just one of us to be on the boat," Blaine said. "Lucky me."

"Or maybe he was using the shooting across the lake as a diversion," Lara said. "Maybe he thought it was his best chance to take back the bridge."

"Well, the poor bastard figured wrong."

"Looks like it," Maddie said. "So, who's gonna clean up this mess?"

"Don't look at me."

"You shot him."

Blaine pretended he didn't hear her and said to Lara, "You guys figured out what all the shooting before was?"

"We don't know, but it was coming from the southern part of the lake," Lara said.

"It has to be Keo. He went in that direction, and the timing's right. Maybe we should go see if he needs help."

Lara didn't answer right away.

"Lara," Blaine said. "He could be hurt."

"No," she said finally. "Keo's on his own." She glanced at her watch. "Besides, we have other work to do now that Boris isn't a problem anymore. It's past noon, which means it'll be dark in less than seven hours."

Maddie and Blaine exchanged a worried look. Maybe they were hoping she'd change her mind about Keo.

"Head back to the island and bring Gage over," Lara said to Maddie. "I need to find out what this boat's fully capable of."

"So we're definitely using it," Blaine said.

Lara nodded. "I don't know how yet—not exactly—but yeah, I think we're going to use it."

CHAPTER 13

KEO

It was eight kilometers from Song Island to the mouth of the channel that connected Beaufont Lake and the Gulf of Mexico. After thirty minutes of traveling at full speed across the wide-open lake, seeing the narrow corridor coming up made Keo slow down to half speed. He instinctively loosened the MP5SD and laid it on top of the console behind the steering wheel.

Better safe than sorry.

Like the rest of the shoreline, the channel was flanked by swaying sunbaked grass on both sides and buildings rose in the distance farther inland. He guessed the channel was about 300 meters wide, which was big enough for most vessels, including the *Trident* that had come through last night.

He cruised the sixteen-footer toward the familiar bridge that arced over the water and connected the two sides of the channel. The metal structure looked as dangerously old now as it did when he had driven over it yesterday with Blaine and Bonnie. After making sure there was no one on top of it, he glided the boat underneath and onto the other side, passing floating red and green buoys marking the edges of the channel.

More flat and uninteresting fields of grass greeted him. It was peaceful out here, but instead of putting Keo at ease, it only made him more alert. He belatedly noticed that the windshield in front of him only went up slightly higher than his waist, which made it useless in terms of protection. Not that he expected a thin piece of clear plastic was going to deflect a bullet, but, well, something was better than nothing.

A kilometer and a half into the channel, the buildings started to become clearer in the distance. He spotted eerily empty marinas and abandoned shrimp barges, and warehouses dotted both sides of the landscape. Cranes and towering equipment, part of whatever industry had once thrived here, crisscrossed the skyline like ancient sentries. He wondered how long they would remain like that before the elements pulled them back down to earth.

He was glad for the motor running behind him. Keo thought he would become used to the silence of an empty world by now, almost a year in, but that was always proven false whenever he went through an area that was, once upon a time, a nest of activity. The marina back at Lake Dulcet was one of those places. The desolation always got to him, a reminder that no matter what he did, how many promises he kept, or bad *(badder)* men he killed, the world as he knew it was gone. And in its place was…this.

Whatever "this" was.

He was too far away from land to make out a group of businesses, but they looked like stores or possibly offices. He hadn't really gotten the chance to explore the area yesterday, and Lara and the others had no reasons to. He did think the two Army Rangers would have at least taken some time to scout their immediate AO for potential dangers, though, and was surprised to learn that they, in fact, hadn't—

Crack!

The windshield in front of him shattered and Keo instinctively grabbed the submachine gun with one hand, pulled back on the control lever with the other, and hit the plywood floor a split second later.

He waited to hear a follow-up shot, but there wasn't one. Instead, there was just the boat continuing to move, its forward momentum keeping it going up the channel even though he had put the shift into neutral. Thank God this part of the lake was wide enough that it would take a miracle for him to run aground—

Crack!

The hull in front of him splintered, and a round *zipped!* to the right of his head and exited the other side before *plopping!* into the water.

A sniper.

Jesus Christ. There was a sniper out there. A pretty good one, too, since the guy was probably shooting at him from 150 meters or more from land.

He's a better shot than me, that's for damned sure.

The boat's momentum had lessened by quite a bit now, but it hadn't stopped completely. How much farther was the channel entrance? If he could reach the Gulf of Mexico, he had an entire ocean to escape into. Even the world's best sniper couldn't hit him out there.

Of course, Keo hadn't lifted his head to make sure of his current position. That would have been a fool move that, quite possibly, also ended his life. Judging by the angle of the first two shots, he guessed he was getting closer to the shooter. The first round had hit from in front of him, and the second had penetrated the boat at an almost 120 degree angle at the port side. Pretty soon, he'd be sidling right alongside the bastard. That, unfortunately, was also going to make it much easier for the guy.

He thought about reaching up and pushing the throttle forward to hasten his trip to the channel's entrance. That might work, as long as he kept going straight like an arrow. Of course, if the boat started to drift to either the left or right side, he might very well run right into one of those barges or hit the shoreline. It was kind of hard to steer when he couldn't even see over the sides at the moment.

He kept waiting to hear a follow-up torrent of gunfire and was again surprised there wasn't any. What was the man waiting for? Maybe the guy couldn't see him. Keo was flat against the floor of the boat, and if he couldn't see above the portside gunwale, chances were very good the guy (or guys, if his luck was really that bad) couldn't see him, either. The fact that the man hadn't fired again was unsettling. A man who didn't shoot randomly was a lot more dangerous than one who just fired blindly at a target.

So how did that help him?

It didn't, really.

He was stuck, and the boat had slowed down to a crawl now even though the engine was still coughing behind him, threatening to shut down at any second. His only available line of sight was up at the open skies, because looking left, right, front, or back only offered up the same ugly navy color.

He realized now how stupid pulling back on the gear had been. The smarter move would have been to pour on the power, because his best chance to survive was to blast right up the channel and stay low. Even a great shooter was going to have difficulty hitting a moving target, and that was what he would have been.

Live and learn, pal.

How good was this guy, anyway? That was the million dollar question. How long would the shooter need to acquire a target and pull the trigger? A second? Half a second? Two? Because that was how long Keo guessed he would need to lift himself up from the floor and expose himself (or, at least, his nice, big juicy head) while he reached for the lever, made sure of his direction, and pointed the boat at the Gulf of Mexico.

Two seconds.

Okay, maybe three…or four.

That was a long time. He had killed men in less time than that, and he was a lousy shot. This guy, on the other hand…

Four seconds.

Damn. Stuck between the Gulf of Mexico and a wet grave. What a way to go.

Keo put the MP5SD down and pushed both palms against the floor and readied to spring himself up. The first motion would get his feet back under him and the second would send him straight up, just far enough to reach the steering wheel and control lever. It wasn't exactly brain surgery, and all he'd have to do was keep from getting his head blown off in the four seconds he probably had. *Probably.* Once he made sure the boat was pointed in the right direction and the motor was at full throttle, he could jump back down and only expose his hand. If the sniper managed to shoot off his arm while he was moving at full speed, then more power to him.

Who needs two arms, anyway?

Keo sucked in a deep breath. It was slightly stale and smelled of dead sea life, not to mention whatever chemical they had been pumping out of those industrial buildings from the nearby areas.

Two breaths…three…

On *five*, he jumped—got both feet under him, pushed up, twisted to his right, grabbed the rubber-covered steering wheel with one hand and the metal lever with the other and—

Oh, crap.

It was a Jeep. About a hundred meters farther up the channel. The vehicle was bright yellow against the brown and green fields, and men were jumping out of the back. He didn't need binoculars to know they were probably all armed, and from the way they were running toward the shoreline, they knew exactly where he was and what they were going to do when they reached it, and he reached them.

And then there was the sniper—

The loud *crack!* of another gunshot split the air, just before something hit him in the right shoulder and spun him slightly. He fought through the pain, ignoring it (or at least telling himself to) and shoved the throttle all the way back up. The motor roared and instead of holding the steering wheel straight, Keo spun it right until the boat turned away from the swarm of men and he was arcing in a wide U-turn.

Water churned under him and he ducked just as another shot *zipped* over his head, right where he had been standing a brief half-second ago. The boat was swinging around in a wide circle—too wide—and he was holding on for dear life. There was a solid *thunk!* as he broadsided one of the buoys, warning him that he was getting too close to the shallower parts of the channel.

He waited for the sniper to shoot again, but the man either didn't have a bead on him or—

Crack! Another round *buzzed* past his head just as the boat completed its U-turn, coming dangerously close to ramming into the other side of the channel. He righted the vessel, spinning the wheel back left as the sixteen-footer fought against the surface while tearing up the lake, back in the direction he had come moments ago.

He expected to hear the *pop-pop-pop* of automatic gunfire as the men from the Jeep opened up on him, but to his surprise, they didn't. Not that he spent more than a few seconds thinking about it. He remained kneeling, steering with one hand, hoping something didn't pop up in front of him and take him out in a collision.

Five seconds...ten seconds...

He had put enough distance between him and the shooter that Keo felt safe enough to stand up. A good thing, too, because he had swerved dangerously too close to the left shore in the last few seconds and had to quickly right the boat again. He slashed underneath the bridge a second time and finally burst back into the wider section of Beaufont Lake.

Then, and only then, did he let himself glance over his shoulder back into the channel.

Silhouetted figures, like twigs in the distance, were scrambling around on land. If the sniper was among them, Keo couldn't tell. Not that he had seen the man during the whole ordeal. But he had to be somewhere in the weeds, close enough to the water that he could see everything in the channel. He knew for a fact the gunshots had all come from ground level. If the guy had been higher up—positioned on one of those cranes, for instance—Keo would have been a dead man.

The *drip-drip* of blood on the console reminded him he hadn't made it out of the channel completely unscathed. The bullet had clipped his right shoulder, taking a quarter inch of flesh for its trouble. He was bleeding, but it looked worse than it really was. A dripping wound was better than a pouring one.

He didn't stop the boat until he had gone for a few more minutes. Keo opened the compartment under the console and fished out the first aid kit. It was a dirty white box, but the contents were clean the last time he checked. He rolled up the sleeve and disinfected the wound, then wrapped it up with gauze and taped it into place. The pain was slight and nothing he couldn't handle. After surviving all those months in the woods with a pair of holes in him, this was more of an inconvenience.

He hadn't finished putting the first aid kit back under the console when he heard a second outboard motor filling the air behind him. Keo glanced back just as a fast-moving white boat blasted out of the mouth of the channel. It was pointed straight in his direction and men clung to it. He couldn't tell how many, or if they were wearing uniforms or not from the distance.

The sight of them set him off. He wasn't sure if it was annoyance, anger, or maybe a little of both. Probably a lot of both, now that he thought about it. He picked up the M4 from the floor and pulled back the collapsible stock. He flicked the fire selector to semiautomatic, then moved toward the stern and balanced himself for a few seconds before settling in behind the red dot scope. The optic wasn't anything fancy, but he could see the moving vessel coming easily enough. Three hundred meters, and closing in fast.

Keo fired, waited, then fired again, then again, and again.

He didn't know if he hit anything, but by the way the boat slowed down before breaking off the pursuit entirely, he assumed he had gotten close enough to spook them.

He lowered the rifle and waited for a response. He didn't have to wait long. They fired back in his direction a moment later. Two shooters, and they were apparently just as bad at long-distance shooting as he was, because while a couple of rounds landed in the water off his starboard and one sailed harmlessly over his head, most of them didn't even come close.

Keo thought about returning fire to let them know he was still standing, but decided they could probably see him just fine. The fact that they hadn't kept coming was a sign they either weren't ready to risk their lives chasing him, or they had orders to stay back. He wasn't keen on either possibilities, but the latter gnawed at him.

By the time they stopped shooting, it was clear they weren't going to chase him anymore, but they weren't moving, either. That meant the channel was blocked off to him. Unless, of course, he was willing to shoot his way through. But even if he could get past these bozos, there was still that sniper out there, lying in wait in the weeds. Keo had a feeling that dickhead wasn't going anywhere anytime soon, and he probably hadn't hopped onto the boat along with these other guys.

Keo slung the M4 and walked back to the console. He pushed the throttle, and the boat jumped back to life and headed off. He glanced back once, to see if they would pursue, but they were just shifting back and forth against his waves, content to watch him go. Soon, they faded into the background.

So much for escaping into the Gulf of Mexico. He'd have to find another way to reach Santa Marie Island and Gillian.

Maybe he could try the roads. That had to be safer, right?

THE *TRIDENT* WAS where he last saw it, next to Song Island, with the long strip of white beaches on the other side. A small boat drifted off the stern next to the swim platform, where the beautiful people gathered to soak in the sun and take a dip when the wind moved them. At the moment, there was just Maddie's small figure facing him, one hand shielding her eyes from the sun. He couldn't tell if that was a smirk or a grin on her face as she watched him near.

Keo felt another pair of eyes and looked up at Blaine peering back down at him through his rifle's optic. He lowered the M4 and waved from the rear of the upper deck, and Keo, feeling like a failed college student returning home to mom and dad, waved back.

"We figured you had something to do with all that shooting," Maddie said when Keo sidled his boat alongside the yacht. "What happened? You ran into more old friends?"

"Not quite."

"What happened to your arm?"

"Mosquito bite."

"Must have been a big ass mosquito."

"You have no idea."

"And my boat?" she frowned. "You putting holes in my boat, Keo?"

"I didn't exactly have a choice in the matter." Then, "Where's Lara?"

"Up here," Blaine called down. "You need a doctor?"

"No, I just need to talk to her. What's happening up there?"

"Lara's doing what she does," Maddie said.

"I don't know what that means," Keo said.

"She's looking for a way for us to survive tonight."

"Did the Rangers show up yet?"

"Not yet."

"When are you expecting them?"

Maddie looked anxiously down at her watch. "I have no idea, but it shouldn't be long now."

Or maybe they're already dead. That seems to happen a lot to people out there these days.

But he said instead, "Yeah, they'll probably be here soon." He picked up his line, said, "Heads up," and tossed it to Maddie.

◄━━▮ ▮━━►

HE FOUND LARA in the captain's cabin behind the bridge on the upper deck of the *Trident*, looking at a large map spread out on a table in the center of the room. Sunlight poured in through two curtainless windows, and she looked up when he knocked on the open door.

"What happened to the bridge?" Keo asked.

"We found the eighth guy," she said. "Or, actually, he found Blaine."

"That explains the mess."

"Yeah." Then, "What happened out there?"

"Soldiers. I guess they weren't keen on me leaving."

She looked from his face to his bandaged shoulder. "You okay?"

"I'll live."

"How many were there, and where?"

He walked inside and slumped down on a felt armchair. Clothes were strewn about the floor, others draped off the large queen size bed behind her. The place looked and smelled heavily lived in.

"A handful of shooters at the channel," he said. "It doesn't look like they want anyone leaving this place. You can assume they've got people on the roads, too. Maybe even technicals."

"What's that?"

"What's what?"

"The last thing. Technicals?"

"Machine gun-mounted vehicles. Usually trucks. I saw a couple of soldiers with machine guns back at the staging area. Along with the M4s, I'm guessing they're flushed with weapons, probably from one of the state armories in the area."

Lara didn't say anything for a while. He saw that mind of hers turning again, absorbing this new information and slotting them in order of importance. It was kind of impressive to see someone who was obviously smarter than him working in real-time.

"You think the *Trident*'s appearance had something to do with why they're cutting off the Gulf?" she finally asked.

"They probably heard the commotion from last night and realized there was a possibility you might take off in that direction."

Which means if I had left when I was supposed to, I would be at Santa Marie Island right now, on the beach with Gillian.

He sighed, and added, "Of course, they probably had no idea you were going to fight to the death to keep the island."

"I don't have a death wish, Keo," she said, sounding slightly annoyed with him.

"Are you sure about that?"

"I'm not the one with a bleeding shoulder."

"It's just a flesh wound."

"Go let Zoe fix it up anyway. You're no good to me bleeding to death. Flesh wound or not."

"You assume I'll still be here by nightfall."

She was already looking back at the map. "Call me Captain Optimism."

"Maybe we should get you a captain's hat, too."

"Go, Keo, before you bleed to death on my fancy new boat."

He got up, but instead of leaving, he walked over to her. "Maddie says you're looking for a way to save everyone."

"She's being overly dramatic."

"So what are you doing?"

"Looking for a way to save everyone."

He chuckled. "What've you come up with so far?"

He looked down at the map. It was spread out with the Gulf of Mexico and its surrounding areas, including the southern United States, with Mexico to one side and the Caribbean Islands on the other.

"Are you staying?" she asked, not looking up at him.

"It doesn't look like I have much of a choice. At least, not today."

"How bad is it?"

"It's a choke point, Lara. The channel's wide and deep enough for a large boat like this, but it's tight enough that a half dozen men with assault rifles could make it difficult for anyone attempting to run through it."

She didn't respond; her mind churned silently next to him.

He nodded at the map. "So, what're you looking for specifically? Maybe I can help."

"Maybe you can. I'm guessing you've traveled more than me."

"Other people go out of the country for vacation, but I go in country for mine. That should tell you something."

"You're an odd one, Keo." Then, "I'm looking for someplace to take everyone just in case we have no choice but to abandon Song Island. God willing, we won't need it."

"I didn't know you believed in God."

"I don't." She hesitated, then, "At least, I didn't use to."

"But you do now."

"Maybe."

"'Maybe'?" He smiled. "You either believe or you don't, Lara."

"I'll let you know when I figure it all out. Anyway, you have any ideas?"

"When was the last time you left the States?"

"I went to Paris when I was twenty-one for summer vacation with my roommate."

He was going to ask, *"What happened to your roommate?"* but of course he already knew the answer, so he kept his mouth shut about that and said instead, "You thinking about sailing this thing to *Gay Paree?*"

"You got any better ideas?"

He scanned the map, noticing just how close the Texas coastline was to his current location. He could easily have reached it by boat. So easily…except for those soldiers waiting to pick him off in the channel.

So close, yet so far.

He looked past the Gulf and moved into the Caribbean Sea. There was Cuba and Jamaica, and nearby, a familiar spot of land that he recognized. It was hard to forget one of the few places where he almost died.

"There," he said, pointing at a tiny dot. It was so insignificant compared to everything else on the map that it didn't even have a name. "Bengal Island."

"Bengal Island?"

"It's actually two islands. Grand Bengal and Little Bengal. The one that shows up on the map is Grand Bengal, but there's a smaller companion island—"

"Let me guess. Little Bengal?"

"That third-year medical school education is finally paying off."

She snorted.

"Here," he said, putting his finger over an empty spot on the map.

"I don't see anything."

"It's a good-size island, about 160 kilometers—"

"I still get my kilometers and miles mixed up. What's that in miles?"

"About 100, give or take."

"Okay. Go on…"

"It's about 100 miles—"

"Give or take."

"Can I finish?"

She smiled. "Sorry."

"I was saying, it's about 100 miles from its big brother, Grand Bengal, and is about ten kilometers in length and one-point-six in width, though the middle is more like two-point-four."

"So, about six miles long?"

"Yeah, about ten times the length of Song Island. Big enough for an airfield on the east section and a hotel resort on the west, with the two sides linked by roads. There's a strand of white beaches in front of the hotels where the rich and infamous bunk. The water is blue and everything is expensive, but depending on the state of the island, you may or may not have to fight for a spot in one of those suites."

"You've been there before."

"I almost died there."

"Which Bengal?"

"Both."

"Hunh."

"Yeah. Anyway, the place used to be a notorious pirate den until the British Empire took it over in the seventeenth century. You know the Brits. Law and order and Queen and Country, and all that good stuff. These days, it's treated as a British Overseas Territory."

"I don't know what that means."

"It's technically a part of the old British Empire, because apparently they enjoy the prestige of being linked to an old carcass, but for all intents and purposes, it's entirely self-governed."

"I've never even heard of it."

"You wouldn't have, because you're a normal, decent person. The main island is only fifty square miles with about 5,000 locals, and the rest are all tourists and criminals."

"You mean tourists or criminals?"

"No, I mean tourists and criminals. Bengal Island is where you put your money if you want to hide it from Uncle Sam or some other government body. As long as you pay for the privilege, the government there will hold pretty much an unlimited amount of funds for you. That includes your own private villa to live out the rest of your miserable, criminal life."

She gave him a curious look.

"What?" he said.

"You really know a lot about this place."

"I've had occasions to go there in my old job. The point is, Little Bengal is a perfect replacement for Song Island. You wouldn't necessarily have to deal with the main island, and the closest countries are Cuba to the east and Jamaica to the southeast. Both are well over 300 kilometers away with nothing but open Caribbean sea in the middle."

"Around 200 miles?"

"Close enough. But you understand where I'm going with this?"

"It's isolated."

"Yes. It's very isolated. Both physically and internationally. That's what makes it so attractive to the criminal element. You'll be able to see anyone coming for, literally, miles away."

"And all that water…"

"There's that, too."

Lara pulled out a marker and circled Little Bengal, then drew a line from it to the channel that connected Beaufont Lake with the Gulf of Mexico.

"How far?" she asked.

Keo did the numbers in his head. "Less than 2,000 kilometers and more than 1,000 miles?"

"Can you be more specific?"

He grunted. "You know there's a bridge on this boat? In it, there are all kinds of neat computer doodads that you can program to tell you the exact distance of places and such. Just sayin'."

She ignored him and continued looking at the map. "I like it."

"You should. It's exactly what you're looking for. The only thing you have to worry about are the criminal elements that may or may not still be there."

"Guys with guns?"

"Without a doubt."

"Well, then," she said, "if we actually do go there, it's a good thing we have plenty of guns of our own."

CHAPTER 14

GABY

As much as she longed for the white beaches and blue waters of Song Island, she dreaded finally reaching it after being away for so long. It was less about the island and more about who would be waiting for her there.

Lara. She would be there.

What am I going to tell her? How am I going to explain Will not being with us?

"You should smile more," Nate was saying from across the back of the moving truck.

She snatched hair out of her face with one hand, the other holding the M4 in her lap. "What did you say?"

"You don't smile enough," he said, shouting a bit to be heard over the roar of the wind. "You should smile more. It brings out the cut on the bridge of your noise."

She smirked. "Funny guy."

"I try."

"Well, stop. This isn't the time."

"So when is the time?"

"I don't know. But this isn't it."

"Relax, Gaby. You're almost home. Look around you. There's nothing but road and grass and fields out here. I haven't seen a building in…ten minutes? Twenty?"

Nate had a point. There was nothing out here except large acres of sun-bleached and overgrown grass to one side and the clear, calm waters of Beaufont Lake on the other. She couldn't see Song Island yet because they were still too far north, but it wouldn't be long now. An hour, maybe less, and the first signs of home would appear in the distance. She found herself getting more anxious and at the same time more alert as they got closer.

How many days and nights now had she been waiting for this moment? It had been too long, and the prospect of finally getting there was overwhelming, both exhilarating and terrifying.

What am I going to tell Lara?

"Maybe it won't be that bad," Nate said.

"What's that?"

"At the island. Tonight."

She looked at him curiously for a moment. Did he actually believe that, or was he trying to make her feel better? Or maybe he was trying to convince himself. Looking at him, she felt guilty all over again. She had to remind herself of all the troubles he had gone through just to find her, and now having done so, she was dragging him straight into another hellish gunfight. Somehow, the fact that he was coming willingly—even anxiously—made it just that little bit worse.

"Do you really believe that?" she asked.

"Why not?"

Because you didn't see them. Back at the farmhouse. The blue-eyed creatures. This is their world now, Nate. We're the trespassers. And they might be coming for us tonight. Are you ready for that, because I'm not.

"I'm sorry," she said.

He gave her a confused look. "For what?"

"Bringing you here."

"I don't understand…"

"They're going to attack tonight, Nate. Will is certain of it. And he's rarely wrong."

"There's a first time for everything."

"Not this. He was so sure of it he risked his life so we could get through the ambush back at Route 13. And as much as Danny and me wanted to come home—and God, we did, desperately—Will wanted to come home more."

He nodded and went quiet for a moment.

After a while, he said, "I never heard anyone talking about it, you know. Song Island. Back when I was with the others in town. I don't think most of the soldiers knew it even existed."

"What *did* you hear?"

"What do you mean?"

"Back at the town. What did the soldiers talk about?"

The question had been nagging at her ever since L15. The guards assigned to watch her back then hadn't been very talkative, and she was confined to a room where she didn't get to interact with the townspeople. She saw them from her window—the way they lived, went about their lives, and sometimes she could hear the tail end of their chatter—but she never really knew them.

"Mostly about everyday things," Nate said. "What they used to do before, that sort of thing. They weren't all bad, you know."

"The soldiers…"

"Yeah." He paused for a moment, looking thoughtful. "Some of them were in it for the power trip, but most of them…" He shook his head, then pursed his lips into a forced smile. "There were a couple of good guys back there."

She didn't ask him if one of those "good guys" had been back at the highway because she decided she'd rather not know. They'd all had to do things these days that they weren't completely proud of. Gaby didn't regret very many things, but sometimes the more violent situations stuck with her for days afterward. Every now and then when she closed her eyes, she still remembered Mercy Hospital back in Lafayette, and the blood and the screams and the gunshots…

This is our existence. Surviving from day to day. Night to night.

Everyone dies, sooner or later. Everyone.

"Gaby," Nate said, smiling across the back of the moving truck at her. "We'll make it through tonight. We'll be around to see tomorrow, and the day after that. We have to, otherwise I won't be able to convince you what a charming devil I am."

She smiled back at him.

Or tried to, anyway. It may or may not have been all that believable, but at the moment it was all she could manage, and he looked like he desperately needed to see it.

<hr />

HER WATCH HAD just ticked to four in the afternoon when Danny finally slowed down and stopped the Chevy in the middle of the two-lane highway. The heavy vehicle creaked as Danny turned off the engine and climbed out.

"Stretch 'em if you got 'em," he shouted.

The girls climbed out, and Gaby hopped out of the back with her M4. She exchanged a brief grin with Claire, who had also come out of the Silverado, still clutching onto her FNH shotgun, ready for battle.

"Are we almost there?" the thirteen-year-old asked.

"Almost," Gaby said.

She glanced around at their surroundings. Every inch of grass looked like the last few thousand they had passed. The same went for the water on the other side. The truth was, without Song Island anywhere in the distance, she had no idea where they were. This side of the lake was all new to her.

Danny had placed the portable ham radio on the hood of the truck and was fiddling with the buttons and dials.

She walked over. "Where are we exactly?"

"We should be directly beside the island if my internal GPS is correct."

"Internal GPS?" she said doubtfully.

"By which I mean, the map."

She looked back at the lake, but despite her best efforts, she couldn't make out any signs of the island in the distance. "There's nothing out there, Danny."

"It's there. Just too far to see from this side of the lake."

"So why did we stop here?"

He showed her his watch. "We don't have time to circle all the way around to the marina. Besides, we're running low on gas."

"How low?"

"I've-been-driving-on-fumes-for-the-last-thirty-minutes low."

Nate had walked over. "We're out of gas?"

"Unless you have a secret stash hidden somewhere, Famous Nathan, that's an affirmative."

"I still don't know what that means."

"That's what ESPN's for," Danny said. He turned back to the radio and pressed the lever and spoke into the microphone. "Song Island, come in. Roger if you roger me, roger."

A male voice answered almost immediately. "Danny? Is that you?"

"It ain't Danny Elfman. Although I was known to play a pretty mean Casio keyboard back in college."

"Holy shit, you're alive," the man said.

"You sound surprised."

"Yeah, well, you know…" The man disappeared from the line for a moment before returning about ten seconds later. "I just told Lara over the two-way. She's still on the yacht."

"Who is that?" Gaby asked. "I don't recognize the voice."

"That's Roy," Danny said. "He came over with a handful of people after you left on your helicopter adventure."

"Danny?" a female voice said through the radio, sounding slightly out of breath. This one Gaby recognized instantly. *Carly.* "You asshole. You had me worried."

Danny smiled. "Sorry, babe. You know I love you. Girls have been throwing themselves at me, but I told them to back off because there's only one redhead for me."

"I want names," Carly said.

Gaby nodded at Nate, and they drifted to the back of the truck to give Danny some privacy. That, and she wasn't sure she wanted to be around when someone on the island got to asking about Will, which they would, eventually.

The girls were skipping rocks across the calm lake on the other side of the truck while Annie watched them. The sight of the girls being so carefree for the first time in such a long time made Gaby smile.

"They look happy," Nate said next to her. "It's been a while since I've seen kids that happy."

"What about back at L17? Did you have kids there?"

"A lot of kids. Most of them were happy to be there. Not all of them, but most. Did both girls come from L15?"

"Just Milly," Gaby said.

She thought about Peter, the man whom Milly had treated like a brother. Peter was gone, and in so many ways Annie had taken his place. That was how it worked these days. You needed someone to cling to, because the emotional loneliness was sometimes worse than the physical isolation.

Gaby glanced back as Danny walked over to them.

"Are we at the right spot?" she asked him.

"Close enough," Danny said. "Looks like running out of gas might have saved our lives."

"How's that?" Nate asked.

"Apparently there is a very strong possibility of bad guys with big guns lying in wait at the bridge up the road. So instead of us braving that snake pit, the kids from Song Island will be coming here to pick us up. It'll take longer, but it'll keep us from being dead, and gosh darn it, that's a good thing."

"How long before they get here?" Gaby asked.

"Long enough. So I need you and the Natester to pull security until they arrive."

"Did you tell her?"

Danny shook his head. She didn't have to say who "her" was; he already knew. "She was busy on the yacht." He pointed down the road. "Former bad guy, you take that side. Gaby, the other one. Stay within shouting distance in case you see or hear anything that isn't us or the fishies."

Nate gave her an exasperated look before heading off to take up position farther down the road. She did the same thing in the opposite direction, with Danny falling in beside her. Gaby made a concerted effort to walk slower to accommodate his limping pace.

"What are you going to tell her when we get back?" she asked.

"I'll think of something between now and then."

"Do you want me to?"

"No," Danny said. "She deserves to hear it from me."

She nodded. As much as coming back home without Will pained her, she knew it was nothing compared to what Danny was going through.

"Keep an eye out, kid," Danny said. "We'll be back at Song Island and drinking ice cold water before you know it."

He turned around and limped off.

"Hey," she said after him.

He stopped and glanced back. "What's up?"

"We made it. I didn't think we'd ever see Song Island again, but we made it."

"We're not there yet."

"Close enough."

"It's never close enough until you're chewing on the cheese."

"That makes absolutely no sense, Danny."

"Of course it does," Danny said, turning and walking back to the truck. "Think about it."

"Yeah, no," Gaby said after him.

AFTER SITTING IN the back of the Chevy with the wind pounding against her face for most of the day, standing in the middle of the road under the sun was a nice change of pace. The combination of warm and cool air was almost enough to lull her into a sense of calm, and for a moment, just a moment, she almost forgot that they were cutting it too close, that it would be dark soon.

Always running from the night. Always running. How long before I get tired of it? How long before I just lie down and decide not to do it anymore?

She pushed those thoughts away. They were defeatist, a lingering part of her old self that refused to completely go away no matter how hard she tried, because she knew the old Gaby could never survive in today's world.

Claire, a reminder of how much times had changed, appeared next to her. The girl cradled the heavy shotgun across her arms and squinted down the barren road. "Do they take the dead, Gaby?"

The question caught her off guard, and it took her a moment to answer.

"I don't know," she said finally.

It was the truth. She really didn't know, and it was one of those nagging questions that she tried not to think too much about it because there didn't seem to be any point.

"Will had some theories about that," she added, "but we don't know for sure. Why?"

"We haven't seen any bodies. I'm just wondering where they all went."

"I'm sorry, Claire, I don't know."

"It's okay." She kept staring down the road, as if she expected to see something (or someone) coming down it anytime now. "I miss Donna."

"I know." Gaby put her arm around Claire, who leaned against her. "Donna's in a better place now."

"You think so?"

"Absolutely," she said, wondering what kind of special hell was waiting for her for lying to a thirteen-year-old. "You still have me, and if you want, I can make fun of how you stink."

"I stink?" Claire said.

"Oh yeah." She sniffed for effect. "The BO's so bad I'm about to barf."

Claire laughed. "You're such a liar."

"Maybe."

They exchanged a brief smile.

"Do I get my own room and bed on the island?" Claire asked.

"Yup."

"I've never had one before."

"Well, first time for—"

"*Incoming!*" Nate screamed behind her.

She turned around in time to see sunlight glinting off the hood of a vehicle driving up the road toward them. It was coming from the southern part of the lake and looked like a Jeep, its bright yellow color making it obvious against the gray of the road and the brown and green of the surrounding fields.

"Into the truck!" Gaby shouted.

Claire took off without a word, and Gaby actually had to run just to catch up to her. The girl was deceptively fast, even hauling that huge shotgun around.

Danny was climbing out of the Silverado, still moving gingerly on his bad leg. "How many?" he called back to Nate.

"Just that big ugly mustard thing coming at us," Nate said, peering through his binoculars.

Gaby also pulled out hers and looked through it. The Jeep was still too far off to make out a lot of details. A mile, she guessed, maybe two. But it was bearing down at them at full speed and they could already hear the sound of its engines despite the distance.

"Gaby," Danny said. "Keep an eye on your side."

She nodded. Danny was worried about a two-prong attack, and so was she. They had been here long enough for the enemy to set up some kind of coherent plan. Of course, these men weren't exactly seasoned tacticians, but it didn't take a combat veteran to know that attacking from two directions was better than one.

Claire, Annie, and Milly had already disappeared back into the truck, and Danny slammed his door shut and unslung his M4A1. "Kid, in the truck," Danny shouted at Nate. "Man Big Bertha."

Nate slung his weapon and ran back, then hopped into the bed of the Chevy. Gaby had to be satisfied with looking back one second for every five she paid attention to her side of the road.

"Wait until they get closer before you shoot," Danny said.

"How much closer?" Nate asked. "I've never fired one of these things before. What's the effective range on it?"

"You're overthinking it, Nateroni. Squeeze the trigger when you can smell them."

Nate grumbled as he perched the machine gun against the closed truck gate and settled down into a crouch. The ammo belt *clinked* against the truck with every movement he made.

Danny had stepped forward a bit and was now looking through his rifle's scope.

"Danny!" she shouted.

"Yeah?" he shouted back.

"Stop messing around and kill them already."

"Yes, ma'am," he said, and fired.

A single shot. She waited for him to pull the trigger again, but he didn't.

Instead, she listened to the shot echo for a second—maybe two—before the Jeep began swerving as if the driver had suddenly lost control. Then the vehicle seemed to make a sharp right and disappeared into the ditch, even as two men in the backseat were flung into the air, arms and limbs and rifles flailing wildly around them. Clouds of dirt plumed briefly about 200 meters from their position.

"Holy shit," Nate said, sitting up in the back of the truck. "Nice shot."

"Eh, I was aiming for the engine block," Danny said. "But I guess that'll do."

A lone figure stood up from the fields, but there were no signs of a second or third man. The survivor picked something up from the ground, seemed to hesitate for a moment, then after stumbling around, turned and began jogging back in the direction he had come.

They waited to see if anyone else would rise from the grass, but no one did.

"Should we go see if there are survivors?" she asked.

"We might be able to use the Jeep," Nate said. "If it's not too damaged."

"Fuck 'em," Danny said. "We're not going to need a Jeep where we're going." He glanced to his left. "Besides, our ride's here. Everyone look presentable. First impressions count and all that."

She looked over at the lake as a vessel appeared, getting bigger as the sound of a boat motor made its presence known. There were two figures onboard, mostly silhouettes against the bathing sun. One of them was pointing a rifle up the road, looking for something to shoot, which meant they had either seen the Jeep or heard Danny's gunshot and were taking precautions.

Nate looked through his binoculars. "Two people. A man and a woman. The woman's short and the man's a blond."

"That'll be Roy, the guy I was talking to earlier," Danny said. Then, to Gaby, "You'll like him. Handsome kid. Good with his hands, and I hear the ladies like that in a man."

Gaby wasn't sure how to respond to that, so she didn't say anything.

"Then, of course, there's Benny," Danny continued. "Face it, kid, you're going to have your hands full with the gentlemen callers when we get back to the island."

"Hey, I'm right here," Nate said.

"So you are, Natepoleon Bonaparte, so you are."

"Give it a rest, guys," Gaby said, smiling anyway, because it allowed her to think about something other than what she was going to say to Lara when she finally saw her again very soon.

◀━▮ ▮━▶

MADDIE STEERED THE old but dependable pontoon around the big white vessel anchored in front of Song Island. It was massive and occupied a ridiculous amount of real estate. Or maybe that was just her imagination, since she'd never seen a yacht up close before, never mind one that probably cost more than her parents made in their entire lifetime. The word *Trident* was written along its side.

Gaby saw a familiar figure leaning over the railing at the top of the boat waving to them. Blaine. She'd recognize his hulking size anywhere. She waved back, as did Danny and the girls. Blaine wasn't alone on the yacht. Two women on the other two decks watched them coming in. They were all heavily armed and looked the part of soldiers waiting for a fight.

Song Island has been getting ready for war. God help us.

Gaby felt the familiar pangs of guilt whenever she looked back at Claire, Maddie, and Annie. The three of them seemed awestruck by the sight of the big white yacht, and then later the beaches of Song Island and the towering solar panels that ringed it. She couldn't shake the nagging fear that she had made a terrible mistake by bringing them here. What was she doing? Song Island might have been a sanctuary once upon a time, but if Will was right and Kate was going to throw her human forces at it tonight, the place might as well be a death trap. And she had led them here with promises of a soft bed, their own rooms, and ice-cold water.

Song Island's not safe. I shouldn't have brought them here. Anywhere but here.

And then they were past the yacht and slowing down as they approached the piers. And there, standing at the end of one of the wooden structures sticking out of the beach, was what Gaby had been dreading since she stepped onto the boat.

Lara.

She was standing with a man Gaby hadn't seen before. Like Blaine and the two women on the *Trident*, Lara and the stranger were heavily armed and wearing assault vests.

Lara looked so different from the last time Gaby had seen her, and she suddenly realized that it wasn't just her who had gone through the kind of metamorphosis that even her parents wouldn't have recognized while she was running around out there trying to stay alive. Lara had changed, too. They all had. You had to, these days, or you didn't survive.

"Who's that?" Nate, standing next to her, asked.

"That's Lara," Gaby said.

"I thought you said she was some kind of medical student."

"She was. I mean, she is."

"Wow," Nate said. "Medical school in Texas is, uh, really different."

Gaby couldn't help but smile a little bit.

"Who's the string bean?" Danny asked Roy. The two of them were standing at the back of the boat.

"Keo," Roy, the blond who had come to pick them up along with Maddie, said.

"What kind of name is Keo?"

"You'll have to ask him. Showed up a couple of days ago. He's the reason the collaborators haven't attacked the island yet."

"So that's Keo."

"Yup. That's Keo," Roy said.

Gaby was listening to their conversation, but she was mostly focused on Lara standing on the pier with Keo. They were watching the pontoon on approach and talking. Gaby wondered how long it would take Lara to notice that Will wasn't among them.

She caught her breath and waited for the inevitable.

"Welcome home," Lara said as Maddie shut off the pontoon's motor and sidled it alongside the pier. "Guys, this is Keo. Keo, this is Gaby and that's Danny and...I don't know who the rest are."

The tall Asian guy nodded at them. Gaby could just barely make out a long, thin scar running down one side of his face, and he seemed to be favoring his right shoulder for some reason. Instead of an assault rifle like the others were carrying, he had a weapon with a long suppressor attached to the end. It looked mean and dangerous, and she wanted one.

"What kind of name is Keo?" Danny asked, climbing out of the boat.

"Lou was taken," the guy said.

Gaby hadn't made it onto the pier yet when Lara said, "Gaby, Danny—where's Will?"

CHAPTER 15

JOSH

"WE ALMOST HAD him," Travis said. "Smiley said he might have even tagged him."

Smiley? Right. The sniper.

Or as close to a sniper as he was going to get out here. Josh had to constantly remind himself that he wasn't actually leading a group of soldiers. It took more than a nice polished uniform to turn some accountant or restaurant manager or, in Travis's case, a construction supervisor, into a full-blooded killer.

Will and Danny would laugh at these guys.

"But he was too fast," Travis was saying. "Lucky bastard somehow managed to do a U-turn in the channel and slipped back into the lake before the others could catch him."

"So where is he now?" Josh asked.

"Back on the island'd be my guess."

"Just one guy?"

"Just one guy."

"I guess one more or less won't matter." Then, "Have you heard back from Mason?"

"Sonia didn't say anything, so I'm guessing not. He's probably still trying to deal with those other guys that popped out of nowhere and laid waste to his group back at Route 13."

"The Dunbar people."

"Yeah."

"I thought we killed everyone in that city."

"That's what Mason thought, too. But apparently not. It's funny…"

Funny? Nothing about this is funny, Travis, Josh thought, but he said, "What's that?"

"I think this is the first time I've heard of them not being able to finish a job."

"First time for everything," Josh said.

The "them" Travis was referring to were the blue-eyed ghouls. They had slaughtered almost everyone in Dunbar a few nights ago and took the women and children. Or, well, most of the ones that were still alive at the end of the night, anyway. Josh didn't want to think about it too much. He accepted what the ghouls were, what they did, but it didn't mean he wanted to dwell on it. As long as he wasn't directly involved, it was easy to pretend it wasn't actually happening.

"I don't know what's giving Mason so much trouble," Travis said. "He's got what, thirty or forty people with him?"

"Something like that."

"He should have had them by now. They were right there for the taking."

Mason.

The man was irritating. Or was that aggravating? Maybe both. The worse part of it was that Mason just didn't care. Sometimes Josh wondered if he should bring it up with Kate during one of their talks. It would serve Mason right. What Josh needed were dependable men, not lazy ones that did whatever the hell they wanted.

Will and Danny could whip them into shape. Maybe I just don't have what it takes. Or maybe some people just aren't meant to be soldiers.

"I've been meaning to ask," Travis said behind him.

"What's that?" Josh said, even though he knew the question, because it always came up.

They were always so curious about how it worked. He couldn't really blame them. Even now, after having gone through it dozens of times, it still freaked him out, though he would never admit it out loud. He had learned in those first few weeks that the only way to lead men was to make them fear your authority. Josh was never the biggest or most imposing kid, and he didn't have to be. He had something better. He had *them* standing behind him. Most of all, he had *her*.

"How does it work?" Travis asked. "How do they contact you?"

"Do you really want to know?"

"Yeah, I do."

"It's dreaming…but not really dreaming. It feels more like reliving a memory."

"Whose?"

"Yours, theirs… Whatever they want it to be."

"So they control it."

"You really have to ask that question?"

"No, I guess not."

Travis paused, and Josh could see him weighing the pros and cons of continuing this conversation. Like the rest of them, Travis was trying to balance wanting to know more and being afraid of the answers.

Finally, Travis said, "And they tell you what to do while you're in these dreams?"

He nodded. "It takes some getting used to, but yeah, that's essentially how it works."

"Freaky," Travis said. He might have also shivered involuntarily.

Josh smiled. He didn't bother telling Travis that in the dreams, Kate always came to him as her former human self, a major change from the first time he had seen her. It was sometimes difficult for him to reconcile the beautiful thirty-something woman, who moved with dreamlike sensuality and elegance, with the ghoul-Kate that had first recruited him not far from where he was standing now.

As much as he told himself he had become used to Kate's presence, or the sound of her voice inside his head, he could never quite shake the feeling there was something odd about her existence that went beyond the skeletal frame, pruned black flesh, and blue eyes. It was as if she was straddling the line between human and ghoul, trying to hold onto something that was long gone.

Why? he always wanted to ask her. *Why bother?*

He knew why *he* was bothering, though.

Gaby. I'm doing this for you. For us.

Josh lowered his binoculars and wrinkled his nose. It had been months since Will burned down the two-story house across the small inlet, but Josh thought he could still smell the damage. The marina had also been reduced to ashes, but the wild grass around it hid the scent better.

He looked down at his watch: 3:36 P.M.

It wouldn't be long now before Josh could finally leave this place and put Song Island into the back of his mind for good. He was looking forward to that. Beaufont Lake hadn't been very good to him. He still remembered getting shot and almost drowning and dying out here. Those were memories he'd rather bury in the past.

"You used to live there, didn't you?" Travis was saying.

Josh didn't need binoculars to see Song Island in the near distance. It was the only thing to break the monotony of calm lake water for miles around, its Tower jutting out like a sore thumb. It looked so insignificant, like a stain holding back progress. How did Will ever think this place could save them?

"I wouldn't say I used to live there," Josh said. "I was there for a couple of days, long enough to know it's just another island."

"Still," Travis said, "it must feel a little weird to be leading the attack on it."

He had thought the same thing, once upon a time. It only took looking at the place from afar to realize it wasn't true at all. Song Island was just another patch of dirt on a lake. That was it. Nothing more, nothing less.

"No," Josh said, turning and walking back to the Jeep, "it doesn't feel weird at all."

Travis jogged after him. "So, it's settled. We're attacking tonight. Even with that guy going back? That's an extra gun."

"You see that big thing sticking out of the island?"

"The lighthouse?"

"Yeah. There's a basement at the bottom. Song Island's always had all the guns and ammo it needs. One more guy isn't going to make any difference."

The former construction supervisor glanced back at the island one more time. "Man, it's gonna get bloody. I was hoping it'd go down easier."

"It could have, but that ship's sailed."

"What about the big boat that showed up last night? Did you tell them about that? Maybe they'll let us delay the attack—"

"They don't care," Josh said, cutting him off. "Besides, if we're lucky, all that shooting last night did was cut down their numbers. Either way, it's going to happen tonight."

Josh climbed into the front passenger seat of the Jeep while Travis slipped into the driver side. He still had to fight back a big smile whenever one of the older men had to drive him around, which was pretty much every time. Nineteen-year-old boys weren't supposed to be leading armies, but here he was anyway, doing just that. All of this, because he was one of the chosen ones.

Soon you'll be one, too, Gaby. Then you'll understand why I'm doing this. I'll make you understand.

◂▬▮ ▮▬▸

SONIA JOGGED DOWN the outer stairs of the two-story red house as he and Travis arrived in the Jeep. She looked excited, which told Josh she probably had news from Mason *(finally)*. Sometimes Josh thought Mason was the most capable man under his command, and other times he couldn't be trusted to look for gas for their vehicles.

Travis parked in the driveway, among the trucks and people in uniforms milling about and talking excitedly among themselves. They were anxious and scared, and they had every right to be. Most of them had never shot anyone or been in real combat. Some of them knew how to use the weapons they were carrying, but the majority had never fired at a living, breathing person in their lives.

He felt almost sorry for them, for what they were about to experience tonight. But whenever that pity threatened to paralyze him into backing out of the plan, he just had to remind himself that this was for the best. He was doing this for them—he and Gaby. He needed to prove himself to Kate and Mabry and the others. And once tonight was over, he could move on and prepare for the future.

With Gaby. Because none of this mattered a lick without Gaby at his side.

Sonia smiled at him as he climbed out of the Jeep. She was here the last few days and had lived through the grenade launcher attack. She was a Southerner, like Travis, minus the accent for some reason. Of course, that could have just been the hormones talking. For all he knew, she sounded exactly the same as Travis, except the visual was throwing him off.

"Mason?" he asked.

"Got word from him about ten minutes ago," Sonia said.

She fell in beside him as they walked across the large yard. Josh liked the fact that she hadn't even acknowledged Travis's existence, and Travis no doubt noticed that, too. He could tell the older man had a thing for the twenty-something. He didn't blame the guy. You had to be dead not to pitch a tent at the sight of Sonia. Somehow, that gun belt around her slim waist only made her more—

Gaby. There's only Gaby!

"What did he say?" Josh asked.

"They lost the trail at the interstate around Lake Dulcet."

"What does that mean?"

"They killed some guys he had stationed outside the city. Apparently, they used a machine gun. One of ours, if you can believe it."

Oh, I can believe it. You don't know half of the things these ex-Rangers are capable of. If you did, you'd be more scared about tonight.

"So where are they now?" he asked.

"He doesn't know."

Josh felt the familiar flurry of annoyance flaring up.

Mason. Goddamn Mason. Simultaneously the most capable man

under him, and the most aggravating.

"What about Salvani?" he asked.

"They haven't seen them," Sonia said.

"So that means they left the interstate at Lake Dulcet." He stopped and glanced north, where he imagined the casino town was in the distance. "They could be anywhere by now. Maybe even on their way down here this very moment. How long ago did Mason say he lost them?"

"He couldn't be sure. He guessed two, maybe three hours ago."

Goddammit, Mason.

"What do you want me to tell him?" she asked.

"Tell him—" He paused, then shook his head in frustration. "What about Will? Did he reacquire Will after the attack by the Dunbar people? Is he even still alive?"

"He says he's working on that."

"What does that mean?"

She shrugged. "He didn't elaborate."

Fuck, shit. Goddamn you, Mason!

He could feel Travis watching him closely to his right and Sonia doing the same thing in front of him. A couple of the other soldiers loitering around were also eavesdropping. They were all waiting for him to blow up, to finally reveal the nineteen-year-old *kid* (because they all thought of him as a kid, despite everything he had done and all the power he wielded) instead of the commander of men he had become since he struck out on his own.

But he was one of the chosen ones, and although Josh was flustered, pissed off, and angry, he reined it all in and tempered down his emotions and didn't let any of them show.

"Tell him to get his shit together, or he'll be answering to me," he said finally.

"Okay," Sonia said.

Josh continued to the house and climbed up the outer stairs to the second floor with Sonia beside him. He was proud of himself. Despite how badly the day was going *(Mason, you worthless piece of shit, you better get it together!)*, he had maintained his composure and was still on track to finish this whole messy affair with Song Island tonight. By morning, he could move on with the rest of his life with Gaby at his side.

Christ, Sonia smelled good. It was just generic soap, but women always had a way of making the ordinary extraordinary. Then again, for all he knew, Sonia could have put something extra on just for him. He had seen the way she looked and acted around him. She gave out all the signs and was all but begging him to make a move.

But he couldn't. Not with Gaby out there. Not with Gaby waiting for him.

I'm doing all of this for you, Gaby. I know you won't understand. Not at first. But one day you'll finally come around and then we'll be together. You'll see.

"Josh," Sonia was saying.

He stopped on the second-floor patio. "Hmm?"

"You're gone again." She frowned. "Gaby must really be something."

"She is," he said. *She's the most beautiful girl in the world*, he thought, but he didn't say it out loud. He liked Sonia and didn't want to hurt her feelings, so he asked instead, "Did you eat yet?"

"Not yet."

"You should, if you're going with us tonight."

"I was waiting for you to come back."

Gaby. There's only Gaby.

"I already ate," he lied. "I need to get some sleep. Wake me up when Mason radios back with news."

"About Gaby, or just anything?" she asked.

"Anything," he said, and slipped into the house before she could keep the conversation going.

AROUND FIVE-THIRTY, HE got good news and bad news.

"Sorry, didn't know you were still napping," Sonia said when she entered the bedroom after knocking once on the door.

Fortunately he had lain down and gone to sleep in his clothes.

The last thing he needed was to be caught in his underwear by Sonia. It was hard enough keeping his hormones in check around her when he was fully clothed.

He sat up and swung his legs off the bed, then absently flicked at the hardened pieces of dirt his boots had left on the mattress. "It's okay. What's up?"

"Mason finally radioed back."

"What took him so long?"

"He didn't say."

Mason. Christ.

"What did he say?" he asked.

"He caught that Will guy," Sonia said. She had sat down on a chair at the foot of the bed. "It took him a while, and he says it was messy, but he got him again."

"And he's still alive?"

"Mostly."

"'Mostly'?"

"He said the guy was injured, but that he's still breathing."

"I guess that's all that matters."

"What's so special about him, anyway?"

Nothing, except she *wants him, and what's important to her is important to all of us, because she's the only thing holding back the sea from drowning us all.*

"He's just a guy," Josh said, standing up and yawning. It was a good nap, and he was glad he had taken it. Tonight was going to take a lot out of him and the more energy he could save up for it, the better. "Anyway, Will's not our problem now. The island's the only thing we should be focusing on."

"Speaking of which, one of the guys watching the other side of the lake just intercepted a vehicle heading toward the bridge."

"Reinforcements?"

"Looks like it."

He picked up a canteen from the windowsill and took a sip. "How many?"

"He couldn't tell for sure. Maybe half a dozen, though he says he thinks some of them were women and children."

"You said 'he'?"

"Yeah. Only one of the scouts came back alive. The rest are dead."

"How the hell did that happen?"

"Apparently the newcomers had a really good shooter with them. He shot the driver of their vehicle from two football fields away, according to the survivor. That forced their vehicle into a ditch, and the crash killed the driver and another guy in the back."

"Aw, shit," Josh said.

"What?" Sonia said, eyeing him curiously. "Does that mean something to you?"

"Danny. It has to be Danny."

"Who's Danny?"

"He's an ex-Army Ranger. He's by far the best shot on the island, and he's one of the guys Mason was supposed to stop at Route 13."

"The one that escaped somewhere around Lake Dulcet?"

"Yeah, I think so."

"So that means…"

"Gaby," Josh nodded. "She has to be with him, which means she's already on the island right now."

No wonder he had felt differently when he woke up just a minute ago. He thought it was just the aftereffects of the nap, but there was a strangeness in the air.

Because Gaby was nearby.

He didn't say that out loud to Sonia. Besides the fact that the other woman was probably a little jealous of Gaby, it might sound a little crazy to tell her that he could feel how the air changed when Gaby was around.

But it wasn't crazy. It was the truth.

Sometimes Josh wondered if he had developed the same kind of connection to Gaby that Kate had with him, this thing that couldn't be explained to people who hadn't experienced it. Sonia wouldn't understand, and neither would Travis, regardless of how hard he tried to break it down for them. It was like something out of a comic book; unreal, unless it was happening to you night after night.

"So what does this mean?" Sonia asked. "Are we still attacking the island tonight? Even with Gaby there?"

Josh didn't answer right away. His mind was whirling, trying to process this new wrinkle in what had, up to this point, been smooth sailing.

Danny was back, but not Will. That was the only bright spot in all this mess. He didn't like that Gaby had returned, though. It was going to make tonight more difficult. Goddammit, why couldn't Mason have taken her on the interstate? Or back at Route 13? They had promised him.

Mason, and Kate. They had *promised* him they would keep Gaby away from the island.

"Josh?" Sonia was saying, trying to get his attention. "About tonight. Are we still going through with it?"

He stood up and walked to the window and peered out at the darkening skies. It was almost time. He could feel it coming without having to look at his watch.

Maybe he was seeing this all wrong. Maybe Gaby returning to Song Island, just as he was about to attack it, was a sign. Maybe it was always destiny that he would find her again at the same place where he had lost her, where everything had changed for both of them.

This is fate. It has to be.

"Tell the men to get ready," he said. "We're taking Song Island tonight."

CHAPTER 16

LARA

SHE WAS NUMB all over and had to summon every ounce of strength to push through it. The others were watching her. Keo beside her, Danny and Gaby in front of her, and the kids whose names she didn't know, even though Gaby had just told her a few seconds ago.

Will. You promised me. You goddamned promised me.

"He's still alive," she finally said.

"The last time I saw him," Danny nodded.

"What kind of shape was he in?"

"I couldn't tell you. He was in a car and so were we, and everyone was going fifty to sixty miles an hour. And, oh yeah, bad people were shooting at us, so that didn't help."

"They wanted us alive," Gaby said. "They were shooting at the tires."

"Which means he's definitely still alive," Lara said.

"Yeah," Gaby nodded.

Lara could see it in the teenager's eyes: Gaby was saying all the right things, but she didn't fully believe in them.

The girl had changed so much since the last time Lara saw her, and she wanted nothing more than to welcome her home like a big sister, but the pier suddenly felt too unbalanced and the air became suffocating, and she needed to leave.

Now. *Now.*

"Okay," she said.

"Okay?" Danny repeated.

"Yeah. Okay."

"Lara...," Gaby said.

"We can catch up later, but right now you guys need to go get cleaned up and eat something. It's going to be a long night." She ignored their searching gazes and turned around and walked down the pier. "Keo..."

Keo followed without a word.

She could feel the others watching after her. Danny and Gaby, even Maddie and Roy, and the newcomers. The woman and the kids, and the young man who stood protectively next to Gaby. Maybe she should have spent a few more minutes talking to them, hugging and making useless welcome-back talk. But there was no time for that. The sun was setting and the hours were dwindling, and soon, very soon, they would have to get ready.

There wasn't enough time. There was never enough time.

She kept walking and didn't look back. She was afraid of what might happen if she stopped. She had never been particularly good at keeping her emotions in check, but Lara had discovered she was capable of a lot of things that would have been unfathomable a year ago. Maybe it was the constant life-and-death choices, or this label of leader everyone had given her the last few weeks, or maybe it was because she knew he was alive.

Out there, alone, maybe even captured, but *still alive.*

Will was the most capable man she had ever known in her life, and as long as he was breathing, he would find a way back to the island. Back to her.

I'll wait for you, Will. I'll wait for you as long as I can.

She snapped another look at the skies. It would be dark soon, except for the halo of lights emanating from the LED lamps around the island. Then it would be just them and the people coming to kill them, using the blanket of night as cover.

"So your boyfriend's not dead?" Keo said. His voice came out of nowhere, and for a moment she forgot he was keeping pace beside her.

"No," she said.

"You sure about that?"

"If you knew Will, you wouldn't need to ask."

"So we're going on faith, then?"

"You honestly think your girlfriend actually made it to Santa Marie Island? That she's wearing a bikini and waiting on the beach every morning, waiting for you to finally show up?"

He chuckled. "Yeah, okay. Hit a guy while he's down, why don't you." Then he shrugged. "One ex-Army Ranger ain't bad, I guess. Even a gimpy one."

"We'll be fine, as long as everyone follows the plan. Including you. Like it or not, you're stuck here with us now, Keo."

"Lucky me."

Carly was running down the beach toward them and jumped onto the pier. Lara didn't know she could even run that fast. She and Keo made room as Carly darted past them—she might not have even noticed they were there—and ran straight into Danny's arms.

Lara turned back around and quickened her pace down the beach.

"How good is he?" Keo asked, still walking beside her.

"Danny?"

"Yeah."

"He's good."

"And the girl?"

"Danny and Will taught her themselves."

"That doesn't answer my question, Lara."

"Will says she's the best soldier on the island after him and Danny. He says she's gotten better since she's been out there."

"What is she, twenty-five?"

"Nineteen."

"Damn," Keo said. "I don't know whether to be impressed or a little scared of you people."

WHILE CARLY AND Benny welcomed Danny and Gaby back in the dining room, Lara spent the rest of the remaining daylight making sure everyone knew where they were supposed to be. Blaine, Bonnie, and Gwen remained on the *Trident* to keep watch, while she sent Roy over with Gage. The captain figured out pretty quickly what she was planning and seemed to be moving fine on the leg brace Stan had made for him. The painkillers Zoe had given him probably helped, though the doctor assured her it wouldn't be enough to dull his ability to pilot the boat.

Lara was in the basement under the Tower, making final preparations. She could have given the job to anyone, but she needed the solitude only the room's concrete walls, floor, and ceiling could provide. Ironic, since she always hated coming down here alone. Now, though, surrounded by the reminders of people who had come to Song Island seeking shelter only to find tragedy, she felt perfectly at home.

Nothing lasts forever. So why did I think this island would?

She remembered a conversation she'd had with Will not all that long ago.

"The island is vital, Lara," he had said to her.

"It's just an island," she had responded.

"But you're on it. And Carly. And the kids..."

The people. That was what mattered. The people on the island, not the island itself. There were other islands out there, like the Bengals, that Keo had shown her. Islands were just patches of dirt and could be replaced. But its people were another story.

She wasn't surprised to hear Danny climbing down the steps behind her. She knew he would seek her out sooner or later. Under the bright LED lights of the subterranean room, the scars along the bridge of his nose and face looked more pronounced, as if he had just stepped out of the boxing ring. He limped across the room, wearing another one of Stan's custom-made leg braces.

"How's the leg?" she asked.

"My dancing days are definitely over," Danny said. "At least until the break heals."

He ran his palms along the leather padding held together by Velcro straps and rigid hinged steel bars. The elastic material went all the way over his knee and down the calf. From what she could tell, Stan had done a marvelous job making it practical, and she made a mental note to ask him to make more, just in case.

Danny was looking at the nearly empty weapons rack at the back of the room. "Been busy, huh? I guess it's true what they say: Give a woman the key to your place, and before you know it, she's reorganizing everything. Should I ask what you've been doing with all the stuff me and your boyfriend collected over the last few months?"

"They're around."

"Can you be more specific?"

"Here, there, everywhere."

"Ah. All part of the plan?"

"Yes."

"So, tell me about it. That is, if you have the time. I mean, if you don't, maybe I can make an appointment or something. I can see you're a very busy gal these days."

"I'm sorry about before. At the pier…"

He waved a dismissive hand. "Water under the yacht. So tell me about this plan of yours that's supposed to keep everyone alive."

She did.

"Hunh," he said when she was finished. "I guess it's a good thing we stocked up on those cheap boats and emergency ladders."

"That's Will, Danny. He's always thinking ahead. That's why he's such a good leader and I'm…barely hanging on."

"You're doing all right from what I can see."

"Barely." Then, "So tell me. Am I going to get everyone killed?"

He thought about it for a moment. "It's risky," he said finally.

"It's very risky. But I don't see any other way. If we need to abandon the island, the *Trident* has to be ready. For that to happen, it can't be involved until we need it."

"It's a big boat."

"We'll have the cover of darkness, and I'm hoping they won't be able to adjust their assault plan on the fly. Or want to, given their overconfidence."

"So many maybes, Aunt Bee would be jealous." He seemed to think about it some more before nodding. "What's the worst that could happen? They try to board the big boat?"

"Keo did."

"Yeah, but from what everyone's told me, that guy is half-dolphin. Besides, I brought something that'll discourage them if they do decide to go that path. Have you ever stared down the barrel of an M240? It's guaranteed to make anyone cry for their momma."

"The other option is to pack everyone and everything onboard the *Trident* now and take our chances at the channel before nightfall."

"And you say they've got that place sealed tight?"

"Keo barely survived."

"He's a merc. You can't really trust a merc. Even one that's half-dolphin."

She sat down on one of the crates and looked over at him. "Tell me the truth. Am I going to get everyone killed, Danny?"

"Like I said, it's risky, but I trust you."

"Why?"

"You're smarter than me." He grinned, and despite the bruises and cuts, she could almost believe he was the same Danny who had left her and Carly to go look for Will. "Let's face it, you're smarter than everyone on this island. I used to think it was just book smarts, but Willie boy's convinced that's not the case. And I've learned to trust his instincts, even though this time it got me a busted nose."

"Funny, because I don't feel so smart."

"Now you know how I feel every day. Wait, did I just say that out loud?"

She managed a smile, but her mind was already elsewhere. She hesitated with what she was going to say next because she had been dreading it, but knew it was inevitable.

"What happened out there, Danny?" she finally asked.

"What do you wanna know?"

"It's her, isn't it? Kate?"

He sat down next to her. "They went to great lengths to take us alive back at Route 13. Kate's orders would be my guess. I don't know what that bitch has up her fleshy sleeve, but it's got everything to do with Willie boy."

"He was only with her for one night. Or did he lie to me?"

"Nah, I think that was it. But it's not like I have a bell around his ankle or anything."

"So what is this, some kind of schoolgirl crush?"

"I don't think so."

"Then what?"

He shook his head, and she could see that Danny had been thinking about it for some time now, too. "Putting on my serious hat here, but I don't think it's something we would understand. You know how she would sometimes show up in his dreams?"

Lara nodded. It was one of the more infuriating things about Kate.

"He used to tell me they had this unexplainable connection," Danny said. "Some psychic shit, or something. Maybe it happened back in the early days of The Purge. The Kate you met on the road wasn't the same Kate we first saw back in Houston. She'd changed a lot by the time you joined us."

Everyone changes. You adapt or perish.

"So I don't know what happened between them," Danny continued. "You should ask him when he comes back."

"I will."

"And he will come back."

"I know."

"Your boyfriend's stubborn. It's one of his most annoying qualities. Sometimes I want to punch him in the face just for being him."

"I'll tell him you said that." Lara reached over and squeezed his hand. "I'm glad you're back. You know I love you, right?"

He grinned. "What would Carly say?"

She kissed him on the cheek. "Welcome home. I'm sorry you're not going to be able to spend a lot of time with Carly."

"Fortunately, I don't need all that much time. Back in college they used to call me Speedy Danny. You don't wanna know."

"I think you're right," she smiled, and this time it came out easier.

"I could tell you."

"No."

"It's a funny story."

"Save it for tomorrow."

"Right-o." Then, "So. Your own little Plan Z, huh?"

"I'm trying to come up with a better name, but yeah. If we need it, that's what I've come up with."

"Eh. I've heard worse."

"When?"

"Whenever your boyfriend opens his mouth."

Lara laid her head against his shoulder. "He'll be back. As long as he's alive, he'll come back to me. He promised, and he knows I'll kick his ass if he breaks that promise."

"Well, that settles that, then."

They didn't say anything for a moment, and the only sound for the longest time was the humming of the lights around them.

Finally, Lara said, "What if they don't do what I think they'll do? What if they're smarter than that?"

"They'll definitely go for the beach," Danny said. "They won't be able to help themselves. They have the manpower and firepower for it. They'll overwhelm us with force. Shock and awe. Or, at least, that'll be the plan. Personally, Willie boy and me could have come up with something better. Like, a billion times better. But we're not talking about professionals here. They'll take the path of least resistance because they'll be overconfident in their numbers."

"Do they really have that many soldiers?"

He nodded. "However many you think they have, they actually have more. Everyone loves a winning side, right? And you don't get any more winning than taking over the planet in one night. Hell, if we're smart, we would have joined them long ago."

"It's a good thing you're not that bright, then."

"Ouch."

"But I love you anyway."

Danny put his arm around her and pulled her tight against him. "One more day. That's all we need. Just long enough for Big Willie to make his way home. I don't like to tell him this, but he's the brains of the operation, you know. If there's a Will, there's a way." Then he added, "Get it?"

"I'm not an idiot, Danny."

"Well, you did drop out of school."

"I had a really good excuse," she said.

SHE FOUND GABY in her room. The same one she had left behind weeks ago when she climbed into the helicopter with Will and didn't come back to until now. It still looked the same because Lara hadn't touched it since, and Carly had visited it once every few days to keep the dust at bay. From the looks of the clean carpeting and bed, Carly had done a good job of it.

Gaby was sitting on the end of the bed, looking at the open bathroom door across from her. Someone was in the shower singing some song that sounded familiar, but Lara couldn't quite place it. It was probably the young blonde girl who had stood on one side of Gaby while the young man, Nate, stood on the other when they arrived on the island earlier. Looking at the two girls was like seeing sisters, and she wondered if that's what people saw when she stood next to Gaby.

A dirty T-shirt and pants lay crumpled on the floor next to the supply packs Gaby and the girl had brought with them. Gaby was still wearing her gun belt, and her M4 rifle leaned against the bed within easy reach. There was an awareness about her, as if she was waiting for something to happen so she could explode into action, that hadn't been there when she had last seen the teenager.

Always the soldier. You trained her too well, Will.

"Hey," Lara said.

Gaby looked over. Despite the bruises, the cuts, and the healing broken nose, she still looked very much like the painfully pretty eighteen-year-old teenager who had come to her and Will not all that long ago. Josh had been with her then, but that was another life. These days, Gaby had other boys scrambling for her attention, and no amount of bodily injury was going to stop that.

"Some homecoming, huh?" Lara said. "'Welcome back. Oh, by the way, we're about to be attacked by an overwhelming force. Can you grab that rifle?'"

Gaby smiled. "Beats what's going on out there."

"You've been through a lot."

"Who hasn't?"

Lara nodded. She couldn't argue with that.

And Will was still out there…

"I was hoping you'd come by," Gaby said. "I wasn't sure if you wanted to see me after…earlier."

"I'm sorry about that. I reacted badly."

"I'm just glad you didn't shoot me and Danny."

They exchanged a brief smile, then Lara pointed at the open bathroom door.

"Claire," Gaby said.

"Mini you."

Gaby chuckled. "I guess we do kind of look alike."

"What's she singing?"

"I think that's a Taylor Swift song."

"I don't know who that is."

"Taylor Swift?"

"Yeah."

"She was a country singer, sang mostly about boys and breaking up and all that girlie stuff. Then she became a pop singer. Then…well, I don't know what she did after that. This happened."

Lara walked over and sat on the bed next to her. Gaby hadn't changed clothes since she arrived. She was still wearing the same cargo pants and long-sleeve shirt, clothes that would make other women look tomboyish or plain, but of course other women weren't Gaby.

"You should have seen me this afternoon," Gaby said. "I was wearing a dead man's uniform."

"Why in the world were you doing that?"

Gaby told her about posing as soldiers in order to get past the barricade at the Lake Dulcet exit.

"Oh," Lara said. She wondered how many of those "soldiers" were running around out there right now. More importantly, how many Will would have to elude *(kill)* in order to come back to her.

However many it takes, Will. You better come back to me.

"From what Carly told us in the dining room, it sounds like you have everything ready," Gaby said.

God, I hope she's right, Lara thought, but she said, "Will has a saying: No plan survives first contact with the enemy. I just hope I don't get everyone killed."

"We'll do fine. I was trained by two of the best, and you guys have been fighting for this island for a while now. We're going to give them a hell of a fight."

They didn't say anything for a while. Instead, they sat quietly and listened to Claire singing inside the shower. Gaby was right; the song was about a boy and heartbreak, and maybe a high school was involved somehow. They could make out Claire's figure behind the curtain, scrubbing herself down as heavy mist drifted through the open door.

"I told her there was a five-minute limit," Gaby sighed. "I think she's way past that."

"It's okay. Let her enjoy it." *Because it might be the last shower any of us gets for a while,* she thought about adding, but didn't. She said instead, "Then you should take one, too."

"I will. I have a lot to scrub off." She paused for a moment, before adding, "Thanks for keeping my room clean, by the way."

"Thank Carly. She did all the work."

Gaby looked toward her patio window. "What are the chances he's out there, you think?"

"Who?"

"Josh."

The question caught her off guard. It had never occurred to her that Josh would be out there right now, somewhere on the shoreline waiting for nightfall. Would Kate send him to do her dirty work? The Josh she knew was still eighteen, tall but gangly, even nerdy, and if she had to pick someone to lead a battle, he would have been the last person on her list. But according to Will and Gaby, that teenage boy was long gone, replaced by a very capable (and dangerous) ghoul collaborator. So who was to say what he was capable of now?

Adapt or perish. Maybe Josh has adapted, too.

"I don't know," Lara said. "Would they let him join in the attack?"

"The Josh I saw out there wouldn't be a part of the attack, Lara; he would be leading it."

"Josh?" She knew he had changed, but had he changed *that* much?

"He's gone, Lara."

"What do you mean?"

"He's gone. He's not a boy anymore. You can't think of him as the same boy who you met in Lancing. If you get the chance—if you see him tonight—don't hesitate. Shoot him, because he'll shoot you."

Lara was speechless for a moment. Finally, she said, "I guess it doesn't matter who leads the attack. One man in a soldier's uniform is the same as another."

Gaby looked over at her. "Just don't hesitate, Lara."

Lara nodded. "I won't." Then she stood up. "I'm going to need you tonight, Gaby."

"That's why I came back. You just tell me where you want me, and I'll be there."

"Meet me in the lobby in—" she glanced at her watch "—half an hour."

"Should I bring my gear?"

"No. And you won't need the M4, either. I'll have something

else for you."

Gaby nodded. "I'll be there."

Lara walked to the door.

"Lara," Gaby said.

She stopped and looked back.

"What about Will?" Gaby asked.

That's the question of the century. What about Will?

"He can take care of himself," Lara said. "Right now, we need to worry about us."

"Danny's convinced Kate's the one pulling the strings out there. Is she capable of something like that?"

"I don't know," Lara said. "Let's save that question for Will when he comes home. Until then, let's make sure he has someplace to come back to."

CHAPTER 17

GABY

THE ISLAND HAD changed. She didn't think it was possible it could look and feel so different since the last time she had walked along its white sandy beach or dipped her feet into the cool blue waters. But maybe it wasn't Song Island that had changed. Maybe it was her. She wasn't the same girl who had left this place. She had killed. More than once. If not for The Purge, the lives she had taken would have made her notorious.

The conversation with Lara hadn't really gone as planned, but in many ways it went better. She loved Lara. She hadn't realized that until they sat together and simply talked. They had both changed a lot, and maybe not all of it for the better. They had become survivors. They always had been, of course, but there was a difference between surviving and being *survivors*.

Was that a good thing? It was hard to say.

Once Claire finished showering, Gaby took her turn. She didn't linger too much. Five minutes, tops, standing underneath the scalding hot spray and letting it cleanse away the days on the road, the night slept in that crypt outside of Dunbar, and whatever remained of L15 and Josh's company.

Are you out there right now, Josh? Are you the one leading tonight's attack?

She didn't want to think about what would happen if she saw

him tonight. Josh in that uniform, with a rifle in his hands, running toward her. Could she do it? Could she shoot him the way she had told Lara to?

Stay away, Josh. Please stay away.

Claire was already gone by the time she came out of the shower. Gaby put on clean black cargo pants and socks, then pulled on an olive green long-sleeve sweater. She dressed silently while sneaking looks at the clock on the wall.

6:15 P.M.

The audible *clicking* of the second hand was like a grenade going off inside the quiet room. One of these days, the batteries were going to die and the hands would stop moving. That was life now. Sooner or later, everything just stopped.

She glanced at the patio window for the fifth time in as many minutes. The curtains were pulled halfway, revealing the falling night outside. Soon, very soon, it would be complete darkness. She should have been afraid, but she wasn't. Maybe it was being back home again, or the fact she was now surrounded by friends.

Tonight felt different somehow. She was calm. Amazingly so.

The lack of activity in the hallway outside was surprising, given how many people were now calling the hotel home. She made sure to close her door before heading up to the lobby with just her pack in one hand. She walked past two doors before stopping at the third.

She took a breath, then knocked on it.

"Come in," Nate called from the other side.

She opened the door and stepped inside.

He stood next to his bed, shirtless, with his back to her. His hair was wet, and fresh steam drifted out of the open bathroom door. His dirty clothes were in a pile on the floor, and Nate looked cleaner than she had ever seen him.

She smiled briefly, remembering the look Benny had given Nate back in the dining room. Benny had burst inside, not expecting to see her sitting next to Nate. The next few minutes had been incredibly uncomfortable, and Gaby felt miserable about not preparing either one of them for that moment.

I'm back in high school all over again, she remembered thinking.

Nate glanced over and gave her a wide smile. "You weren't kidding about this place. Your own room, a big soft bed, and working plumbing. I could definitely get used to all of this."

If we're still alive after tonight, she thought, but asked instead, "How was your reunion with Mary, Kendra, and the others?"

"It was good to see them again. A lot of questions, though." He pursed his lips. "I didn't know how to answer most of them."

"Mary must be especially happy to see you back."

Mary was the teenage girl who had been a part of Nate's group back when they were still out there on their own. The girl had stuck close to Nate the entire time, and Gaby used to feel a little guilty about Nate just leaving them behind to go with her. That guilt was compounded by what happened to him afterward.

"She was," he nodded. "I was happy to see her, too. They all look healthier than I've ever seen them. Coming here was a good thing."

Gaby wasn't so sure about that. She couldn't help but think about Claire, Milly, and Annie, and bringing them to a place that was about to be attacked. It must have shown on her face, because Nate gave her a reassuring look.

"We'll get through tonight," he said. "We'll be fine. You'll see."

He turned around and picked up a shirt from the bed. She was so used to seeing him with that stupid Mohawk that not to see it perched on top of his head still took some adjusting. She was staring at his head when her eyes fell down to his arms as he pulled the shirt on.

Teeth marks.

They covered both his arms, extending from the wrists to the shoulders blades. There were dozens of them, like tiny mazes crisscrossing his flesh, or poorly thought-out tattoos. Most looked healed, but some still looked fresh. *Too* fresh. She stared and couldn't look away, and couldn't stop herself from wondering where else they were on his body that she couldn't see at the moment.

Nate looked back and saw where she was staring. The look on

her face must have betrayed her thoughts, because he quickly grabbed a knitted black sweater and pulled it over the T-shirt.

"It looks worse than it really is," he said.

"Do they hurt?" she asked, feeling stupid as soon as the words blurted out of her mouth.

He didn't look offended, though. If anything, she had the impression he had been waiting for this conversation.

"Not anymore," he said. "In the beginning, yeah. Back at the pawnshop, when I was still conscious. I could feel their teeth breaking skin." He seemed to drift off a bit, maybe flashing back to that night. "But after a while, I blacked out. When I woke up, they told me that was how it usually worked. Once they put you under, you don't feel anything anymore."

"Usually?"

"Some of the guys had stories…"

"What kind of stories?"

"You know all those scary stories people tell about how some coma patients in hospitals are still awake when everyone else thinks they're asleep? But in reality they're trapped inside their bodies and can still see, hear, and feel everything? But they just can't move or talk? I think there's a medical term for it, but I can't think of it right now."

"Maybe Lara knows," she said absently.

"Probably. Anyways, some guys said they could still feel the ghouls drinking them when they were unconscious." He shook his head. "But I didn't, so I can't really say for sure either way."

"Then you woke up…"

"Yeah."

"I'm sorry, Nate," she said quietly.

"What for?" he said, smiling across the room at her. "You don't have anything to be sorry for, Gaby."

"You wouldn't have been there if it wasn't for me."

"Oh, come on. It's not like you forced me to. Or even asked me to. I volunteered, remember?"

"I know. Still…"

"Gaby," he said, and there was a forcefulness in his voice she hadn't heard before. "You didn't do this. Understand? Those things did. Everything else was my choice. Okay? You don't ever have to apologize for what happened to me. I don't blame you. I never did, and I never will."

She didn't know what to do or what to say, so she just did what felt right at the moment, and that was to walk silently to him. Nate opened his mouth to say something, but before he could, she slipped her arms around his neck and pulled him down and kissed him. His arms slipped anxiously around her waist, and he pulled her body to his and ground his mouth down against hers with a hunger that momentarily took her breath away.

They kissed for the longest time. Or maybe it was just a few seconds. It wasn't until she couldn't breathe anymore that she pulled slightly back, but she was still so close to him that she could feel his warm breath against her face. He was, she noticed, breathing harder than usual. Maybe even harder than her.

"You wanna see this wicked scar I have on my back?" he asked with a grin.

She gave him a confused look. "Why would I want to see that?"

"I dunno, but you saw the scars on my arms and I got this. I figured, scars must turn you on."

She shook her head. "They don't."

"Wow. Totally read that signal wrong, then." He glanced at his wall clock. "We still have a few minutes—"

"Not nearly enough for everything I want to do with you," she said, and pulled him down and kissed him again.

SHE SENT NATE to the lobby ahead of her to join the others while she made a detour to the infirmary first. Carly had given them a quick tour of the new rooms as they were walking through earlier, so Gaby didn't have any trouble finding it again. It was also close enough to the lobby that she could hear voices on the other end of the hallway. Muted conversations, part anxious and scared, but there was a determination among them that heartened her.

The only person in the infirmary was a blonde woman sitting on a stool at a counter, her back to Gaby. When she entered and knocked on the open door, the woman turned around and Gaby smiled at Zoe.

"Long time no see," Gaby said.

Zoe smiled back, which was something Gaby found amusing, since the last time they were in the same room, she had threatened to kill the other woman. More than once, actually.

"Gaby," Zoe said. "Welcome home."

"Glad to be back." She walked over and sat down on a stool. "You look pretty healthy. Will told me you were shot."

"Yeah. Word of advice? Don't get shot."

"Good advice." She looked around the room. "Not bad. Beats working out of a tent in the woods."

"I know, right? It only took the end of the world to get my very own medical practice. And on a tropical island, no less. I still don't know where they got those palm trees from, though."

"They were here when we showed up."

"That's what Lara said. This place was supposed to be a resort for the rich and famous. I bet they didn't expect it to become a refuge for humankind's last holdout."

"Wow. I never thought of it quite like that."

Zoe laughed. "What, too ominous?"

"Just a bit," she said, pinching her fingers together. "You're not going to the lobby for the big powwow?"

Zoe shook her head. "That's just for the badass warriors like you. The rest of us already got our marching orders. I'm just finishing up here before heading off. Lara's got it all figured out."

Gaby had seen the way Lara took control of the island, giving orders with the kind of authority she'd only seen Will exert.

You would be proud of her, Will. She's like you—only prettier.

"I spent most of this afternoon following Lara's orders," Zoe was saying. "She's got me running back and forth from the yacht."

She looked thoughtful, adding, "I can see why Will likes her so much. She's the female him."

Likes her? Will doesn't like Lara. He loves her. We should all hope for something close to that at least once in our lives.

"So," Zoe said, "what can I do for you? Or is this just a friendly visit?"

"I was hoping to stock up on something for tonight."

"What kind of something?"

"You have any painkillers you can spare?"

"Is it your nose?" Zoe leaned forward slightly. "Does it hurt? It looks like it was broken recently."

"It doesn't hurt anymore."

She thought about complaining to Zoe about her shoulder, which still bothered her if she sat around in one place for too long, but decided the occasional numbness wasn't worth mentioning.

She said instead, "I want to make sure I have something to fall back on if I need them. Maybe a field first-aid kit. Just in case."

"Just in case," Zoe repeated. "You sound like Lara."

Gaby smiled. "I'll take that as a compliment."

BY THE TIME she reached the lobby, the only people left were Danny and Lara. They were talking quietly next to a large granite table in the center of the room, which looked cavernous with just the two of them inside at the moment. There were extra gun belts, magazines, and two ammo cans on the table between them, along with a pair of M4s and shotguns that hadn't been claimed yet.

"Where is everyone?" Gaby asked. "I didn't know I was that late."

"You're not," Lara said. "Everyone's where they should be."

She looked at Lara, then Danny, and realized they had stayed behind on purpose. They were waiting for her.

"What's going on?" she asked.

Lara picked up one of the M4s. It looked like the one she had left behind in her room except for the long and slightly bulky scope mounted on top. She took it from Lara and turned it over under the harsh lobby lights.

"Night vision," Danny said. "You're going to need it. It doesn't have the range of the ACOG, but it'll do in a pinch."

"How many of these do we have?" Gaby asked.

"Not nearly enough," Lara said.

Danny held up his M4A1, the same rifle he had been carrying around ever since she had known him, though it had gone through plenty of fixes and replacement parts. It was also equipped with the same scope as hers.

"Just you and me, kid," he said. "Keo's going to have to make do with a laser pointer and NVD."

"NVD?"

"Night-vision device. Basically, goggles with glowing green beer cans for lens."

"The laser sounds cool."

"This is cooler."

"I feel so special."

"That's because we are special. Special snowflakes in an ocean of dripping crap."

"Oh, nice vision, Danny."

He grinned. "I'm here to serve."

"How's the leg?"

"How's the nose?"

"Still busted."

"There you go."

"Wise ass," she said. Then to Lara, "What about Nate?"

"Don't worry about your boyfriend," Danny said.

"Shut up, Danny."

Danny chuckled.

"Benny and Nate have everything they need," Lara said. "They'll be fine."

"So who's going to be in the Tower?" Gaby asked. "I thought Danny and I were the best shooters on the island."

"Long-range isn't going to get it done tonight, kid," Danny said. "We'll be on the beach. Up close and personal. When those little buggers show up and ring the doorbell, we'll be the ones to greet them. *With a face full of lead.*" He grinned. "I always wanted to say that. Did I get the tone right?"

"I got chills," Gaby said.

"Awesome."

"So how is this going to work?" Gaby said to Lara.

"I'll fill you in on the way over," Danny said.

He picked up an ammo pouch and tossed it to her. It was a lot bigger than the ones she was used to, with two slots already filled with two magazines each, for a total of four.

"Shove what you can carry into your pack," Danny said. "Just pretend you're a really well-armed pack mule."

She strapped on the pouch, then begin grabbing extra magazines for the Glock in her hip holster. "Silver bullets?"

"Nothing but," Danny said.

"Are we expecting ghouls tonight?"

"We're not expecting them, but we're not *not* expecting them."

"That doesn't make any sense."

"Of course it does. Think about it."

"I'd rather not." She sensed Lara watching her and looked over. "What's wrong?"

Lara smiled. "You've grown up."

She grinned back. "That's a good thing, right?"

"Tonight? Absolutely."

"What if they don't come tonight?"

"Everything points to it happening. I wish I was wrong. But they're coming."

Gaby glanced reflexively at the wall clock. 6:46 P.M.

"The funny part is, they know that we know they're coming, but they're coming anyway," Danny said. "If I was a betting man, I'd say they're a lot more scared of not attacking than they are of facing the Wrath of God, a.k.a. Danny and Gaby's Shoot-o-rama."

Kate. He's talking about Kate.

"Meet me outside when you're done getting all dolled up," Danny said. He slung his M4A1 and headed across the lobby, whistling as he went. He still had a noticeable limp, but he was either doing his best to hide it or the contraption on his leg was actually doing its job.

"Here," Lara said, handing Gaby an LED flashlight. "It's going to get really dark out there."

"No moonlight tonight?"

"That's not what I meant."

Gaby shoved the heavy Maglite into her pack, then slung it. "How long have you been thinking up tonight's plan?"

"Since noon. But I've been considering it for a while now. I call this Plan D."

"Plan D?"

"Will has his Plan Zs, but I never liked that name. It's too…"

"Last resort-ish?"

"Yeah."

They both chuckled.

"Plan D," Gaby nodded. "I like the sound of that. Not quite as last resort-ish."

"That's the idea."

"If that's Plan D, then what's Plan A?"

"You, Danny, and Keo," Lara said, patting her on the shoulder, "saving the island."

"Oh," Gaby said.

No pressure. No pressure at all.

◂━▪ ▪━▸

DANNY WAS WAITING for her on the raised front patio when she stepped outside the hotel. "We good?"

She nodded. "We're good."

"You ready to kick ass and ignore the whole taking names part?"

"Not so much."

"That's my girl."

She followed him down the steps and they continued along the cobblestone pathway toward the beach. The silence of the island, except for the steady and ever present hum of the lamps, was the first thing she noticed. That, and the blanket of darkness that had fallen around them. Instead of making her anxious, she felt growing excitement.

God help me, I'm ready for this.

There was no activity around them except for her and Danny's movements, as if the entire island had shut down. Which, she guessed, wasn't far from the truth. She looked behind her at the Tower, literally a beacon of light shining on the northeast cliff. Two shadowy figures moved around on the third floor.

"Where's Nate, Danny?" she asked.

"Don't worry about your boyfriend. He's doing his job."

He's not my boyfriend, she thought about saying, but it sounded too much like something a high school teenage girl would say, so she said instead, "Where are the girls? Claire and Milly and the others?"

"They're safe and sound and tucked away. Don't worry about them, either."

"What should I be worried about, then?"

"Shooting straight and reloading fast."

She grunted. "Thanks for the advice. You're full of pearls of wisdom tonight."

"I aimsta please."

"So what's the objective? Besides not dying, I mean."

"The objective tonight is to put enough hurt on them to convince them to back off."

"And if that doesn't work?"

"Well, that's what contingency plans are for, kid. Any more questions?"

"Yes." She glanced around them. "Where's that Keo guy? Lara said he was going to be on the beach with us."

"He's around."

"What's your opinion of him?"

"He's a merc."

"Merc?"

"Mercenary."

"I take it that's not a good thing."

"A year ago I would have said yes, but these days?" He shrugged. "Times change, pants go out of style, and everyone's suddenly wearing long johns again. Plus, Carly seems to like him." Then he added, with what sounded like a slight annoyance, "Just a tad too much, if you ask me."

They reached the corridor between the woods, with the smell of lake water wafting from the beach in front of them. It wasn't a full moon tonight, but there was enough to see with. Coupled with the solar-powered lamps that lined the island, it would be incredibly difficult to miss them from any part of the lake.

Men are coming. Men with guns.

So why am I so calm?

"Danny," Gaby said.

"What's up?"

"Are we really going to survive this?"

"I'd say the chances are pretty low, but hey, stranger things have happened. Like, say, the end of the world. Who saw that coming? But here we are."

She frowned. "That isn't very reassuring."

"I got a joke that'll take your mind off it. Wanna hear it?"

"No."

"A priest, a rabbit, and a horse walk into a bar," Danny said anyway. "The bartender sees them and exclaims, 'Whoa, whoa, didn't you read the sign outside? This is a No-Animals bar!' To which the priest harumphs, puts his fists on his hips, and indignantly replies, 'Animals? I'm not an animal, good sir!'"

"'Good sir'?"

"He's a priest. They talk old-timey like that."

"Since when?"

"Since forever. Now shaddup. You wanna listen to the rest of it or not?"

"Are you saying I have a choice?"

"No," Danny said, and continued. "So the bartender reaches under the counter and pulls out a shotgun..."

CHAPTER 18

KEO

I'M SO SCREWED.

Gillian was so going to kill him. If she was even still alive out there, and if he ever made it to her if she was. There were a lot of maybes. He really was just operating on faith, and had been for some time. Maybe he always knew it, but it took Lara trying to convince him—and herself—that her boyfriend was still alive to bring it home.

She wants to believe it. Badly. Just like I want to believe Gillian's still out there waiting for me.

We're both suckers.

Between the two of them, he was definitely the bigger sucker. After all, he was the one stuck on a doomed island. It didn't get any worse than that. It might have been different if he had a battalion of soldiers fighting with him. Or, hell, he would have settled for some seasoned mercs. But no, just kids and women and…more women. Way too many women. Maybe it was a sign from God that he'd end up surrounded by double X chromosomes. A really sick and perverted sign. He'd be angry about it if he actually believed in a higher power.

So screwed.

He had to admit, when it came to suicidal plans, Lara had him beat by a mile. His friend Norris would have had a heart attack if he'd heard what she was planning. Then again, Keo recognized his own shortcomings when it came to tactical decisions, so what did he know? Maybe this was the only way out. Could he have come up with something better? Probably not. Most of his ideas ended up with him nearly dying anyway.

The lights up and down the beach had buzzed to life by the time darkness enveloped the island in a nice thick blanket, and soon even the quiet hum of the lamps was drowned out by the *sloshing* of water against the sand. The wind was picking up, and a nice breeze washed over him. He was glad for the long-sleeve wool sweater he'd found at the hotel's lost-and-found room. Even the lake seemed to know something was about to happen as soon as night fell.

He heard their footsteps against the cobblestone pathway before someone called over, "Shouldn't you be hiding with the women and children?"

They looked like brother and sister with their blond hair, matching broken noses, and facial scars. The girl, Gaby, was gangly but obviously athletic, and actually looked comfortable with the M4 for a civilian. The gun belt sagged a bit against her narrow hips, mostly thanks to the heavy ammo pouches she was carrying.

"Apparently I'm neither women or children enough," Keo said.

"Coulda fooled me," the guy, Danny, said.

Keo smirked.

"See what I mean?" Danny said to the girl. "Mercs have no sense of humor. It's always shoot this, shoot that, and where's my money with them."

"Not all of us get to live off Uncle Sam's teats," Keo said. "Some of us actually have to work for a living."

"You good at keeping the lights on, Kia?"

"I've sent a few Army Rangers packing in my time."

"Oh ho, don't mess with this guy."

They walked over and stood next to him, and the three of them stared off at the darkening lake in silence for a moment. It wouldn't be long now until the shoreline in the distance became indistinguishable from the nothingness gathering beyond the lights of the island.

"Wind's picking up," Danny said.

"Is that a good or bad sign?" the girl asked.

"Depends…"

"On?"

"If you believe in good and bad signs. Me, I just pay attention to the ones that say 'Stop' and the ones with dresses on the door."

Gaby was focusing on the white yacht at the end of the piers. It looked like a sleeping whale waiting to be awakened, moving slightly against the waves. "What exactly are we going to do with that thing?"

"Part of Lara's Plan Z," Danny said.

"Plan D," the girl corrected him.

"Plan D?"

"Yeah. She says it sounds better than Plan Z. Less last resort-ish."

"Sure, if you want to take all the fun out of it." He looked over at Keo. "What about you, Karaoke, you prefer Plan Z or Plan D?"

"As long as it keeps me alive at the end of the night, I don't really give a shit," Keo said.

Danny chuckled. "Listen to this guy," he said, jerking a thumb at Keo. "He actually thinks we're going to survive tonight. Looks like someone wants the Captain Optimism title."

◀━━▌ ▐━━▶

AT EXACTLY 7:00 P.M., the earbud in his right ear, connected to the throat mic and Motorola radio clipped to a stripped-down assault vest, *clicked*, and he heard Lara's voice. "Stan, come in."

Stan was the Mexican electrician, who as far as Keo knew was at the power station on the western part of the island. "I'm in position," Stan said through the radio.

"It's seven," Lara said. "Do it."

"Shutting down the power in five, four, three, two…*one*."

Then it got dark.

Really, really dark.

The lamps that lined the beach and stretched out into the lake along with the three piers shut down one by one. Even though they were all solar-powered, the lighting system had a built-in manual power override, or so he'd been told. In a matter of seconds, the white sand and blue water of Beaufont Lake seemed to blink out of existence.

His heartbeat actually accelerated as he sat there in complete darkness, waiting for his eyes to adjust to the sudden shift. It had been so long since he found himself outside and exposed at night that for a very brief moment, Keo remembered what fear was.

It took about thirty seconds, but he'd be damned if it didn't feel more like thirty minutes before his vision finally adjusted to the new reality, and he could once again make out the waves lapping against the beach in front of him under the moonlight.

"*And so it begins*," Danny said in his right ear. Then, "Was that ominous enough?"

"I give it an eight out of ten," Gaby said through the comm.

"I was going for at least a nine."

"Better luck next time."

"Yeah, that's me. Better Luck Next Time Danny. That's what they called me in college, you know."

"What school did you go to?" someone else asked through the radio. A woman. It sounded like either Bonnie's little sister what's-her-name or one of the other women whose names he hadn't bothered to learn yet.

"Um, I don't know," Danny said.

"You don't know?" the woman said, slightly amused.

"Well, no one's ever had a follow-up question before."

"Shouldn't you have thought of one just in case?"

"Everyone's a critic."

"Hey, everyone, leave my boyfriend alone," someone else said. Keo recognized Carly, the redhead. "Don't listen to them, baby. Your jokes are awesome."

"Ah, thanks, babe. You're the bestest. Have I told you lately how much I love you?"

"Not yet, but the night's still young."

"I think I'm going to throw up," Gaby said.

Keo tuned them out, which was difficult because he was connected to the same channel as the entire island. After a while, their playful back and forth faded into the background and he was able to focus on…absolutely nothing.

He was sitting on the ground, his back pressed against a tree. The beach started less than a meter in front of him, and from his position he could see all of the piers, including the *Trident*, its white paint easily distinguishable in the darkness. Gaby was all the way on the other end of the beach, with the ex-Ranger somewhere in the middle.

Finally, Lara's voice cut through all the jokes that were still going back and forth. "Blaine, come in."

"Read you loud and clear," Blaine answered.

"Is he there with you?"

The "he" in question was Gage, the boat captain.

"In front of me now," Blaine said.

"Is he listening?" Lara asked.

"He's listening…"

"Good. If he does something you don't like—if it even *looks* like he might be thinking about doing something you won't like—I want you to put a bullet in his other kneecap."

"I hear you loud and clear." There was, Keo thought, almost giddiness in Blaine's voice when he answered.

No one likes you, Gage. That's what happens when you go around marauding at the end of the world, dipshit.

"All right, it's time for you guys to go," Lara said.

"Roger that," Blaine said. "We'll see you when we see you."

The *Trident* came alive, its whisper-quiet engine and 1,400 horsepower starting as a low whine before rising in volume. A moment later, its anchor rose out of the water like a metal serpent.

Keo hoped for their sake that whatever eyes the enemy had along the shorelines at the moment couldn't make out the boat against the now-darkened island despite the white paint. The fact that the luxury yacht had powered up without turning on any of its lights would help to keep it invisible from a distance.

The large vessel began moving, turning and sending waves crashing against the beach as it did so.

"Thar she goes," Danny said.

"How's he doing that without lights?" Gaby asked.

"I guess that's how he earned his captain's hat. The rest of us have to parallel park, but they have to navigate by total darkness."

"Are you just making that up?" Carly asked.

"Pretty much," Danny said.

Keo held the night-vision goggles up to his eyes in order to see the vessel more clearly. It was cautiously moving away from the island, the water under it churning, before it turned completely around with all the speed of a bloated metal whale. For a one-legged marauding asshole with no redeeming values, Gage was a hell of a boat captain, because the man was doing all of this without the benefit of a single spotlight on or off the vessel.

"He's wearing night-vision goggles," Lara said through the comm. "That's how he's able to pilot in the dark."

"I guess he's not that special after all," Danny said.

Keo could just make out Bonnie, the leggy ex-model, moving along the side of the main deck on the *Trident*. There was a third figure on the lower deck, but she had ducked inside as soon as the boat started moving. Probably Gwen, the short one with the impressive rack. He had yet to memorize everyone by name, and a part of him didn't want to know.

A *click* in his ear, and Gaby's voice. "Can't they still see the boat from shore?"

"Can you see it without your night vision?" Lara asked.

"Let me see…" A brief pause, then, "Barely."

"And you're closer. If we're lucky, they won't be able to see it from the shorelines even with night vision."

'If we're lucky,' Keo thought with a slight smile. *If you're lucky, someone will survive tonight. If you're unlucky, everyone will be dead, including me.*

Which sucks for all of us, but especially me.

"We should have painted the whole thing black," Danny was saying.

"There was no time," Lara said.

The *Trident* was turning, before disappearing completely around the western corner of the island. He could still hear the engine, but it was already fading.

"Seven-thirty," Lara said in his right ear. "If they're coming, it's going to be soon. Everyone buckle down for the night. No one goes anywhere unless I give the order."

"Sheesh, who died and made her boss?" Danny asked.

"Everyone," Carly said.

EIGHT O'CLOCK CAME and went, and nothing happened.

The chatter over the radio had since died down, with only the occasional updates between Lara and the others spread out across the island. Or, in the case of Blaine, off-island. Everyone who didn't have a gun and wasn't in position to shoot something had been given explicit instructions not to break into the radio channel unless absolutely necessary. Much to his surprise, they were actually obeying protocol. Keo wasn't used to civilians having that kind of discipline, but then he had to remind himself that everyone here had survived the end of the world. That, he guessed, took more than just dumb blind luck.

"Nate, come in," Lara said around 8:17 P.M.

"Nate here."

The kid who had just arrived on the island with Gaby and Danny was patrolling the northern cliffs, with Carrie and Jo (or was it one of the other girls?) moving around in the same general vicinity. The beach was the obvious target—it was wide and easily accessible—which was why he and two others equipped with night vision were watching it. But there was a chance the collaborators might risk scaling the cliffs, the way they had the last time the island came under attack.

"Anything on your end?" Lara asked.

"Nothing so far," Nate said. Keo could hear a slight wind in the background from Nate's side. He guessed the kid was very close to the cliff.

"Stay sharp, everyone."

"Will do," Nate said.

The other two women echoed him a second apart. He still couldn't tell if one of them was Jo.

"Danny," Lara said.

"Yes, milady," Danny said.

"How's it going down there?"

"No complaints. It's a real beach."

"Nice," Gaby said.

"Thanks, kid."

"Stay sharp," Lara said.

"Don't worry," Danny said. "I'm so sharp they used to call me Danny The Really Sharp Guy back in college."

"And what college would that be?" someone asked.

"Ah, man," Danny groaned.

NINE O'CLOCK CAME and went.

Then ten…

Click. "Maybe they're not coming after all," Carly said in his ear.

"Babe, I'm Captain Optimism here, remember?" Danny said. "I just wrestled the title back from Kazaam over there."

"Who?"

"Kazaam."

"I don't know who that is," Carly said.

"Shaquille O'Neal?"

"Okay, now you're just making it worse."

"Nineties movie. Shaquille O'Neal played a genie named Kazaam."

There was silence over the radio.

"You know who I'm talking about, don't you, Kablooey?" Danny asked.

"I don't watch a lot of movies, sorry," Keo said.

"Ah, you guys suck. Remind me never to invite any of you over to movie night."

"Promise?" Gaby said.

"That hurts. That really, really hurts."

"Hey, if you can't take the heat," Gaby started to say, when she stopped and said instead, "Danny."

"I see it," Danny said. "Karaoke, your ten o'clock."

Keo had no trouble making them out against the green phosphor of the night-vision goggles he had put on an hour ago. Lara had given him a first-generation device, which was not nearly as bright or clear as the third-generation he was used to working with back in his old job. It was good enough, though, to let him spot the bright circles of light—at least a dozen of them—moving in their direction.

They were spotlights at the front of a fleet of boats.

He clicked his radio's Push-To-Talk switch. "I see them."

"You have the better angle," Danny said. "What's the count?"

"Ten."

"That's more than last time. Looks like they're going to love us to death with sheer numbers."

"You guys must be really special."

"It's the special sauce. Everyone wants the special sauce."

"Ten boats?" Lara said through the radio. "Or ten spotlights, Keo?"

"Boats," Keo said. "Ten boats. Confirmed."

"Can you see what kind of boats?"

"Not a chance. Give them ten more minutes."

"Benny, Carly?" Lara said.

"Keo's right," Carly said through the radio. Carly was in the Tower with Benny, using night-vision binoculars to keep an eye on the surrounding lake. "I see ten separate lights moving from the southeast shoreline. They're launching from the old marina."

"That doesn't make sense," Lara said. "They have the entire lake to launch from. Why the marina?"

"Crazy kids be doing crazy things," Danny said.

"You think it's a trick?" Gaby asked.

Lara didn't answer right away. After awhile, she said, "It doesn't matter. What matters is where they're headed. Nate, Carrie, and Jo, report in."

"I don't see anything back here," Carrie said.

"Nothing here, either," Jo said. "I can't hear a single engine or see anything moving out there."

"Confirming the big fat nothing," Nate said. "It looks like they're going to hit the beach straight on, just like you said." Then, sounding slightly anxious, "I'm heading over there now."

"No, stay where you are," Lara said.

"I'll be more useful down there."

"Nate, I need everyone exactly where I put them. That's an order."

"There's nothing back here," Nate said. "You were right. They're going to assault the beach. That's where I should be."

"Stay where you are."

"I'm coming—"

"Nate," Gaby said, "do what Lara says. We'll be fine over here."

"I can be more useful down there," Nate said.

"Please, hold your position. Lara knows what she's doing."

"Gaby…"

"Nate," the girl said. There was a surprising hardness to her voice. "Please, stay where you are. We'll be fine down here."

There was a brief pause, then Nate said, "Roger that."

Keo had to admit, he was impressed with the girl. He didn't know a lot of nineteen-year-olds who had that kind of control over not just her emotions, but others as well. Nate might as well be putty in her hands.

"Blaine, Bonnie," Lara said through the comm. "What do you see?"

"Confirming that everything's clear back here," Blaine said.

"Night vision?"

"Yeah, and still nothing."

"Ditto for me," Bonnie added. "You were right, Lara. They're going to attack the beach with everything they have."

"Weekend warriors," Danny snorted. "These yahoos wouldn't know a sound tactical plan if it bit them on their keisters."

"Everyone maintain your positions," Lara said. "Everyone has a job to do, so *do your part.*"

She sounded firm and in control. To listen to her, Keo could almost believe she wasn't scared shitless at this very moment. Of course, he knew better, but she was doing exactly what she needed to—giving off the aura of confidence that the others needed to hear. Not bad for a third-year medical student.

"Lock and load, boys and girls," Danny said. "Shoot first, shoot straight, and shoot often. And if all else fails, shoot some more."

"You practiced that one, too, Danny?" Gaby asked.

"Yeah. How'd I do?"

"I'll give it an eight."

"Sweet, just two short of perfection," Danny said.

THE HECKLER & KOCH MP5SD had been a lifesaver, but right now it wasn't going to do him a lot of good until the bad guys actually stepped foot on the sand.

Oh, look who's calling other people 'bad guys' now. My, my, how times have changed.

He slung the submachine gun and slid it behind his back and picked up the M4 leaning against the tree next to him. He patted the ammo pouch along his left hip to make sure it was still there—six mags in all, loaded with silver bullets. Not that he was going to need anything that special on the people coming in the boats now.

Better safe than sorry, I guess. Seems to be the island's other motto, right after 'just in case.'

He slipped the night-vision goggles back on and moved closer toward the tree line until he was less than a yard away. In his dark clothes, he would be completely invisible (or pretty damn close) even if the men on the approaching boats had their own night-vision gear. Which, of course, they did. He remembered seeing them when they were prepping a few days ago back at the staging area. Even so, the tree line would provide him plenty of cover. That was his one and only advantage when the soldiers stormed the beach.

Should have left when you had the chance, pal. Live and learn.

Finally, after what seemed like forever, the sound of the first boat motor reached him. It had taken them a while because they weren't moving very fast. He guessed the fact that the island was pitch dark was the reason for their cautious approach. That, or they were dragging it out, dreading what awaited them. So maybe they were smarter than he gave them credit for.

A *click* in his right ear, followed by Danny's voice. "Hey, Keo."

"Yeah," Keo said. He didn't bother whispering. There was no point. The enemy was still too far away and the closest person to him was Danny, further down the beach.

"Carly tells me you're on your way to see a girl in Texas."

"Uh huh."

"How's that going?"

"About as well as you and this island."

Danny chuckled. "That good, huh?"

"Yup."

The boats had begun to spread out, which signaled they intended to hit the entire length of the beach at the same time instead of concentrating their forces into one spot. Too bad, because he would have loved to see what ten boats landing a few yards apart would have looked like, especially while he, Danny, and Gaby were pouring as much lead as they could manage at them.

"You're all right, for a merc," Danny was saying.

"You're not bad, for a soldier."

"You don't like soldiers?"

"Never had much use for them."

"Oh, I don't believe that. I bet it goes deeper. Parental involvement, perhaps?"

Keo grinned. "I don't know what you're talking about, grunt."

"Heh heh, I knew it. What's the matter, the old man rode you too hard?"

"Something like that."

"You should have rode him back. Old people hate it when you ride 'em like a horsey."

"Yeah, I should have thought of that."

Watching the boats moving against the phosphorous green of his night vision was a surreal experience. The way the spotlights were bouncing up and down as the vessels picked up speed (and the rumble of motors gaining in intensity as a result) made him think of a legion of BMX bikers doing stunts as they charged.

"You wanna hear a joke?" Danny was asking.

"No," Keo said.

"So this couple are out on a date and the guy realizes he's out of condoms. He decides to make a pit stop at a grocery store and runs inside…"

"Hey, Danny," Gaby said.

"What's up, kid?"

"I'll give you a buck if you shut up."

"Tough beach," Danny said.

PARTY BOATS, KEO thought when the first vessel emerged out of the black canvas like some demon from the pits of hell.

It was white and long, with red-hot rod flames along the sides, and flat. The driver sat in the middle, guiding the steering wheel while two men crouched at the stern and two more manned the bow. They were wearing battle gear, complete with ballistic Kevlar helmets and knee and elbow pads. Keo could almost see their faces constricted into tight grimaces as they held onto the speeding boat as it burst out of the water. Like him, they were all wearing night-vision goggles, the long lens bobbing up and down like extra appendages.

Hot rod was the first boat to hit the beach fifty meters in front of him, its sharp front hull digging a trench as it was driven forward by a roaring motor. The driver was battling with the steering wheel, looking almost spastic, while the passengers hung on to keep from being thrown off by the erratic vessel. When they were closer, he saw that the two up front were actually attached to the boat by coiled cables clipped to their belts. Flurries of sand arced through the air as the propellers came into contact with the beach.

Still on one knee, Keo lifted the M4 and switched on the laser pointer underneath the barrel. A red beam pierced the darkness, clearly visible through the green of his NVG. Keo stood up and focused on the boat that had made landfall first; it just happened to be directly in front of him. He watched the two on the bow struggling furiously to free themselves from the cables. One of them finally got himself unattached and was standing up when Keo settled the half-inch red dot on the man's chest and put two rounds into him. Despite being unsuppressed, unlike his MP5SD, both shots were barely audible against the raging storm of ten boat motors roaring in his ears at the same time.

The dead man slumped off the boat and his partner, seeing his comrade go down, decided to give up trying to manually detach himself and began ramming the butt of his rifle into the hook that held him hostage.

Losing your cool during the heat of battle is a good way to die, pal.

Keo shot him in the right thigh, then squeezed off two more rounds even as the man was going down. He was pretty sure he hit the guy at least one more time. Fifty meters should have been a difficult shot for him, even with the long-range ability of a rifle, but the red laser dot made it a cheat. Not that he spent more than a nanosecond giving a damn.

The two on the stern had already decoupled themselves and were hopping off the boat, even as more vessels shot out of the water and made landfall to the left and right of them. More sand arced into the air, and the roar of the motors became deafening.

Meanwhile, the driver of the hot rod had ducked his head behind the steering wheel, and the only thing Keo could make out from him was the twin protruding lens of his NVG over the console. Keo ignored the hidden man and turned his attention to the two running up the beach, one of them struggling to maintain control of his rifle while the other had lost his night vision along the way.

They weren't the only two trudging their way forward, their heavy boots and equipment causing them to sink into the soft beach, further slowing them down. They should have considered that when they were gearing up for the attack. He thought of something the British used to say called the 7 Ps: Proper Planning and Preparation Prevents Piss Poor Performance.

More boats were landing one by one now, hitting the long stretch of sand many meters apart. He wondered if that was part of the plan or a byproduct of the drivers trying not to crash into each other in the darkness.

As soon as he fired his first shot, Danny and Gaby immediately joined in, pouring bullets into the surging mass of black-clad bodies trying to jump off their vessels up and down the beach. The *pop-pop-pop* of automatic gunfire clashed with the continuous whirl of machinery, creating an odd melody that was painfully out of tune.

They had plenty of targets to choose from. Too many, in fact. The surging men looked like ants trudging and falling and stumbling as they attempted to flee from the open. They might not have any combat experience, but he couldn't fault their tactical awareness. They knew just enough to understand that standing on the beach right now was a death sentence. Most of them hadn't even returned fire, probably because they had no idea where he or Danny and Gaby were.

Keo flicked the fire selector on his M4 to full-auto and emptied the remaining magazine into the group of black-clad figures directly in front of him. They were already angling left toward the opening in the woods that led to the hotel grounds. Most of the soldiers were irresistibly drawn to it like moths to the flame, while only a few stayed behind to use the beached boats as cover and to return fire into the woods.

He didn't know how many had already fallen, and he didn't bother counting. He just knew that men were going down as he oscillated his fire from left to right, shearing the leaves and branches that had kept him hidden until now. The smell of burning foliage filled his nostrils and Keo was still smelling it as he emptied his weapon.

He hustled to his right, ejecting the magazine and slamming in a new one as he went.

A group of charging men was returning fire. They didn't know where he was exactly inside the tree line, but even an idiot could tell his general vicinity after his last barrage. And that was where they were concentrating their fire now. Fortunately he wasn't there anymore, and was still moving right, continuing to use the woods to his advantage.

He took a step closer toward the beach, stopping only when he could see out again, and went down on one knee, ignoring the *zip-zip-zip* of bullets slamming into the section of the woods where he had been just seconds ago. He was now a good twenty meters from his last position and the soldiers were still stuck in no-man's land. The group of battle-dressed figures that had unleashed on him was reloading, while others continued running toward the passageway.

Fallen black-clad bodies zig-zagged the length of the beach, stretching from the parked boats to the trees. That was a sign Danny and Gaby were doing their part. Not that he expected any less from the soldier, though the girl continued to be a revelation. The *pop-pop-pop* of automatic gunfire continued back and forth, still smashing against the roar of motors that had been left unattended as their drivers darted for safety.

The group that had returned fire on his last position had just finished reloading when Keo stepped outside of the trees and onto the beach, opening up on them. He felt the sand sinking under his boots as he pulled the trigger. He was so close to them that he didn't even need to use the red dot this time; he just kept the trigger depressed until all four men had fallen down and stopped moving.

Keo quickly searched for more targets, but there were none to be found. The rest had already made it into the opening at the center of the beach and were on their way to the hotel grounds right this moment.

How many had gotten through? He couldn't tell. If there were at least four per boat (five in some), that meant over forty soldiers, easily. And he was pretty damn sure he didn't see forty-plus bodies lying on the beach at the moment.

He tossed the carbine, then unslung the MP5SD. The familiar feel of the submachine gun immediately reassured him, and Keo took hurried steps back into the tree line where he wouldn't be exposed. He hadn't gotten completely back inside cover when he heard the hellacious explosion of gunfire coming from the cobblestone pathway to his right.

It seemed to go on forever, and Keo found himself standing still and listening, wondering how many were dead or dying. That would depend on how many had managed to survive the beach.

Ten? Twenty?

A lot.

He looked back at the bodies lying under the moonlight. Too many to count. Some were his, some were Danny's, some were Gaby's. It wasn't anything he hadn't seen before. Soldiers died— often. Even weekend warriors. And these poor bastards were only shot with small-arms fire. It beat having an arm or leg amputated by a large-caliber round from close range. He'd seen plenty of that, too.

You pick up a gun, this is what happens. Sooner or later, someone has a bigger gun, or has a better fighting position. Either way, live by the gun, die by the gun.

One of these days, that same thing would happen to him. Keo was fully prepared for it. He had been ready, even before the world ended. Surviving when so many had perished that first night had been a miraculous event. It was akin to making it through the Rapture. He was pretty sure someone, somewhere, had screwed up.

Keo looked back at the beach, past the unmoving figures and at the boats. Almost all of the motors had shut down except for a couple still running, still sending streams of sand and water into the air behind them.

He could take one of those boats and leave right now, take his chances back at the channel...again. *(Second time's the charm, right?)* Would the sniper still be there? What about the men in the Jeep? Or was everybody already here, storming the beach? It made sense for the collaborators to throw everyone at them at the same time. That's what he would have done—

BOOM!

The island shook under his boots and continued for at least two full seconds before settling again.

An explosion. Not a big one, judging by the short duration of the aftershock, but big enough for him to hear it over the continued churning of the few remaining motors on the beach.

Keo looked back into the woods, toward the northwest part of the island. He knew the sound (and feel) of an explosive device going off when he heard one, even from a distance.

"What was that?" a voice gasped in his right ear. *Lara.* "Anyone know what that was or where it came from? Someone answer me!"

No one answered for the longest time. Or maybe it just seemed like a long time. It could have been only a few seconds.

Keo looked back at the boats again. Nine of the vessels had gone silent, leaving a lone one to continue spinning sand into the air. It was a nice white bass fishing boat, just big enough to take him wherever he wanted to go.

So what was he waiting for?

He sighed, turned around, and waded through a sea of black and green and shadows, dodging trees and pushing his way north as fast as he could. He was carrying a noticeably lighter load now without the M4 and most of its ammo. The MP5SD was gripped tightly in front of him, and he used it to bat at branches in his path.

"The shack!" Carly finally shouted through the radio. "It's the shack!"

"Shack?" someone else said. Male. It sounded like Nate, but it was hard to tell because his heart was beating too hard against his chest. "What shack?"

"The one at the power station!" Carly shouted. "It's open! Lara, the shack's open!"

CHAPTER 19

JOSH

"IT'S DARK; I think they turned off the lights," Travis said, his voice partially obscured by the harsh sound of wind rushing against him. "I can't see shit."

"It's an island," Josh said, his own voice slightly muffled by the gas mask over his face. "It's not going to start moving now. Just keep going straight and you'll run into it eventually. Besides, that's why I ordered everyone to pack night-vision goggles."

"Have you ever assaulted an island with night vision?"

"Just get the job done," Josh said, slightly irritated.

Travis might have laughed at the other end of the radio. Or snickered. It was a little difficult to tell, because sounds echoed inside the close confines of the tunnel.

"This is a stupid plan," Travis said.

That's your part of the plan, but it's not the plan.

"Keep going," he said. "We're taking Song Island tonight—" *even if I have to sacrifice you to do it* "—because that's what she wants."

That did it. Just mentioning her was enough to shut Travis up.

Next to him, Sonia shifted her legs again, the soft *plopping* sound of her boots moving against the puddles of water that had settled and still continued to *drip-drip-drip* lazily from the ceiling above them. It wasn't nearly as bad as when they were moving through the length of the tunnel about an hour ago. He was glad he was wearing combat boots because there was no telling what types of infestation had taken root inside the concrete structure ever since Will and the others sealed it up months ago. Or thought they had, anyway.

The gas mask he was wearing helped, the breathing apparatus filtering out all the suffocating stink of the long tube that connected the shoreline with Song Island, eventually opening up onto a large shack next to the power station.

Josh glanced down at his watch and was glad it had glow-in-the-dark hands. Travis and the boats had just started off from the marina a few minutes ago. It would take them a while moving at their current speed to reach their destination. Making them take off from the familiar marina was on purpose; Josh wanted the island to see them coming, to draw all their attention.

"How long?" Sonia called up the stairs.

"Five minutes!" a voice shouted back down at them.

Josh could see and feel the staccato glow of the cutting torches working their way against the steel shack door above the stairs right now. At one point, the people responsible for constructing Song Island had used the tunnel to bring supplies over from the mainland, transporting them by trucks to this cavernous room that looked like some kind of tomb at the moment, even with strategically placed LED portable lamps to light their way. The door was going to be a tight fit, and he would have preferred to use the wider cargo elevators, but those weren't going to work without any power available down here. No, it would have to be the stairs and the shack.

He spent the next few minutes glancing at the gas-masked faces standing, sitting, or leaning against the thick walls around him. Thirty. That was how many heavily armed soldiers in battle gear he had brought with him through the tunnel, unnoticed by whoever was in the Tower at the time.

It hadn't been easy, but once darkness fell and the island, predictably, went into action to get ready for the impending attack on the beach, Josh's people were able to sneak over to the tunnel entrance and remove just enough of the rubble to gain entry. Under the cover of night, and wearing all-black while carrying nothing that would give them away against the blackness, they had made the almost mile-long walk from their vehicles to the tunnel entrance. Josh had been counting on whoever was in the Tower tonight being accustomed to movement on land by Kate's creatures as soon as darkness fell. Removing the debris took time, but he had plenty of men to make short work of the necessary labor.

After that, it was a matter of jogging through the tunnel that extended under Beaufont Lake like an unused limb. The thought of moving under the large body of water had been unnerving at first, but that was just the side effect of having once "died" out here. It had been one of his worst experiences, and the idea of being trapped down here was almost paralyzing. But all he had to do was remind himself that the others were watching him, waiting for signs of weakness, and he was able to power through.

Drip-drip-drip.

Most of the men gathered round him looked anxious, and some were clearly terrified. They tried to hide it by looking away or chatting quietly among themselves, but he could hear the quivering in their voices even behind their gas masks. They had every right to be afraid. Even if their approach to the tunnel entrance had been discovered, Josh would have still stuck to the plan. He had brought plenty of men for just that possibility. Even if every gun on Song Island was concentrated outside the power station at the moment, Josh would have ordered these men out there anyway.

And they would have gone through with it, because *she* had given the order through him, and these men had sold their souls. Guns were scary, but a legion of mangled teeth coming at you relentlessly, night after night, was more terrifying.

Josh didn't blame them. He remembered those nights before he saw the light and stopped fighting the inevitable. This wasn't a war, as Will falsely believed; this was conquest. It was already over, and only the stubborn kept pretending it wasn't.

Except for Sonia and a few others crouched nearby, Josh didn't know the names of most of these people he was leading at the moment. If not for the name tags, he wouldn't be able to tell one man from another, which, Josh had found, was a good idea. What was the point of memorizing the names of dead men?

What's that old saying? Can't make an omelet without breaking a few eggs. Or killing a few guys.

Okay, a lot of guys.

He remembered the looks on their faces when he told them their roles in the attack. Half of them wanted to curse him, and the other half wanted to shoot him right then and there. Travis, he was certain, wanted to do both.

But they did neither of those things. Because they knew who Josh was. He was one of the chosen ones. To disobey him was to disobey the ghouls. To disobey *her*.

"*Take the island,*" Kate had said to him last night in his dream (*nightmare?*).

"*I will,*" he had replied.

"*Whatever it takes,*" she had said, "*Song Island has to fall. It's become a symbol. It has to fall at all costs.*"

But not at the cost of Gaby's life, Josh thought to himself now.

Drip-drip-drip.

She was on the island right now. His Gaby. He knew it with absolute certainly, even if he had no visual confirmation. She would have returned with Danny and the new arrivals from earlier, all because Mason had screwed him over and was solely concentrating on capturing Will. Josh guess he couldn't really blame the guy. Mason was doing Kate's bidding, just like he was. Just like they all were. At the end of the day, Kate's needs were the only things that mattered.

He looked back at Sonia. "How much longer?"

She leaned into the stairwell and glanced up. "How much longer?"

"Almost done!" a voice shouted back down.

"Almost there," she repeated to him.

Josh nodded and turned back to the gathered men. They had heard, too, and the ones who were sitting had stood and the ones leaning were straightening. Electricity filled the room, emanating from the almost three dozen bodies squeezed into the tunnel. They were ready, anxious, and terrified at the same time.

Drip-drip-drip.

"Take the hotel," Josh said to them. He wanted to be loud and commanding, but his words came out flat and echo-y to his own ears. He gathered himself and continued. "That's your job. That's your only job. Once the hotel falls, the island will follow. Got it?"

Some nodded, but others were too scared to do much besides fumble with their rifles or equipment in an attempt to stop their hands from shaking. Josh didn't quite understand why he was feeling so calm. Like these men, he'd never (willingly or not) gone into a war zone before, which was what he was about to do right now.

And yet, and yet...

I'm one of the chosen ones. Whatever happens, I'll be fine. Because it's fate. Just like Gaby and me. We belong together.

Always. Forever.

"What about them?" one of the men said. He was looking behind them at the wide half-circle entrance that connected the large room they were inside now with the rest of the tunnel.

He couldn't see them, because they were keeping their distance just as she had ordered them to. He wasn't quite sure how many were back there, invisible in the darkness beyond the ring of LED lamps spread out across the large room, but there had to be hundreds, maybe more. They had entered the tunnel only after Josh's people had begun moving through the over-half-mile-long concrete structure.

Kate's ghouls. Or were they his?

Maybe ours...

Josh pulled the gas mask off and breathed in the stench. It reeked in here, made worse with the creatures nearby. One of them was bad, but so many crowded into one room without ventilation was unbearable. He pushed through the smell and sucked in a large lungful of the stale air anyway.

"Forget about them," he said, hoping the confidence came

through in his voice that time. He couldn't be sure if he had succeeded, though a couple of the men did look comforted, even if he could only see their eyes behind their gas masks. "They're only here as a last resort—not that we'll need them. We'll get this done, men. Everyone just do your jobs, and this will be over in a few hours."

He must have been pretty convincing, because that seemed to placate most of the men; there might have been one or two (or a dozen) that weren't moved. It was less about him and more about being so close to the creatures gathered en masse behind them. They might not have been able to see those black eyes, but their stink…

Josh slipped the gas mask back on and was grateful for the filtered air that flowed to his lungs.

"They're done," Sonia said.

Footsteps echoed as two men wearing welding masks, rivers of sweat dripping off their faces and clothes, trudged down the stairs carrying heavy portable equipment, the two cylinders inside *clinking* with every step. They looked exhausted and were leading two more men hauling a thick metal plate between them. The door. Or a part of it that had been cut free. It must have been extremely heavy by the way the men's eyes were clenched behind their gas masks.

Josh and Sonia stepped aside to let them exit the stairwell. Then he leaned inside and glanced up, not that he could see much of anything even with the portable LED lamps sitting at the very top step.

After Will and Danny closed and then locked the shack, they had sealed it with two layers of brick and mortar. That was why Josh couldn't see anything now, even with the hole where the door used to be.

"You ready?" Sonia said to someone behind him.

Hank and two others walked over to his position. They were carrying backpacks, and while Hank seemed comfortable with the items, the other two couldn't hide their nervousness. It almost looked as if they might both bolt at any second.

"Relax," Hank said. "Nothing's going to blow up unless I want them to."

That didn't make the other two relax at all. Josh stood aside to let the three men go up the steps.

Sonia leaned closer to him. "What's in those bags?"

"C4," Josh said.

"Explosives?"

"Uh huh."

"Should we, uh, move farther away?"

"I think that's a good idea," Josh nodded.

He took a couple of steps back, and Sonia did the same. They stopped, looked toward the stairs, then at each other, before taking another half dozen more steps backward.

Around them, the other black-clad figures tried to move as far away from the stairwell as they could, though of course there weren't a whole lot of places for them to go. The only possible way to retreat further was the adjoining tunnel, and it was already occupied.

HE KNEW TRAVIS and the others had finally landed on the beach when the *pop-pop-pop* of automatic gunfire penetrated the thick walls around him. The gunshots sounded wet and echo-y, like everything else around him at the moment.

He was heartened that the battle seemed to be getting louder, which was a sure sign Travis (if he was even still alive) and the men were pushing inward, just as planned. Josh didn't know how many guns Lara would have on the beach waiting for them, but he knew she would have everyone she could afford over there right now.

That's it, Lara. Concentrate on the beach. Just like I want you to.

Where else was he going to land people, after all? Was he going to make them climb up the cliffs? That wasn't going to work. Besides the fact that his soldiers weren't really soldiers, they had seen armed guards walking around everywhere. Not to mention in the Tower. They could see every damn thing from that building. Besides, Lara and Danny would remember that Karen had sneaked onto the island that way the first time, and they'd be ready for it.

No. It had to be the beach. It was the most obvious access point to the island. Everyone knew it; there was no point in getting cute. That knowledge, more than anything, was why he was down here at the moment.

Josh had an idea about how things were going up there, but he hadn't been in contact with Travis in almost twenty minutes. He didn't really need to know all the details anyway. The men had their orders: Attack the island and take the hotel. What could be more simple than that? Did he really expect them to reach the hotel? Not really. Even without Will, there was still Danny. The guy was an ex-Army Ranger. He would know how to coordinate a proper defense. With enough people and enough rifles, you could do a lot of damage. Even an idiot could fire a gun.

Josh was crouched next to Sonia, with Hank's large form in front of them. The older man, a former demolitions expert in his past life, had his gas mask perched on top of his head and was wrestling with a thin, bright-yellow plastic rope that snaked all the way around the stairway entrance ten yards in front of him. The detonation cord. The rest of the line was connected to a six-inch-long tube. Josh had expected something more dangerous looking given what was on the other end of the wiring, but apparently all you needed to set off C4 was something that looked like a Roman candle.

Finding Hank among the soldiers had been serendipitous. Locating the C4 had been more troublesome, but with the army depots open to them, all it took was some searching. Fortunately for Josh, he had plenty of manpower to throw into the simple job.

When he was finished, Hank threw a quick look over his shoulder. His bright red beard and hair stood out even in the semidarkness. "Better cover your ears. It's gonna get real loud in here."

Josh took out the earplugs Hank had given him earlier and slipped them on. Sonia did likewise. The rest of the men had to make do with pressing their hands over their ears. Some were curling up into a ball on the floor as if that would protect them if Hank misjudged and the ceiling caved in on them.

He glanced up. The entire room was made of concrete, and the faded gray looked surreal against the LED lights. What if the room actually caved in on him? After all, it had been a while since Hank blew something up, and maybe his skills had gotten rusty?

That last thought, more than anything, made Josh shiver slightly.

"You okay?" Sonia said quietly next to him. She had said it just low enough that the others *(hopefully)* couldn't hear.

Josh nodded back. Then, to Hank in front of him, "Are you sure this is safe?"

"Should be," Hank said. The man sounded just a bit too glib for Josh's tastes. "I put just enough to blow through the walls."

"'Should be'?" Sonia said.

"You've done this before, right?" Josh asked.

"Of course," Hank said, sounding almost offended. "I used to do this for a living, remember?" He squinted at Josh in the semidarkness, his heavily lined face covered in sweat and grime. "You want me to do this or not? It's up to you, kid. You're the boss. You want me to shut this down?"

Josh stared back at him.

I am the boss.

He saw the challenge in Hank's eyes. It was the same look all the others gave him whenever he told them to do something. They despised the idea that a nineteen-year-old "kid" was leading them, giving orders. They couldn't stomach that he was chosen and they were not, even though, like him, they had all sold their souls to the ghouls.

But he had done it for Gaby. In order to save her and to ensure their future.

I'm the boss. I'm in control.

"No," Josh said, staring back at Hank. "Do it."

"You're the boss," Hank said.

You're damn right I am.

Hank slipped the gas mask back down over his face, while Sonia slid closer until she brushed up against Josh. He didn't know if she'd sought out the contact or if it was an accident. Not that he minded. He enjoyed the warmth of her closeness.

"Fire in the hole!" Hank shouted, just before there was a soft *click*.

Almost instantaneously, there was a loud, crashing *BOOM!*

The walls and floor and even the ceiling shook, and continued to shake for what seemed like an eternity. Despite the earplugs, the explosion was earsplitting in the close confines of the tunnel, and he actually flinched even though he knew it was coming. Thank God it was just dark enough and everyone was probably too busy keeping their heads down to notice his response.

Pek-pek-pek as debris trickled down the stairs in front of him, followed by a thick cloud of dust—red and white from the brick and mortar—that plumed out of the stairwell opening like some kind of smog monster. Josh snapped his eyes shut, expecting to be hit full in the face by the spreading aftermath, but of course he didn't have to because the gas mask protected him.

He continued to breathe normally, even though men were coughing erratically around him. Sonia had moved even closer, and he fought the urge to wrap one arm around her slim body to keep her safe.

He thought about Gaby instead.

I'm doing this for you. Everything I've done, it's for you. Please be safe up there. If anything happens to you, all of this will be for nothing.

He summoned all the courage he had and stood up in the swirling smoke. "Go!" he shouted. "Get your asses moving now! Move move move!"

To his surprise, they burst into action. Maybe he was more convincing than he gave himself credit for. Or maybe they were too shocked and disoriented and were looking for the first voice to give them orders, and it just so happened to be him. Or maybe, finally, they recognized his authority and were reacting accordingly.

I'm the boss. I'm in control.

They ran past him and up the stairs, boots *crunching* debris as they went. It was a long stream of black-suited figures, one after another, and for what seemed like forever, Josh stood tall and proud and watched them go.

"Take the hotel first!" he shouted after his men (his soldiers!). "Take the hotel, and the island will fall!"

CHAPTER 20

LARA

"IT'S OKAY TO be nervous. When they come, just shoot straight. Don't be afraid of friendly fire. No one we know will be coming up this path. It'll just be the bad guys. Okay?"

Stan nodded and tried to smile back at her. She could just barely make him out on the other side, with just the moonlight to keep the both of them from standing completely in darkness. He was much older than her and could have been her father, and she wondered if he found the idea of her attempting to comfort him just as absurd as she did.

She was crouched next to some trees and listening to the sound of boat motors getting closer. It seemed as if they had been coming for hours now. What was taking them so long?

Be careful what you wish for.

It wouldn't be long now before heavily armed men began rushing up the beach in an attempt to kill her and everyone on the island. It was going to be bloody. Even more so than the last time. And back then she had Will, and there weren't nearly as many men coming.

Ten boats. At least four men to a boat. At least.

How were they going to kill so many? And could they really go through with this? Could she? The idea of spilling so much blood just to keep the island should have horrified her, but it didn't. That, more than anything, made her hands tremble so much she had to rub them against her pants just to give them something to do.

This wasn't what she had envisioned doing with the rest of her life. Not that she had any choice in the matter. The decisions had been made for her. Out there. By Kate.

Where did you get so many men willing to die for you, Kate? Was this the plan all along? Make us kill each other?

She pushed those useless thoughts away and focused on the here and now. It didn't matter where these men came from or who they were. They were coming fast and armed and they had only one goal, and she couldn't allow that. Not with everyone's lives at stake. Carly, Vera, Elise, and all the poor souls who had come here hoping for a new start.

As afraid as she was about what was about to happen, Lara was also angry. More than that, she was pissed off. She wondered if this was how Will felt whenever he went into battle. No, probably not. Will was always pragmatic. He wouldn't really look at the men coming on boats now as anything but obstacles to overcome.

You should be here with me right now, Will. Where the hell are you?

You promised you'd come home…

She remained crouched behind the wall of trees, next to the ten-yard-wide pathway that connected the beach and stretched about half a football field until it reached the wide open grounds behind them. Without the lamps that serpentined across the island, everything was blackened, including the hotel and the unfinished swimming pools. The only structure on the entire island that still had lights was the Tower, glowing brightly behind her, and that was only because of the LED lamps on the third floor.

Even the birds that usually chirped away, oblivious to human presence on the island, had gone uncharacteristically quiet tonight.

Did they know? Of course not. How could they?

Behind her, Sarah shifted back and forth on the balls of her feet, apparently unable to decide whether she wanted to sit down or remain standing.

"You okay?" Lara whispered over her shoulder.

Like Stan a few seconds ago, Sarah tried to smile, and just like Stan, it came out poorly. "I've never shot anyone before."

"You'll do fine. Just follow my lead."

"What's it like?"

"What?"

"Killing someone. What's it like?"

"Don't think about it. Shoot, reload, and keep shooting until there's nothing to shoot at anymore. They're coming here to kill us. Just keep reminding yourself of that. Do it for Jenny. For Mae. For everyone who is counting on us right now."

Sarah nodded mutely, then went back to trying to decide whether to sit or stand, and constantly changing up her grip on the M4.

"You'll do fine," Lara said again, and hoped it was at least convincing. Judging by Sarah's face, she guessed she was only halfway successful.

There was a time when Lara had been just like Sarah—scared and uncomfortable with a gun in her hands. Those days were long gone, and even as she turned back to the darkness, she wished Will's face was looking back at her.

You promised me, Will. Where are you?

But he wasn't there. Instead, she saw Roy, his blond hair easy to spot in the semidarkness. He had moved away from the trees and was standing next to Stan in a spot that allowed him to remain behind cover while still able to peer down the pathway and at the moonlit beach on the other side. Compared to Stan, Roy looked strangely serene, the M4 hanging almost naturally from a sling in front of him. She knew better, of course. Roy was a former IT man, and the closest he'd ever come to holding a gun in his life before The Purge was playing *Call of Duty* on the PlayStation.

Roy glanced over and grinned at her. "Remember that time in the woods? When we were chasing West?"

She smiled back. "Yes."

"Man, I was so unprepared back then."

"Not anymore."

"Not anymore. What's that motto of yours again?"

"Which one?"

"'Adapt or perish'?"

"Ah."

"I guess you can say I've successfully adapted."

And not a moment too soon.

"They're taking their sweet time," Roy said. "I wish they'd get here already. My legs are cramping up from the waiting."

Be careful what you wish for, Lara thought for the second time as the sound of motors seemed to increase in decibel on cue.

It wouldn't be long now…

There was a *click* in her right ear, and she heard Blaine's voice through the earbud connected to her radio. "Lara."

Lara pressed the PTT dangling from her vest. "Yeah, Blaine."

"They're getting closer, right? We can hear them all the way on the other side of the island."

"Yeah, they're getting closer."

"Keo said ten boats?"

"Yes."

"I don't understand why they're just attacking the beach with ten boats. Is that all they have?"

"I don't know," Lara said. Then, "Keo."

"Yeah," Keo said through the radio.

"How many boats did you see when you were at their staging area?"

"I didn't exactly do an official count. Most of them were already in the water." He paused, seemed to think about it some more, before adding, "Remember what we talked about? How they've been going around sinking boats for a while now, trying to keep everyone on land? Maybe these ten are all they have left in the area."

"What a bunch of asshats," Danny said. "I bet a lot of people paid good money for those boats."

"What are you thinking, Blaine?" Lara asked.

"I don't know what I'm thinking," Blaine said.

"Spit it out," Danny said.

"It's just that…this is pretty bold of them, to just think they can invade Song Island by hitting the beach," Blaine said. "Especially knowing how it all turned out last time."

She didn't blame Blaine for being suspicious. That was all she had been doing since they spotted the ten boats. But there was no way to alter the plan now, not with the attackers bearing down on them.

"Blaine has a point," she said into the radio. "This could all be one big diversion. There could be more approaching from the other sides. Report in as soon as you see or hear anything out of the ordinary. Anything at all. Understand?"

The others responded one by one.

"I wish Will was here," Sarah said quietly behind her.

So do I. God, so do I.

On the other side of the trees, the sound of boat motors seemed to have picked up in volume. She knew what that meant: They were getting closer.

"Look alive, boys and girls," Danny said through the radio. "Here they come. Shoot straight, shoot often, and keep moving. Do not—I say again—do *not* let them get a bead on you. It's a big beach. Use it."

KEO FIRED FIRST. She knew it was him because the gunshot came from the other side of the pathway. Danny was in the middle, while Gaby was camped to her left.

Once Keo let go with the first shot, the shooting didn't stop. It sounded like thunder crashing against the beach over and over again, first concentrated on one side, then the other, and before she knew it, it was impossible to pinpoint where the bulk of the gunfire was coming from because it seemed to be coming from everywhere.

If Sarah was nervous, she was on overdrive now. Lara could feel the other woman's anxiety in the warm breaths hitting her in the back of the neck. Across from her, Stan was equally anxious, gripping and ungripping his M4 at least a dozen times in as many seconds. Roy seemed to be faring better, though even he had gone into a crouch to keep his feet from fidgeting.

Lara had to fight her own instincts. She wanted badly to peek into the pathway, to see if they were coming yet, or get a glimpse of the gunfight that was taking place on the beach at this very moment. But she didn't, because doing so might give away her position. That, and the prospect of getting hit with a stray bullet flying from the beach was more than enough motivation to keep her rooted in place.

Staying still became more difficult when bullets began pelting the trees behind and around her. Branches snapped off and whenever a round *zipped!* nearby, she flinched, while Sarah gasped audibly. The assaulters were pouring everything they had into the woods, obviously trying to hit Danny, who was somewhere in front of them, moving constantly and using the trees as cover. That didn't stop them from firing into the woods anyway, and branches were continually snapping around her, some just a little bit too close for comfort.

She exerted every ounce of control she had to remain perfectly still, even if every instinct she had told her to move, move, *move*.

No one was talking—not Danny or Keo or Gaby, or anyone else plugged into the channel, which was everyone on the island with a radio. Like her, they were mesmerized by the chaotic back and forth, the never-ending *pop-pop-pop* of assault rifles crashing up and down the length of the beach.

It went on and on, and whenever she thought it would calm down, having run its course, it picked up again.

My God, how many men are out there? How many have they killed already? How many more do we have to kill? I don't want this. This bloodbath.

God help me, I never wanted this...

Then, through the tumultuous pounding of gunfire and her own thrumming chest, she heard the *click!* that she had been waiting for, followed by Danny's voice, slightly out of breath, shouting into her ear. "Hot Gates! Persians in the Hot Gates!"

Lara snapped her eyes shut and counted down from *ten*.

The first step was to rein in her heartbeat. It was racing too fast, threatening to overwhelm her.

Nine...

She clutched and unclutched the pistol grip under the M4's barrel.

Eight...

Made sure the fire selector was on full-auto.

Seven...

Behind her, Sarah whispered, "Oh, God."

Six...

Opened her eyes back up.

Five...

Roy was staring across the pathway at her, and he managed a nervous smile.

Four...

She smiled back at him, hoping the confidence she was faking came through all right, but knowing it probably wasn't even close to being convincing.

Three...

"Oh, God," Sarah said again.

Two...

She located the trigger on her rifle.

One...

"Now!" she screamed.

She might have run or walked really fast. She wasn't quite sure. One second she was hiding behind the trees, the next she had moved out from behind cover and into the open, spun around sixty degrees until she was facing the beach, and even before she saw the first black-clad figure rushing up the cobblestone path right at her, she was already squeezing the trigger.

There had to be a dozen of them—maybe more—racing up the ten-yard-wide opening with wild abandon, the adrenaline of the beach landing clearly surging through them. She didn't need the lamps to see they were wearing black uniforms and helmets. Moonlight glinted off the rifles swinging back and forth in their hands as they charged forward.

They had no idea she was there. Or Stan, running out from behind his part of the woods and going into a crouch. Or Roy, positioning himself behind the electrician. Sarah might have followed her out from cover and into the open, too, but Lara didn't have the second or two it would have taken to make sure.

She was too busy shooting.

They fell like dominos. She was glad it was too dark to make out each individual man, because that would have meant thinking of them *as* men. Right now, she couldn't afford that, because killing was still unnatural to her even as she tried to convince herself this was necessary, that it was kill or be killed. The anger that had carried her through the last few minutes flooded out of her with every bullet she poured into the mass of bodies, replaced by pity and horror.

But none of that made her take her finger off the trigger—all she had to do was think of Elise, of Vera, of the teenagers who had come with Bonnie—and she was able to hold on as the rifle bucked and the magazine emptied at a dizzying rate. She wasn't shooting at any one person—she was shooting at all of them.

Roy and Stan were still firing into the ten-yard-wide pathway when Lara ejected her magazine and grabbed a new one, slamming it home. She became vaguely aware of Sarah crying while the rifle in her hands was bucking again and again. The other woman still had her weapon set to semi-automatic for some reason.

They were crumpled in front of her, the closest one having gotten halfway up the road before she felled him. She didn't count the number of lumps lying across the cobblestone floor. She didn't want to.

(A dozen? Two? Too many…)

She finished reloading and started shooting again. She didn't even know what she was shooting at. There may or may not still be men moving around in front of her. She might have simply been firing into the pile of bodies now, looking for survivors that might not even exist.

She thought of Elise and Vera again and didn't stop shooting until she was empty a second time. Then she instinctively ejected the magazine and groped for a third one from around her waist.

Roy and Stan were frantically changing magazines to her right, but Sarah was holding her M4 uselessly at her side. The woman had stopped crying, and the sudden quiet was deafening, with the only noise coming from the *clicking* of metal as they reloaded their weapons.

"Oh, Jesus," Roy said.

He was looking at a lone black-clad figure crawling out of the pile of bodies. It was a man, but he might as well have been a ghoul because that was all they could see—a twisted, bloodied black thing moving slowly, painfully toward them. He might have been groaning, or moaning, or even saying something, but it was hard to tell. Or maybe she just didn't want to know for sure. The man was having trouble pulling his legs out of the unmoving bodies stacked on top of him.

Roy put away his rifle, drew his handgun, and aimed at the man.

Lara waited for him to shoot, but the gunshot never came.

Roy finally let out a sigh and lowered the gun to his side. "I can't," he said, almost breathlessly.

Lara drew her own sidearm slowly. It was the only way she could get it out because her hand was shaking, her fingers having a difficult time gripping the Glock.

She took aim at the figure, even as the man lifted a hand toward her, but before she could fire there was a loud *bang!*

One side of the man's head exploded and showered the cobblestone. The body slumped to the ground and didn't move again.

A figure walked calmly out of the tree line to their left side, and a voice said, "I come in peace."

Danny.

Lara gratefully holstered her gun. Her hand was still trembling slightly, and she had to grip the M4 to give it something to do.

Danny walked toward them with a noticeable slight limp. He opened his mouth to say something when—

BOOM!

The ground shook for a few seconds, and Sarah gasped loudly behind her.

"What the hell was that?" Roy almost shouted.

"That was an explosion," Stan said.

"What was that?" Lara said into her radio. "Anyone know what that was or where it came from?" When no one answered, she shouted, "Someone answer me!"

She waited for a response, but there wasn't one for what seemed like an eternity, until Carly finally said, "The shack! It's the shack!"

Oh, God, did she just say the shack?

"Shack?" Nate said through the radio. "What shack?"

"The one at the power station!" Carly shouted. "It's open! Lara, the shack's open!"

The power station was halfway between the hotel and the western cliff. It was a large but unremarkable gray building that controlled the island's power source. Without it, Song Island was just another dry patch of dirt. But the station itself wasn't "the shack" Carly was referring to. That was the building next to it—a structure no bigger than what you'd find in someone's backyard. It was locked and sealed, because on the other side was a tunnel that connected the island to an entranceway along the shoreline of Beaufont Lake. There hadn't been any activity there for months. Even if someone had managed to sneak their way into the tunnel unnoticed, the door was sealed. It would take…

"The explosion," Lara said breathlessly.

She was still trying to wrap her mind around the last few seconds when a new burst of gunfire ripped across the island. It wasn't coming from the beach, because the landing had failed and the invaders were dead. This time it came from the other side of the sprawling but darkened hotel, from the direction of the power station.

Lara spun around and almost bumped into Danny.

"It's time," he said.

He was amazingly calm despite everything that had happened, despite what he must know (because she knew, too) what was about to happen.

"Will," she said, her voice coming out in gasps. "What about Will?"

"He can take care of himself," Danny said. "We have to go. *Now*."

"Lara, what do we do?" Roy asked.

"The shack," Stan said. He was looking in that direction. "Without the shack…" He didn't finish.

"Lara?" Sarah said. "What should we do?"

She glanced at Danny one last time.

He nodded.

She turned around and fumbled with the radio, found the right switches, and shouted into it.

"This is Lara! Everyone who isn't already there, head to your designated exit points now! I repeat! Head to your exit points now! The island is lost! I repeat! The island is lost! We're evacuating Song Island!"

BOOK THREE

ALL GOOD THINGS...

CHAPTER 21

WILL

HE WAS ALIVE, and as long as he was breathing, things weren't completely hopeless. It would take some doing, but it could be done. He could be on his way back to Song Island by the morning and finally see Lara again after being away from her for so long.

I've been in worse situations.

He couldn't remember when exactly, but it would come back to him eventually. Besides, he was dealing with two grunts who were far from home and isolated from their unit. If Mason were around, things might be different. That midget was smarter than he looked. These two, on the other hand, maybe not so much.

"You see that?" Rick asked.

The second guy, whose name turned out to be Millard *(Close enough)*, had stood up and taken a step away from the pools of moonlight pouring in through the gas station's glass curtain wall. Will wondered if he had done that intentionally or if it was an involuntary response. Either way, the reaction of both men told him that despite whatever deals with the devil they had struck, the fear of the creatures amassed outside hadn't gone completely away.

"What?" Millard said.

"I thought they moved," Rick said. He had risen from the floor but remained in a slight crouch, his M4 resting at his side like a crutch.

That's no way to treat a rifle, soldier.

Of course, Rick wasn't really a soldier. Despite the fact that the former paramedic had essentially saved his life, Will didn't feel very warm toward the man. Besides, it would make having to kill Rick easier.

"I don't see anything," Millard said.

"No, I swear, I thought I saw them move," Rick said.

"You said 'thought.'"

"I saw it."

Millard had retreated completely into the shadows at the back of the store. Will didn't know what Rick saw (or thought he saw), but the creatures outside didn't seem to have moved in any way. They continued to stand, shoulder to shoulder, their numbers so thick that it was impossible to see past them and at the I-10 highway in the background.

It didn't help that this part of the world was pitch black with no source of artificial light for miles. Not that he minded that, either. Given the shape he was in now, Will wasn't excited about seeing what he looked like anyway. The bandages, the bloodied clothes he was still wearing, the pool of dried blood he had been sitting on ever since he woke up. What part of him wasn't covered in blood?

At least Rick had been nice enough to give him back his pill bottle as promised. Will tilted it up to his lips now and swallowed the last three remaining lifesavers. He swore it worked almost right away, but maybe that was just his mind trying to convince him his entire body wasn't about to shut down from the pain of the last few days.

"They freak me out, man," Millard was saying while clutching the carbine as if it were a baseball bat.

"So don't look at them," Rick said.

"I can't help it. Can you?"

"No..."

Millard was skinny and tall, whereas Rick was thick and slightly pudgy. "Man, they must really want you bad," he said to Will.

"They don't want him," Rick said. "She does."

"She?"

"Yeah. *She.*"

"Oh," Millard said, turning back to the window. "So what happens when she shows up? We just give him to her or something?"

"Mason says to stay out of her way. We're just here to make sure he doesn't run off again."

"What about them?"

"They're here to make sure he doesn't run off, too."

"I doubt he's going anywhere. The guy looks like a bad extra from *The Mummy.*"

"Yeah, well, he's done it before. So we just sit tight until she shows up."

"Freaky," Millard said. He looked at Will again. "I don't know what you did, buddy, but you must have fucked up bad."

Will chuckled.

That prompted a glance from Rick. "What's so funny?"

"Nothing," Will said.

Rick walked over and crouched about a foot in front of him, leaning the rifle across his knees. Will fought every instinct to grab at the weapon. It was so damn close…

"Come on," Rick said, "I wanna hear what the dead man thinks is so funny."

"Have you ever met her in person?" Will asked.

"Who?"

"*Her.*"

Rick and Millard exchanged a look.

I guess that's a no.

"She's not like the others, you know," Will said. "She's different from the ones outside."

"Yeah, we know," Millard said. "Blue eyes, right?"

"That's right."

"What else do you know?" Rick asked him.

Apparently more than you.

"They like to play," Will said.

"Play?" Millard said. "What the hell does that mean?"

He thought about Harrison and how the blue-eyed ghouls had toyed with him. Then there were the people from Mississippi who had suffered the same fate. Gaby had also told him and Danny an interesting story about a man named Peter, whom she had escaped L15 with. Peter had fled the town because he was afraid for his life, because men had a bad habit of going missing, never to be seen again.

And there it was.

He had been searching for a way out ever since he opened his eyes, and it was right under his nose the entire time. Now all he had to do was tell a convincing enough story because his life depended on it.

"It means she's not going to just come and take me," Will said. "It's not how this works."

"'This'?" Millard said. "What's 'this'?"

"This is Mason, leaving you here for a reason. This is Mason, offering you up to her." Before they could respond, he added quickly, "You've heard the stories, haven't you? About people going missing in the towns? Men who are never seen again?"

He watched their reaction: The way they exchanged another quick glance, the way their shoulders trembled ever so slightly, and the way they gripped their rifles as if their life depended on it, because maybe it did. They didn't really understand their ghoul overlords, he realized now, but they had heard the whispers. The rumors. Maybe they'd even talked about it amongst themselves in quiet rooms when they were certain no one could hear.

God, I hope this works.

"You've heard the stories," Will said.

"Maybe," Millard said hesitantly. "Guys have said they've seen some crazy things."

"About the blue-eyed ones."

"Yeah…"

"The stories you've heard? No matter how crazy they sound, I can tell you this: They're not even close to the real thing, because the truth is worse."

"Bullshit," Rick said.

"When she comes, it won't be just me that she takes," Will said, keeping his focus—directing everything out of his mouth—at Millard, and Millard only. He could feel Rick staring at him, but he ignored the other man. He didn't have to convince both of them—he just needed one of them on his side. "The ones outside? Those are pets. The blue-eyed ones are the masters. And masters take what they want. Me, I'll survive this, because *she* wants me to. But you two? I don't see it. You're not here to protect me, or to keep me from running off. Look at me. I'm not going anywhere. You two are here for a reason. You're snacks."

"He's lying," Rick said. "Don't listen to him. He doesn't know anything."

"Where's Mason now?" Will said, pressing on as if Rick hadn't said anything. "Did you ever wonder why he left just the two of you behind? Let me guess. You got on his bad side recently? Maybe talked back one time too many?"

"How do you know all this?" Millard said. His mouth twitched, which was either a sign Will was getting to him or…the guy just had a twitch.

"I've been around," Will said. "I've seen things you wouldn't believe. I've fought the blue-eyed ones. More than once. And I've lived to tell the tale. What about you two? You really think you're supposed to survive this? Wake up."

"Shut up," Rick said. Then to Millard, "Don't listen to him. We're rejoining Mason in the morning."

"Where?" Millard said. "Where's Mason now?"

Rick didn't answer right away.

"He doesn't know," Will said.

"He's at Lake Charles," Rick said.

"He's lying," Will said. "Look at his face."

Millard peered at Rick in the semidarkness, almost leaning forward with his entire body. "He's at Lake Charles?"

"Yes," Rick said. "He told me himself."

Will laughed. Loudly. When both men looked back at him, he

said, with all the conviction in the world, "You're a shitty liar, Rick. Mason's gone. He never told you where he went because you didn't need to know. Because he won't see you or Millard again after tonight."

Millard looked at Rick, then at Will, then back at Rick. "He's in Lake Charles right now?"

"That's right," Rick nodded. "He's just messing with your head. Don't listen to him. Mason told me to be careful with this guy. He's slippery."

Will snorted at Rick, then smiled at Millard. "What did you do?"

"What?" Millard said.

"You must have done something to piss Mason off."

"I didn't—" He paused, then seemed to think about it. "I had no choice."

"What did you do?" Will asked again.

"Don't tell him," Rick said.

Millard ignored him, said, "Back at Route 13. When those people from Dunbar attacked us. There were too many of them, and they had a machine gun. I…ran."

"Mason doesn't strike me as the kind of guy who forgives something like that," Will said. "No wonder he sent you here."

Almost there, Will thought when he saw the conflicted look on Millard's face. *Just a little more…*

"Stop talking to him," Rick said. "He's just filling your head with lies. I should have left him bleeding on the floor instead of saving his life."

"What were Mason's orders?" Millard asked Rick.

The question caught Rick by surprise. "What?"

"What were Mason's orders?" Millard repeated, his voice growing slightly in volume, almost threatening. "He didn't tell me. He just said to stay here with you. But he never told me how to reach him in the morning."

"I told you, we're supposed to meet up with him at Lake Charles tomorrow," Rick said, looking noticeably more irritated by the second.

There was a flicker of movement outside the window. It was the ghouls. They seemed to be reacting to the growing agitation inside the store. It was just a slight tremor that rumbled across the field of black pruned flesh. Will wouldn't have noticed it at all if they hadn't been so still just seconds ago.

"We're just supposed to stay here and wait for her to come get him," Rick was saying.

"That's it?" Millard said.

"That's it. Just sit tight and it'll be over soon."

"Nice story," Will said. "A bald-faced lie, but I'll give you points for trying. Then again, you might actually believe it, which is pretty sad if you ask me."

Rick looked back to him. "No one asked you, dead man."

"If I'm the dead man, why are the two of you ready to piss your pants? Maybe it's because you know I'm right. Mason's gone. He may or may not be at Lake Charles, but he sure as hell doesn't expect you to link back up with him in the morning. The rest of your unit is gone. They left you behind. Face it."

"You don't know a damn—" Rick said, but he never got the chance to finish because there was a loud *bang!* from the back of the store and Rick collapsed to the floor in a pile.

The gunshot was still echoing off the walls, causing the windows to vibrate slightly, when a voice said, "Move and you're dead."

Millard stood shaking over Rick's crumpled form, desperately trying to control his breathing. He looked wide-eyed, as if he'd just run a marathon and was not quite sure if he should sit down and rest or have a heart attack. His right hand had also begun to inch toward his holstered sidearm—

Bang!

Millard dropped and laid still.

"Christ," Will said.

"That's two you owe me," the voice said as its owner stepped out of the shadowed back part of the gas station.

She had looked better, but then she could probably say the same thing about him. There was a gash along her left temple that had left thick clumps of blood along the side of her face, and she moved with a noticeable limp. Other than that, it was still the same woman who was a trigger pull away from shooting him dead when they had first met back at the Palermo along Route 13.

Natasha lowered the M4 rifle and smirked at him. "That's some silver tongue on you. I thought for sure you had them convinced."

"Almost," Will said.

"Listening to you back here, it occurred to me everything you might have told Leo and the others was bullshit, too." She narrowed her eyes. "Well? Was it?"

"I needed to get to Song Island."

"So that's a yes."

"Not everything. The part about the ghouls avoiding bodies of water is true. I've been on that island for three months and they never once crossed it."

"Not once?" she said doubtfully.

"Not once." He turned back to Rick's and Millard's still bodies. "Nice shot."

"I've had practice."

She walked over and took out a knife. The sharp edge gleamed in the moonlight and Will waited for her to strike.

Natasha snorted. "Relax. If I wanted to kill you, I would have just shot you."

She sliced his hands free, then did the same to his legs.

"Thank you," he said.

"Can you even stand? You look like shit."

"I can stand."

"I'll believe it when I see it."

Will stood up, even as every joint in his body popped and creaked. He had been sitting for so long that he didn't realize just how much his entire body still ached and throbbed from the events of the last twenty-four hours. Just moving his arms to rub his wrists to get the blood flowing again made him wince. He couldn't tell how bad his hands had been shredded by the highway underneath the gauze, and frankly he didn't want to know. Every time he touched something, there was a painful jolt.

I should be dead.

How many times have I said that this week?

He sucked it up. None of it mattered because he was still far from his destination.

Song Island.

Lara.

Gotta get back home.

"Motherfucker," Natasha whispered.

She was staring out the store windows at the ghouls outside. The wall of dark flesh and gleaming black faces was stirring, moving slightly left and right and front and back. The eyes that peered back at them seemed to have grown with intensity since he last looked.

It had to have been the violence. They were reacting to the deaths of Millard and Rick. So what was still keeping them back? What was holding them in place?

Not what. Who.

Kate...

"I've never seen so many of them in one place," Natasha said.

She had lowered her voice to almost a whisper for some reason. He wondered if she knew that the doors weren't even locked, that there was nothing—absolutely nothing—keeping the monsters at bay this very moment.

Will hurried forward—grimacing, trying not to scream out with every step—and turned the locks on the doors before retreating quickly back into the darkness.

When he was in the moonlight, he had spotted his reflection in the glass door and was glad he had only seen himself for a split second. The sight of a dead man wearing bloodied clothes and covered in bandages, limping badly, wasn't something he wanted to see again.

"Are you shitting me?" Natasha said. She might have been hyperventilating a little bit. "Those doors were never locked?"

"They are now," Will said.

"Jesus Christ," she said breathlessly. She was still staring out the windows, unable to take her eyes away from the throng of creatures outside.

Will picked up Rick's M4 and slung it, then rolled the man onto his back, careful to avoid the blood dribbling out the side of Rick's head. He unclasped the gun belt with the Smith & Wesson semi-automatic in the hip holster and found a nylon sheath stuffed behind Rick's waist. The knife inside was a tantō style model about a foot long with a seven-inch black stainless steel blade. It looked overly stylish and nothing he would have been caught dead carrying in combat or elsewhere, but you never knew when an extra weapon might come in handy.

"What are you doing back here, Natasha?" Will asked as he finished going through Rick's pockets. "Not that I'm complaining."

When he was done with Rick, he went through Millard's belongings. The two men didn't have any extra ammo on them besides the magazines already loaded in their rifles and sidearms.

"What else was I going to do?" Natasha said. She had walked back to him, but kept glancing over her shoulder and out the windows. "Figured I'd follow these assholes and kill as many of them as I could before they get me."

"What happened?"

"You mean how did I survive?"

"Yeah."

"I was thrown clear. Landed on the side of the highway in some thick grass. Thank God no one's done any mowing for a year, otherwise they'd have spotted me. I woke up in time to see them hauling you away."

"What about the others?"

She shook her head before looking behind her again.

"You limped all the way here?" he asked.

"We're only half a mile from the crash site. I didn't even know you were in here until I climbed in through the window in the back room just before nightfall."

"So you heard everything."

"Most of it. Was it true? What you said? Or were you just feeding them a line to try to turn them on each other?"

"What do you think?"

She grunted. "You're such a fucking liar."

"I'm just trying to get home."

"Song Island."

"Yeah."

"So how are you going to get there now?" Another quick look at the ghouls behind her, before she added, "How are you going to get through that."

Will didn't answer her. He was too busy looking down at Rick and Millard.

No, not at the two dead men. More, specifically, at their uniforms.

"What?" Natasha said. "What are you looking at? You already took everything they have. What's left?"

"Their uniforms," Will said. He kneeled back down and began unbuttoning Rick's shirt.

"Why?"

"You know why."

"Because they leave the soldiers alone," she said. Then, with something that almost sounded like hope in her voice for the first time since he'd met her, "You really think it'll work?"

"Only one way to find out," he said.

IT DIDN'T TAKE them long to strip the two men down to their underwear. Rick was the smaller of the two, so Natasha took his uniform into the back room. Will pulled on Millard's, grateful to shed his own bloodied clothes.

He didn't realize just how bruised and purple and yellow he was until he was standing in his boxers. He quickly put the uniform on and cinched the gun belt in place, covering up the scars and bandages and everything else that reminded him he was probably not going to last very long in this condition. The painkillers he had popped earlier were starting to work, but what he wouldn't give for a little bit more pep.

He told himself he'd get the help he desperately needed when he finally made it back home. Lara could treat him. Or Zoe, though he'd insist Lara do it.

Have to get home. Get back to Lara.

Have to get home at all costs...

Natasha came back out, still doing up the buttons on Rick's shirt. "It kind of fits. For all the good it'll do."

"That's it, think positive," Will said.

Millard's clothes actually fit him pretty well, and he shoved the sheathed knife behind his back.

"I'm being realistic," Natasha said. "These two didn't even know why the uniforms work. They just accepted it because that's what they do; they're followers. Look how fast the tall one was willing to buy your bullshit."

They were adapting so they wouldn't perish. It's human nature.

"What's in the back room?" he asked.

"Just some empty boxes. The window was unlocked, and it was just big enough for me to crawl through."

Then Natasha went very quiet.

"What's—" he started to ask.

She was staring past him and out the windows again, at the creatures gathered outside. Nothing had changed that he could see. There were still too many of them, overflowing out of the parking lot and onto the feeder road. No matter how hard or long he stared, it was impossible to make out the gray concrete of the I-10 in the background. Was it even still there?

"What's happening?" Natasha asked. Her voice had dropped noticeably again.

"Nothing," he said.

"Nothing?"

"I don't see anything."

"They don't look different to you?"

He shook his head, then glanced back at her. Natasha had retreated until she was standing (almost leaning) against the far wall, now little more than a silhouette in the shadows. He didn't know how, but he could actually see her terrified face in the darkness.

"I swear I saw them move," she said.

"Move?"

"Yeah. They moved."

"How?"

"I can't explain—"

Bang!

He spun around, lifting the M4 just as the ghoul picked itself up from the concrete sidewalk. It had smashed itself, skull first, into one of the twin glass doors and left behind a crack about an inch long. The figure slowly straightened up, tar-like black eyes finding Will and focusing in, as if it knew—it *knew*—who he was.

"That can't be good," Natasha said breathlessly behind him.

Yeah, I think that's the understatement of the century, Natasha.

Will took another step back, then another one, when a second ghoul raced forward and flung itself into the other glass door. It struck headfirst, like the other one, and instantly fell to the sidewalk before picking itself back up. Like the first one, it had left an inch-wide crack across the glass.

What the hell were they doing? They weren't going to break through the doors. Most convenience stores had tempered glass designed to withstand this kind of brute force attack. It would take forever to shatter unless you had a pickup truck moving at full speed. And right now he didn't see a vehicle—

Oh, fuck.

He stumbled back as they began flinging themselves into the glass walls—*bang! bang! bang!*—all across the length of the store.

One after another—

Bang!

—after another—

Bang!

Each impact rang out like a gunshot—

Bang!

Worse than gunshots, because this weapon could be reloaded again and again, because they never died, they didn't feel pain, and shattered limbs and broken bones meant nothing to them. The windows, along with the doors, were starting to chip little by little with every strike. They would break. Sooner or later, they would break.

"What now?" Natasha shouted behind him.

He didn't answer her, because there was nowhere to run. If there were this many ghouls outside that he could see, there were probably even more surrounding the building that they couldn't. Because it was night outside, and the night was theirs.

It was *hers*.

"I'm coming, Will," she had said. *"I'll be there soon…"*

"What the fuck is happening?" Natasha shouted, her voice drowning in the maddening fury of ghouls spearing the glasses with their bodies.

The constant hammer pounding, growing…

Bang!

"Hey!"

BANG!

"What now? What do we do now?"

BANG!!!

CHAPTER 22

GABY

"THIS IS LARA! *Everyone who isn't already there, head to your designated exit points now! I repeat! Head to your exit points now! The island is lost! I repeat! The island is lost! We're evacuating Song Island!*"

She might have stopped breathing for a moment as Lara's words echoed through the earbud. Her body was still trembling from the sight of men dying on the beach—and the fact she had contributed to that body count—when the explosion ripped through the island, followed by Lara's voice over the radio.

"*The island is lost! We're evacuating Song Island!*"

It couldn't be possible, could it? She and Danny and Nate had risked everything to get down here just to save the island. They had left Will behind in order to do it. All that sacrifice had resulted in these bodies lying on the beach, the lapping waves of Beaufont Lake flooding the white sand with crimson blood that looked shockingly bright even with just the moonlight. At first she thought shooting men behind the night vision of her optic was surreal, like playing a videogame. The men stumbling and jumping out of their beached vessels didn't look like actual human beings; they were more pixilated CGI.

But they were real, just like the round after round she had sent into them from the safety of the tree line. She had lost count of how many times she moved from spot to spot, never giving the black-clad assaulters a single location to shoot at. Eventually, they started believing there was more than just her in the eastern half of the beach and began spraying indiscriminately into the trees.

All of that, and for what?

"The island is lost! We're evacuating Song Island!"

This can't be how it ends. All this blood. All those lives...

"Gaby!" someone shouted in her ear. *Danny*. "Get your ass moving!"

How did he know she wasn't already moving?

Because he was Danny, and he knew her. Just like Will knew her. They had trained her themselves on this very island, where she had dreamt about coming back to night after night. Only to have it end now...like this?

"Gaby!" Danny again. "Move your ass! That's an order! *Vamos!*"

How the hell did he know she wasn't already moving?

She pushed up from the slightly damp ground and onto her feet, then spun around and began running through the woods. She was glad to go, happy to be leaving the beach behind. If not figuratively, at least literally. She was going to have nightmares about tonight for years to come, she knew that much, and the less she could remember the images—the blood, the dead...but especially the dead—the better.

She tried to do that now—push the sight of those men falling as she shot them—as Danny and Keo shot them—out of her mind. But they were still too fresh and the best she could do was tell herself it was either her or them, because they hadn't come here to talk. They had come here armed and ready to kill.

The wind against her face, the branches slapping her legs and arms, brought her back to the present. Back to the here and now. And right now, they were evacuating the island—

Wait, how was she moving so fast? Oh, right; because she wasn't as weighed down by ammo as she was when the night started, because she had used up all her spare magazines. The one in the M4 at the moment was only half full, and once she used it up she would be down to just the Glock in her hip holster. At least she had two spare magazines for that.

The bodies on the beach. I did that. I killed those men.

God help me, I killed those men.

For a second or two, she entertained the idea of stopping and turning around and running back to the beach and collecting spare magazines from those very same men who she couldn't stop thinking about.

Did they want to come here? Were they forced? Did they have friends or family waiting for them back in the towns? She remembered the woman with the boy in L15 and the countless other people walking along the sidewalks. Couples. Families. Was there a husband among the dead on the beach right now? Maybe she had killed him. Or maybe it was the man next to him—

Stop it. They're gone. You did what you had to do.

Focus!

The *clicking* in her right ear helped her to concentrate on the moment, on the branches still slapping against her arms and legs, and the chill that pervaded the island and soaked her to the very bones despite her clothing.

"Lara," a voice said.

"Keo!" Lara shouted back. "Where are you?"

"Southwest corner, just beyond the power station."

"What do you see?"

"More assaulters. They're coming through the shack next to the power station and heading right at you."

"How many?"

"Too many. But if we coordinate a defense—"

"No," Lara said, cutting him off. "It's not the humans we have to worry about. Without the shack, there's nothing to hold them back. Do you understand? Get to your exit point. We're getting off the island!"

"Roger that," Keo said, and the radio went quiet again.

Gaby burst out of the woods a moment later and into the almost pitch-black state of the hotel grounds. Even the Tower in the distance was barely visible, a hulking and darkened spire sticking out of the cliff, the familiar floodlights that usually adorned its exterior missing. Not gone, just turned off like the rest of the island, along with the LED lamps that had been inside the third floor a few hours ago.

For the first time in a long time, Gaby felt alone. The others were gone, moving toward their exit points. Soon, they'd all be converging on the *Trident*, anchored somewhere on the other side of the island. Lara's Plan D, just in case everything went to hell.

I guess this means everything's gone to hell.

She jogged across the tall grass, trying to get her bearings as she went. She had exited the woods at a random point and was much further away from the hotel than she had expected. She could see its squat one-story shape in the distance, the walls visible against the deep black of a lightless world. She was so used to seeing the grounds around the hotel lit up by bright LEDs that not having those markers now was startling.

She turned away from the hotel and ran in the direction of the Tower, where her designated exit point was. Even without lights, it was hard to miss, its structure looming against the moonlit sky. Carly or Benny would have already put the escape ladder in place over the cliff and climbed down, where two cheap aluminum boats, each with a pair of paddles inside, awaited them among the rocks. If both of them had left at the same time (which made sense), they would have left one boat down there for her. Or, at least, she hoped.

She was halfway to the Tower when the *pop-pop-pop* of assault rifles made her slide to a stop in the tall grass. The shooting was coming from her left, where the hotel was. The vicious back-and-forth paralyzed her, and Gaby didn't know whether to keep running to her exit point or turn toward the hotel.

"*The island is lost! I repeat! The island is lost! We're evacuating Song Island!*"

Orders were orders, but the sound of gunfire seized her and refused to let go. Maybe it was the ferocious nature of it, or its proximity—so close, and yet so far away. Who was shooting? Lara and Danny and how many assaulters? It was definitely concentrated inside the hotel, she was sure of it. There was a hollow almost echo-y quality to the gunshots, hints that they were coming from enclosed spaces.

"We're pinned!" someone screamed in her right ear. *Lara*. She was shouting to be heard over the continuous roar of rifles firing at close proximity. "Blaine, take off now!"

"What?" Blaine shouted back through the radio. "We're not leaving without you! Get over here!"

"We're not going to make it!"

"Then we'll come back to you!"

"Don't be stupid!"

"Lara!"

"That's an order, Blaine! Move your ass now or I'm sending Danny over there to kick it!"

"Yeah, what she said!" Danny chimed in.

"Danny!" *Carly*. "What are you doing? Get over here, you dumbass!"

"Get going!" Danny shouted back. "We'll catch up! I promise, babe!"

"You goddamn better!"

"Scout's honor!"

"You were never in the scouts—" Carly started to say, when a loud explosion drowned out the voices all trying to speak at the same time.

The blast had come from the hotel, almost a football field away from her, but it sounded much closer. Thick plumes of smoke were drifting into the air, looking almost poetic against the black canvas of night. But she knew there was nothing lyrical about it, especially when the gunfire temporarily halted in the aftermath.

Gaby was running full-speed toward the hotel before she even realized she had made the decision. About ten seconds into her run, the shooting started up again, the back-and-forth still as frenzied as they had been before the explosion. As horrific as it was to think so, the fact that two sides were exchanging gunfire was a good sign that either Lara or Danny (or both) were still alive.

She hoped, anyway.

To keep her mind off the fact that she was running *to* the sound of automatic gunfire, Gaby tried to imagine how many assaulters were waiting for her in there. They had sent anywhere from thirty to fifty on the beach alone. So how many more had gotten through the tunnel? Another thirty to fifty? God, she hoped not. The very idea of having to kill that many more made her want to stop and vomit into the grass.

But she didn't stop. She couldn't. Lara and Danny were in the hotel right now. *(What happened to Roy and Stan and Sarah?)* And they clearly needed her help, or Lara wouldn't have ordered Blaine to go. She had done that to save them, Gaby knew, because for whatever reason, she and Danny weren't going to make it to their exit point.

Gaby ran until her lungs were burning, and still the hotel seemed to remain just as far away as when she had counted the distance a few seconds ago. As she drew closer, she realized the shooting wasn't just coming from the building in front of her. It was coming from the other side, too, as well as from her right. That was where the *Trident* was, waiting to shove off. There were, as far as she could tell, at least two or three gun battles going on simultaneously across the island.

And here she was, running right into the middle of one of them—

BOOM!

Another explosion tore through the hotel just as she was about to reach it. This time she was close enough to feel the ground trembling as the blast blew a hole in the roof near the middle, almost directly in front of her. It sounded like a grenade had gone off. Christ, who was throwing around grenades on the island? Was the first blast a grenade, too?

Gaby dived to her left as debris—chunks of the ceiling and God knew what else was up there at the moment, left behind when the workers abandoned the place—rained down around her. Something hard pelted her head and shoulders and she threw herself against the hotel wall and clung to it, trying desperately to make herself small against the falling pieces of the building.

She could smell the pluming smoke and hear the still-rattling gunfire from the other side of the wall she was pressed up against. *Right on the other side.* Even a grenade going off hadn't stopped them for very long.

The side door was to her right, within easy reach. Even without lights to point her way, she knew there would be one around here and there it was. She moved toward it now, trying in vain to keep track of the back-and-forth clatter of assault rifles inside the hotel.

What was going on in there? Some kind of running gunfight? Although at the moment it sounded like it had stalled in one spot. The first explosion had come from her left—very close to where the lobby would be—and moved right toward the back, through the hallways. So why had it stopped now?

Stop thinking and move!

She grabbed the doorknob and took a breath, then counted to five—

One.

She pulled the door and slipped inside—raising the M4, peering through the night-vision scope—even before the door had swung completely open. It would have been pitch black inside the narrow passageway except for the staccato *flash-flash-flash* of assault rifles firing in the connecting hallway ten meters in front of her. She easily picked up the distinctive *clink-clink-clink* of ejected shell casings pelting the hotel's smooth tile floor.

The endless flashes filled her vision while the continuous slamming of gunshots dominated her eardrums, and the lingering sting of sulfur in the air, combined with the suffocating smell of gun powder in the closed confines, threatened to overwhelm her sense of smell. There was a big hole in the ceiling in front of her where the two hallways joined, though it hadn't done very much to vent out the place.

Gaby pushed through until she was almost at the corner, when there was a flurry of movement in front of her. A man clad all in black, with a thick beard that might have been red (though it was hard to tell when everything was awash in green), took a step backward and stopped in front of her and began reloading. The man's night-vision goggles protruded forward from his aging face like a pair of alien eyes. She guessed he had to be in his forties, and he looked a bit like her Uncle Bill.

He must have sensed her, because he turned his head and saw her—

Gaby shot him once in the chest.

Even as the man fell, she was running up the hallway and flicking the fire selector on her rifle to full-auto. She reached the corner and stepped over the crumpled body, turning right to find three men crouched further up the narrow passageway—two on one side, the third on the opposite—with their weapons aimed at a door that had already been perforated by at least two dozen bullet holes. The backs of all three men were to her, their black uniforms glowing green under the phosphorous lens of her night-vision scope.

Once upon a time, Gaby might have hesitated. Certainly, the Gaby from a year ago, who depended on Matt (and, to a lesser extent, Josh) to keep her safe would have been horrified at the thought of shooting men in the back. That Gaby would never have made it off the beach earlier tonight.

This Gaby, at this very moment, only saw three enemies trying to kill her friends.

She emptied the remaining rounds in her magazine into the three figures. She didn't let go of the trigger until she couldn't feel the rifle bucking in her hands anymore. Then she immediately slung it and drew her Glock and looked for something else to shoot.

The men lay still on their stomachs and she was glad she couldn't see their faces in the semidarkness, though one of them had his head turned slightly to one side, revealing the side profile of a young man in his twenties, the brim of his helmet riding low over his eyes, the night-vision device thrown askew against his face during the fall.

Her heart was racing, battling to be heard over the continuous *pop-pop-pop* of other gun battles taking place outside the hotel, on other parts of the island right this moment. She imagined the *Trident* engaged in its own fight. Did Nate make it to the yacht? What about Keo? What about Carly and Benny, who were at the Tower earlier—

There was a *click!* behind her and she spun around, finger tightening against the trigger, as a familiar voice said, "Stop, or my mom will shoot."

He was pushing his way out of a badly damaged door at the end of the hallway. She recognized the infirmary on the other side and the owner of the messy blond hair and blue eyes looking back at her.

"Danny," Gaby said.

"That's me," he said. "Aren't you supposed to be gone by now?"

"What about you?"

"Point taken."

While Danny struggled with the bullet-riddled door, she holstered her gun and crouched, then went through the dead bodies looking for spare magazines. She had done it instinctively, the need to have a loaded rifle overwhelming the part of her that was still squeamish about going through a dead man's pockets.

"Where's Lara and the others?" she asked.

"Lara's in here with me," Danny said. He had returned to the room, and now came back outside with Lara leaning against his shoulder. "They caught us out in the open, forced us into the hotel. Fearless leader and I stayed behind to give the others time to make their exit points."

"Did they make it?"

"I have no idea. Too busy trying not to die. And that last grenade fried both of our radios. And, ah, other things."

She was able to salvage three magazines and shoved two into her ammo pouch, using the third to reload her carbine. She stood up and watched Danny and Lara walk over to her.

Or hobbled. Danny was moving on his one good leg, using his rifle as a crutch, while holding Lara against him. Blood dripped down his temple, and there were cuts along his right cheek. His neck was covered in blood, as was almost the entire right side of his clothes.

"Jesus, Danny," Gaby said. "How are you still alive?"

"It's not mine," he said. "Well, most of it isn't mine."

She didn't have to ask whose it was. Lara had a field tourniquet wrapped around most of her left shoulder and right thigh. Blood was already seeping through them, and she leaned back against the wall and sighed, catching her breath and somehow managing to grin back at Gaby anyway. She didn't have her rifle and her hip holster was empty.

"They threw a grenade into the lobby," Lara said. "Looks like we're going to have to redecorate."

"Let's get some better wallpaper this time," Gaby said, trying her best to smile back. "Are you okay? Where's your rifle?"

"Lost it. My Glock, too. Got this big piece of shrapnel in my shoulder, though." She touched the bandage over her thigh and shook her head. "And I think I was shot here. I don't remember."

"She was shot down there," Danny said. "I'm the one who wrapped it up. Trust me, that was a bullet hole."

"If you say so," Lara said.

"I do, I do. And I also say we gotta go."

"Where?" Gaby asked. "Lara told Blaine to leave in the *Trident*, remember? The exit points are useless now."

"The beach," Lara said. "There are boats on the beach, remember?"

◄■■▮ ▮■■►

THEY LEFT THE hotel through the same side door she had used earlier and stepped back out into the chilly night. The world looked different behind the night-vision goggles attached to her head. She thought things were surreal peering behind the scope mounted on her rifle, but it was nothing compared to actually wearing one of the NVGs she had taken from one of the soldiers.

Gaby went outside first, then let Danny and Lara move in front while she brought up the rear. She wasn't looking forward to returning to the beach and seeing all those dead bodies again, but they didn't have any choice now. Blaine and the *Trident* were already moving and the last thing Lara wanted was to stall them, to make them vulnerable again. There were too many people on board. The kids, the adults…and Nate.

As they moved away from the hotel, they could hear isolated bursts of gunfire continuing from the other side of the island. It was difficult to pinpoint the location, almost as if the battle was constantly moving.

Gaby pulled her earbud out of her ear and disconnected the wire before keying the radio. "Blaine, come in."

"Jesus, are you guys still alive?" Blaine said. His anxiety came through her radio's speakers loud and clear, along with the *brap-brap-brap* of machine gunfire in the background, echoing what they could hear from across the island.

Gaby held the radio out for Lara, who said into it, "We're heading to the beach for one of the boats. Is Keo with you?"

"No, I thought he was with you guys."

Lara exchanged a brief look with Gaby, then she said into the radio, "We'll meet you at the rendezvous point as planned, Blaine."

"Good luck! We'll wait as long as it takes!"

"See you soon."

Gaby clipped the radio back on. "What about Keo?"

Lara glanced across the hotel grounds. Gaby saw the conflict on her face.

"Keo's resourceful," Lara said finally. "He'll find a way off the island. I'm more worried about us."

"Don't forget, the guy's half-dolphin," Danny said.

They continued to the beach, moving as fast as Lara and Danny could manage, while essentially keeping each other from falling. Gaby wanted to lend a hand, but she was their only security at the moment and she had to make do with keeping an eye on them while also scanning the blackened grounds.

Soon, they had left the hotel behind and were moving down the cobblestone pathway that cut through the woods. She could already feel the colder air from the beach wafting up in their direction. She shivered slightly before realizing it wasn't from the dropping temperature. No, it was the prospect of seeing those bodies lying across the sand one more time. She had wanted to avoid that at all costs, but that was impossible now.

"Watch your step," Danny said in front of her.

"Why?" she asked, turning around and almost stepping on a helmet.

The owner of the helmet (or, at least, one of the possible owners) lay in front of her among a pile of dead men in black clothing. There must have been two dozen of them, their arms and legs draped over each other's bodies and limbs, like friends that had fallen asleep during some kind of commando sleepover.

Gaby flinched. She always knew this was part of the plan, that the objective was always for her, Danny, and Keo to kill as many as possible on the beach while funneling the rest into the pathway where Lara and the others laid in wait for them. But knowing and being faced with the reality of what they had done…

She pulled the NVD off and sucked in a lungful of cold air.

"Gaby," Lara said. She was standing with Danny on the other side of the bodies looking back at her. "Come on, we have to go. There's no telling how many more of them are running around the island. Sooner or later, they'll find their dead friends at the hotel and start looking for us."

She nodded and started moving again, but made sure to go around the dead as much as she could, skirting along the edges and doing her best to ignore the lingering smell of almost-vomit on her lips.

The bodies, the death, the blood…

All of it made her glad they were abandoning the island, despite doing everything possible to hold it. Even if they had been successful and repelled the attack, she wasn't sure if she could look at Song Island in the same light ever again. In the morning, the dead would still be there, and the knowledge she had contributed to the body count weighed on her.

She had helped to do this. One year removed from high school.

If her friends could see her now, she wondered what they would say. Would they be impressed by her growth or horrified by what she had become?

And what was that? A shooter? A killer? A survivor?

Even she didn't know for sure—

Bang!

She was almost beyond the pile of dead and looking back to make sure she didn't step on a pale arm covered in blood when the gunshot exploded behind her. She spun around, lifting her M4, just as Danny and Lara collapsed to the ground in front of her.

There had just been the one shot, so her mind couldn't reconcile why both of them were falling. That quickly gave way to the sight of the dark figures standing at the other end of the pathway, blocking the exit to the beach. With the night-vision goggles dangling around her neck instead of over her eyes, all she could see were shadows. Although she couldn't make them out, she could see the rifles in their hands just fine, and they were all pointed at her. That wasn't entirely true. Four of them were pointing weapons at her, but the fifth one—in the center—was pointing a handgun at Lara and Danny.

She waited for them to shoot, to get it over with. She would fire back, even knowing she had no chance of surviving this, especially at this range. She could probably take out one, maybe two. If Danny or Lara weren't too badly hurt, they would chip in. Together, maybe the three of them could kill the rest, or enough to make this a pyrrhic victory.

"Gaby," one of the silhouettes said. It was the one in the middle. He had lowered the handgun and was looking across the darkness at her. The way the others flanked him, she guessed he was their leader.

And his voice!

She would recognize his voice anywhere.

"Thank God you're still alive," Josh said, taking a step toward her until she could see his face in a sliver of moonlight. He picked up Danny's rifle from the ground, then pulled out Danny's sidearm and tossed both weapons into the woods. "This whole thing has been a real mess. Everyone's shooting at everyone; no one's following orders. I was even hoping you'd gotten on that yacht, just so you'd be safe."

Somehow, she knew it would be him to lead this invasion. Somehow, just as Will could never escape Kate, she knew she would never be rid of Josh.

Gaby took the opportunity to glance down at Danny and Lara again. Lara was kneeling, with Danny lying on his back on the cobblestone floor, his head resting in her lap. Danny's body was very still, and Lara was moving her hands frantically around his midsection.

She looked back at Josh, her forefinger never leaving her rifle's trigger. She thought she'd know what to say when this moment came, but staring at him now, she didn't have a clue. All she could remember was what she had told Lara back at the hotel, hours ago.

"He's gone. He's not a boy anymore. You can't think of him as the same boy who you met in Lancing. If you get the chance—if you see him tonight—don't hesitate. Shoot him, because he'll shoot you."

And she was right. Josh had done exactly that—shot Danny.

So why didn't she pull the trigger? Why didn't she do what she told Lara to do? Why was she hesitating?

"You shot Danny," she said. "Jesus, you shot Danny."

"I'm sorry," he said. "I didn't know it was Danny. It's dark…"

"You *shot* him."

"I had to stop you from getting to the beach. I knew you'd come down here." He gave her that cocky smile that she was so familiar with. "The yacht's gone. The only place with any boats left is the beach. I knew any survivors would come down here sooner or later. It was easier than going into the hotel after you." He was beaming, looking so very young at the moment. "I'm glad you're alive, Gaby. I was really worried. Things have spiraled out of control so fast…"

"Let us go, Josh."

The word came out a lot calmer than she had expected. She thought her voice would crack, maybe quiver slightly, but there was none of that. She was so still, and she wasn't even breathing hard.

Maybe it was because somehow she always knew it would end this way, with Josh in front of her and the two of them holding weapons on each other.

Josh frowned. "I can't do that, Gaby."

He took another step forward, then another, leaving the other four behind. They didn't follow but stood obediently in the background, though Gaby detected a slight movement from one of them—the shortest of the four—almost as if the figure wanted to follow Josh but somehow managed to restrain itself, if just barely.

"Put the rifle down, Gaby," Josh said. "I'm sorry about Danny. That was a mistake. An accident. Don't do anything crazy—" He stopped and his eyes darted down to Lara. "What are you doing?"

"Saving his life," Lara said. She had pulled a roll of gauze out of one of her pouches and was wrapping it around Danny's waist. His shirt was pulled up, exposing his blood-slicked stomach. He groaned against her, but Gaby couldn't tell if he was still conscious.

"Stop that," Josh said.

"No," Lara said.

"What?"

"I said *no.*"

Josh looked confused, and for a moment he reminded her of the old Josh—young and inexperienced and awkward. Then the gun in his hand started to move…

"Don't, Josh," she said.

Josh looked at her, then back at Lara, who hadn't stopped treating Danny's bleeding wound despite the threat. The four behind Josh fidgeted—the shortest of the four even more prominently—as they moved their rifles from Lara to Gaby and back again.

A part of her wanted all of this to end right here, right now. After all the bloodshed of tonight, this would be poetic. Now, while standing with all those poor souls on the beach behind them, in a burst of gunfire. Wasn't that how all violent men's lives ended in the history books? Bonnie and Clyde? John Dillinger? Every bank robber she had seen on TV caught in the act by the police?

"Gaby, put down the rifle," Josh said. "It's over."

"I almost died ten times tonight, Josh," Gaby said through clenched teeth. "If you came here to save me, you're not doing a very good job."

He sighed. "You don't understand. It would have been worse if I hadn't been leading the attack. Kate would have sent someone else, someone worse. And believe me, there are worse people than me out there. That's how badly she wants this island."

"She can have it," Lara said. "Let us go."

He shook his head. "I can't do that. She doesn't just want the island, she wants you too, Lara. But it's not for the same reason she wants Will. I'm sorry. This is the end of the line for you and Danny."

"Josh, don't," Gaby said.

He turned back to her, and she thought he looked almost apologetic. "It's not my decision. You have to know that. It's Kate's. It's always been Kate's."

"She's not here. You are."

"She's everywhere. You don't understand. She's *everywhere*," he said, almost whispering the word "everywhere" as if he was afraid someone (Kate) might hear it.

She could see it in his eyes: Josh was scared. Not just him, but the four behind him blocking their path onto the beach. Gaby had very clearly seen a couple of them shifting their feet nervously at the sound of Kate's name.

No one wants to say the devil's name out loud.

"I'm sorry," Josh said again. "It has to be this way."

"If you get the chance—if you see him tonight—don't hesitate. Shoot him, because he'll shoot you," she had told Lara earlier.

So why couldn't she do it now?

Because he was Josh. No matter what he had become, or what she told others he had become, when she looked at him she still saw the eighteen-year-old boy who spent nearly a year trying to keep her safe. As much as he had changed, as much as he had done, he was still Josh.

And as she stood there watching Lara trying desperately to save Danny's life, working diligently despite the presence of the man who had just shot him standing close to her on the verge of shooting her too, Gaby realized she couldn't have loved Lara and Danny any more than she already did.

And she didn't want it to end. Not for her, and not for them. Not even for Josh. But most of all, not for her friends.

She wanted Danny to run into Carly's arms again, the way she had earlier today at the pier. She wanted Lara to finally see Will one more time after being apart for so long. She wanted the two of them to take little Claire and Milly to someplace better and start all over. Even if she couldn't go with them, she wanted that for these people, her family.

No, she didn't want it to end tonight after all. Not this way.

It can't end this way.

"Lara," Gaby said. "How is he?"

Lara looked back at her and shook her head.

It shouldn't end this way.

Gaby lowered her rifle and placed it on the ground, then did the same with her Glock. Josh sighed with relief at the sight. Even the four behind him seemed to relax a bit.

"Gaby," Josh said, "you're doing the right thing."

"Let them go," she said.

"What?"

"Let them go, and I'll come with you."

"Gaby, no," Lara said, looking back at her again.

"It's okay," Gaby said, and smiled at her. "It's just Josh."

Lara didn't believe her. Gaby could see it in her eyes.

"You'll come with me?" Josh said, sounding so young again.

Gaby nodded. "If you let them go."

"And you won't try to escape?"

"No."

"Ever."

"I won't try to escape. Ever."

His eyebrows furrowed, and he looked down at the road. This was what he wanted. This had always been what he wanted. The young boy whose family lived across the street from her for all those years. The teenager who secretly admired her from the back of the classes they had together. The survivor who did everything he could to keep her safe.

It won't end this way.

Finally, he looked back up and nodded. "I'll tell her everyone died on the island during the assault."

"What about them?" Gaby said, nodding at the four standing behind him.

"She talks to me, not them," Josh said. Then he nodded again, as if to confirm what he had already decided—or maybe to convince himself he could get away with it. "All right."

"All right?" she repeated.

"All right," he said again. Then to Lara and Danny, "Go. Hurry."

Lara looked back at Gaby, but before she could say anything, Gaby crouched next to her and embraced her as hard as she dared, keeping in mind Lara's hurt shoulder and that she was still cradling Danny's unmoving form in her lap. Lara put a hand on her arm, covering her in some of Danny's blood.

"I'll be okay," Gaby whispered. "Go. Please. Danny needs you to go now. I've already left Will behind and there won't be anything left of me if Danny dies, too. Please, save him. Save us. Save *everyone*."

She stood up quickly before Lara could say anything and nodded at Josh.

He held out his hand.

She forced a smile and reached for it when Josh's entire body suddenly stiffened.

"What is it?" she said.

"I...," he stammered, tried to say something, but couldn't get it out. Then he stared past her and back down the pathway at the black emptiness on the other side.

"Josh," Gaby said. "What is it? What's happening?"

"She knows," Josh said. His voice was soft, almost a whisper. "Oh God, she knows. She *knows*."

"Who? What does who know?"

He whirled on her, his eyes wide and seized with terror. "She knows!" he shouted. "She's in my head, Gaby! She's always been in my head! She knows everything!"

Lara had struggled up from the ground with Danny, his weight threatening to collapse the both of them. But somehow Lara was holding them up, though Gaby couldn't fathom how since Danny had to be so much heavier, especially now that he looked completely unresponsive.

"She knows!" Josh shouted again. "And she's pissed off!"

"Kate?" Gaby said. "Are you talking about Kate?"

"Yes!" He looked back down the pathway at the darkness. She couldn't see anything. What was he looking at? "She's in my head, Gaby. We're connected. I didn't realize—I didn't know how much— Oh my God, she *knows*."

"Josh…"

He seized her wrists and his fingers dug into her skin. "Run," he said breathlessly.

"Josh…"

"*RUN!*"

Gaby was looking at Josh, trying to understand, when the hotel grounds behind him seemed to have come alive…*moving*.

Then she saw them. Black pits of tar piercing through the night, rays of moonlight gleaming off pruned flesh and emaciated forms. The familiar *clacking* of bones and the *tap tap tap* of bare feet against cobblestone.

Hundreds, maybe thousands of them, pouring into the opening on the other end.

Ghouls.

CHAPTER 23

KEO

BLOOD. DEATH. AND bullets.

So what else was new?

Even the island locale wasn't anything he hadn't experienced before. Of course, back then he had a team behind him. Men who were grizzled beyond their years and killed with a glee usually reserved for butchers wearing plastic aprons. Tonight, all he had was a gimpy ex-Army Ranger, a teenage girl, and a bunch of civilians he wouldn't have trusted to watch his back in a snowball fight, much less a gunfight. And the cherry on top? A third-year medical student was calling the shots.

It could have been worse, though. People could have been looking to him for leadership. Now that would have been a nightmare.

At the moment, there was a lull in the radio channel, so he assumed Lara and the others were trying to figure out what was happening. He had already darted through the woods and stepped out into the opening at the western part of the island, with the big power station visible to his left in the open field. At one time it had been surrounded by hurricane fencing but was now left exposed. A red and brown mist had gathered around the area, the result of a few layers of brick and mortar being disintegrated by explosives.

It was hard to miss the silhouetted figures pouring out of a building the size of a backyard shack next to the ugly gray structure. They were clad in the same black uniforms and Kevlar helmets as the ones that had assaulted the beach. He was too far to count their exact number, but he guessed more than ten. Maybe two dozen. Who knew how many had already made it out before he arrived?

Keo crouched just beyond the tree lines and watched the figures racing across the open field. They clearly knew where they were going—east, toward the hotel. At least the figures weren't heading north where the *Trident* was currently anchored. That meant they hadn't spotted the yacht yet. Then again, for all he knew the first stream of invaders might have gone in that direction before he arrived.

There was a *click* in his right ear, and he heard Lara's voice through the comm. "This is Lara! Everyone who isn't already there, head to your designated exit points now! I repeat! Head to your exit points now! The island is lost! I repeat! The island is lost! We're evacuating Song Island!"

Oh, so now you want to leave?

Women. Can't make up their minds.

A part of him wanted to laugh. They had gone through all this effort to hold the island, but all it took was one well-placed explosive to change everything.

"Lara," he said into the radio.

"Keo!" He heard ragged breathing, which meant she was moving fast. "Where are you?"

"Southwest corner, just beyond the power station."

"What do you see?"

"More assaulters. They're coming through the shack next to the power station and heading right at you."

"How many?"

A shitload, he thought, but said, "Too many. But if we coordinate a defense—"

"No," Lara said, cutting him off. "It's not the humans we have to worry about. Without the shack, there's nothing to hold them back. Do you understand? Get to your exit point. We're getting off the island!"

"*Them?*" Oh. *Right.* Them.

"Roger that," he said.

He didn't move right away. Instead, he bided his time and let the stream of black-clad figures race across and vanish one by one into the waiting woods that separated this part of the island from the hotel on the other side. There was no point engaging that many men. He had done more than enough killing in the last hour to last a lifetime, and that was saying something given his past—

A lone figure, clearly not part of the invading horde, had appeared on the other side of the open ground. Keo was still trying to figure who it was (it had to be one of Lara's islanders, given how the man was trying to stay hidden), when the guy decided to ruin Keo's night by opening fire. Two men running full speed toward the woods fell instantly.

The man kept firing, but was smart enough to start moving sideways at the same time. He darted behind trees only to pop out on the other side and shoot again.

Keo ran through the island's inventory of men in his head. He discounted Danny because the man had come from the wrong direction. Stan the electrician would be near the hotel with Lara and Sarah, the cook. Roy would also be there with them. Benny, the other gimpy guy on the island, would be in the Tower with the redhead—or was, since Lara had given the abandon ship signal. Blaine, the big Mexican, had the important job of keeping Gage and the *Trident* in play.

So who did that leave?

The shooter had the right height for the kid Dwayne, but it was stretching it to think a twelve-year-old had the tactical ability he was witnessing now. No, that was a full-grown man out there who had just moved behind cover as the invaders returned fire on him.

Keo would have preferred to stay out of it, let the whole group pass him by before he made his way to his own exit point. That, unfortunately, was on the other side of the open clearing. The only other way to get to the yacht was to go around the power station using the western cliff, then circle over to the north side.

He would have liked to use the more direct approach because it was much, much faster, but as he observed the men in black starting to diverge toward the north and at the lone defender, his choices became very limited.

Remember when you were on your way to Gillian at Santa Marie Island?
Yeah. Live and learn, pal.

Keo ripped the NVD off and let it hang around his neck, then lifted the submachine gun and flicked the fire selector to full auto. He was more than a hundred meters from the closest assaulter when he stood up and unleashed all thirty rounds across the open field.

To his surprise, one of the men actually stumbled and fell to the ground, even though Keo had just fired randomly into the jagged line of attackers hoping to draw their attention away from the islander. They didn't hear his gunshots with the attached suppressor, but they either saw one of their own going down or they recognized someone was shooting at them from behind. Half of them turned around, night-vision goggles seeking him out in the darkness.

Keo spun and ran back into the tree line as they opened up on him, the loud clatter of a dozen or so assault rifles firing at the same time crackling across the air. They were armed with M4s and firing on three-round bursts. Unlike the carbines the islanders were using, the soldiers' weapons hadn't been converted to full-auto, it seemed. The difference between having a pair of Rangers on hand who knew their guns…and not, he guessed.

The problem was that those M4s, fully auto or not, still had the long-distance shooting ability that his MP5SD didn't. Fortunately for him, he was moving before they started shooting, though that didn't stop bullets from slamming into trees and snapping branches and kicking at the ground around him as he dived the last few meters into the sanctuary of the woods.

Daebak!

He scrambled to his feet, turned right, and ran as hard as he could. The air was filled with *buzzing* and gunfire, branches being reduced to splints all around him. Either they knew the direction he was taking or they were shooting at everything. Not that it mattered. He was still in one piece with no extra holes in him, which was good enough.

He didn't slow down until he could hear the lapping of the lake against the rocks at the bottom of the western cliff. Cool air floated through the trees and he stopped to catch his breath, then slipped the night-vision goggles back on. Running through a sea of trees with something blocking your vision, even if it gave you artificial night vision, wasn't a good idea. He had learned that the hard way outside of Caracas a few years back—

BOOM!

Keo turned back around. He knew instinctively the explosion had come from the hotel even before he glimpsed the gray-white plume of smoke rising lazily into the air. It sounded like a grenade.

This night just keeps getting better and better. Now aren't you glad you stayed?

So the bad guys had grenades, too. He guessed he shouldn't have been surprised. They had blown up the brick wall around the shack with something pretty strong. Maybe C4 or Semtex. Probably C4, since he was on American soil. Uncle Sam's boys in uniform hoarded those things in bunches.

The rattle of gunfire had picked up again, but this time not directed at him, thank God. He listened and judged their distance.

The hotel.

That was a bad sign, because Lara and the others were at the hotel. Or would have to go through it in order to reach their exit point as fast as possible. So he was right. More soldiers had come out of the shack before he even got there. He knew the sound of a ferocious firefight when he heard one, and he was listening to that right now.

He turned around and pushed north, even as the fight back at the hotel continued, the gunfire crashing like rolling thunder from one side of the island to the other. It was much louder than it really should have been, given the distance.

Beaufont Lake grew in volume to his left, but it wasn't enough to replace the clatter of another running gunfight ahead of him along the northern side. That would be where the *Trident* was waiting. How long before Blaine decided to take off? That would probably depend on how much fire he was taking. With his luck—

His right ear *clicked* and he heard someone screaming through the comm, "We're pinned!" *Lara.* "Blaine, take off now!"

Oh, hell no.

"What?" Blaine shouted back. "We're not leaving without you! Get over here!"

Good call. Just wait a little longer until I get there, Blaine ol' buddy.

"We're not going to make it!" Lara said.

"Then we'll come back to you!" Blaine said.

"Don't be stupid!"

No, Blaine. Be stupid. Be really stupid.

He picked up his pace just in case tonight was the night Blaine decided to start being smart.

"Lara!" Blaine shouted.

"That's an order, Blaine!" Lara said, most of her words drowned out by gunfire on her end. "Move your ass now, or I'm sending Danny over there to kick it!"

"Yeah, what she said!" Danny chimed in.

Then Carly said something before another *BOOM!* cut her off.

Keo stopped moving and glanced back toward the hotel. Another plume of smoke was rising into the air, wisps of it like a dragon's breath.

Well, that's not good.

He gripped the MP5SD and looked north, then east. The *Trident* was north. If he didn't get there soon, Blaine was going to obey Lara's orders and take off without him onboard. But Lara and Danny were pinned in the hotel. The bad guys also had grenades. They had made use of it twice now. What kind of chance did they have against that kind of firepower? What kind of chance did *he* have?

He looked north again.

I'm the dumbest man alive.

He sighed and took a step back toward the hotel, but he hadn't completely stepped out of the tree lines when a new round of gunfire ripped across the air nearby. He dropped to the ground reflexively, expecting the trees around him to be sliced in half by the rapid *brap-brap-brap* of a machine gun blasting away.

The *Trident*.

Danny had brought the M240 with him and it was now perched along the rails of the yacht, with either Blaine or one of the islanders behind it firing away. He was trying to pinpoint the location of the machine-gun fire when it started to get louder.

Oh, for the love of God.

Keo remained pressed against the cold ground, stretching out the MP5SD in front of him, when he heard the heavy *crunching* of combat boots tramping grass with wild abandon as they came toward him. They were shooting as they ran, the *zing-zing-zing!* of bullets stripping away leaves and branches as they attempted to hit—

The yacht, its stark white color like a metallic beast swinging around the curvature of the island. He glimpsed the staccato effect of the M240 firing away from the upper deck railing, the light show blinking in and out as the boat moved across the row of trees between him and the cliff. Keo imagined the stream of empty brass casings falling into the ocean as the MG razed the column of woods as it passed.

Two men, both clad in black, burst through a pair of trees in front of him. They were somehow moving while crouched and trying to get a shot on the *Trident*'s machine gunner through the trees. They were ten meters away and closing in when Keo dropped both of them with a squeeze of the trigger. Rifles clattered to the ground just before a third man, out of breath, slid to a stop at the sight of his dead comrades.

Keo shot him twice in the chest, then scanned the woods, waiting for more pursuers.

The yacht had continued on behind him, its weapon still firing nonstop into a section of the woods in front of Keo. He stayed low against the ground as 7.62mm rounds, coming at 700 to 900 rounds per minute (give or take), sheared the trees around him like axes chopping down branches and reducing bark into clouds that stung his eyes.

Keo didn't move his head for fear of getting it shot off. He didn't breathe or move at all until the *brap-brap-brap* finally faded and a large branch *plopped* down in front of him. The smell of burnt wood filled his nostrils, and he had to switch to breathing through his mouth.

Only then did he allow himself to hop back up to his feet.

He glanced back and saw the white of the *Trident* fading through the trees. Keo ran after it, moving closer toward the edge as he went, but not so close that he'd run right off the cliff with one false move. He could already feel the cool swirls from the lake brushing against his face as he neared the end of the woods.

There. The yacht, like a white missile, gliding across the calm lake water and getting smaller as it went. The damn thing was picking up speed and it wasn't going to stop for him. Nosirree. He thought about shouting after it, maybe tell it to *Get the hell back here*, but decided that probably wasn't going to work. The boat was too far away and besides, shouting might bring more men in black uniforms after him.

Not daebak. This is definitely not daebak.

He headed back to where he had left the three bodies. He slung his MP5SD and snatched up one of the M4s, knowing the magazine was almost empty by how light the rifle was. He searched the bodies and found two spares, pocketing what he could. You could never have too many bullets, especially on a night like this. He was about to swap in a full mag when—

"Hey!" a voice shouted from behind him.

A man. It didn't sound familiar, but it was close.

Keo stiffened, kept his back to the man, and didn't move. Unfortunately for him, he was still holding the rifle at hip level.

"Terry?" the man asked.

The *crunch crunch* of boots on grass as the man neared. The name was clearly accompanied by a question, so the guy wasn't certain who Keo was. Then again, he was surrounded by shadows and trees. In here, the moonlight picked and chose what it wanted to reveal, and at this very moment he was standing in one of those patches of darkness and wearing black.

"Yeah, what?" Keo said, keeping his voice as level as possible. He just hoped "Terry" didn't have a deep voice. Or a feminine one. Hell, for all he knew, "Terry" could have been a girl.

But apparently not, because the guy said, "Where is everyone?" and the *crunch crunch* of grass got louder as the man got closer.

"I don't know," Keo said, spinning around.

He fired the carbine without lifting it first, just in case the guy had a rifle pointed at him. The first three-round burst knocked a man in a black uniform to the ground…and revealed *four more* standing about twenty meters behind him.

Keo pulled the trigger again but only got a *click!*

He turned and ran as all four opened fire at the same time.

◄■■■ ■■■►

HE WASN'T SURE how long he'd been running, but sometime between either the third or fourth time he bent down to keep his head from getting blown off, he collided with a large tree that popped out of nowhere. Well, that wasn't true. The tree was always there, but he hadn't seen it because he was essentially running blind through the woods, too afraid to put on the night-vision goggles for fear of limiting what little vision he had.

Southeast.

That was all he knew; he was heading back toward the beach.

Then the tree said "Hi" and Keo bounced off it, but the impact knocked the radio loose from his hip and it went flying. He thought about trying to find it—for a brief nanosecond, anyway—but when the *crack!* of rifles sounded behind him, he decided he didn't really need it and kept running instead.

With the radio now lying in some bushes behind him, Keo ripped out the earbud and throat mic and tossed them. He had also dropped the M4 to further lighten his load, because he needed the extra speed more than he needed firepower at the moment.

The four chasing him were fast and relentless, and they apparently had plenty of ammo, because they kept shooting. A couple of rounds came dangerously close to detaching his head from his shoulders, but he credited that more to dumb luck than skill. It was hard enough hitting a running man, but it was next to impossible to hit him while you were running, too.

He did manage to lengthen his lead by turning suddenly left, which threw them off a bit. About half a minute later, he righted his direction until he was running toward the beach again.

He could almost feel the lake water somewhere up ahead. Almost there. All he had to do was reach one of the boats and get the hell off this island and forget this night ever happened. Or the last few nights. Dammit, where would he be now if he hadn't picked up Carrie and Lorelei? Probably on his way to Gillian. Or maybe already there, drinking piña colada. Did they have piña coladas on Santa Marie Island? He preferred to think they did.

To get off the island, he had to traverse about fifty meters of open beach while being shot at, which was why he was sticking to the woods for as long as possible. It had been a while since a bullet *buzzed* near his head, though he could still hear his pursuers crashing through branches and stomping the ground with their heavy boots behind him.

He couldn't hear the loud mechanical roar of boat motors anymore, but that wasn't surprising. After a while, the motors would turn off by themselves. As long as there was enough fuel left in one of the tanks, he could always turn them back on. There would be keys in the ignitions still. He didn't remember any of the soldiers taking the time to pocket those before leaping off the beached vessels.

He was certain he was back at his old spot, where he had been lying in wait for the assaulters, when he saw moonlight glinting off spent shell casings on the ground. That was good, because a man could only run for so long. How long had he been in constant motion, anyway? He had no idea. Time had a way of slipping by when you were trying to keep from getting shot.

The sudden burst of *pop-pop-pop* from behind him made Keo duck his head instinctively, praying for the twentieth time in as many seconds that one of those bullets didn't get lucky and take out his legs. Except he didn't have to duck, because nothing was coming at him. Bark on the trees around him weren't flying, and branches weren't snapping into kindling. Instead, the gunfire continued behind him but, for whatever reason, it wasn't being directed at him.

He told himself to keep running, to keep going—

Then someone screamed.

Then someone else joined in…

Keo slid to a stop and twisted around, lifting the MP5SD to fire. He was breathing hard, all the running finally catching up to him. He expected to see the four men in pursuit, but instead there were only two of them, and they were backing up toward him while shooting at something *behind them*.

It took only a second for Keo to see what they were shooting at.

He stared, because the sight was too much. Too…*insane*.

There had to be hundreds of them, so many there was no room for the trees, for the branches, for him and the two poor saps standing twenty meters in front of him, firing regular bullets into the creatures. Keo couldn't see the other two, but he didn't have to know where they were or what had happened to them. He could hear them screaming from inside the thick mass of moving ghouls.

I guess the uniform's not working anymore, Keo thought before he turned and lunged out between the trees and felt mushy white sand under his boots a second later.

Run! Run, run, run, run!

Behind him, from inside the woods, the screaming and the gunfire continued, but Keo didn't waste a second looking back. He didn't have to. He knew what was back there. God knew he had seen plenty of it to last a lifetime. Tens of lifetimes. Right now, there was just the blood-soaked beach under him, the bodies left behind where they had fallen, and the boats still perched on the other side waiting, so close and yet so, so far away.

Christ, he didn't remember the beach being this wide. Had it always been this wide?

Keo pushed harder, leaping over bodies and dodging rifles buried in the sand. There was so much blood it looked as if Song Island had soaked up all the plasma and was trying to give itself some kind of Grand Guignol makeover. And yet, and yet, the air still smelled fresh and clear, as if he could lie down and go to sleep right here and now and never notice the horrors.

Then the ground under his feet started to rumble. It felt like an earthquake, but of course he knew better. It wasn't a natural disaster. Hell, there was nothing natural about this.

He didn't have to look over his shoulder to know what was back there, but he did it anyway.

Because he had to be sure.

Because there was a chance he could be wrong—

He wasn't wrong.

They came out of the woods, between the trees, and the sight of the beach being swallowed up by the wave of pruned black flesh, like a living flood, sent a shiver up and down his spine. This was the stuff of nightmares, and Keo might have given in to his instincts and let out a loud mindless scream if he still had any energy left to make his mouth do anything besides gasp for breath.

To keep himself from freezing with fear, Keo looked forward instead and counted the steps to the nearest boat.

Twenty meters. Not too bad.

Then what?

Jump up into the boat. Turn the engine. Pray the motor still worked. Then somehow back out into the lake—

Dead. I'm dead meat.

He didn't have to look over his shoulder this time to know they were almost on top of him. He could *smell* them. The air had changed, shifting from that pleasant clean lake aroma to something thick and grimy that made breathing difficult. His lungs continued to burn from all the running he had done, and his legs became dangerously wobbly.

Ten meters…

Gunshots rang out, and Keo glanced left without breaking his stride. Someone else was also moving toward the row of boats further down the beach. Because of the distance and with only moonlight to see with, he couldn't tell if it was a lone figure or multiple people huddled together. Or hell, an entire basketball team.

But at least they knew where they were going.

The water. Get to the water!

Five…

Four…

Three…

Then he was there, the splash of wetness against his boots, letting him know that he had made it. He ran past the closest boat without looking at it, because the air behind him crackled and he felt warm, tainted breath hit the back of his neck and what sounded like a guttural squeal of delight—

Keo took a leap of faith. Or maybe he just leaped. Through the air. He imagined he must look like some kind of dolphin.

He hit the water headfirst and went under, unable to squash the laughter even as he sucked in a mouthful of Beaufont Lake water, because this was the third time he had gone for a swim in as many nights. He sank with his entry, but thank God he was a strong swimmer, because Keo quickly righted himself.

"They will not cross bodies of water," Lara had said in her broadcast. *"An island, a boat—get to anything that can separate you from land."*

Why, exactly, wouldn't the ghouls cross bodies of water? Lara didn't know. No one knew. The creatures just didn't.

Well, it was time to test that theory. Up close and personal.

Hello, Guinea Pig Island!

He was halfway to the bottom of the slanted lake floor when he whirled around and almost choked on more of the clear water when he saw them dive bombing into the lake around him, shattering the surface one by one by one. They looked like missiles falling from the sky, but they were so light *(bags of bones)* that they didn't sink right away.

Keo counted.

Five...ten...

Twenty!

Maybe one more. Maybe one less. Twenty or more (or less) ghouls in the lake with him were more than enough to make this a very short swim.

He was reaching for his MP5SD, hoping the German gun would still prove effective. He had never actually fired it under water before. But hey, there was a first time for everything. Like the end of the world. Like keeping a stupid promise to a woman he hadn't seen in half a year. Like almost giving up his life for an island full of strangers run by a third-year medical student—

Keo never had to try shooting the submachine gun under water, because one second the creatures looked as if they would right themselves at any second and the next they seemed to be convulsing, desperately trying not to swallow the lake water. Their arms and legs were thrashing about wildly and one or two, maybe more, of them began trying to swim back toward the shore. Or what appeared to be an attempt to swim. It actually looked more like frantic kicking and clawing, movements he'd seen more than once from dumb tourists who got to Mission Beach and realized, too late, that they didn't know how to swim.

He watched with a combination of fascination and exhilaration as the closest ghoul struggled to stay afloat, its dark eyes bulging as water poured into its agape mouth, bony fingers reaching out toward him as if for a handhold. Keo treaded water, neither sinking nor going up, too mesmerized by the sight to go anywhere.

Then they stopped moving entirely, and one by one they began to sink toward the bottom. They looked like stones, blackened gargoyles with arms and legs frozen in mock surrender. These creatures that he always thought of as being entirely devoid of humanity were suddenly very human and he saw, to his surprise, what looked like terror frozen across their faces. They sank and sank, before resting softly, almost delicately, against the angled incline of the lake floor.

He waited for more of the creatures to drop down from the sky after him, into the water, and die, too. But there were no more. He could see them on the other side of the surface, like staring through a murky, flickering mirror. They crowded the beach, black shapes easy to make out, and looked after him but unwilling to pursue.

"They will not cross bodies of water. An island, a boat—get to anything that can separate you from land."

Keo turned around and continued swimming. He stayed under for as long as he could before finally breaking the surface to suck in a lungful of fresh air.

He wasn't surprised to find that he was surrounded by darkness. When he turned around, the island sans lights was barely visible in the distance. He couldn't even see the beaches anymore, and it took him a few seconds to realize why.

The ghouls. There was nothing on the beaches at the moment but those shriveled black things that used to be human, so many that they blotted out the white sand.

He was staring at them when he thought he heard the sound of a motor droning somewhere behind him. Keo glanced around, but there was no boat in sight. At least, nothing on the water. There were plenty on the beach, but given what was also waiting for him there, they might as well not exist.

He pointed himself in the direction where he thought the shoreline was—even though it was impossible to see right now—and started kicking toward it.

He always liked swimming in the ocean at night anyway. You had to, in order to avoid the crowds during tourist season along San Diego's beaches. Of course, if he had known he'd spend this much time in the water at night, he would have put in even more time.

Live and learn, pal.

Live and learn...

CHAPTER 24

WILL

"WE'RE GOING TO die," Natasha said. "I should have stayed in the back room and not come out to save you. You're going to get me killed. Jesus, you're going to get me killed."

"I thought you didn't care about dying," Will said.

"I changed my mind." She was visibly shaking, even in the semi-darkness of the store. "I changed my mind, you hear me? I want to live. I didn't think I did, but now I want to live."

Check out Captain Optimism here, Danny.

"Shut up and listen," he said.

"Listen to what? That? I can hear *that* just fine!"

The constant *bang! bang! bang!* of ghouls smashing themselves into the glass curtain wall hadn't let up, not even for a second for him to catch his breath. There were so many of them, and they were raining blow after blow on the windows that the cracks were now stretched from one end of the frame to the other and connecting like river veins along the way.

It wouldn't be long now. Soon, very soon, the windows would break and there would be nothing to stop them. Then it would be over. He would never reach Song Island. Never get to see Lara after so long. Never hold her hand or walk on the beach with her again.

Kate. This is your doing, isn't it?

"Yes."

Her voice echoed inside his head. It was unnatural and yet so intimate. *Too* intimate. It was like talking to a lover. Pillow talk. He shivered at the thought.

"*How sweet.*"

Had she just laughed? Giggled? Was it possible to project that sort of thing through...what was this? Telepathy? ESP? Insanity?

"*Don't be so hard on yourself, Will.*"

Where are you?

"*Close.*"

You're coming here.

"*Yes...*"

You know.

"*Yes...*"

How?

"*I can see you,*" she said. "*Inside that store. In that uniform with the woman. You've looked better, Will. But we can fix that. Imagine: No more wounds, no more scars, and no more illnesses.*"

The uniforms aren't going to work, are they?

"*Haven't you figured it out by now? It only works when I tell them it works.*"

He stared out the cracked *(breaking)* windows at the creatures, past the ones flying into the glass like raindrops falling to the sidewalks, and at the wall of skeletal figures standing like good soldiers in the back. The sight of them, unmoving in the moonlight, was somehow more distracting than the ones smashing into the windows.

For some reason, he wasn't really frightened. Disappointed and saddened, yes, but the fear wasn't there. Even if everything ended tonight, he could take solace in one thing: At least Kate was here and not on Song Island. If nothing else, there was comfort in knowing she was too busy to pay attention to Lara—

"*Oh, Will.*" He sensed, even if he couldn't actually hear it, amusement dripping with every word that echoed inside his head. "*I don't have to be there to be there. Will, Will, Will. How did you ever think you could beat us when you know so little?"*

You're attacking the island now, aren't you?

"Not me. The island is an annoyance, but it's not worth my time. I have people for those things."

Like Josh. Like Mason...

"Two of many. So, so many. You have no idea."

It made sense she wasn't at the island in person, because she didn't have to be. There was a legion of human collaborators willing and anxious to do her bidding. People like Rick and Millard, dead on the floor in their boxers behind him. Opportunists like Mason. Then there were all the poor, easily malleable souls like Josh, who didn't know any better.

She laughed inside his head. *"You, on the other hand...I can devote time to you, Will."*

What do you want from me, Kate?

"You're living in the old world. It's time to join me in the real one."

No...

"Don't be so naïve. You don't have a choice."

CRASH!

The first section of windowpane shattered and fell in streams to the tiled floor. The creature that had used itself as the final hammer flopped through among the shower of cubed glass, like sand pebbles, but only thicker and sharper. It rolled forward, bones *clacking*, shards of shiny glass sticking out of its cheeks and body and shoulder and chest—

"Run!" Will shouted.

By the time he turned around, Natasha was already racing toward the back room, arms swinging wildly in front of her. She had apparently forgotten all about her injuries. Like her, he couldn't feel his own wounds anymore. His legs had stopped hurting (or, at least, that's what he told himself) and every cut and bruise had ceased to matter. Everything faded into the background except the need to flee.

He glanced back as the ghoul rose from the floor, even as more of its brethren gave up on assaulting the other parts of the window and converged on the opening. They attacked the entrance with wild abandon, slashing their flesh against the jagged glass, thick rivulets of tainted blood arcing through the air and splashing the tiles and counters and shelves.

Run run run!

He darted into the last aisle and saw the open backroom door waiting for him at the very end. The brass handle stuck out in the semidarkness, gleaming with promise.

Natasha, already inside, was shouting at him. "Move your ass! Move your ass now!"

Gee, thanks for the suggestion, Natasha. I was just going to lollygag out here for a few minutes and then—

TAP TAP TAP!

He glanced over his shoulder again—

A flying swarm of twisted limbs and seemingly rippling flesh leaped onto the top of the shelves and knocked over products as they hopped their way toward him. Black eyes pierced the darkness and he imagined Kate, somewhere out there, looking through those very same hollowed holes at him.

"*How did you ever think you could beat us when you know so little?*"

She was right. She was so right. He knew so little. After all these months, he still knew so little about them. How did he—

"Come on!" Natasha's voice cut through his thoughts.

He turned and lunged into the backroom and spilled against the cheap tiled floor. He landed on his outstretched arms and spun around until he was on his back, his hands scrambling to unsling the M4. Pain from the torn flesh underneath the bandages roared, but he pushed them aside and concentrated on getting a solid grip on the weapon.

Natasha was slamming the door—*BANG!*—then groping for the deadbolt and shoving it into place. She turned around and pressed her back against the slab of wood as if that would be enough to keep it shut.

It wouldn't be. He knew it, and she knew it, too.

He looked into her eyes and knew that she wanted to live. Desperately. The woman he had met earlier, who had murdered Michael in cold blood and had some kind of death wish, really had come to an epiphany. She didn't want to die.

He wished he could tell her that she had a choice at this moment.

Thoom-thoom-thoom!

Natasha was stunned by the ferocity of the attack and staggered forward before regaining her composure and shoving herself back against the door. The sections of the wall that flanked the door quivered as the creatures assaulted it from the other side, over and over again, a ceaseless pounding of flesh against wood. Weakening wood. There was no way in hell the door was going to last the entire night. Not even close.

"Now what?" she shouted at him.

Thoom-thoom-thoom!

He picked himself up from the dirty floor and glanced around the semi-dark room. He saw it right away—a small pool of moonlight shining inside through the three-by-three-feet window at the back. The same one Natasha had climbed through earlier.

"Will."

There was an ethereal quality to her voice that seemed to sing only for him.

"It's over, Will. Stop fighting and open the door."

No.

"Open the door."

No!

"Why do you always have to fight?"

Why? Because that was who he was. He didn't surrender. He couldn't. Lives were at stake. His. Natasha's. Lara's. Because he had to get home to her. Get back to Song Island. Whatever it took. However long. He had to get home.

Thoom-thoom-thoom!

"Hey!" Natasha shouted behind him. He looked back at her, still pressed against the door, both feet sliding each time the creatures crashed against her on the other side. "Do something, goddammit!"

Good idea. Do something. Why didn't I think of that?

"Will..."

Get out of my head!

"No."

Get out of my head, damn you!

"Open the door, Will."

No!

"Open the door!"

NO!

"Hey!" Natasha's voice again, loud and raw, drawing him constantly out of Kate's soothing embrace. "Don't just stand there! Do something, for God's sake!"

Thoom-thoom-thoom!

"This door's not going to last! Hey! Can you hear me?"

Thoom-thoom-thoom!

"Do something!"

He nodded back at her. Or thought he did.

What do to? What to do?

The window. Use the window.

And then what?

Later. No choice.

Out there, he had a chance. A tiny chance. Miniscule. But it was better than in here. There was absolutely zero chance within the confines of this small backroom. Out there, in the wide open, maybe...

You almost believed yourself that time. Ha!

He slung the rifle and hurried across the room to the back.

Thoom-thoom-thoom!

The window was locked by a simple latch at the bottom. Will stood on his tiptoes and looked out at the darkness, expecting to see a pair of black eyes staring back at him. Instead, there was just the pitch-black of night.

Was it possible the creatures were all converging on the front windows, trying to get in through the door? Was the back of the store really clear? His heart actually raced at the possibility of surviving.

Thoom-thoom-thoom!

"Are you kidding me?" Natasha shouted behind him. "Aren't there more of those things out there?"

"I don't see any!" he shouted back.

Thoom-thoom-thoom!

He swore he could feel the entire room trembling with each crash, and he pretended that he couldn't hear the sounds of pieces of the wall falling apart around the door. Not long now. A few minutes, at the most...

Thoom-thoom-thoom!

"Do it!" Natasha shouted. "Whatever you're gonna do, do it!"

He flicked open the latch and pulled the window up and open. Cold wind rushed inside and swamped him. He shivered, though he wasn't sure if that was from the chill or something else.

"Will."

He ignored it.

"Why do you persist?"

There was such a lyrical quality to her voice that made it difficult to shut out.

"This is for the best."

He stuck his head out through the opening and looked left, then right.

"This is inevitable."

Nothing. Emptiness.

"Song Island is gone. And Lara and Danny with it."

There was nothing out there. He had expected to see a legion of them, but there was...nothing.

Just...nothing.

"Will..."

He didn't answer the voice. Instead, he looked back at Natasha and nodded.

"Oh, God," she said.

Thoom-thoom-thoom!

"Come on," Will said.

"You first."

He gave her a grin. Or close. It might have been something awkward or half-assed. Or maybe both.

Thoom-thoom-thoom!

He turned around, got a good grip on the windowsill, and pulled himself up and—

—over.

He landed in a crouch and quickly unslung the M4, scanning the darkness behind the iron sights of the weapon.

There was just the black shroud of night staring back at him from every direction. The gas station was flanked by a thick wooded area to his right and Interstate 10 to his left, its gray concrete form just barely visible under the moonlight about a hundred meters away on the other side of a feeder road and overgrown grass that swayed in the breeze. The real jungle was on the other side—thick patches of shadows, like walls, that was as inviting as stepping into a wood chipper.

He stood up just as Natasha made an *oomph!* sound as she landed a few inches next to him.

It didn't take long for the door in the backroom to go. In fact, the loud *crash!* caught him off guard because Will expected it to last just a little bit longer. Had Natasha really been the only thing keeping it from collapsing all this time?

"Oh, shit," Natasha said breathlessly. She stumbled, turned around, and lifted her M4, ready to shoot the first thing that came through the open window behind them.

She didn't get the chance because the darkness behind her shifted, moving in ways that shouldn't be possible. Natasha fell. As she did, she pulled the trigger and the carbine fired a three-round burst into the air, the staccato effect of the discharge lighting up the immediate area for a second and a half, illuminating the half dozen ghouls that were pulling her down, bony fingers clutched around her legs and arms and waist.

Natasha let out a shriek that pierced Will's soul.

Then she was gone, swallowed up by the shadows. The air crackled and the stench of death filled his nostrils as she screamed and screamed and screamed...

He started moving toward Natasha instinctively, but froze when they emerged out of the blackness. There was just enough moonlight to make out their emaciated forms, hollowed black eyes, and the sound of bone joints *popping* as they scrambled toward him.

He took a step back and fired, the first three-round burst shredding the chest of one of them. The second burst drilled three holes into the head of a second. Of course he knew it wouldn't stop them. Why should it? The bullets weren't silver, and he might as well be throwing sand pebbles at them for all the good the rounds were doing.

But he didn't have a choice. Will kept backing up along the wall, moving left, even though he didn't know why left would be any better than right. Left took him toward the highway, but he had no illusions he was ever going to reach it. He should have stopped then and there to catch his breath, but that would mean surrendering. Will hadn't given up when the world died, and he'd be goddamned if he was going to do so now.

He kept shooting, because there was nothing else to do. But it wasn't just the ghouls coming out of the nothingness around him now; they were also pouring out of the small gas station window, dropping to the ground one after another, after another...

He shot the legs out from under a ghoul, and it fell and was instantly stepped on by two—three—*a dozen* others.

"Will, stop."

There wasn't the sound of triumph in her voice that he was expecting. There was almost...what was it? Concern? No. That had to be a trick of his mind, giving her human traits when he knew damn well Kate was no longer human. She was a monster, like these poor bastards coming at him from every direction at the moment.

He was hoping the continuous gunfire would drown out her voice, but he had no such luck. He could hear her just fine. More than fine, actually. Her words were so loud and clear despite everything that he might as well be trying to shut himself off from his own thoughts.

"Why do you keep fighting me?"

He smashed the butt of the rifle into the head of the first ghoul that reached him. He heard a *crack!* as its skull gave way. The blow sent it reeling, though whether he had actually hurt it or not (or maybe just annoyed it), he couldn't tell. And he didn't have time to find out because the others were already closing in from the right and left—

Left. Christ, the left!

"You always were so stubborn."

He spun and started shooting in that direction, but that meant he was now cut off from the highway.

"Always so...Will."

Click! as the rifle went empty.

Already? He didn't have time to breathe or reload because they were everywhere, converging on him in an unending tide. He dropped the rifle and drew the Smith & Wesson, shooting the closest one point-blank in the face. The bullet drilled through its right eye and hit another ghoul behind it in the forehead. It, too, snapped back momentarily.

"The world turns whether we're here or not."

He shot another one in the chest, spun around, and blew out the forehead of another, and then they were all over him. One had gotten a grip on his right arm and was pulling it back, along with the gun. He punched it in the face, staggering it. That forced it to let go of his arm, but it just gave another ghoul—*two*—the opportunity to take its place.

"There is order in acceptance."

He could only see the tops of their pruned foreheads as they climbed over him, and soon they were pushing him down to one knee. He fired another shot, but it was like throwing a pebble into an ocean of black tar. Nothing. Absolutely nothing happened.

"You don't have to lose your humanity. Not all of it, anyway. I can show you how."

Then he was kneeling, trying to rise, but unable to against their sheer number. One or two, or even a dozen wouldn't have done it, but there was more than that. There were two, maybe even three dozen, crawling over him. Whatever had happened to them—this infection, this deviant transformation—it had shrunk them into husks of their normal size. They were shorter and lighter, but that didn't matter when there were *so many of them.*

"*Let go.*"

He fell. He had no choice. He went down on the grass, trying desperately to punch and kick at them, but he could barely move any of his limbs.

"*Just let go…*"

No.

"*It's over…*"

No!

"*Yes…*"

He couldn't see anything—just a world of black, even darker than the night itself. This nothingness, this void was complete and suffocating. He waited to feel their teeth penetrate his skin, to inject their poisoned blood into his veins and turn him from who he was into what they were—

"*No, Will. You're not for them. You were never meant for them.*"

There was a sadness in her voice. He didn't know how he knew, but he felt it in every fiber of his being that this Kate was once again the Kate he knew, the survivor of The Purge and not the one that had become a monster. Or maybe he was fooling himself again.

"*Soon you'll understand everything.*"

They had pinned his right arm against the ground near his hip, bony fingers wrapped around every inch of his skin like pricking needles.

Never.

"*Yes.*"

Never…

It took every ounce of muscle, but he was able to move his hand partially up the length of his body despite the arms—so many fingers, and so strong—tugging at him the entire way. Or maybe they weren't strong at all. Maybe it was just their sheer number. How many now? Three dozen hands? Four?

It didn't matter. There were too many. There were always too damn many.

He kept pulling anyway, willing every muscle to work, and slowly, very slowly, turned the gun in his hand until it faced up instead of down.

Lara, I'm sorry. I tried to make it back home.

He wrapped his finger around the familiar cold trigger.

I tried, baby. I really tried.

The gun wasn't exactly right under his chin where he could be guaranteed of a killing shot, but it was close enough. Or it would have to do, anyway.

I can't become one of them, Lara. I won't *become like her.*

He wished he could see where the barrel was pointing, just to be sure. He wished, he wished, he wished…for so many things at the moment.

Please understand.

He had to get it right with the first shot, because he wouldn't have a second one. If he just wounded himself, he might not have the strength to try again.

I hope you'll be able to forgive me.

He started to pull the trigger…

"What are you doing, Will?"

He didn't remember the trigger being so strong, so difficult to pull. It felt as if the gun was purposefully fighting him. Or was he just weak from all the struggling? That could have been it.

"No."

He ignored her and closed his eyes, shutting out the sight of the wall of black flesh. He didn't need to see them to know this was the right thing to do. He couldn't become one of them. Never. Lara would understand.

"You can't do this."

At least Danny and Gaby had made it home. At least there was that. If nothing else—all the failures, the near-misses—at least he had done that one thing right.

Take care of her, Danny. I'm counting on you.

There, almost there—

"Stop it," the voice said, and this time it wasn't inside his head. This time it was coming from *outside*. "It can't end like this."

The ghouls pinning him to the ground unraveled, their thick layers dissolving like liquid around him. They released his arms and legs and slithered backward on their hands and knees.

He could breathe again, and sucked in a deep lungful of biting cold air.

He was still on the ground, his chest heaving, the thickness of the night sky exposed above him. It was ironic that it would end here—out in the open and under the stars. The Purge had begun inside an apartment building for him, and it seemed as if he had been hiding inside back rooms and basements ever since.

Except for all those wonderful times when he was at the island with Lara. Those were the best days of his life. The best nights, too. Because of her.

Lara...

Something moved in the darkness, flickering in the corners of his eyes. He sat up and scrambled to his feet, backing up until he was pressed against the brick wall of the store, the Smith & Wesson clenched tightly in his hand.

Almost. He'd almost pulled the trigger.

He didn't shoot the approaching figure right away; not yet, not until he could see what he was shooting at. He could feel the weight of the gun even through the gauze covering the raw (and probably bleeding again) flesh underneath—the magazine was half empty, and he knew with absolute certainty he wouldn't have time to reload if he emptied it now.

Not yet, not yet...

The lone ghoul emerged out of the black canvas like a ghostly apparition; it was taller than the others, and it stood straight. It walked toward him with a preternatural fluidity that shouldn't have been possible and had the obvious hips of a woman even though anything resembling breasts were long gone, replaced by a sunken chest that, nevertheless, managed to still look strong and boastful.

The way it moved was undeniable: It owned this moment with every step, and it knew it.

Bright blue eyes pulsated in the darkness.

He knew this day would come. Somehow, some way, he knew it would end this way, with the two of them face to face in the middle of a lonely, dark night.

"Hello, Will," she said. "It's been a long time."

CHAPTER 25

LARA

"*Run!*" THE KID shouted.

Kid? Why was she calling him a kid? The Josh who had come back to the island after supposedly dying wasn't a kid anymore. Far from it. The fact that he had just shot Danny with a pistol erased any doubts about that.

Lara was struggling to pick Danny up when Gaby grabbed him on the other side. They exchanged a brief look and as much of a smile as they could manage before they lifted Danny up from the cobblestone road.

"Run!" Josh was shouting behind them. "Get out of here, Gaby! Leave him, and get out of here now!"

But Gaby didn't leave him, and Lara couldn't be any more prouder of her. The girl who had come back to her was hardly recognizable, but it wasn't because of the bruises and cuts. Gaby had changed. She had grown up. She might have still been nineteen, but Lara saw a woman when she looked across Danny.

She's a soldier, Will. You'd be proud of her.

And she was going to need Gaby, too, because Danny was heavy. God, he was so heavy.

She hadn't taken more than a few steps when the air became drenched with a nauseating smell. It was indescribable, and though she hadn't seen them in such a long time, she knew exactly what the stench was a harbinger of even before she glanced back over her shoulder. She had to see for herself—the proof that all of this was happening, that Song Island really was lost to them.

The wall of pruned flesh moved against the night, blackening the already dark background on the other side of the open pathway. She swore she could hear them not just in front of her, but through the woods to both sides, too—the loud and stampeding *crunch!* of grass and the *snap!* and *thwack!* of branches assaulting every one of her senses.

"Faster," Lara said, the word coming out in a breathless whisper. "Faster, Gaby!"

Gaby didn't answer, but she did pick up her pace, and together they pushed their way through the four soldiers staring, a couple of them already lifting their rifles at the legion of creatures swarming down the pathway toward them.

Run! Lara wanted to shout at them. *Run, you fools! Bullets don't stop them! Even silver bullets only slow them down until the next hundred more take their place!*

She didn't, because she didn't care what they did or didn't do. She didn't have any interest in their lives at all. They were the enemy—people who had come here to kill her and her friends—and she didn't give a damn what happened to them. But a small part of her that thought maybe, just maybe, having the soldiers between her and the ghouls would slow the creatures down.

What was that old joke? *"I don't need to outrun the bear. I just need to outrun you!"*

She wanted to laugh, but of course when she opened her mouth, the only thing that came out was harried breathing. She was already out of breath and they hadn't even gone a few yards yet.

"Run!" someone was shouting behind them.

Josh. He wasn't talking to her or Gaby; he couldn't be, because they were already running. So who was he screaming at?

The soldiers. Of course.

"I can't control them!" Josh was shouting. "Run! For God's

sake, run!"

Lara risked a second look back.

Josh was running after them even as his soldiers opened fire on the creatures bounding down the pathway at them. She had forgotten just how unnatural they looked in motion, like a flip picture book colored all in black.

"Go!" Josh shouted at her. "Don't stop! Kate sent them! They're not going to stop! I can't stop them! No one can!"

"Lara, she's coming," Will had said. *"She's coming..."*

Kate. Lara remembered how the woman had chased them from Starch, Texas to Beaumont, then all the way into Louisiana and finally, Song Island. She wouldn't let them go. No, that wasn't true. She was more than happy to let them go. She just wouldn't let *Will* go.

You and your exes, Will, she wanted to laugh.

If Lara went another day without having to hear that creature's name, she would die a happy woman.

As Josh chased them—no, not chased, followed—the soldiers he had abandoned were still shooting behind them. The men, anyway. The only woman among them—the twenty-something with the black ponytail—was looking after them. After Josh. There was an expression on her face that Lara had seen plenty of times before.

Hurt. Regret. *Betrayed.*

"The boats!" Josh shouted at her. "Get to the boats! They won't go into the water! Get to the boats!"

Lara didn't know what he was doing, or why. She only knew that he wasn't shooting at them with the gun clenched in his hand, and that was all she cared about.

She turned around and got a better grip around Danny's waist just as they stepped off the pathway and she finally—*finally*—felt the squishy beach under her. The sand seemed to sink under her boots and she wasn't running nearly as fast as she had been just a second ago.

It wasn't that she was running slower, it was Danny. He was too heavy even with her and Gaby carrying him at the same time. His head hung against his chest, his eyes closed, and sweat dripped off his temple and down his painfully pale, unresponsive face. She couldn't help but wonder if he was already dead, if she and Gaby weren't carrying around a dead man with them at this very moment.

Bang! Bang!

Two quick gunshots from almost directly behind her. Lara didn't have to look back to know who was shooting. Josh. She recognized the sound of his handgun from earlier, when he'd shot Danny.

"Faster!" Josh was shouting behind them between gunshots. "Get to the boats! Gaby, get to the boats!"

Lara looked over at Gaby on the other side of Danny, but she couldn't see the teenager past Danny's bouncing head. She could hear Gaby's heavy breathing just fine, though, even over the *pop-pop-pop* of assault rifles and Josh's earsplitting gunshots behind them.

The water! Get to the water!

She willed herself not to look back a third time (it was hard, so hard) and kept running—or ran as much as she could, anyway. The fact was, she was mostly stumbling, Danny's weight like a giant boulder on her shoulders. It was his feet—they were dragging across the sand like an anchor. But that couldn't be helped. He was simply too heavy for her and Gaby to lift completely off the ground.

Josh was still firing behind them. She didn't know why he was wasting his time. Did that handgun of his (some kind of black semiautomatic) even have silver bullets? If they didn't, he mind as well be picking up handfuls of sand and throwing them at the ghouls for all the good he was doing.

Of course, she didn't bother to tell him that. If he fell now, that was one more thing for the creatures to waste a precious second or two on. Another speed bump on the road to salvation.

Speed bump of the dead. Ha ha. Good one, Lara.

She might have chuckled to herself that time.

I've finally developed Danny's morbid sense of humor. God help me.

They were halfway to the water when Gaby began to slow down noticeably. Lara thought about shouting encouragement when she realized the teenager was only mirroring her own flagging pace. It wasn't just that they were both tiring, they were also literally sinking into the beach with every step.

She didn't know why it felt as if they were running in quicksand until she looked down and saw the blood. It was all over the beach, supplied in generous amounts by the dead men that had assaulted the island. The dozens of bodies lay across the white sand, multiple jagged lines of lost lives thrown away by Kate as if they were little more than expendable sacks of meat.

That's all we are to them. Meat.

What chance do we have? Why do we keep fighting—

The shooting behind them had suddenly stopped and there was just her and Gaby's labored breathing, along with Josh's (he was so close behind her that she swore she could feel his warm breath brushing against the back of her neck) crashing against the lapping waves in front of them.

My God, it was still so far away.

The water—she could see it, even smell and taste it in the air, but it was still so far away. Why was it so damn far away?

She thought about handing Danny off to Josh. He was a man now—bigger and taller and stronger. He could help Gaby carry Danny faster than she could. The two of them were uninjured and would have a better chance of reaching the boat than with her. Besides, she was pretty sure she was bleeding again. The question was, was it both her wounds or just one? Given how badly her night was going, it was probably both.

Her left shoulder and thigh were screaming at her at unimaginable decibels. It had started when she first picked Danny up, and it had only gotten worse—and louder—as she trudged across the length of the beach. Her shoulder in particular howled and bounced off the insides of her skull. Both of her legs were throbbing—and not just the one that was injured and wrapped in gauze at the moment.

She wanted to stop and sit down. No, lie down. That would be so much better. It was time to rest, anyway. She had been fighting for so long, and now she just wanted to stop for a moment and take a breath that wasn't so labored that it felt as if her chest would cave in with every gasp of air.

Why fight it? We can't win.

Why didn't you tell me, Will? Why didn't you ever tell me the truth?

We can't win. We can't—

She looked across and saw Gaby on the other side of Danny. Her face was locked in a tight grimace, and every inch of her was flushed with pain. But she hadn't stopped—not even for a second. She pushed on, fighting through whatever physical hell was trying to suffocate her at the moment.

The sight of Gaby filled Lara with pride.

You're right, Will. We have to keep fighting. Not just for us, but for everyone. For all the Gabys of the world. The Elises and the Veras and the Dwaynes.

Goddammit, you're right. You're always so damn right…

She could do it. She could take the pain and keep moving, because there were no other choices. It was stop and die, or keep moving and live. It didn't matter if they only survived for another second. Or minute. Or hour.

Survive!

"The boat!" Josh's voice, so much louder than before, as if he was almost on top of her. Had she and Gaby really slowed down that much? "Get on the boat!"

"Lara!" *Gaby?* Why was Gaby shouting at her? "Ready?"

Ready? Ready for wha—

Oh.

The boat. One of the ten boats that lined the beach, coming up on them. It was one of the smaller ones, and it had only partially slid up onto the sand before its occupants bailed. There was blood along the sides, and a man in a black uniform lay half-in and half-out of the water nearby, like a permanent fixture.

Then she did a stupid thing and looked back again.

They were coming out of the trees, an oozing black blob of moving limbs and black eyes. There wasn't a single part of the beach behind her that she could see that wasn't already turning black, as if someone had poured a giant bottle of ink that was now swallowing up the white sand inch by inch.

She couldn't take her eyes off them—these impossibly twisted and emaciated things that were once human beings. Their speed was incomprehensible, and for a moment she was sure her eyes were lying to her. But no, they really were that fast, it was just that she hadn't seen them for so long that she had forgotten.

"Lara!" Gaby's voice again. "Hurry!"

She looked forward just as wetness swamped her feet.

Water?

The lake!

The boat wasn't so tall that they couldn't have climbed over without help, but Danny was heavy and all the running had tired her out, and her wounds were screaming inside her like banshees. Every inch of her ached, so Lara had no idea where both she and Gaby found the strength, but they hoisted Danny up—

—he went over and landed on the other side of the beached boat with a loud *thump!* that she hoped wasn't a bad sign. To have gone through all the trouble to save him, only to have him land on something sharp, was a terrifying thought.

Gaby grabbed the side of the boat and disappeared up it with surprising fluidity. Lara wondered where she'd learned that. She'd ask her later…if there was a later.

She gripped the side and pulled herself up, somehow managing not to cry out as pain exploded across her body, her left arm feeling as if it would snap in two—or maybe three or four—pieces at any second.

She might have either cried or screamed (or both) as she climbed over the side and dropped to the floor on the other side. She didn't remember, because she was scrambling to her knees next to Danny, who had fallen on top of an M4 rifle that had been left behind by one of the assaulters.

Lara grabbed the rifle and jerked it out from underneath Danny, then she made the mistake of looking back up the beach again.

They were still coming (of course they were, what did she think, they were going to give up when she wasn't looking?) and there was so many that she imagined this must be what it was like to stare into the heart of a living and breathing black hole. There was nothing in front of her but death.

Josh. Where's Josh?

Not far, as it turned out. He was in front of her, firing the last of his bullets into the incoming horde before dropping the gun.

He spun around, his face wild, screaming. "Go! Go!"

Go? she wanted to ask him. *Go where? We're stuck. The boat won't move—*

The roar of the engine filled the air as Josh rammed himself into the front of the boat. What was he doing? What—

"Go!" Josh was shouting. He was pushing and screaming, digging his boots into the sand for leverage and howling like a madman. "Go, get out of here! Get out of here!"

He was pushing them back into the water.

She didn't know how he was doing it. This skinny kid who had come to her and Will months ago, who couldn't do much of anything right. It was Gaby who had saved his life not once, but twice, because Josh was one of those kids in school who you ignored. He was average in every way—not tall enough, not big enough, and certainly not handsome enough for a girl like Gaby— and there shouldn't have been any possible way he could actually be *pushing the boat back into the water.*

"Josh, what are you doing?" Gaby screamed, most of it lost over the roar of the outboard motor.

The boat kept moving, because Josh was still pushing even though she couldn't see him in front of the vessel anymore.

This isn't possible. How is this even possible?

And the beach got darker and darker, until there was nothing left—

Then the sound of the motor changed noticeably as the propeller finally found water to churn against, and the boat was now reversing faster off the beach and into the lake.

She could finally see Josh again. He stood on the beach, his legs buried in the sand up to his knees. He was looking after them, gasping for breath, his chest heaving with all the effort and strain of what he had just done. And yet there was something strange on his face.

It wasn't fear. Or terror.

Was he smiling? No, not smiling. Josh was beaming as he looked back at her—or maybe he was trying to find Gaby behind her. That was probably it. At that moment, Lara didn't think she actually existed in the teenager's eyes. He was so serene, as if his entire life had led to this moment and he had finally achieved something that had eluded him all this time.

Then he was gone.

Josh disappeared under the tidal wave of surging pruned flesh and hollow eyes. He didn't scream, but simply vanished under the pile of twisted limbs and blackened flesh, as if he had never existed at all.

But Josh had done it. The boat was reversing at faster speeds, moving back, back, *back* from the beach and away from the unending tide of creatures that blanketed it—

Not all the creatures were converging on Josh. There wasn't enough space for all of them, so the rest kept coming. She didn't know what they were doing.

The water. They couldn't go into the water…could they?

As she looked on, breathless, one of the ghouls launched itself into the air and at the boat. It spilled against the side of the vessel and groped desperately for something to hold onto, but couldn't, and went tumbling into the water.

Two—no, *three* more—catapulted themselves at the V-shaped front of the boat, but they too didn't land at the right spots and failed to find something to hold onto and disappeared over the side.

The rest began *plop-plop-plopping* into the lake around them. They looked like kamikaze pilots sailing through the night air only to miss their target. She watched them sink into the lake water and thrash about. A few managed to break the surface again, only to drop back under like…*stones?*

She was still staring off the side, trying to process what she was seeing *(The water! They really can't survive in the water!)*, when one of them sailed across the distance and managed to land on the boat in a ball of *clacking* bones. It rolled forward and slammed into the bench in front of the steering console, unraveling its limbs.

As soon as it lifted its head, Lara shoved the barrel of the M4 toward it and pulled the trigger. The first half dozen bullets obliterated its eyes and nose and mouth, and the next half dozen shattered its skull and sent it stumbling back, back. She didn't expect it to go down *(no silver bullets)*, and it didn't disappoint her.

Mostly headless now, it continued coming.

Lara spun the rifle around and smashed the stock into its chest. That, more than the bullets, made it reel backward. She followed it and hit it again, this time aiming for what remained of its lower jaw, sticking out like one half of a crushed watermelon. That kept it staggering back and off balance. She hit it a third time on the side of its leftover "head" and heard the stock of her rifle *cracking* with the impact.

She kicked it squarely in the chest, putting as much strength as she could muster (or as much as the rippling pain from her thigh would allow her) into the blow. The creature had nowhere else to go, and the force of the kick sent it toppling over the side. There was a satisfying *plop!* as it disappeared into the water.

Lara hurried over and looked down and could see the creature sinking, reaching out with its bony arms for her. Then it was gone, and the waters of Beaufont Lake settled over the spot where it had vanished.

"Lara," Gaby said behind her.

She looked back at Gaby, saw her staring past her and at the island. She followed Gaby's gaze back to the beach—or where she thought it was supposed to be. Normally she would be able to see the long stretch of white sand from anywhere, even at night without lights. That wasn't the case this time. Everywhere she looked, there was just shifting, moving darkness.

Lara shivered, even though they were already forty to fifty yards from land and there was no way they could throw themselves that far. Or, at least, she hoped not.

She looked away. She didn't need to see anymore. The island was gone. Lost. She had fought against it—tried like mad to keep it—but the truth was staring back at her now.

Song Island was lost. Truly, truly lost.

She crouched next to Danny instead and felt along the side of his neck. To her great relief, he still had a pulse, but it was very weak. He was alive, though, something she hadn't been entirely certain of earlier.

"Is he okay?" Gaby asked.

"He's alive," Lara said.

She looked up at Gaby, who was still staring back at the island. But Lara knew what she was really looking for. Josh.

Lara couldn't wrap her mind around what he had done. He had saved their lives. Pushed the boat back into the water. How? That was the question. Could Will, even at full strength, have done something like that? She remembered seeing Josh buried up to his knees in the sand as they were backing up. What kind of strength had the kid possessed to do something like that?

"Gaby, we need to go," she said. "Blaine and the others will be waiting for us."

Gaby nodded and spun the steering wheel. She looked back at the island as long as she could until they had turned completely around. The boat started moving smoothly under her, and Lara fumbled her way to the bench at the front and sat down.

She was tired, and sitting down seemed to help, even though every part of her was threatening to come apart at any second.

"Lara," Gaby said. She looked back as Gaby threw her a white pill bottle. "Don't read the label; just take two."

Lara nodded. She didn't have the strength to argue, anyway. She opened the bottle, took out two pills, and swallowed them. She had never been good about taking medicine without a glass of water, so she felt a little proud of herself when the pills went down surprisingly easy.

"I think I saw someone on the other side of beach," Gaby said. "At the same time we were running for the boat."

"Who was it?"

"I don't know. He was wearing dark clothes." She shook her head. "It could have been one of Josh's..." Gaby stopped in mid-sentence, then said instead, "How long will Blaine wait for us? I don't want to leave anyone behind, Lara. Not again. Not ever again..."

CHAPTER 26

WILL

KATE.

He used the wall behind him as a crutch, because he wasn't confident in his legs. The sight of her in person after all this time left him speechless, confused, and unable to fully understand how the last few months had all ended up with him here, face to face with her.

She was taller than he remembered. Thin, but not quite as skeletal as the others. He recalled seeing this new version of her in the town of Harvest that morning at the water tower. But that was from afar, and though he recognized her (even now, he didn't know how, he just did), it wasn't the same as seeing her standing before him.

The blue of her eyes was ethereal and nothing like the crystal blue of Lara's. These seemed to actually pulsate, as if they were living organisms in and of themselves.

The creatures were gone. All of them. They had slinked away into the night, leaving just the two of them, like children abandoning the room to bickering parents. He couldn't even smell them anymore, and in their place was just the crisp night air. He didn't know how that was possible. Usually when the ghouls were around, there was always the stink of compost.

Maybe it was Kate. There was an iciness about her presence, an almost regal vibe that made him want to fall to his knees and bow. But of course he did no such thing, because this wasn't the Kate he knew. That Kate was gone—dead. He would know; he had shot her in the chest himself.

This Kate wasn't anyone he knew. This Kate was…more.

But even new Kate could die.

"Shooting them doesn't work, not even with silver bullets," he had told Danny. *"But taking out the brain seems to work just fine."*

"You still need silver for that, or will any ol' bullet do?" Danny had asked.

"I have no idea. Let's just use silver to be sure."

Being sure was a luxury he didn't have at the moment, because he had no silver bullets on him. But he still had the gun, and the magazine was half-full. So there was that.

He measured the distance between Kate and him: Three meters.

Not too far, but not too close, either. If last night was any indication, the blue-eyed ones were fast. Much, much faster than the black eyes. (What had Kate called them? Her "brood"?) But how much faster was Kate? Could she dodge a bullet—

"Yes," Kate said. Her voice was almost a hiss, not the same soft and melodic sound that it was inside his head.

"Yes"? he thought. *Yes what, Kate?*

"Yes," she said again, as if he should know.

Because he did know.

Yes, she was fast.

Yes, she could take him before he could put a bullet in her head and splatter the brain inside. Because Kate, like the other blue-eyed ones, still had brains. That was their weak spot.

All he had to do was hit the brain…

Captain Optimism, amirite, Danny?

"He's dead, you know," she said.

Dead?

"Danny," the ghoul said. The creature. Kate. "On the island. He was shot, and he's dead. Everyone's dead, Will. Song Island is lost."

"You're lying."

"Am I?"

"Yes."

"Lara is gone, too. But you don't have to join her."

Was she lying? She was certainly capable of it. She was a monster, after all. There was no such thing as honor among monsters. Everyone knew that.

She might have snorted. Or made some other derisive sound. It was hard to tell because the noises that came out of her *(it)* were difficult to interpret.

She hadn't moved from her spot. Three meters, that was all that separated them, though it felt so much closer because he could hear her voice like a sharp knife. He didn't have to strain, even though her hisses were unnaturally soft, almost whispers. Or was he hearing her inside his head, too? That could have been very possible.

Three meters for a head shot...

"More than enough time," she said.

He smiled at her. He didn't know where it came from. Maybe it was the clown in him, or the gung-ho asshole he thought he had whipped out of his system since the first weekend of Basic Training.

"Are you sure about that?" he asked. "Are you really that fast?"

"Yes," she said simply. "I'm not the one who's dying tonight, Will."

"You mean dying again?"

Thin creases, like cuts rather than lips, formed something that might have resembled a smile. He wondered how long it had been since Kate—this new Kate—had performed such an act that the result was so horrendous.

"Do you really want to die, Will?" she asked. "Is that what you want?"

"You think I'm scared of dying, Kate? If you think that, then you really never knew me at all."

He pointed the gun at her, and the moonlight glinted off its smooth side. He expected some kind of reaction, but there was none; Kate stood perfectly still, as if he were armed with nothing more than a water pistol.

"Let's find out how fast you really are," he said.

She sighed. Or seemed to sigh. He couldn't be sure. "You're so human, Will."

"When did that become a bad thing?"

"Have you looked around you?"

He grinned. She had a point there. "Tell me one thing: Why?"

"Why?" she repeated.

"Why? Why are you in my head? Why can't I get rid of you? Why, Kate?" He was almost shouting now. "What the hell do you want from me?"

She didn't answer for the longest time. In fact, she seemed almost taken aback by the questions. Or was that all in his mind? Was he subscribing human traits to her again in an attempt to understand her?

"It's lonely," she said finally, her voice dropping to a mere whisper, so low he wouldn't have heard if she wasn't standing so close to him.

Three meters...

"I'm surrounded by billions of us," she said, "and it's still so lonely."

A head shot at three meters. Just under ten feet. That was all it would take to end this. Maybe, like with the farmhouse last night, if he could kill Kate and use her as a shield to keep the black-eyed ones back, he could survive tonight. The other creatures were still out there, waiting—always waiting—even if he couldn't see or hear or even smell them *(Is that your doing too, Kate?)*.

Maybe, just maybe, this might work.

Then in the morning, he'd find a vehicle and make his way down to Song Island. Or he'd walk, if he couldn't find a car. It didn't matter. As long as he was breathing, that was all that mattered. As long as he was still sucking in breath, he could get home to Lara, because Kate was lying about Song Island being lost. She had to be.

He almost smiled, because there it was. The opening he had been waiting for. He knew it would come sooner or later as long as he bided his time. Like always, the trick was to recognize it and jump through feetfirst.

Kill Kate and use her to keep the black eyes back. Repeat what he had done at the farmhouse last night.

Easy peasy.

The only thing standing between him and seeing Lara again was a bullet and three meters. He'd made harder shots in his life. But he was only going to get one shot *(Haha, good one)* at this. If he missed, and she proved to be just as fast as the others (or faster), then he might not get a second try.

The shot of your life.

No pressure.

"There are others," she said, when he didn't respond. "Like me. Like Mabry. But it's not the same. This colonization—it'll be over soon. We're bringing order to the chaos, and the future is bright. You must know that this was how it was always going to end, Will. You can't win. You must know that by now."

It doesn't matter how fast she is. You can't outrun a bullet.

Hopefully.

"I think you do, Will. You might deny it out loud, but deep down, in your private thoughts, you know I'm right. You can't win. You never could. You never will."

He focused on the stunning glow of her blue eyes, the windows to her soul. If she even still had a soul. He imagined he could see the old Kate through those eyes, the one that existed beyond the black flesh and gangly frame.

"When it's over, we'll rebuild," she continued. "We've already begun. Humans will serve us and provide for us. There'll be no more fighting. No more violence. We'll rise above it all." She smiled again. Or attempted to. "And when it's over, when it's finally all over, I'll need someone with me. By my side. You, Will. You should be that someone."

Me?

The reality of what she was saying eluded him. He understood every word of it, but he couldn't grasp the concept. Maybe it was the idea of being with her after all of this. Or just being with her at all. It was...unnatural.

How did she ever think it could be possible?

How did she ever think he would agree to it?

"I was content to let you waste your time on the island with that little girl until I could convince you to see the truth," she continued, unbothered by his lack of response. "But then she had to go and make things difficult. That radio broadcast made Mabry angry, and he gave me no choice. And here we are."

She held her hand out toward him, the palm facing up, the flesh so impossibly tight that he could only see the curvature of bones underneath.

"Fate brought us here, Will. But you don't believe in fate, do you?"

I believe in what I can touch, and see, and hear, and shoot. I believe you're not the same Kate, even though you pretend to still be her.

"No," he said.

"You should. Remember the first time we met? Most of the world was gone, but we still found each other. Something led me to you, and something made you stop there to wait for me. It was fate, Will. Nothing happens without a reason. Everything works to achieve a perfect balance. Order out of chaos. That's what this is. This is order."

He stared at her and knew she believed every word of it. That, more than anything, was surprising. The Kate he remembered was mature, smart, and would have laughed in his face if he started talking about destiny and fate and strange, unexplainable psychic connections.

And yet here she was, trying to convince him all of this was...fate?

He pitied her. He hadn't realized what he was feeling until now. There was something sad about Kate—despite her millions of ghouls, her brood—because she longed for a connection that she couldn't have.

You're gonna get a good laugh out of this one, Danny ol' chum.

Her fingers moved as she prompted him. "Give me the gun,

Will. Let it be your token of surrender. You have no choice."

"No," he said.

"No?" she repeated. There was a stunned look on her face. Or, at least, something he interpreted as stunned. It could have been anything, really.

He grinned again. It was reckless, and he must have known she wasn't going to receive it well, but he couldn't help himself.

"Sorry," he said, "but Lara would kick my ass if she found out I was cheating on her with a corpse."

He caught the sudden movements out of the corner of his eye just before the ghouls came back, bringing with them the terrible smell; a swarm of them appearing from the darkness, as if oozing out of the night itself. There were too many to count, so he didn't bother. He always knew they were out there so he wasn't surprised, but how the hell had they appeared so fast?

His eyes were drawn back to Kate because something had changed with her *(it)*; a flash of emotion flickering across her blackened face, the skin so constricted it might as well have been satin over a skull in a medical lab somewhere. Even her eyes seemed to flare up, growing in size, the blue doubling (tripling?) in intensity. He might have even believed they were on fire if they weren't so blue.

"Lara," she hissed, practically spitting the name out. "Always Lara. Lara. *Lara.*"

Will wasn't ready for it. He wasn't even remotely close to understanding what was happening even as it occurred in front of him in real-time. His reaction was delayed, and it cost him dearly. The blue-eyed ghouls had been fast, but Kate (Not really Kate, this thing that used to be Kate) was beyond them.

She was more. So, so much more.

(*"How did you ever think you could beat us when you know so little?"* she had said to him.)

She didn't so much move as explode into a blur of motion.

He fired—

Three meters. Just under ten feet. He'd made tougher shots

before in his career.

—*and hit empty air.*

Then she was there, in front of him, so close that when she opened her mouth and hissed *"Lara!"* he felt the icy cold of her breath, and goose bumps raced through every inch of his flesh.

He was still trying to process what he was seeing, hearing, and feeling when her hand encircled his and she squeezed, mashing his fingers against the grip of the Smith & Wesson as he reflexively fired another shot. Like the last one, the bullet sailed harmlessly past her scrawny shoulder and vanished into the night.

She kept folding her hand over his until his fingers were so crushed against the gun's grip that he couldn't have squeezed the trigger a third time even if he thought it might do any good. Her other hand slithered around his neck and pushed, and he stumbled back in shock, the breath rushing out of him in a single, devastating spurt. It wasn't so much the pain of the impact against the wall that jolted him, it was more the ferocity of her attack. That and the sheer speed of it overwhelmed all his senses until he couldn't focus on any one thing.

The hand around his throat was viselike, and it was all he could do to grab her wrist with his free hand and try to keep her from tightening it any further. He didn't know if he was succeeding or if she just decided not to crush his windpipe at that very moment.

But as suffocating as the bones wrapped around his throat were, it was nothing compared to the pressure being exerted against the fingers of his right hand. She was crushing them as if they were brittle candy. He didn't know how that was possible given how bony her own fingers were, but there was a strength in them that defied the laws of physics. She shouldn't have been as monstrously strong as she was, but if he was imagining this whole thing, then why was he screaming?

"I gave you a chance," she hissed, the icy cold of her breath hitting him in the face and piercing through his screams. Her face was so close, her eyes mere inches away, that he found his entire vision swimming in a blue irradiated ocean. "But I realize now that

Mabry was right. Free will *is* overrated."

She finally let go of his neck and pulled back. He gasped for breath and managed half of it before she hit him in the face with a balled fist. Or, at least, he thought it was a fist. It could have been something else, maybe a hammer. Or a sledgehammer, given how easily his nose broke and the metallic taste of blood flooded his mouth. His head snapped back from the blow, and she grabbed his left hand and broke it at the wrist with a casual twist.

Will had endured pain before. He had been shot more than once, for God's sake, but actually hearing his wrist breaking—the *snap!* like firecrackers in the cold, still night—was a new revelation.

He opened his mouth to scream again but only sucking sounds came out, any noises he might have made drowned out by the blood pouring down his face. He swallowed as much of it as he could and did his best not to choke on his own plasma.

She still had a firm grip over his right hand, the one with the gun pointed at nothing—less than useless—and she was pressed so close to him that instead of the heat of her body, there was just the unnatural cold emanating from every pore. Why was she so cold? The other blue-eyed ghouls hadn't been. Or was he misremembering? That was entirely possible. At the moment, the only sure thing was that he was going to die and he would never reach Song Island and never see Lara again.

He wasn't sure when it happened, but he was sitting again, the uneven brick and mortar wall pricking against his back, keeping him upright. His right hand was on the ground, the gun lost somewhere in the grass. He didn't remember if she had taken it from him and thrown it away, or if he had simply dropped it.

He thought about looking for it (*The head. Shoot her in the head and end it!*), but soon the only sensations he was aware of were coming from the side of his neck, where Kate was bent over and—

Teeth.

He felt teeth penetrating skin. Strangely, it didn't hurt quite as much as he thought it would.

Those are teeth.

She's...

"*Don't fight it,*" Kate said.

Her voice was inside his head again. They weren't hisses anymore, but the Kate he remembered. No, that wasn't true. The Kate he had known didn't really sound like this. This was an artificial version of her. This was the voice of the Kate-that-never-was.

Stop it.

"*It's too late.*"

Lara...

"*She'll never accept you now.*"

No...

"*But I will.*"

No!

There was no response that time. Maybe she was busy, or maybe she realized it was pointless to argue with someone who didn't have a choice.

Instead, there was just the sound of *slurping*, of Kate drinking him.

Lara.

His thoughts were filled with Lara on the beach of Song Island, walking side by side with him because they always snuck away before the others woke up. Even before Danny could rise, which was not an easy feat.

He was back on the beach with Lara, holding hands like teenagers. Not really talking, but doing a lot of smiling. Because he was happy. He was most happy when he was with her.

Lara...

I'm not coming home.

I'm so sorry, baby, but I'm not coming home after all.

Please forgive me.

He came back to the present when Kate finally pulled herself off his neck. Her blackened mouth was covered with blood. His. It dripped from teeth that were crooked and devastated and brown and black.

She smiled gleefully at him, cradling his painfully broken right hand in hers as if they were lovers. "Let it wash over you, Will. Don't fight it. Accept it. This is the way of things now. We'll build the future together, beside Mabry. You and I."

No.

"Yes," she hissed, that hint of anger flashing across her eyes again like blue fire.

No...

She frowned. "Why do you keep resisting? When the transformation is over, there'll be no more pain. No more diseases or illnesses or wounds to worry about. You'll finally be *free*."

No!

He summoned what strength he had left and lunged at her, seeing the surprise register on her face. Maybe she was still drunk from his blood, and it made her slow to react. Or maybe it was because she was too close, and was crouched and wallowing in her triumph. Whatever the reason, and despite all her preternatural speed, she couldn't move fast enough.

He barreled into her with his entire body and knocked her back, reaching behind him and wrapping his hand around the hilt of the knife (Millard's knife, the one he wouldn't be caught dead carrying around, if he had a choice). He screamed as he forced his mangled fingers to tighten around the grip and he pulled, pulled until the blade came out of the sheath. Crushed fingers were not meant to be moved, much less grab something, and the pain was unbearable and speared him like a thousand bullets.

Below him, Kate glared, her lips moving like worms underneath the wet coat of his blood around her mouth. Her body rose, but he threw himself into her again, and though she was longer, he was still bigger and heavier. He used his body as a blunting instrument and knocked her back to the ground. He wrapped his left arm—the one with the useless broken wrist—around her long, thin neck and held on for dear life.

"What are you doing, Will?" she screamed inside his head.

He ignored her and swung the knife from behind his back. Moonlight gleamed off the sharp seven-inch blade, and Kate's eyes were drawn irresistibly to it.

Recognition spread across her face and her straining under him grew exponentially, but he held on with his left hand and continued to crush down on her with his entire body. He refused to give an inch, to let her curl her legs underneath him in order to kick him off. As inhumanely strong as she had become, she had no leverage, and he saw something that looked amazingly like fear flicker across her eyes.

"Will!"

Her voice boomed inside his head, ricocheting off the sides of his skull. Just his name, in that feminine, unreal voice that was the real Kate but at the same time belonged to the Kate-that-never-was.

"Will!"

There was a sudden and fierce stabbing pain in his gut as she drove her fingers into his stomach. She shoved and pulled—

He screamed the flesh-rendering sensations away and drove the knife into the center of her forehead, even as her fingers wrapped around something inside him—maybe a kidney, maybe a lung—and tried to pull it out. He forced the knife to go deeper and deeper, until the guard bumped against her skull and refused to go any further.

Her hand, buried somewhere inside his stomach, went limp, and so did her body. Her eyes, once full of *(unnatural)* life, faded quickly, as if someone had hit a light switch, and her head lolled to one side, taking the knife with it.

He gasped for air, every inch of him shuddering, and crawled off her still form. He slid against the wall. He would have reached for his midsection to stem the flow of blood if he could, but he no longer had any control over either one of his hands. Instead, he let them dangle from his sides like the two useless limbs they had become.

Breathing hurt too much, and the air had become impossibly frozen. His insides burned, as if trying to make up for the cold outside, and he wasn't entirely sure how his intestines weren't already splayed in his lap.

Kate's body lay in front of him, still so close to him that his legs were touching her malformed ones. Her head had ended up turned in his direction, the eyes—with the knife buried in the forehead between them—staring accusingly back at him.

Well, Danny, I guess any ol' bullet (or knife) would do it, as long as you get them in the brain.

Mystery solved, ol' buddy.

He coughed up blood and didn't bother to wipe it from his lips or stop it from dripping off his chin. There was going to be more where it came from in the next few seconds or minutes, or however long it took him to die. Not only had she bitten *(infected)* him, but the human body was not designed to survive someone shoving their hand into your gut.

Soon. Very soon.

He closed his eyes. It hurt too much to keep them open.

Besides, he didn't need to see them. He could smell them just fine and hear them shuffling against the grass. They were everywhere, their stench overwhelming his senses, trying to suffocate him in their thickness.

How long before they ripped him limb from limb, then drank him dry? If he was lucky, they would kill him before he could turn. He didn't want to become one of them. Worst, he didn't want to turn into something like Kate.

Was that how it even worked? He didn't know. Shit, he didn't know anything.

"How did you ever think you could beat us when you know so little?" Kate had said to him.

She was right. As much as he had learned about the enemy in the year since The Purge, he still didn't know enough.

It was too late to change that now, though. Way too late.

Will relaxed and let his mind drift. He detached himself from his convulsing body and floated away from the gas station, then glided across the night sky and headed southward, back toward Song Island.

Back to Lara.

Instead of the sight of his guts spilling into the grass in front of him, he focused on the color of Lara's crystal blue eyes, the shade of her skin under the morning Song Island sun, and the gentle sway of her blonde hair in the crisp wind.

Instead of the *clacking* of bones as the creatures moved closer, he concentrated on the sounds of Lara's laugh when she allowed herself those rare moments to enjoy life again, the feel of her body against his when they came together at night and never wanted to come apart, but knowing that inevitably they would have to.

Because the days would go on, the nights would come to an end, and there would always be another sunrise on the other side.

Lara.

Lara...

CHAPTER 27

KEO

HE WASN'T SURE how far he had gotten toward the shoreline in the last five or ten minutes since he lost track of time. Frankly, he was just trying not to drown. Keo had learned to adapt to the water long ago, and a part of that was forgetting about everything else except the waves pushing against you.

He had taken off his boots, socks, and assault vest, and had been swimming in pants and a T-shirt for the last kilometer or so. Just as it was difficult to tell time, it was next to impossible to gauge how far he had come and how much further he had to go before he reached the nearest land mass. His vision was limited by darkness; which was to say, he couldn't see shit at the moment.

He had, though, managed to hang onto the MP5SD.

Have German gun, will swim.

Just because he was tiring didn't mean Keo stopped. Besides, he was used to being tired. Hell, the last year was one long run after another. What's that old saying?

"It's not a sprint, it's a marathon."

Whoever came up with that hadn't been living in his boots for the last year. Sprinting from one spot to another was all he had been doing. Screw the marathon.

He couldn't remember the last time he wasn't tired. It seemed like just yesterday when he had taken Delia to a motel after she got off work at that terrible country and western bar. Things went downhill fast from there.

But there had been some good spots, too. Gillian, for one. Norris wasn't such a bad guy, either. But for every Gillian and Norris, there was a Pollard and assholes in black commando uniforms trying to kill him.

None of that did anything to help with the lead weights someone had attached to his arms and legs when he wasn't looking and were trying to pull him down to the bottom of the lake. He was pretty sure his cargo pants had ballooned to five times the size (not to mention the complimentary bloated weight), and he had drunk more of the lake than any fish that ever existed. At least he wasn't a ghoul. If he were, he would have turned to stone and sank to the bottom.

Now *that* was something you didn't see every day. He still couldn't get over the sight of watching fear flashing across their eyes.

I guess they still remember fear. Welcome back to the human race.

Well, sort of.

He was doing calm, slow breaststrokes, simultaneously hoping to find shore and dreading it. He hadn't figured out yet what he would do when he finally got there. Climb up and…then what? There were going to be creatures waiting for him. He had seen them from the Tower, racing back and forth like little speed freaks along the shoreline.

Where the hell was he going, anyway? Dammit. He'd lost track of his direction again. The closest shoreline would be the marina and the burnt-down house, but he couldn't see signs of them at the moment even after stopping and twirling around in a circle.

Then again, it was so dark he could barely see more than a few meters in front of him, so that certainly didn't help. For all he knew, he had been swimming around in circles these last few minutes…hours? No, minutes. It couldn't have been hours yet. Could it?

He sighed. Maybe he should be grateful he couldn't locate land.

Drowning might be preferable to fighting a horde of those things, even with the silver bullets in his submachine gun and two spare magazines.

One year. He had survived for one year. Not so bad. Most of the world's population had turned into ghoulish creatures overnight, except him. Certainly no one would have put money on him making it through this long. Only God knew how he had made it when so many hadn't.

God.

That was funny. He didn't believe in God, and he was pretty sure the old guy didn't believe in him, either. Keo didn't blame him. He had too much blood on his hands to think anyone—any*thing*—floating on a cloud up in the sky was looking out for him.

Keo looked up at the twinkling stars. It was peaceful tonight, with only the waves *sloshing* against him to fill the silence. Everything was so serene he didn't know why he was even still treading water. It was time to just stop and let go. He, too, would sink to the bottom of Beaufont Lake and join those pesky black-eyed bastards. Some people would call that poetic, but Keo was just lazy and felt like giving his legs and arms a rest.

"*See the world. Kill some people. Make some—*"

The gradual whine of a motorized device intruded on his thoughts.

He spun around and caught the white spotlight as it danced across the water and blasted him in the face. Keo flinched and held up one hand to keep from being blinded. He managed to peer through his fingers at a white boat. Long and sleek, being powered in his direction by what sounded like a trolling motor. He wouldn't have heard it at all if it wasn't the only thing running in the entire lake at the moment, and was almost on top of him.

Keo lowered his hand and gripped the MP5SD under water. The boat's passengers hadn't fired yet, so he assumed whoever was onboard wasn't shooting on sight. That was good, because it meant he had the advantage.

Yeah, right!

He slipped his forefinger into the trigger guard but kept the barrel of the submachine gun under water as the boat neared. A little bit closer and he'd find out, once and for all, if the German gun could fire while partially submerged in water.

"Keo!" a voice shouted from the boat.

He relaxed at the sound of the voice and grinned against the spotlight. Of all the people he expected to see out here right now, she was definitely not one of them.

The vessel slowed down as it reached him, waves jostling him around and making staying in one place difficult. They angled alongside him and he saw the familiar tall blonde figure behind the steering wheel, two hands frantically trying to keep the boat from running him over and under. Keo had a sudden image of being saved, only to be accidentally shredded by the propellers. Now that would have been ironic.

The girl stopped the boat, hurried over to the portside, and leaned over. "You're alive," she said, grinning down at him.

"So are you," Keo said. "I thought you were on the yacht."

"No, we never made it."

"That makes two of us. Who else made it?"

"Later. Get up here first."

He grabbed her extended arm and let her pull him up. She was a tall kid, but lean and not very muscular. It didn't help that he had been soaked in water for all this time and "gained" weight as a result. He crawled over the gunwale like a crab, snaking arms and legs over every stable piece along the boat he could find. Finally, he slumped over the side and landed on the floor, then struggled to sit back up with his back against the side, water pouring out of every inch of him.

Gaby wasn't alone in the boat. Lara was in the back, using a second spotlight to treat Danny's wound. It looked like a big ugly gunshot to the side. There was already a thick stack of bloodied gauze next to them, and it was clear Lara had been working on him for some time. She looked pretty shot up herself and was grimacing with every little movement she made.

"Glad you made it, Keo," Lara said.

"You came looking for me?" he said, not able to hide his surprise.

"Gaby swore she saw someone else making a run for the water while we were fleeing down the beach. We weren't sure if it was you or one of the soldiers, but we thought we needed to find out before rejoining the others."

"What if I'd been a soldier?"

"Then I'd have run you over," Gaby said.

He chuckled. "My lucky night, then."

"You and I have very different definitions of 'luck,' Keo," Lara smiled.

"Hey, any night where I'm alive at the end of it is a lucky night," he smiled back. He nodded at Danny. "How's Jokes-a-lot doing?"

She frowned. "He's lost a lot of blood."

"What about you?"

"I'll live." She looked over at Gaby, that steely resolve he had come to respect so much returning in the blink of an eye. "Let's find the *Trident*, Gaby. Zoe will be able to do more for Danny there."

"We know the *Trident* made it?" Keo asked. "The soldiers didn't attack it?"

"Not as far as we know," Lara said. Then, "I guess we'll find out soon."

Gaby switched off the trolling motor, then hurried back behind the steering wheel and switched on the outboard motor. It coughed, then caught, and the sound of it powering up was like an explosion against the silent lake.

"Why the trolling motor?" Keo asked her, shouting over the roar.

"In case there were soldiers still around!" Gaby shouted back.

"And now?"

"We've been circling for almost thirty minutes. If they're still around, we would have run into them by now!"

Just in case, Keo thought, and slipped the MP5SD in front of him and looked off the side as the boat started moving.

Gaby pushed on the throttle and the stern dipped slightly as the vessel picked up speed until they were racing across open water, the spotlight at the front lighting their path.

THE *TRIDENT* WAS exactly where it was supposed to be, drifting half a kilometer from the opening into the channel that connected Beaufont Lake with the Gulf of Mexico. He saw silhouetted figures moving on the main and upper decks as soon as they were within sight of it and wondered if one of them was manning the M240 right now, ready to blast away like they had back at the island.

The luxury yacht looked like a ghost ship afloat on the lake with all of its lights still switched off, and only the moonlight to hint at its presence. That is, until the people onboard saw the much smaller boat approaching with its spotlight shining in the darkness. The *Trident*'s industrial strength lights quickly blasted on at full intensity, nearly blinding Keo in the process.

All three of them (and Danny) had lost their radios in the rush to escape Song Island, so they didn't have anything to contact the yacht with to let them know they were coming in. Fortunately, no one onboard had a happy trigger finger, and Keo was still in one piece when a figure on the main deck waved them in. Gaby, one hand shielding her eyes from the bright lights, guided the boat alongside the yacht and toward the back.

Two figures were waiting for them at the large swimming area as Gaby maneuvered over. There were already other crafts onboard, including the lightweight aluminum boats they had used to abandon the island. The two shadows turned out to be Maddie and Nate, and as they stepped into the large pool of floodlights, both were beaming back at them. The boy only had eyes for Gaby, who looked equally happy to see him alive.

True love in the apocalypse lives.
There might be hope for us yet, Gillian.

Gaby moved as close to the yacht as she dared before turning off the engine. They climbed out one by one, then Keo and Nate took Danny from Lara and carried him between them while Gaby stayed behind to help Maddie tie the twenty-footer up.

The ex-Ranger looked more dead than alive, and Nate knew it too when they grabbed the unconscious man. Keo didn't realize he and Nate were rushing through the deck until he glanced back and saw Lara struggling to keep up with them, half-limping and half-running.

He looked over at Nate. The kid "got it" without Keo having to say a word, and they slowed down just enough for Lara to catch up.

"You okay?" he asked her.

She nodded, which was a big lie. He could see her trying to hide the pain. It was all over her face, even if she didn't think it showed.

"You?" she asked.

"Better, now that I'm dry. Mostly dry, anyway."

"Good," she said, and looked away.

Keo didn't say anything, but he pegged the chances that he'd be carrying both her and Danny over to Zoe in the next few minutes at fifty-fifty.

Nate's radio squawked, and they heard Blaine's voice. "Are they onboard?"

Nate unclipped the radio from his waist and handed it to Lara. "It's for you."

Lara took it and said into the radio, "We're onboard, Blaine."

"Thank God you guys are fine," Blaine said. "We were seriously debating about going back there. I had the boat turned around and ready."

"I'm glad you didn't." She wiped at a bead of sweat and grimaced. "Is everyone onboard?"

"Almost everyone. Sarah's here."

"What about Stan and Roy? Danny and I sent them ahead with Sarah while we held the attackers back at the hotel."

"They didn't make it, Lara. Sarah said they were ambushed on the other side of the hotel, and Roy and Stan stayed behind to make sure she could reach the exit point."

There was silence behind him. He thought about shooting one of those cursory, *"You okay?"* questions back at her, but didn't. It would have been a stupid thing to do because she wasn't okay. How could she be, when she had just found out two people she had sent ahead didn't make it to their destination? Even seasoned commanders took the loss of their soldiers hard, and Lara wasn't anywhere close to being a soldier.

He was surprised, though, that her voice was calm when she finally said, "Let's go, Blaine."

"Are you sure?" Blaine asked.

"Yes. Follow the plan."

"What about Will? What about the island?"

There was a brief moment of silence before she said, "Follow the plan, Blaine."

Blaine didn't answer, but it didn't take long for the *Trident*'s engine to power back on. Then the boat began turning, back toward the channel.

THEY LEFT DANNY inside the makeshift infirmary, which was really just one of the guest cabins, with the doctor, Zoe. The rest of the islanders, who had been on the *Trident* ever since the yacht moved from the beach to its hiding place, were confined to other rooms to keep them out of the way as Keo and the others got ready for the channel.

They had to brave it, regardless of who was waiting out there, because on the other side was the Gulf of Mexico, an ocean big enough that even the yacht could get lost in it. To get there, though, they would first have to traverse a 300-meter wide section of water, which would put them easily within shooting distance of well-armed men on both sides. Given the size of the yacht, once they started through there was no turning back.

Keo climbed up to the roof of the bridge with the M240. The damn thing was already heavy, but he had to struggle with the ammo belt the entire way, too. When he finally reached the highest point on the yacht, he crawled forward and laid down near the edge, over old dried blood and bullet holes he had put there himself. He tried looking through the holes and into the bridge below, but since Blaine had turned off the lights to make himself and *Capitan* Gage into harder targets, he only saw small halos of lights generated by the console illuminating nothing in particular.

He turned his attention back to the channel and situated himself behind the machine gun, getting as comfortable as possible, which was harder than he had expected with the wind whipping at him. Unfortunately he wasn't nearly as dry from his long swim as he had thought earlier, and the combination made for a cold night out. He perched the MG on its tripod and peered through the iron sights. It would have been nice to have a night-vision scope. Then again, it would have been nice if he could fly and shoot laser beams out of his eyes, too.

He was unclipping the radio and about to set it on the roof next to him when it squawked and he heard Lara's voice. "Keo, you set?"

"I'm set," Keo said into the radio. "You?"

"Yeah."

"No, I mean, can you do this?"

"Yes," she said, with just a hint of exasperation. Apparently he wasn't the only one who had asked that question. "I'm fine. Don't worry about me. You're the one up there in the open."

"Thanks for reminding me. I had forgotten that I'm a goddamn idiot."

"You're welcome," she said, with just a tiny hint of amusement in her voice. Then, "Blaine, maintain our current speed and keep the lights moving in case they try to put some kind of obstruction in the water."

"Did you see any of that last time, Keo?" Blaine asked.

"I didn't get that far," Keo said.

"How many snipers?" Lara asked.

"Just the one."

"But he had backup."

"Yeah."

"What are the chances they actually left someone behind?" Gaby asked.

"They're not exactly tactical geniuses," Nate said. "I think there's a good chance they would have thrown everything they had at the island."

"Let's hope so," Lara said. "Until then, everyone stay alert. No one blinks until we make it into the Gulf."

Gaby and Nate were defending through windows on the port side, while Benny and Maddie had starboard. Lara was moving around the boat. Or limping around, anyway. Keo had caught her taking a couple of pills from a bottle after they finally delivered Danny to Zoe. He didn't have to ask what she was taking. Lara might have been a (surprisingly) tough customer, but the way she was moving around, he kept expecting her to fall down at any moment.

She never did, though, which doubled his respect for her, and it was already high to begin with after last night.

"Entering the channel now," Blaine announced.

Keo stiffened and pushed himself even flatter against the roof.

He hated coming back to a place where he had been shot before; it was the whole pushing your luck aspect of it that didn't sit right with him. He wondered if Blaine and Gage could hear him moving around up here. Hopefully not. He didn't want them to think he was fidgety, even though he was. The best-case scenario was that the height, combined with the spotlights blasting away around him instead of on him, would be just enough to make him invisible. He was heartened by the fact that when the *Trident* had first approached Song Island, there was a sniper up here and no one had spotted him.

He sucked in a deep breath and settled behind the M240 and did his best to ignore the wind that seemed to have picked up, causing the night to get even colder. It reminded him that he should have changed out of his wet clothes when he had the chance. Or at least put on dry boxers.

A boat the size of the *Trident* had a maximum speed of just fifteen knots, and fourteen when it wanted to cruise. Of course, it wasn't going nearly that fast at the moment. Lara was right when she said to watch out for obstructions in the water. It wouldn't have taken much to throw a barge or large fishing boat or two into their path. The soldiers would have been fully aware of the yacht's existence and how it had entered Beaufont Lake previously. That was probably what had prompted them to put a sniper at the channel in the first place.

Swell. If it wasn't for bad luck…

Unlike the last time he was here, the colored buoys that warned of the shallower ends of the channel reflected back the yacht's bright lights, allowing them to easily navigate the dangerous terrain. He wondered if the soldiers knew about that or if it never occurred to them to sink the markers. Either way, he was glad to see them, because a boat the size of the *Trident* needed all the space (and depth) it could get.

He scanned the pitch-black buildings and swaying fields of grass to his left and right, wishing he had taken Nate's spot down there instead. He'd be standing next to a pretty girl right now and not freezing his ass off up here. Even if there was a shooter lying in wait, he wasn't going to see a damn thing until they started firing (hopefully not at him). Once that happened, and only then, could he unleash the machine gun's 900 rounds a minute capability, which, admittedly, would do wonders to overcome his long-distance shooting handicap.

"How long is this thing?" Gaby asked through the radio.

"Gage says it's just over eight kilometers," Blaine said.

"How many is that in miles?" Carly asked.

"Five," Lara said.

"And where are we now?" Gaby asked.

"He says just over a kilometer in," Blaine said.

Keo reached for the radio. "Heads up. This is where they took their potshots at me."

He imagined everyone below him sliding just a bit further away from the windows they were supposed to be manning. Where was

Lara now? Probably still moving around, trying to pick out a target with her M4. Too bad they had lost the night-vision carbines back on the island. They could really have used those at the moment. Of course, they could have used a lot of—

Damn.

They were like cockroaches, sprinting through the tall fields of overgrown grass on both sides of him. More were darting in and out of the warehouses, and he swore there were a dozen or so climbing up one of the cranes. Thin silhouetted figures stood along the rooftops of buildings and watched them pass. The ones on land, racing along the sides of the channel, kept vanishing and materializing out of the moonlight.

There had to be thousands of them out there, just beyond the water's edge to both sides of him. He shivered, reminding himself that if Gaby hadn't found him in the water, he would have had to climb out of the lake and into…*that.*

"Jesus," Gaby said through the radio, her voice barely audible. "You guys see what I'm seeing?"

"Yes," Lara said. "Blaine, make sure Gage stays in the middle of the channel. Don't veer too close to the edges."

Keo remembered how the ghouls had dive-bombed into Beaufont Lake after him, knowing full well they were going to die but unable to stop themselves. He waited for these to do the same thing, and thank God the channel was over 300 meters wide and the *Trident* remained in the very center, as directed.

"Steady," Lara was saying through the radio. "Stay on course. Steady…"

"Can they jump?" Nate asked.

"Yes," Gaby said, and he thought her voice might have quivered a bit there.

"Stay on course," Lara said again. "Stay on course…"

Keo tested the trigger on the M240 and waited for the creatures to start flinging themselves through the air. The ones back on Song Island had risked it—either because they had forgotten they couldn't survive the water, or they had simply given in to their primal instincts.

"Dead, not stupid," Blaine said through the radio.

"What?" Nate said.

"Something Will used to say," Gaby said. "He always reminded us that the creatures were dead, but they weren't stupid. It was his mantra, and something we should all keep in mind if we want to stay alive."

Dead, not stupid. I like it.

It might have been the mention of Will's name, because the radio went silent after that.

It turned out they didn't have to worry about the ghouls or soldiers. There was no ambush, no obstructions in the water, and nothing at all to keep them from cruising straight into the Gulf of Mexico.

Keo sat up and looked back at the channel and the surrounding land mass, at the peaks of warehouses and towering cranes that had been abandoned a year ago. He could still see them racing back and forth, their thin forms flickering against the moonlight as if they weren't actually real and might have just been a figment of his imagination.

He wished he were that imaginative.

He picked up the machine gun and climbed down from the roof.

Lara was leaning on the railing at the back of the upper deck, looking at the channel as the coastline of Louisiana was absorbed into the darkness. She looked at peace, even though he knew there was a lot going through that mind of hers at the moment. Not least of which was the ex-Ranger they had left behind who had never made it home.

He recalled their conversation when the other ex-Ranger and Gaby had arrived back on the island. He had asked about Will, and if she actually believed he was still alive out there.

"If you knew Will, you wouldn't need to ask," she had answered.

"So we're going on faith, then?" was his smartass response.

"You honestly think your girlfriend actually made it to Santa Marie Island?" she had countered. *"That she's wearing a bikini and waiting on the*

beach every morning, waiting for you to finally show up?"

That last part had been a real kick in the balls, because she was right. He was—and had been for some time now—just operating on faith, like a sucker.

Keo put the M240 down on the floor and leaned against the railing next to her. He didn't say anything, and she didn't, either. They looked back at the dwindling coastline, almost completely swallowed up by the blackness now. Entering the Gulf of Mexico was like voyaging into the Bermuda Triangle, because at that moment they couldn't see much of anything beyond the halos of the *Trident*'s lights.

Finally, he said, "You left a message for him back on the island?"

"I did," she nodded. "It's in a place only he'd think to look. When he finds it, he'll know it's from me."

"So it's only a matter of time before he follows you to the Bengals."

"Yes."

"*Are* you going to the Bengals?"

"I don't know yet. I'll make a decision after we reach the refueling depot. After that..."

"What?" he said.

"Can you stay awhile, Keo? I know it's asking a lot, after everything you've already done. But I have to ask anyway. Not for me, for the others. Can you stay a little longer?"

He knew it was coming, and he was fully prepared to tell her no. But standing there next to her, hearing the desperation in her voice and knowing this was the last thing she wanted to ask him, he couldn't pull the trigger.

Christ, you've gotten soft.

Like a big ol' marshmallow...

"How long?" he asked.

"As long as you can."

He sighed. "Hell, why not. I've already invested a lot of time keeping you guys alive, wouldn't want all my efforts to go to waste now." He nodded. "I can stick around until the Ranger's back on his feet."

"That might take a while."

"Then I guess it'll take a while."

"What about Gillian?"

"She'll understand. Probably."

"Thank you, Keo."

"Sure."

He looked out at the Gulf of Mexico churning against the *Trident*'s propellers. It would be a few more hours yet until sunrise, though for the first time in a long time, he didn't feel the internal conflict of watching darkness staring back at him.

Beside him, Lara was quiet for a long time before she finally said, "When you jumped into the lake, did you see what happened to the creatures?"

"They sank."

"Yeah."

"Silver, bodies of water, and…what was the third thing?"

"Ultraviolet light. But we haven't been able to replicate what happened back at Starch."

"Maybe you should go back there."

She nodded. "One of these days. Right now, the lives of everyone on this boat is more important."

She did a marvelous job of hiding it, but Keo could hear it in her voice and see it in the way she leaned against the railing. She was tired. Dead on her feet.

He knew how she felt; it had been months since he could say he was sufficiently rested. He hadn't gotten any at the island, which was supposed to be safe. But out here, on this boat, maybe he could finally get a full night's sleep.

"Why?" she said.

"Why?" he repeated.

"Why?"

"What's the question?"

She gave him a knowing look, and he smiled back.

"You needed my help," he said, and shrugged, hoping she'd let it go.

"We did," she said. "We still do. In the worst way. But you didn't have to do any of it. You don't have to do it now. So why?"

"I've done things..." He hesitated, turning the words over, searching for the right ones. Or at least, the least objectionable ones. "I have a lot of blood on my hands, Lara. A lot. You have no idea."

She didn't interrupt and just listened.

"I didn't use to do what I did for God, country, or apple pie," he continued. "I wish I could say I was a true believer. Or at least a jingoistic moron. But I can't."

He paused again. Why was he even bothering to tell her any of this? What was the point? He guessed maybe he just needed to say them out loud more than he needed her to understand, because he didn't really think she could understand.

"I have a lot to make up for," Keo said. "I don't know. Maybe I figured you and your friends were a good start."

He stopped talking and waited for her to respond. He was both afraid and longed for it.

"Thank you," she said.

"You already said that."

"I don't think I can ever say it enough."

I'll take it, he thought, and said, "You should get those wounds properly dressed. How'd you get shot twice, anyway?"

"I just got shot once. The other wound is shrapnel."

"Hurts?"

"Everyone's hurt. Pain lets you know you're still alive."

He smirked. "*Daebak*, Rambette."

"One of these days you're going to tell me what that really means."

"Ask nicely and I might."

"Deal." She leaned over and surprised him by kissing him on the cheek. "Go get some rest, Keo. You've earned it," she said, and pushed off the railing and hobbled through the door back into the upper deck lounge.

She moved gingerly, and though he couldn't see her face, he

imagined she was grimacing with every step. She wasn't trying to hide the pain anymore, he realized, because there was just him around to see her vulnerable. He took that as a compliment and looked back at the ocean.

Or the big black spot where the ocean was supposed to be, anyway.

He thought about his mantra, the three sentences he had been basing his life on for the last ten years.

"See the world. Kill some people. Make some money."

Not all that much had changed if he really thought about it. He was still seeing the world, still killing people, except no one was paying him to do it anymore. Or, well, not in stacks of green rectangular pieces of paper, anyway. Instead, there were just kisses on the cheek.

He'd take it.

CHAPTER 28

GABY

"GO, GET OUT *of here! Get out of here!*"

She couldn't stop thinking about him. The sound of his voice, the way he had screamed the words at her. There was a look on his face: terror, regret, and an absolute certainty that defied logic.

She didn't know how he had done it, and she still didn't despite running it over in her head again and again for the hundredth time. Josh had never been the strongest kid; it was one of the reasons they had defaulted to letting Matt call the shots after The Purge. There was no reason why Matt should have been the leader. He wasn't older by that much and he certainly wasn't smarter than either one of them. But he was bigger and stronger.

And yet, Josh had pushed the boat *with them onboard* off the beach by himself.

How? How did you do that, Josh?

She was reminded of all those stories about mothers lifting cars to save their child after an accident. Was that where Josh had summoned his strength? Had he dug deep because he wanted to save…

Her.

She found it difficult to reconcile the Josh in the uniform who had shot Danny (even if he did claim he didn't know it was Danny) with the one that had ultimately saved her. They were the same man—and yet, so different. It didn't make any sense, and her inability to understand him—what he was, what he had become, and what he had done at the very end on that stretch of beach—kept Gaby up all night.

After a while, she stopped trying to sleep and lay on her back, looking up at the ceiling. It was quiet outside despite the hum of the yacht's engine everywhere. Even the gentle waves of the ocean under her didn't lull her back to sleep.

She finally got up from the floor where she had been trying to sleep with nothing but a pillow and walked across the cabin she was sharing with some of the other girls. Bright lights from outside splashed through the windows and over Bonnie's and Gwen's snoring forms. The *Trident* ran on diesel but also had its own electric generator, which was how they still had lights now.

There were no signs of Jo, even though Gaby had seen her in the room earlier. Mary and the kids who had come with Bonnie were on the edges of the bed or spread out along the floor on the other side. She stepped around the bodies, then slipped out into the hallway, grateful she had gone to sleep—or had tried to go to sleep—with all her clothes on, including her gun belt. She didn't have her rifle, but Gaby felt at ease enough not to go looking for it.

She stopped at another one of the cabins and peered inside at a pair of sleeping figures on the bed. She recognized the older woman who had arrived with Bonnie and Jo, sleeping with Sarah and her daughter, Jenny. The two women who had come to the island with Keo (their names escaped her) were sleeping on the floor at the foot of the bed. They were snoring, and she didn't think anything could possibly wake them.

She closed the door back up and moved to the next one, Josh's words still echoing inside her head.

"Go, get out of here! Get out of here!"

She found another door and opened it and leaned in.

Gaby smiled at Claire's thin figure, curled up on a couch in the corner of the room with the FNH shotgun leaning against the wall next to her, within easy reach. She looked cold and her body was trembling slightly, even though the room was warm. Gaby slipped inside and picked up a blanket from the floor that the girl had kicked off her sometime during the night and re-draped it over Claire's shivering body.

Gaby took a moment to look over at the bed where Annie and Milly were asleep in each other's arms. Elise, who Gaby always thought of as Lara's "other little sister," was asleep with Vera, Carly's sister, the two of them snoring lightly next to each other. They looked almost like twins.

She walked to the door and was about to step into the hallway when a small voice said, "Gaby."

She stopped and looked back at Claire, peering at her through the semidarkness. "Go back to sleep."

"Where are you going?" Claire asked. She reached up from under the blanket to rub her eyes.

"I just came over to make sure you were all right."

"I'm fine," Claire said, and smiled.

"I can see that."

"Can't sleep?"

Not for a while, Claire. I don't think I'll be able to close my eyes without having nightmares about tonight and all those men I killed on the beach. About Josh and what he did. About Danny, half-dead somewhere on this boat. And Will, out there somewhere, maybe dead, maybe alive...

She smiled at Claire. "No, but I'm going back to sleep now, and you should, too."

Claire nodded and closed her eyes. She was asleep again almost immediately.

Gaby slipped into the hallway and closed the door soundlessly behind her.

She found Zoe in the last cabin up the hallway, keeping a vigil over Danny from a chair next to the bed. She was half-asleep and only perked up when Gaby opened the door and leaned in.

"Hey," Zoe said, sitting up in the chair. "I know why I'm not asleep, so what's your excuse?"

"I wanted to check up on him," she said.

Danny was on the bed and Gaby was glad most of his body was hidden in shadows, because she wasn't sure she could stand seeing him so helpless and near death. Danny and Will had always been invincible in her eyes, but after tonight she'd never be able to think of him in that way again. Will, too. She hadn't realized it until now, but throughout the night she had always expected Will to come riding home just in the nick of time to save the day.

But he hadn't, and Danny had proven less than bulletproof.

Zoe and Danny weren't the only ones in the room. There was a third figure asleep on the floor at the foot of the bed. Carly, curled up into a ball with a blanket draped over her. She looked restless, and her lips moved as if she were stuck in some kind of endless conversation loop, though she made no sounds.

"She wouldn't leave," Zoe said. "I don't think she's had a lot of sleep these last few days."

None of us have, Gaby thought, but said, "Has he woken up?"

"Not yet."

Gaby leaned against the wall next to the door, just far enough from the bed so she couldn't see Danny's face. She remembered how unresponsive he had been during their race down the beach, and then on the ride over to the *Trident*. She had no trouble seeing the blood bag hanging from a steel coatrack next to the bed though. A tangle of wires connected it to one of Danny's arms.

"How is he?" she asked.

"He lost a lot of blood," Zoe said. "Unfortunately, only Lorelei is O-negative like Danny, so she was the only one who could give him a transfusion. But she's not exactly Keo or Blaine, so Danny didn't get as much as he needed. I'm going to need more from the poor girl in the morning if she's up to it."

"But he'll be fine?"

"Maybe. I don't know." She shook her head. "If he's like Will, he'll be too stubborn to die, but...," Zoe paused and seemed to choose her words carefully when she said, "I'll be able to tell for sure in the morning. I don't know how she knew, but if Lara hadn't insisted I had all of this stuff ready just in case things went bad..." She let it trail off, before finishing with, "I guess she knew what she was doing, after all."

"Lara's smart. Sometimes I don't think she realizes just how smart she really is."

"After tonight, I'm a believer." Zoe stood up and walked to a mini fridge and took out a bottle of water. She took a sip and sighed. "What I wouldn't give for some cold water right now."

"The galley has a refrigerator. The water bottles we put in there should be cold."

"Galley?"

"That's what Maddie called the kitchen."

"Oh."

It was all part of Lara's plan in case they had to abandon the island. Even before she and Danny had arrived, the others had been transferring some of the hotel's inventory over to the boat and storing it. A lot of the nonperishable food, as well as supplies, ammo, and even vanity items like shirts, shoes, and personal hygiene were scattered among the rooms on all three decks. It had taken them hours, and according to Lara, they had only managed to move barely twenty percent of the island's resources.

You would be proud of her, Will. Lara saved us. She saved all of us tonight.

Zoe sat back down in her chair. "I'll keep an eye on him, Gaby. That's why I'm here, remember? If things go bad between now and morning, I'll do the best I can."

"But you don't know for sure if he'll make it through the night."

"I don't usually believe in prayers, but if you do...well, it probably wouldn't hurt."

Prayers? That required faith, didn't it?

She had faith in Will and Danny, but even that was shady these days.

"Go get some sleep," Zoe said. "You look like you need it."

Gaby nodded and left the room.

"Go, get out of here! Get out of here!"

Zoe was right; she did need sleep. But needing it and getting it weren't the same things.

She climbed up the spiral staircase to the upper deck instead, stepping over some dried blood along the steps. She found Nate asleep on one of the couches in what looked like an entertainment lounge, alongside Benny. The two of them hadn't exactly gotten along yesterday, and she wondered if they had been talking before falling asleep. Just what she needed—two men who both liked her exchanging war stories.

She glimpsed a figure moving along the railing outside through one of the windows, and Gaby stepped out just as Blaine rounded the corner.

"Hey, kid," he said.

"Hey, Blaine. Anything?"

"Just water. Lots and lots of water." He had his assault rifle slung over his back and a pair of night-vision binoculars hanging around his neck. "Can't sleep?"

"Nope."

"Yeah, me too."

He leaned against the railing and looked out at nothing in particular. Their world at this moment began and ended in the halo of lights that encircled the *Trident*. It was as if the rest of the universe no longer existed; or, if it still did, it had gone into hiding.

"Did Lara say where we were going?" Gaby asked, leaning next to him.

"There was talk of some Caribbean island, but I don't think she's decided yet." He shrugged. "Doesn't matter, I guess."

"No?"

"Nah. One island's the same as another."

She didn't think that was exactly true. Song Island had been unique.

"Where's Lara?" she asked.

"In the captain's quarters next to the bridge."

"Thanks."

As Gaby started off, Blaine stopped her with, "Hey, kid." And when she looked back, he said, "I'm sorry about Josh."

"*Go, get out of here! Get out of here!*"

"We move on," Blaine said. "It's hard at first, but eventually the pain hurts less. Don't make the same mistakes I did by closing yourself off for too long. There are people who care about you."

She gave him a pursed smile. He was talking about himself. About Sandra.

"Thanks, Blaine," she said.

"Don't mention it."

Gaby went back inside.

She walked past Benny and Nate again, but this time stopped to linger on Nate for a moment. He looked peaceful, and she was glad he was still alive. Not just after tonight, but after the pawnshop. Had she ever made that clear to him? If not, she could always fix it, maybe starting this morning.

But that was for later.

Now, she continued on, finding the hallway at the back. She knocked on the first door that came up.

"It's not locked," a voice said from inside.

Lara was alone, looking over a heavily annotated map spread out on a table with a lamp turned on next to her. The rest of the room was dark except for sections that were lit up by moonlight filtering in through the windows.

Like Gaby, Lara hadn't changed out of the blood-splattered clothes, and her shoulder and leg remained heavily bandaged. Gaby didn't know how she was even still standing despite all the painkillers she had been taking throughout the night. Had she even gone to see Zoe yet? She had washed the dirt and grime (and blood) off her face, though there were still spots that she couldn't get to or didn't know were there.

Gaby made a mental note to talk to Keo and Blaine about forcing Lara to take a break—or at least get her off her feet. Now that Keo would be staying around for a while, they could afford to take turns getting some rest. God knew they all needed it. A lot of it.

"Can't sleep either?" Lara asked.

Gaby shook her head. "You?"

"No rest for the weary."

"Amen, sister."

Gaby leaned against the table and looked down at the map.

"You checked up on Danny?" Lara asked.

"Just came from there."

"How is he?"

"Zoe thinks it wouldn't be a bad idea to start praying."

"She doesn't know him the way we do," Lara said. "He'll pull through. He has to. We need him now more than ever without—" She stopped herself in mid-sentence and didn't finish.

We need him now more than ever without Will here, Gaby thought, finishing for her friend.

"Who's watching our fearless captain?" she asked instead.

"Jo."

"Jo?"

"Gage is handcuffed to the steering wheel. He's not going anywhere or doing anything. I would have preferred Roy—" She stopped again and shook her head. "Dammit."

"What?"

"No matter what we do, where we go, we keep losing people."

Like Will. Dead or alive, somewhere out there by himself.

"He'll be back," Gaby said. She didn't have to say who "he" was, because Lara already knew. "He'll return to the island, find your message, and come look for us. Have faith."

Lara nodded. "I do have faith." Then, as if to convince herself, "I do have faith…"

Gaby reached over and took Lara's hand and squeezed. They exchanged a brief half-smile. It was the best either one of them could manage at the moment.

"Is that it?" Gaby said, looking down at the map. It was covered in Lara's notes, with a barely-visible dot in the middle of the ocean heavily circled. "Bengal Island?"

"Bengal Islands. There's a main one and a smaller companion island."

Lara hadn't said it with a lot of enthusiasm—or, at least, not as much as Gaby had expected when talking about a place that was supposed to be their salvation.

"What's wrong?" Gaby asked.

"We don't know what's waiting for us there," she said, staring at the map as if she could see all the bad things lurking if she just stared hard and deep enough.

"Isn't it like that everywhere?"

"Yes, but this place…it has everything we need, and everything we don't want."

"Like?"

"People with guns. A lot of guns. Bad people."

"Badder than us?" Gaby smiled.

"According to Keo…yes. Way badder."

They didn't say anything for a moment, and Lara seemed to drift off with her thoughts again. They were standing across the table from each other, but her friend might as well be on the other side of the continent.

"So what do we do?" Gaby finally asked.

"We'll figure it out," Lara said. "Whatever happens, whatever's out there, we'll adapt and survive."

"He said something similar to me back on Route 13." Again, she didn't have to say who "he" was. "He said, 'Whatever happens, keep moving forward. Don't stop to look back. Keep moving forward, because that's how we survive.'"

Lara pursed her lips, then walked around the table and embraced her. Gaby wrapped as much of her arms around Lara as possible, careful to avoid her bandages. She was fighting back tears and could tell Lara was doing the same thing, Lara's body trembling noticeably against hers.

"Adapt or perish," Gaby said, just barely able to contain herself. "We should make a banner and hang it somewhere."

Lara laughed and pulled back. The two of them took turns exchanging embarrassed smiles. "I like the sound of that."

Gaby pushed off the table, needing to go before she ended up bawling like a little kid. She couldn't allow that to happen, because that childish version of her had been excised and she couldn't afford to let her back in. Not now.

"Anyway, I'm going to go keep Blaine company," Gaby said. "I don't think he's slept at all the last couple of days."

"That's a good idea."

Gaby walked to the door.

"Hey," Lara said.

She stopped and looked back.

"He saved us," Lara said. "Josh. Despite what he did to Danny, if he hadn't pushed the boat off the beach…"

Gaby smiled at her and was surprised how easily it came out. "That was the Josh I always wanted you to meet. That was him back there. Not the one in the uniform, or the one that shot Danny, but the one that I grew up across the street from."

"He was a good kid, that Josh."

"He was."

Lara nodded. "Okay, enough chick talk. Go check on Blaine, make sure he doesn't nod off and drop into the Gulf of Mexico."

"Aye aye, boss," Gaby said, giving her a mock salute as she left.

She closed the door behind her and walked along the hallway, her footsteps seemingly louder than even the hum vibrating along every inch of the yacht, originating from the engine room three levels below.

"Whatever happens," Will had said, *"keep moving forward. Don't stop to look back. Keep moving forward, because that's how we survive."*

She owed it to Will to keep going. And Josh too, because for all his faults—and there were many—the boy she knew had returned to her last night when it mattered. And there was Nate, and Carly, and Danny, and everyone else onboard the *Trident* at the moment. She owed it to them, and to herself, too.

We'll keep going, Will, because that's what you taught us.
We'll adapt, and we'll keep going…and we'll survive.

EPILOGUE

"COME HOME."

Night after night, and sometimes even in the day, they chased him. Hunted him. It didn't matter how many times he got away; they always picked up his scent again, and the chase would resume. It wasn't the other blue eyes he had to worry about. They weren't any faster or stronger or smarter than him. No, it was really just the one person *(thing)* he couldn't escape, regardless of how high he climbed, how deep he dug, or how long he ran.

Mabry.

The name echoed inside his head. It was always there, lingering at the corners of his mind, waiting to spring. Its voice was like that of a patient father, whispering to him, cajoling him to do things he didn't want to.

"Come home," it would say. *"You took her from me. Now you have to take her place."*

He wouldn't answer, because responding would be to give himself away. He didn't know how he knew, he just did.

"You can't run forever."

Escape was impossible, because Mabry was a part of him, the way he *(it)* was a part of Kate and the ghouls that stalked the darkness, that chased him even now. They all came from Mabry, like the veins of a river.

Thousands of veins.

Tens of thousands.

Millions.

The war was lost. He knew that now, even though he once tried to delude himself into thinking otherwise. Or maybe he had really, truly wanted to believe it. Not for himself, but for her. For the others, too. He had come to his senses days ago.

Or was it weeks ago?

Months?

Impossible. It couldn't have been months. Or even weeks.

Could it?

How long had he been running, trying to stay one step ahead of them, one step ahead of Mabry? Time was fluid, especially when all he could see was darkness. That was his life now. Racing through the blackness, the nothingness. He had forgotten the feel of the sun against his skin, the warmth caressing his flesh…

Flesh.

…and bones.

Thinking about it only made it worse, so he concentrated on surviving instead. He was good at it. Had always been. Even now, when he was a remnant of what he used to be, he still knew how to stay alive.

He crouched in that always present darkness now, listening to them moving in front of him. They had come down the stairs a few seconds ago, somehow tracking him across the last three cities and dozen towns and hundreds of miles of countryside and woods. All the way down to this basement, in a house that hadn't been lived in for a year. It didn't matter how far he went, how deep he hid, they always found him.

"You can't hide forever."

A small splash of moonlight intruded on the basement from a high window just above his head. Not that he needed light of any kind to see with. His eyes were different now—they were made for the darkness.

There were two of them, and he recognized what they were almost immediately, even before he saw the deep blue glow of their eyes. He could feel them. Sense them when they were nearby. It wasn't the same as with the black-eyed ones. Their thoughts may have been shut off from him, but the air was different—it smelled and even moved differently—when they were around. He could always tell how many there were just by the way the wind moved, their aura like a living thing pressing against his flesh.

They were talking, but their lips weren't moving. No. They had a more efficient method of communication now. Sometimes, when he was close enough and they let their guards down, he could hear their thoughts and eavesdrop on their conversations.

And he learned.

"How did you ever think you could beat us when you know so little?" she had said to him once.

But he was learning. Slowly, he was learning.

In the quiet moments when he found shelter and was safe from pursuit, he let himself think about all the things he knew about them. He knew so much now that he didn't know before, but it still wasn't enough. Not nearly enough.

Not yet, anyway.

That was always the tricky part: Seeing the options and choosing the right one to exploit. But in order to do that, he had to have more information.

More. Always more—

One of the creatures had turned its head in his direction. It had sensed him, maybe in the same way he could always tell when they were around. Why hadn't he realized that possibility earlier?

Before the first blue eyes could act, he leaped out of the corner and straight at it. He was fast. So much faster than he used to be. At first it had frightened him, but now he embraced it because his survival depended on it. The speed, the ferocity, the ability to move almost instantly as soon as his mind conjured up the idea.

The skinny thing, eyes blazing blue, made to lift its arms in defense, but he smashed into it with everything he had. It crashed into the second one, and all three of them tumbled in a tangle of limbs and *clacking* bones to the floor.

Before the first one could right itself underneath him, he drove his fingers—all five digits pressed flat against each other like steel knives—into the side of its neck and pushed, pushed, *pushed* until it came out the other side. With his other hand, he gripped the creature's head, fingers digging into its eye sockets, and pulled.

There was a soft wet *pop!* as the head came free, and black blood arced through the air, splashing the walls and floor of the basement and his chest. He ignored the thick liquid, the taste of it against his lips, and flung the head across the room. The body slumped back to the floor with a dull *thoomp*, black tainted blood *slurping* out of the stump that used to be a neck.

The second blue-eyed ghoul had risen, and it looked at its dead brethren. Then it sneered at him.

"*Come home,*" it said inside his head.

But it wasn't this creature standing in front of him talking. No, it was someone *(something)* else.

Mabry.

He *(it)* was speaking through the blue-eyed ghoul standing in front of him now.

"*It doesn't matter where you run,*" it said. "*I can follow you to the ends of the Earth. Come home. Come take her place by my side. You belong with us now.*"

"Never," he hissed, and leaped at the creature.

3-31-15

Ls

Mannington Public Library

Made in the USA
San Bernardino, CA
17 March 2015